RE

Please return/renew this item by the last date shown

worcestershire
countycouncil
Libraries & Learning

Johannes Cabal
the Detective

By Jonathan L. Howard and available from Headline

Johannes Cabal the Necromancer

Johannes Cabal the Detective

JONATHAN L. HOWARD

headline

Chapter heading illustrations by Snugbat

Vehicle illustrations by Graham Bleathman

Map by the author, using Campaign Cartographer 3

First published in Great Britain in 2010 by
HEADLINE PUBLISHING GROUP

1

Cataloguing in Publication Data is available from the British Library

ISBN 978 0 7553 4795 7 (Hardback)
ISBN 978 0 7553 4796 4 (Trade paperback)

Typeset in Goudy by Avon DataSet Ltd,
Bidford on Avon, Warwickshire

Printed in the UK by CPI Mackays, Chatham, ME5 8TD

Headline's policy is to use papers that are natural, renewable and
recyclable products and made from wood grown in sustainable forests.
The logging and manufacturing processes are expected to conform to
the environmental regulations of the country of origin.

HEADLINE PUBLISHING GROUP
An Hachette UK Company
338 Euston Road
London NW1 3BH

www.headline.co.uk
www.hachette.co.uk

Dedication

For Louise

Contents

Do you not weep?
Other sins only speak; murder shrieks out.
The element of water moistens the earth.
But blood flies upwards and bedews the heavens.

John Webster

Chapter 1

The condemned cell stank of cats.

There were no rats and no cockroaches, for which Johannes Cabal – a necromancer of some little infamy – was grateful. But the cost of vermin control was an army of cats who crept in and out of his cell and wandered throughout the dungeons of the Harslaus Castle with complete impunity. Even the cell doors had cat flaps cut into them. It was no secret that the warders had a much higher opinion of the animals than they did of the inmates. When Cabal had been given his introductory tour, which took the form of being thrown down the stairs and shouted at, he had been left in no doubt that any harm that he might cause the cats would be returned to him plus interest.

So now he sat and waited for the authorities to find a window in their very busy schedules to execute him, and he did so covered in cat hair in a cell that countless genera-tions of toms had proudly and extravagantly claimed as their own. Things could probably be worse but, despite some careful thought, Cabal couldn't put his finger on how.

1

So, instead, he considered how he had come to be in such a circumstance.

Strictly, necromancy was the telling of the future by summoning up the spirits of the dead and asking them searching questions. This, believed Cabal, was a singularly poor way of finding out anything. The dead were moderately strong on history, weak on current events and entirely useless for discerning what was to come. They were, after all, dead. Still, that was the dictionary definition.

Over the years, however, it became apparent that necromancy, necromancer and necromantic were fine words wasted on useless definitions and the lexicological group consciousness gently slid them over a few notches so that they now pertained to something interesting, i.e. magic *involving* the dead. This was far more satisfying: summoning up the ghost of Aunt Matilda for an insight into next week's lottery numbers was dull; a maniac with a pointy beard unleashing an army of skeletal warriors, however, was fun. Thus, we see the evolution of a language and a gratifying sight it is to be sure.

Johannes Cabal had no time for the Aunt Matildas of this world or the next. He fitted neatly into the newer definition of *necromancer* – he dealt with raising the dead (although skeletal warriors he left to those of a more theatrical bent). First and foremost, he considered himself a scientist embarked upon a search for a cure for a terrible disease: death. This would seem laudable if it were not for his methods, his manner, and his failed experiments, the latter tending to hang around the countryside, dismaying the yokels. Even this might have been forgivable – pharmaceutical companies have done worse – if one ignored the bad reputation that the more melodramatic necromancers have given the profession. Skeletal warriors are all very well when they're chasing Jason and the Argonauts around on the silver screen but when they're battering down your door . . . Well, that's a different matter altogether. So, the necromancers were all besmirched with the same gory brush and Cabal, who just wanted to be left alone to his research, found himself in a profession proscribed in the most capital terms. It was very galling. Especially when you got caught.

Cabal had been caught trying to check out a book from the library of the Krenz University. The book was in the Special Collection and Cabal had intended the loan to be for an extended, open-ended sort of period. Anticipating resistance from the library authorities, he had made the loan at half past one in the morning of a national holiday and might have got away with it too if it hadn't been for an enormous mastiff that patrolled the corridors and of which his contacts had unaccountably failed to warn him. When the library had been reopened, they'd found Cabal pinned down by 180 lbs of overfriendly dog in the reading room, half drowned in slobber. Just out of reach was a well-travelled Gladstone bag that was found to contain an enormous handgun, a collection of surgical instruments, a closely written notebook, a padded case holding several sealed test tubes full of murky fluids, and the library's own demy quarto copy of *Principia Necromantica*.

Nobody wanted a long drawn-out trial. In fact, nobody who mattered wanted a trial at all, so Johannes Cabal didn't get one. He was just told he was going to be executed and taken to Harslaus Castle. That had all been almost a month ago and Cabal was getting bored. He knew full well that his execution was unlikely to be any more formal than his sentencing and at any time, probably in the wee small hours, the door would thud open, he'd be manhandled off to some dark cellar, his throat would be cut and his twitching cadaver thrown down an oubliette. But there was nothing he could do about it, so why worry? Still, it hadn't happened yet; they were still feeding him with nearly edible food and the more intelligent cats had long since learned to stay out of his cell. So why were they waiting? He had a vague and uncomfortable feeling that somebody somewhere had plans for him.

Then it happened just as he'd expected after all, in the wee small hours of the morning. He was awoken by the sound of the cell door being thrown open and, before he could recover his wits, a sack was pulled over his head and he was bundled off down the labyrinthine corridors. He didn't try to fight; there were at least four of them of whom even the slightest might be described as 'burly'. He could only stay calm, wait for any small opportunity to escape should one arise and hope that, if all failed, and he was to die, that the entry procedures for Hell had at least been rationalised since his last visit.

He was half dragged, half carried for a short time and then thrown into a chair. The sack was whipped off him and, as he blinked in the hard light, he caught a glimpse of a dour, portly man stropping a cut-throat razor on a leather strap. He had the presence of mind to be impressed that such clandestine executions were so common they seemed to have somebody employed to commit them. This sang-froid slipped slightly when brutal hands stripped him of his stinking clothes. Any complaints he might have wished to make thus provoked were drowned when he was thrown into a tub of soapy water and belaboured with sponges. He was still coughing bubbles when he was dragged out again, held down in the chair, slapped in the face with a quantity of lather and the portly man – glowering fiercely – grabbed him by the throat and slashed at him with the razor.

Cabal stopped struggling immediately. The man slid his eyes sideways to look at the quantity of bristles and soap scum that hung from the blade. He twitched the razor and the scum flew in a discrete body off into the shadows where it fell with an indistinct *plap*. His eyes swivelled back to regard Cabal.

'Warm for the time of year, isn't it, sir?' he grated. The razor swept in again.

Ten minutes later, Cabal – cleanly shaven, bathed and dressed in freshly pressed clothes – regarded himself in the mirror. He stood a shade over six feet tall and, although he'd have preferred his blond hair cut back a little and the suit they'd given him was a dark grey rather than his habitual black, he wasn't altogether displeased with his appearance. It was sober and Cabal was a very sober man. 'Not bad,' he said, running his hand over his chin. 'Not bad at all. You're the prison barber, then?'

'No, sir,' said the man as he put his razor and strap away. 'I'm the executioner. But it pays to have more than one feather in me cap. Good morning.'

Cabal watched him leave with mixed feelings.

'Feeling more human, Herr Cabal?'

Cabal turned his head to look at the newcomer and instantly suspected that he'd been there the whole time, in the shadows. An educated voice. Cabal sighed inwardly: this was probably going to become political, and politics and politicians bored him immeasurably. 'No more than usual,' he replied. 'I gather I am to be released?'

'You gather incorrectly,' said the newcomer, stepping into the light. He was in his late thirties, slim, moustachioed and beautifully turned out in the uniform of a captain of the Imperial Hussars, the jacket over his shoulders, the busby tucked under his arm. His bearing and the order hanging at his throat stated very loudly 'landed aristocracy'. He walked to the table upon which Cabal's old clothes lay, swept them to the floor and perched on the corner. He produced a cigarette case, took one for himself, and then offered the case to Cabal. 'Do you smoke, Herr Cabal?'

'Only to be antisocial,' replied Cabal, making no move.

The hussar smiled, put the case away, and lit his own cigarette. 'Do you know who I am?' Cabal shrugged noncommittally. 'I am Count Marechal of the emperor's own bodyguard. Yes?' Cabal had raised a finger of query.

'Perhaps it's just me being a stickler for nomenclature but doesn't the title of "emperor" presuppose some sort of empire? I wasn't aware that Mirkarvia has ever gained so much as an inch of land from its neighbours, excepting that business with the faulty theodolite a few years ago. And that, you had to give back.'

'I thought you an educated man, Herr Cabal. You've never heard of the Mirkarvian Empire and the Erzich Dynasty? You disappoint me.'

'Of course I've heard of them, but that was all centuries ago. You can hardly hearken back to some medieval golden age as if it happened yesterday.' He looked at the count and reconsidered. 'Or perhaps you can. My mistake.'

The count twisted his head as if working a crick out of his neck. 'Do you believe in history repeating itself? That what has passed will come again? I do. Names and faces will change but their rôles will be the same. Wars will be fought with new weapons and new tactics but for the same goals and objectives.'

Cabal thought it was nonsense but could see it might be a very comforting theory to cling to for a third-rate backwater with dust on its laurels. Bearing in mind that if this interview didn't go just *so* then he might well not live much longer and bearing in mind what a great nuisance that would be, he instead said, 'I'm not a historian. I can make no comment.'

'But you disagree. No matter.' Something in the way he said it made Cabal think that it was a comment frequently on the count's lips and that a lot of the people who didn't matter ended up floating out of town face down. With an effort, he made a stab towards diplomacy.

'You know my profession. I have to think in the long term. There may be something in what you say. In my own researches I've noticed repetitive patterns developing down the centuries. But my interest is not history. I've never had the desire to analyse these patterns.'

'Patterns? Patterns.' The count mused for a moment. 'Yes, I like that. Patterns forming through time. Destiny, as manifest as geometry. As irrefutable as Pi. Yes!' His eyes gleamed oddly as he grinned and started pacing up and down, drawing fiercely on his cigarette. 'Yes!'

Cabal started to have a bad feeling about the count. In his experience, military aristocrats fell into two classes. The great majority were in the army because they liked the uniforms, were unpleasant to their batmen, spent fortunes on moustache wax and did it all to appeal to the sort of woman who is envious of a cavalryman's horse. A tiny minority, however, were in uniform because they had plans, *military* plans. And a minority of this minority actually had the wits to do something about it too. Whatever else Count Marechal was – mad, for instance – he was also intelligent. Thus, despite his characteristic impatience with the rest of humanity, he let Marechal pursue his train of thought to its conclusion, or at least until he ran out of cigarette.

Marechal threw the fag end to the floor and crushed it out beneath the heel of his gleaming boot, taking its successor from the case even as he did so.

I'm at the mercy of a demented chain-smoker, thought Cabal. *Oh, happy day.*

'Mirkarvia has plans, Herr Cabal. Great plans. The Mirkarvian Empire is not just a footnote of history. It is a blueprint for the future.'

7

Cabal remembered what little he could about the excesses of the Mirkarvian Empire and thought this was a future only Mirkarvians could enjoy.

'In ten days time the emperor, Antrobus the Second, will make an announcement to the people in Victory Square from the balcony of the palace. He will tell them that the time of our hiding in the shadows of our neighbours is over, that foreign spies and agents will no longer be tolerated within our borders, that our climb back towards greatness starts now. At the same time, the secret police will move against known spies and their sympathisers. Their corruption of this country's spirit will cease immediately and patriot shall work with patriot to ensure that . . . Am I boring you?'

Cabal finished yawning. 'My apologies. My sleep was disturbed. So, you wish to turn your country into a police state and eliminate any dissent. You're not the first and you certainly won't be the last.'

'You disapprove.'

'I don't care. People are cattle. Do as you will, it's your country. I'm just wondering where I fit into your plans.'

'You're focused. I like that. I respect clear thinkers. These dissident factions have poisoned the people's minds. We must act quickly or it will be too late.'

'A revolution.'

'A rebellion. Civil war. Which is, of course, what our enemies want. I . . . *we* cannot permit that to happen. The emperor's announcement will nip these rebellious move-ments in the bud. The police actions will remove the possibility of their reoccurrence. Then, we can get on with making destiny manifest. But, there is a small problem.'

Ah, thought Cabal. *Now we come to the crux of it.*

Count Marechal looked at the ceiling for a moment, frown-ing slightly as he tried to couch his next words as best he could. Finally he said, 'The emperor is as dead as a doornail.'

'For how long?' asked Cabal bluntly. There seemed little point in being coy now it was plain what they wanted him to do.

'Three hours. He has been unwell for some time. We suspected the worst but hoped for the best. To no avail.' His upper lip twitched savagely. 'The stupid old bastard. He only had to last long enough to make the speech and then he could have died right then. It would have become a crusade on the instant. 'We must fulfil the emperor's dying wish!' Yes, that would have been grand. And that . . .' he looked meaning-fully at Cabal, 'is the way it is going to be. The emperor will make his speech. Then he will die. In that order. Mirkarvia's future depends upon it. As does yours.'

'Can't you just declare, 'The emperor is dead, long live the emperor'? Don't you have a spare for emergencies?'

'The emperor's son is eight years old, and none too bright. His Imperial Majesty dropped him on his head at an early age, and it shows. It would be necessary to declare a regent . . .'

'Who would be you, no doubt?'

'Who would be me, yes, but by the time such things were in hand, we would be up to our necks in revolting peasants. The speech *has* to go ahead as planned.'

Cabal straightened his jacket. 'I shall need my bag with *all* its contents. That includes the *Principia Necromantica*.'

'The book you tried to steal? The university greybeards won't like it.'

'They don't need to. Tell them they'll have to make sacrifices for the greater glory of Mirkarvia. If they still don't like it, offer to have some of your secret policemen come calling to explain patriotism in detail.'

The count smiled wryly. 'You should have been a politician.'

'I shall ignore that comment. I shall need a laboratory and I shall need it now.'

'Naturally. Assistants?'

'I work alone. If you insist on having a spy present to report on my actions, he can sit quietly in the corner and stay out of my way. I give you your emperor doing a reasonable impersonation of a living person and you give me my freedom. That is the deal.'

'Very nearly. I'm afraid there is one item I cannot let you have. That handgun of yours, for obvious reasons. Tell me, why do you carry such a cannon? Its bullets are more than half an inch in diameter.'

Cabal shrugged. 'A gun is a tool for killing. It isn't an enterprise calling for subtlety, only certainty.'

'Guns don't kill people. People kill people.'

'But guns make it *so* much easier. Shall we go?'

They were ready for Cabal. He was taken from the prison and smuggled into the Imperial Palace via an impressively abstruse secret route. A bathroom larger than some ball-rooms he had seen had been scrubbed, disinfected and fitted out with surgical tables and equipment. Plainly, his execution had been put off in anticipation of the emperor dying inconveniently. The knowledge irked him; he disliked being a pawn in somebody else's game.

The late Antrobus II lay flat out and stark naked on a sluice table, a trolley of instruments standing by. Sitting by them was Cabal's Gladstone bag and as he reached the table, he realised that the instruments arrayed were his own, sterilised and ready. Out of interest, he opened the bag and found that Marechal had been as good as his word; everything else was there – *Principia Necromantica* included – but for his gun.

He cast an eye over the dead man. Antrobus hadn't been a great believer in exercise and diet by the look of him. One leg looked gouty and his gut settled about him like unset blancmange. Cabal made a swift estimate of the cadaver's weight, counted the number of test tubes of reagent he had and decided it wasn't enough.

Marechal had sat down on the marble edge of a geyser and was just tapping a cigarette against his silver case when Cabal raised a cautionary finger. 'No smoking. Does this place have a meat freezer?'

The count looked longingly at the cigarette before replacing it. 'Yes.'

'Excellent.' Cabal drew a tiny amount of liquid from one of his phials into a five-millilitre syringe and injected it into the cold, motionless, imperial carotid artery. 'This will start a catalytic reaction throughout the emperor's cardiovascular system to slow down deterioration. The freezer will do the rest.' He took up his notebook and wrote rapidly. 'While the emperor is on ice I shall be synthesising the necessary reactants. I shall require these components.' He tore off the sheet as he went across to Marechal and placed it in his hands. The count read the list. Then he read it again, his eyebrows raising. 'Time is of the essence, Count,' added Cabal sharply.

The count tapped the paper. 'Two pounds of fresh human pituitaries. I don't believe the imperial grocers stretch to fresh human pituitaries. This isn't an easy list to fill.'

'That,' said Cabal, walking back to the emperor and taking off his jacket as he went, 'is hardly my problem. If you want this vast quantity of blue-blooded lard to make his speech on schedule, fill it you will.' He hung his jacket from a wing nut on the surgical light stand and started to roll up his sleeves. 'And fill it promptly.'

The count looked like he might say something for a moment. Then he changed his mind and stood up. 'I'll see to it you have your,' he glanced at the list again and curled his lip, 'components.' He marched out, his boots making sharp clicks that echoed around the tiled walls.

Out in the corridor, Count Marechal snapped his fingers and his adjutant was at his side on the moment. The count handed over the list. 'Get these together as soon as possible and have them given to Cabal.'

The adjutant, who was very much of the majority of aristocratic soldiers and maintained an apiary dedicated to the glory of his moustaches, silently mouthed the list as he read it. 'I say, sir. What *is* a pituitary when it's at home to visitors?'

'It nestles in the middle of the human brain and it's not the sort of thing one can voluntarily donate. Scour the mortuaries. We want them fresh, mind!'

'They don't sound very big. It might take quite a few to make a couple of pounds of the blighters. What if we can't find enough in the mortuaries?'

The count fixed him with his gaze. 'Then find some donors,' he said with an emphasis that even Lieutenant Karstetz could fathom.

'Right ho!' said Karstetz, and clattered out in boots that were a lot brighter than he. He paused at the door and turned back. 'Incidentally, sir. If this necromancer chappie delivers the goods and old man Antrobus sits up and does the business, d'you still want me to bump friend Cabal off?'

The count thought about it for a very short moment. 'No, that's one small change to the plan. When Cabal's done his best, whether he succeeds or fails, you are not to kill him.' He let his hand drift to the hilt of his sabre. '*I* shall.'

All over the city, causes of death were altered to allow the taking of brain samples. Men carried in with knives in their backs were pronounced dead of strokes. Some of the more principled mortuary staff saw fit to complain. 'This is a nonsense!' barked a district coroner at Lieutenant Karstetz as they stood by a slab upon which lay a fresh body of a young man. 'I utterly refuse to open this man's head when the cause of death is obviously a sword wound to the chest! He may have needed his head examining before he got into the duel but it's far too late now.'

'No, I assure you, sir,' said Karstetz. 'This man died of a seizure caused by a morbid condition of the . . .' he took a crumpled piece of paper from his sabretache and read from it, '. . . pituitary gland.' He put the paper away again. 'That's in the brain, you know.'

'I know where it is! I simply fail to see how you can possibly see a sword wound and associate it with . . . Urgh!'

For Lieutenant Karstetz had lost patience, drawn his sword and run the coroner through. He wiped his blade clean on a handy shroud and scabbarded it. 'See?' he asked the assistant coroner who had gone a horrible shade of frightened. 'Sword wound to the chest and what did he die of?'

'A morbid condition . . . of the pituitary?' ventured the assistant.

'Good show! Knew you were the man for the job after poor old,' he waved vaguely at the dead coroner, 'Herr Poor Old here turned up his toes. Anyway, be a sport and fish out the offending organ. Pop it in a jar when you've done and a little man will be around shortly to pick it up. Got to go, there's an absolute epidemic on. Cheerio!'

Cabal worked slowly but surely as the necessary elements came in. He hardly slept, hardly ate, hardly spoke but to demand some new substance or piece of apparatus. His every move was reported to Count Marechal: every drop from every pipette; every process observed; his notes were stolen, copied and returned every time he napped. The count studied them but found them impenetrable, some sort of personal cipher, and he passed them on to the Imperial Intelligence Section for cryptanalysis. Less impenetrable, to the count's shrewd eye at any rate, had been Cabal's demand for fifty pounds of freshly shaved cat hairs. The gaolers of Harslaus Castle would be wearing bandages for weeks. The sack containing the fruits of their painful labours sat, ignored, in the corner. The count knew petty revenge when he saw it and he welcomed it here; it showed Cabal was more human then he liked to pretend, and that lurking somewhere within him was a sense of humour, albeit a cruel one. A man is known by his actions and the count liked to know those he dealt with.

The day of the speech approached and Cabal finally sent for the late emperor's mortal remains. He thawed it in a circle of lamps that he had had manufactured to his specifications, fuelled with a blend of oils that baffled and disturbed the small army of chemists Marechal had assembled. Cabal had Antrobus carefully placed on the cold, white floor before surrounding him with a circle of five of the lamps – their glistening reflectors facing inwards – each vertex of the precise pentagon joined to its neighbours with fluorescent tubes filled with gases that theoretically shouldn't fluoresce. The gas mixture had cost one of the artisans charged with their construction his sanity. Now he lay in a padded cell screaming about the infraviolet and the corners in time. Marechal deliberately left the technical report unread and ordered the destruction of all Cabal's equipment when it had fulfilled its purpose.

The lamps and the tubes burned for exactly twenty-three hours before abruptly extinguishing themselves. All through the time, Cabal had sat cross-legged and muttering some sort of mantra beneath his breath in a light trance.

'Well, I don't know if he's the real thing or a fraud,' Karstetz commented late that evening, 'but he's frightfully good at whatever it is he's doing. More Bikavér?'

The instant the lights went out Cabal's eyes rolled back

down in their sockets and he jumped inside the line of tubes. He plucked a syringe case from his pocket, drew a quantity of faintly shimmering liquid from a bottle and started injecting the corpse at specific points: the temples, the base of the throat, the solar plexus. Marechal had the misfortune to be the only person handy when Cabal needed part of the Emperor's bulk moving out of the way so he could get at some of the less savoury locations. 'What are you doing?' asked the count making conversation in an attempt to distract himself from what he was doing and where his hands were.

Cabal said nothing as he drew a full fifty millilitres of the fluid, carefully placed the point of the great steel needle and pushed it in with some effort and the sound of separating gristle. 'Do you know what the Ka is?'

'No.'

'Ki?'

'No.'

'Chakra?'

'Ah, now that's a sort of round throwing knife from somewhere or other on the subcontinent. Fearsome thing in the right hands,' Marechal said with enthusiasm.

Cabal paused for half a second before carrying on. 'And that's all?'

'Yes.'

'Then I can't explain it to you. Come back when your education includes the details of life as well as the commission of death.'

Count Marechal looked at Cabal, paling with anger. Cabal looked back at him evenly, noting both how very easy Marechal was to provoke, and the scar on his cheek that only seemed to be visible when he was angry. 'You duel, Count?'

The count brought himself under control. 'I did, when I was at university. You mean the scar? Yes.'

Cabal seemed to have lost interest. He'd moved on to the corpse's legs and was inserting the needle behind the patella of the right knee. 'You can put that down now. Unless you've developed a personal attachment, of course.'

The count let that comment pass, stood up, and walked to a sink to wash his hands. 'You really believe you're some sort of obscene parody of a doctor, don't you? Saving lives after they're already lost for the good of humanity.'

' "Obscene parody"?' repeated Cabal without rancour. 'I'm not sure that particular phrase was in my mind when I decided on my career. As for humanity, anything I do for it is purely by accident.'

'Then why? Immortality? Perhaps you should have become a vampire.'

Cabal stopped and looked at the count very coldly indeed. 'Perhaps I should,' he said finally.

'These lands used to be full of them,' said the count conversationally, having entirely missed Cabal's look. 'Tottering old castles on craggy mountain tops packed to the rafters with them. More Nosferatu than you could shake a stake at. Not any more. They had to go. They wouldn't pay their taxes.'

'I beg your pardon?'

'They thought that just because they'd dodged the certainty of death that dodging the certainty of taxes somehow went by on the nod.' He snorted. 'They were wrong.'

Cabal momentarily considered the sight of bailiffs armed to the teeth with stakes, garlic, and court writs. Then he stood up and stepped out of the pentangle. 'Finished.'

'What?' The count was incredulous. 'Just like that?'

'He's alive. Or at least, he's doing a convincing impersonation. I need some sleep. Then I shall require the text of the speech he is to deliver.'

'Why?'

'Because,' snapped Cabal, his tiredness catching up with him, 'he's nothing more than a heap of walking offal. He can't possibly read the speech himself, it will have to be conditioned into him like teaching a parrot.'

The count had gone over to look down on the emperor. The corpse was undeniably breathing. He shook his head; he'd only half believed all this mumbo-jumbo could possibly work. 'He doesn't look very well.'

'He's *dead*. He's hardly going to be a picture of vibrant health. Just before he gives the speech, I'll give him something to make him look a little less like a side of beef and more like a head of state. Now,' Cabal sighed, wilting slightly, 'I'm very tired. We shall continue this tomorrow.' He started to walk out.

The count stayed where he was. The plan to resurrect the emperor had always been a desperate contingency plan. It was very hard to accept that it seemed to be coming off. 'Shouldn't you put him on, I don't know, a saline drip? Or glucose or something?'

'He's only performing basic respiration. I think he has enough reserves to last a few hours,' said Cabal without even turning. Then he was gone.

Count Marechal was left with the undead emperor and his grand schemes.

JONATHAN L. HOWARD

CENTRAL MATRICULATION BOARD: LEVEL 5 HISTORY PAPER
SECTION 4: THE SECOND GALLACIAN CONFLICT

Read the following brief description of the Second Gallician Conflict, its results and ramifications, and then answer the questions that follow it. This section is worth 10% of your overall mark. Show all working.

Some four hundred years ago in Eastern Europe, Mirkarvia made significant inroads into the territories of two of its neighbours – Senza and Polorus. These conquests were accompanied and succeeded by a series of atrocities, mostly carried out under the pretext of counterinsurgency actions. Over the following decades, these acts settled into a pattern of ethnic discrimination and violent suppression. Finally, Senza – newly resurgent after the discovery of major gold deposits in the southwest and a generally burgeoning economy – militarised its border with Mirkarvia. The Mirkarvian emperor, Dulcis III, listened to the council of his hawkish generals, armchair strategists all, and declared war. This was exactly what the Senzans had anticipated; several secret treaties were triggered that ultimately resulted in Senza and Polorus, with support from their neighbouring states of Ruritania and Graustark, forming an alliance against Mirkarvia. The antiquated Mirkarvian army was quickly routed, and the captured lands recovered.

Polorus argued for the occupation of the Mirkarvian capital of Krenz with the implied erasure of Mirkarvia as a state. Senza, however, had no desire to try to control lands containing ethnic Mirkarvians. Therefore, the Mirkarvian exchequer was emptied, large quantities of art treasures and transportable wealth were seized, and swingeing trade concessions were taken as reparation.

It took Mirkarvia generations to recover financially from

18

these humiliations, and the scars still run deep in the national character. The days of the Mirkarvian Empire are domestically regarded as a golden age for all, the terrible crimes of that period expunged from Mirkarvian schoolbooks. Politically, the ramifications of the empire's collapse are still evident in Mirkarvian's dealings with its neighbours. Her only local ally is the notoriously backward Katamenia to the north. They share no borders, however; travel between them must go through a mountainous isthmus of Senzan territory extending from the bulk of the country off to the west, where strict customs inspections are the rule. The only other route would require travelling through the Gallaco Sea, but Katamenia has no coastline. Thus, any such journey would still require some travel through either Senza or Polorus.

(A) In what year did Mirkarvia invade Senza?
(B) i) With hindsight, what was Dulcis Ill's most serious error?
     ii) And without hindsight?
(C) Discuss any two (2) of the following statements:
     i) Mirkarvia behaved like a right bunch of bastards.
     ii) Polorus behaved like a right bunch of bastards.
     iii) All countries behave like right bunches of bastards.
(D) Write a political treatise – not to exceed 250,000 words or 500 sides, whichever is less – detailing your solution to stabilising relations in the region, Military force above brigade level is not permitted, nor is divine intervention. You may include diagrams.

Chapter 2

IN WHICH A SPEECH IS DELIVERED AND
THERE IS A FALLING OUT

'I should like my own clothes back,' said Cabal. 'And my cane.' He was setting up an odd device consisting of a small diamond-shaped mirror on an armature over the recumbent emperor's head. Cabal spun it experimentally with the tip of his finger and the reflected light flickered rapidly across the emperor's eyes. The eyes, which had been showing no inclination to cooperate or even an acceptable job of tracking objects individually, twitched crazily before finally settling their gaze on the mirror.

Count Marechal watched, his arms crossed. 'Your cane?' He remembered seeing it among Cabal's possessions; an elegant ebony stick topped with an ugly silver skull headpiece, the high sheen of the smooth surfaces contrasting strongly with the tarnish in the eye sockets and between the teeth. 'Sentimental value?' he said sarcastically.

'As it happens, yes.' Cabal walked over to the count and took the emperor's speech from him. 'I bludgeoned my first failed experiment back to death with it. Thank you.' He returned to linking the mirror to a small electrical motor.

The count went to where Lieutenant Karstetz waited. 'Get him what he wants, lieutenant,' he said. Then added softly, 'We won't have to put up with him for very much longer.'

'Good thing, too,' whispered Karstetz back. 'The people are getting very troublesome. We're having to put down little demonstrations almost constantly.'

'That will all change in a few hours when the emperor gives his greatest – and last – speech.' He nodded in Cabal's direction. 'It would be a useful trick to be able to trot dead people out when necessary. Has any progress been made on Cabal's notes?'

'All a bit technical for me, I'm afraid,' said Karstetz, who found getting dressed unassisted all a bit technical for him. 'The cipher boffins are very impressed that he does it all in his head, though. They said something about a rolling key but they lost me after that.'

'What's a "rolling key"?'

'That's the bit that lost me. Sorry.'

'It hardly matters if they take a little while to break it. Anybody who's going to be dying in the next week or so can stay that way with my blessing.'

Cabal folded his legs under him into a corrupt lotus position by the emperor and flicked through the speech. 'Your work, Count?'

'Yes, as it happens. Yes, I wrote it. Why?'

'No reason,' said Cabal, holding the paper with his fingertips. 'Very . . . rabble-rousing. Very appealing to the mob.'

'All the best speeches are,' said Marechal, scenting dissent. 'The intention is to get the hoi polloi behind a little healthy expansionism, not dazzle them with a philosophical discourse.'

'No danger of that,' said Cabal. He leaned over and

flicked the mirror with his finger. It started spinning rapidly, powered by the motor. The late emperor's gaze settled on the glittering object and stayed focused there. Cabal leaned forward and read in an intense whisper, 'People of Mirkarvia. Friends. I come before you today to share a vision I have of the future. Not just the future of our own great and noble country but also that of our neighbours . . .'

Marechal gestured curtly at Karstetz and the two men tiptoed noisily out, their boots clacking and squeaking in the great echoing room. When they were gone, Cabal paused. He looked at the emperor, then at the door through which the two officers had just left. Then he smiled a smile that had no intention of getting anywhere near his eyes.

'Brocade, your Imperial Majesty, your favourite!' It is always a little disappointing when somebody fulfils a stereotype to several decimal places. Prezof, the emperor's tailor – more of a costumier, really – would have been laughed off the stage if he'd ever played his job. Tired, dull clichés, the critics would have said. Isn't the playwright living in the present? Surely no respectable theatre would dare turn out a production of anything other than farce in which a personal tailor is a flouncing, pompadoured, powder puff? A pathetic, simpering, mincing . . . and so on and so forth. Prezof was all these things. He lived alone but for an obese cat that he called *Felice*. He had a well-thumbed copy of *The Castle of Otranto* with his favourite passages underlined in green ink. He had an impressive collection of embroidered antimacassars on all the armchairs in his house that he changed daily whether anybody had sat there or not. There was nothing more important than the creation of fine clothes for his Imperial Majesty and not an hour went by when he wasn't actively pursuing the muse. The materials were of the finest, the workmanship superlative, the design execrable. For Prezof may have been dedicated, hardworking and diligent but he was not in the least talented. It summed up Mirkarvia very nicely that nobody noticed. Even Cabal, whose artistic eye had been allowed to atrophy, found it painful to be too close to the exquisite robes in which the emperor was due to make his speech. As Prezof bustled the unusually silent emperor into his new clothes, Cabal took his blue-glass dark spectacles from his pocket, polished them on a small piece of chamois that he kept handy and put them on. That was much better.

Prezof favoured him with a sour glance. Cabal's black suit had been returned to him, repaired, cleaned and pressed. A new white shirt, cravat and shoes made him feel like himself again. His cane lay across his lap. He'd stunned Karstetz by thanking him for its return and almost sounding as if he meant it. All Prezof saw was an unexciting, conservative ensemble. Still, black was always good but perhaps as a cloak? Yes, a cloak! Cabal tended to stride, a cloak would look marvellous billowing about him as he did so. So far, so obvious. Then Prezof demonstrated that he hadn't lost his knack by mentally adding mauve galoshes and a tall fez with a feather. Cabal was not a vain man but he did stand upon his dignity and if he had only been able to see that image in Prezof's mind, he would certainly have considered murder.

'Your Imperial Majesty is very quiet today,' said Prezof. 'And a little pale, if I might make so bold. You are well?'

Antrobus looked down at Prezof and his eyes were black ports into an empty pit where a soul used to live. His lips slowly formed the words, 'People of Mirkarvia . . . Mirkarvia . . .' Prezof prided himself on being a sensitive person, but then again he prided himself on being a great artist and he was deluding himself there too. He smiled at the dead man and told him there was a bit of mild flu going around and that was certainly the problem.

Cabal was getting bored waiting. He had one last syringe to inject just before they presented the imperial carcass to its public that would give the grey, marbled flesh the semblance of humanity. After that . . . well, he would have to see. The Count Marechal was clearly a career soldier, a political meddler, and an ambitious aristocrat and any of these occupations would have boded ill in itself. How he managed to be all three simultaneously without tearing down the seams, and the mendacity and ruthlessness with which he was stuffed leaking out was a small miracle. Cabal briefly wondered what mendacity and ruthlessness looked like as stuffing and imagined something like wet poppy seeds before his personality turned up and quashed such frivolous whimsy. He had to stay focused if he were to stay alive.

Lieutenant Karstetz came in and stamped to attention because he liked it. 'The Count Marechal requires your presence, Herr Cabal, at the imperial balcony. Oh, and take the corpse with you,' he added as an afterthought.

'Corpse?' said Prezof, appalled, stepping out from behind Antrobus's bulk where he had been brushing nap. Then he looked up at the pale emperor and a penny audibly dropped. He gasped and stepped back.

'Oh,' said Karstetz, miffed, 'I say, the dressmaker. That's a bind. This is all supposed to be terribly hush-hush. The count will have my guts for garters for letting the cat out of the bag.' He went up to Cabal. 'Be a brick and take his Imperial Deadness to the balcony, will you?' He looked at Prezof without rancour and drew his sabre. 'Fraid I've got a bit of cleaning up to do here, don't y'know?'

Cabal took the emperor by the elbow and guided him to the door and out in the corridor. As he turned to close the door behind him, he saw Karstetz bearing down on the terrified Prezof. He loathed unnecessary killing but, on the other hand, he loathed Prezof.

Still, he felt it was necessary to at least register his disapproval. 'You can't go around killing people to cover up your mistakes,' he said. 'You'll kill off half the country at that rate.'

Karstetz paused. 'You're right, of course,' he admitted, apparently missing the implication. 'I think that's a very good point. I shall start being more careful . . .' he turned back towards Prezof and raised his sabre '. . . tomorrow.'

Cabal narrowed his lips and closed the door behind him. Halfway down the corridor, he heard a reedy scream from the room.

'This is a fine country you've got here,' he said to Antrobus II. '*Such* a fine place. A nominal leader who should have been in a sepulchre a week ago and a military full of inbred psychopaths.' They walked a little further. 'A little bit like Imperial Rome, really.'

Marechal was crushing a dead cigarette out in an overflowing ashtray when Cabal entered. 'Where have you been?' he demanded, thrusting a thumb over his shoulder at an ormulu clock. 'Have you seen the time? Is he ready? *Gott*, look at the state of him.'

Cabal produced a syringe and jammed it in Antrobus's neck. Antrobus seemed wholly unconcerned. After a few seconds, a spreading perimeter of good skin colour was expanding out from the needle mark. Where it passed, the pallid corpse tones were replaced with a glow of rude health, the dead eyes twinkled, the hair bristled.

Lieutenant Karstetz entered as the transformation was well underway. 'I say, I could do with a jigger of that stuff after a heavy night.'

'I'll give you the formula,' said Cabal in the full knowledge that the stuff was toxic to the living.

'Does he know the speech?' asked Marechal.

'He knows every word he's been taught,' replied Cabal. 'He can be relied upon to play his part.'

'Excellent.' The Count Marechal went to the curtain that divided the room from the balcony. It was a good day for a speech. The weather was clear and cool without being cold. A national holiday had been called and the people were feeling well disposed to the ruling class. They showed this by milling around eating sausages, swilling beer, and slapping each other on the back while laughing too loudly. This, from Marechal's perspective, was a vast improvement on them running around with flaming brands, torching government buildings, and stringing up tax collectors. He watched the crowd for a few moments, the faint sneer that lurked about beneath his nose twisting his moustache.

Across the square, the basilica clock sounded the hour and the people grew quiet. Marechal moved away from the window. 'It is time,' he said, purely for effect. 'This had better work, Cabal.'

'I've done my work properly,' said Cabal as he led the emperor forward. 'You should be worrying about the standard of the speech.'

The curtains were drawn back, Cabal whispered a word of command into Antrobus's ear, and the dead man stepped forward for his finest hour. Cabal retreated into the shadows as Marechal and the other dignitaries formed up into a line behind the emperor. Marechal curtly gestured to Karstetz. 'Watch Cabal,' he whispered.

'Bit late in the day for him to try anything, isn't it, old man?'

'A bit late?' He looked at Karstez with mild disbelief, as if just realising that he was talking to a chimp in a cavalry officer's uniform. 'Just watch him, will you?' He joined the line.

Karstetz moved back into the room and perched on the corner of a table, an unconscious echo of how Cabal had first seen the Count Marechal. But where Marechal had watched him closely, Karstetz only grinned amiably, looked around the room with little interest and started to hum an unlovely melody for the tuba. Cabal found an antique high-backed chair and made himself comfortable.

The crowd went deadly quiet as the emperor, Antrobus II of Mirkarvia, made his appearance. Plentiful rumours of his death had been floating above; despite Marechal's threats and Karstetz's enthusiasm, the imperial household leaked gossip like a buckshotted bucket. The people had been half looking forward to a nice revolution. And now up popped Antrobus and quite spoiled things. Still, they gave a cheer. The beer and sausages *were* free and they didn't wish to appear churlish. They'd let him have his say and then start a revolution next week, after a decent interval. They were a downtrodden mass but they had been brought up nicely.

Antrobus stepped up to the balcony rail and paused. And paused. The moment grew to impolite and impolitic length. The dignitaries in the line shot glances at one another. The crowd began to mutter, a distant susurration of uncertainty. Marechal's expression never changed but he made sure that the captain of guards down in the square would be able to see his signal to shoot into the crowd if need be. Then things would need to be done and done quickly. Still, it would only take a moment to shoot Cabal through the middle of his supercilious face and blow recondite grey matter over the walls. He'd intended to do it anyway but it would be so much more satisfying seasoned with revenge. Then he forgot about the pale pleasures of cheap brutality as the emperor raised his hands and the crowd fell silent once more.

'People of Mirkarvia,' he spoke in a pleasing baritone that carried easily across the square. 'Friends,' he said it with such sincerity that commoners who had long referred to him as 'lard arse', 'flobber features', 'cancer borne on the backs of the proletariat' and other things less kind, suddenly felt unfamiliar but not unpleasant pricklings of admiration for their emperor. They hung on his every word. This was going to be important. 'I come before you today to share a vision I have of the future. Not just the future of our own great and noble country but also that of our neighbours . . .'

It was powerful stuff and those of a romantic, nationalistic nature in particular were borne along by it. Karstetz was all that and stupid to boot. He rose from the table and walked slowly towards the fluttering curtains as if drawn by siren song. He stopped and listened, transfixed. Cabal watched him as a scientist watches a beetle on a tombstone. After a few seconds, it was plain that Karstetz had forgotten all about him. Quietly, Cabal climbed to his feet, picked up his bag and cane, and walked softly, keeping to the thick carpet, in the direction of the door.

On the balcony, Marechal glowed inwardly. This was exquisite, far better than even his fondest hopes. The crowd were eating this with an even more avaricious appetite than the one they'd used to demolish several tons of state-owned sausage. The rumours of the emperor's death could now be skilfully twisted into the people 'knowing' about the emperor's fragile health. Yet he'd heroically torn himself from his deathbed to deliver this, his last and greatest gift to his people, his wish for the future. This wasn't going to be some grubby little land-grabbing campaign. It was going to be a *crusade*.

'The disputed lands are *ours*,' roared the emperor.

'Historically ours. Rightfully ours. They shall be ours again!' In the crowd's collective consciousness, their neighbours turned from trading partners and allies into a bunch of thieving gypsies, ripe for extermination.

Marechal smiled and looked at the others in the line, the generals, the marshals, the admirals of the Aerofleet and the commodore of the tiny Gallaco Sea Fleet. They were entranced, enraptured. War was in the air and it smelled good.

Then he noticed Karstetz standing behind the curtains, his whole attention given to entirely the wrong subject. Cabal was nowhere to be seen. Marechal felt suddenly cold. So Cabal had escaped, so what? Marechal remembered a sack of cat hair and Cabal's strange sense of humour, his loathing of war in general, and Marechal's ambitions in particular. His suspicions deepened.

Karstetz didn't respond to Marechal's attempts to attract his attention while not distracting the crowd. He didn't feel the intense gaze, see the sharp flicks of the head, hear the snapped fingers. He only had ears for the emperor's speech. 'Make no mistake,' Antrobus was saying, 'these fair-weather friends with their deceitful ways and foul plans are our enemies!' The crowd roared. 'Our mortal foe!' They screamed for blood. 'Our prey!' They gave voice to a full-throated howl of fury. It went half-throated when they belatedly realised what he'd said.

Marechal flicked his attention from Karstetz to Antrobus. Prey? He'd never written that.

'We shall hunt them! Kill them! Eat them!' cried Antrobus in a passion. 'They are our meat! We shall tear the flesh from their bones with our bare teeth and devour them!' Marechal realised with horror that the emperor was drooling, dark saliva bubbling from his lips. Down in the square, the people were looking suspiciously at their sausages.

'Ach, *du lieber Gott*,' he whispered. Then to Karstetz he barked, 'Lieutenant! Get him!'

'Wha'?' Karstetz looked around as if waking. 'What? Who?'

'The emperor, you dolt! Get him inside before it's too late!'

'Brains!' The emperor was shrieking now. 'If we eat their brains, we have their strength, their very souls. Brains!' The strength of his voice was going, quickly turning to a shambling imbecilic tone. 'Human brains ... must eat ... brains ...'

'There, there, old fella,' said Karstetz, appearing beside him. 'Let's get you indoors and in your coffin, shall we? Have a lovely state funeral. That'll be nice, won't it?'

'Brains,' said Antrobus unheeding, the drool dripping into a dark stain on his robes. 'Must eat ... brains ...' He finally noticed Karstetz and decided to start with a light snack.

The crowd gasped and gagged and bits of it fainted as its Imperial Majesty fell upon a surprised cavalry officer. Karstetz may have started to scream before Antrobus smashed his head open on the marble balcony rail, threw him to the floor and started to feed. It was so hard to tell amidst all the other screams.

Marechal's mind worked quickly. He needed a ploy and he needed it now. The French gambit, it had to be. 'We are betrayed!' he shouted and signalled to the captain of guards. Sporadically at first and then with increasing discipline, rifle fire started to pour into the crowd. Marechal signalled three volleys and ran into the room. The door at the far end burst open and guardsmen rushed in. 'Get that thing in here,' he bellowed at them.

'The emperor?' asked the sergeant at their head.

'Emperor? That's not our emperor! We are betrayed! Drag it in here and kill it!'

He left them grappling with the foul thing that screeched and whooped at them. The situation was still controllable. The massacre in the square could easily be put at the door of enemy agents. The sudden panic he had caused would drive those last few moments into a strange world of uncertain memory. Had the emperor really turned into a monstrous cannibal before their eyes? Of course not. He'd been attacked by . . . by . . . a traitor! Karstetz had attacked the emperor. A life and death struggle, the heroic efforts of the emperor killing his own assassin even as he breathed his last. Yes, yes! It could work!

It *was* a shame about Karstetz, though. He'd owed Marechal money.

He ran through the palace unheeding of the precise course he was taking, uncertain even what he was looking for. He swung two doors open and found himself in the great banqueting hall of the palace. It was one of the more medieval parts of the place, a long table positioned down its centre, a balcony running round from the end of the great staircase on the northern wall, a minstrels' gallery. At the far end, unsuccessfully trying the doors there, it also had Johannes Cabal.

Marechal smiled bitterly, closed the doors behind him and loosened his revolver in its holster. This was what his subconscious mind had been up to, hunting this man, this hated man. Sometimes, he got a great sense of job satisfaction.

Cabal had heard the sound and already turned to face him. He drew his pocket watch and studied the face. 'Have the emperor's dietary mores changed already?' he asked in a tone of polite enquiry. 'Test batch 295 always was unreliable.'

'You knew this would happen?' Now the Count Marechal could relax a little. What was occurring outside could wait

31

for a few minutes. He had time to pause a moment, take stock, kill Cabal.

'Two ninety-five yields remarkable results. Right up to the moment the subject becomes a maniacal cannibal. I had hoped for a few more minutes' grace, though. Any casualties?'

'Lieutenant Karstetz.'

'No loss there, then.'

'None at all.' Marechal drew his gun. 'What am I to do with you, Herr Cabal?'

'It would seem that you've already made up your mind on that point.' Johannes Cabal placed his bag and cane on the end of the long banqueting table, took off his jacket, folded it and put it down too. Then he unbuttoned his cuffs and rolled up his sleeves.

Marechal watched him with curiosity. 'You seem to be taking this very well.'

'Not at all,' replied Cabal. He picked up the cane, twisted the head and drew three feet of razor-sharp steel from it. Before Marechal's bemused eyes, he placed the cane body on top of his jacket, presented himself as a fencer to Marechal and saluted him with the sword cane.

Marechal laughed. 'You simply cannot be serious, Cabal! Are you challenging me?'

'I appreciate that it is customary to slap you with a glove or some such but I think you would shoot me long before I got near you.' He studied his stance and corrected the position of his feet slightly. 'You must forgive me, I'm rather rusty.'

'Don't be a fool and think *I'm* a fool. Why should I waste any more time with you?' He levelled the gun. 'You don't deserve a chance.'

Cabal flicked the tip of his sword through the four quarters. '*Sixte. Quarte. Septime. Octave.* It's got nothing to do with chances, Count. At least not from your perspective. You're a petty little man. You could just shoot me. Indeed, the probability is that you will. And you will spit upon my corpse and walk away. And in a week or so, the situation outside these walls will probably have deteriorated to the point where controlling your unimpressed civilians will be taking up much of your time. You will curse my name and wish me dead a dozen more times. But, in truth, you will not have killed me even once. That, Count, will gall you more than you can bear.'

'A student of human nature, are you now?' The count drew back the hammer of the revolver. 'You will die and I will be the one to kill you, make no mistake.'

'No, Count. You won't have killed me. Several grains of lead will have killed me while you stayed snug and safe on the other side of a large hall. That gun will have killed me. You won't have the satisfaction. You're a soldier, Count; that I don't dispute. But I also believed you to be a warrior. There, I was wrong. You're no more interested in the martial art of it than a conscripted peasant with a musket shoved into his hands.'

'You cannot goad me, Cabal. I'm past that stage.'

'A drunken grognard of the levy.'

'It would be a shame to lose your dignity in your final seconds.'

'An artillery officer.'

Marechal's skull tightened with rage. '*What* did you just call me?'

'An artillery officer. Safe behind the lines.' Cabal lowered his sword and gestured at the gun. 'A *mechanic*.'

Marechal knew that it was sheer foolishness to throw away a great advantage for a slightly smaller one. Madness. But there are only so many slurs a cavalryman can countenance. When Cabal died, when his face took on that delicious expression of mortal surprise, Marechal wanted it to be because there was a sabre through his heart. More than anything, Marechal wanted to feel Cabal's ribs grating on the edges of his blade as he twisted it in the hated necromancer's chest. That would be a thought to keep him warm in the difficult times that were surely coming. His rage settled and became cold and hard. With economical movements, he opened his revolver and ejected the cartridges. They bounced sharply, sending echoes around the hall. Then he threw the gun to one side. The next sound was the hiss of his sabre leaving its scabbard.

'What have you got there, Cabal? A foil? A rapier? A sword for boys. This,' his sabre whirled in a vicious figure of eight, 'is a man's weapon.' His free hand fisted on his hip, he advanced. *'En garde.'*

Cabal's blade flicked up to quarte. 'I'm always on guard, Marechal, one way or the other.' He watched the count advance for a moment more before adding, 'You're sure you're up to this? I fenced for very nearly a year in my youth. I was considered quite competent.'

'Don't patronise me, Cabal.'

'It's just that I wonder how much technique a man can learn, cutting down unarmed yokels from horseback?'

Marechal stopped just before the blades crossed. 'This isn't one of those effeminate fencing sabres the Italians came up with. It is a real weapon and it really kills and it shall be my very real pleasure to hack you into pieces with it, Cabal.'

Before Cabal had a chance to reply, Marechal launched into a progressive attack. Cabal fell back immediately under the ferocity of the advance. Marechal was a strong man, stronger than Cabal, and the beats that rained down upon his rapier struck sparks and generated vibrations to his wrist that felt like they might numb it with enough time. If he lived that long.

Cabal considered his options. Marechal was no sporting fencer. He fought to kill. The strength of his attack was clearly intended to destroy Cabal quickly, and the physical power of the heavy horse sabre might do it too. Fortunately, his sword cane was designed for practical combat, being far more *forte* than *foible* but without brittleness. Still, he was already running out of room into which he could retreat. He needed to make Marechal think again if he were to stop this dreadful hail of steel. A poor feint, followed by a quick step back to give him the room for a stop hit with *rassemblement*, allowed him to pink the top of Marechal's wrist. Cabal used the moment of surprise to run past the head of the table and gain more space.

The count didn't follow him at first but paused to pull up his cuff and check his wrist.

'First blood, Count Marechal?' called Cabal as he returned to his guard position.

'Touché, Herr Cabal. A scratch,' he said and Cabal could see that it was no understatement. 'I can see that I've underestimated you again.' He saluted and allowed the wry smile to evaporate from his face. 'But now I have your measure.'

'Really? Tell me, Count, how did you learn to fence? Correspondence course?'

Marechal said nothing but moved to reengage, his face like thunder. This time there was none of the brutal slashing that had accompanied the first attack. Cabal suspected that had as much to do with the count regaining his strength as anything else. He would certainly employ it again should he spy an advantage in doing so.

They traded attacks and parries for a few moments, the count clearly probing Cabal's defences. Although he didn't show it, Cabal was getting more worried with each clash of steel. His sword cane was outweighed by the sabre, his experience was outweighed by the count's, and his aggression was a pale shadow in comparison. He was defending, Marechal was getting all the information that he needed for a telling attack, and there was always the chance of guards wandering in at any moment. Cabal needed a way out of this situation quickly and he doubted it would hinge on his skill on the piste. He needed to look at the whole picture and see an escape. For the moment, however, it eluded him and then Marechal launched an attack and Cabal didn't have time to think about anything else.

It ended with a cutting blow that Cabal parried with difficulty although he made it look easy – half the psychological game in fencing. He countered with a type of sabre riposte he'd seen the count make, from tierce to the head. Marechal parried it easily but made it look difficult – the other half of the psychological game.

Cabal had looked death in the face before on numerous occasions but had always been careful to give himself some chance of survival. There were very few grounds for hope here, though.

'You look worried, Herr Cabal,' said Marechal. 'Something on your mind?'

'There is, since you ask. I was just thinking that this is all a dreadful waste of resources. I appreciate that you intended to kill me whether I succeeded or not but that was politics. But think! Nobody else knows about me. Wouldn't it make sense for you to supply me with a laboratory and I work for you? I'm sure I could be of use.'

Marechal made no attempt to hide his sneer. 'Are you begging for your life, Cabal?'

'Not at all. Just attempting to make something constructive of this debacle. By the same coin, if I were to kill you,' the count laughed contemptuously, '*if* I were to kill you, Count Marechal, this country will certainly fall to pieces.

There's nobody around to take your place. Think on it.'

The count thought for a moment, their sword tips just touching. 'I've thought about it. You've forgotten two important details. First, I'm not going to lose this duel. Second, I want you to die. Now.'

Cabal considered. 'I suppose I *could* see my way clear to begging for my life as long as you don't insist on any outright grovelling?'

Marechal's blade supplied his answer. Cabal tried to break ground and disengage but Marechal covered the distance with an impressive *flèche* that Cabal had to dodge, followed immediately with a *passata soto* – known outside fencing circles as ducking – to avoid being decapitated.

This was an unwelcome development. Cabal had gained the impression that Marechal had probably started duelling as a student in the fashion of the Prussian *schläger*, a bizarre contest in which the main goal is to supply one another with scars about the face that impress the ladies no end. Apart from the armour the combatants are covered with to reduce all wounds to a cosmetic level, its notable feature is that the duellists never move from the spot. The count's unexpected and unwelcome entrée into the world of combat ballet – that damn *flèche* must have carried him the best part of ten feet – was just one more thing that Cabal didn't want to have to deal with right at this precise moment.

It was only when Marechal said, 'Touché, Herr Cabal,' and smiled malevolently that Cabal realised he'd been hit. His shirt was ripped high on his left breast, the thrust having gone through the cloth, scored his chest, exited beneath the shoulder and done the same to his left upper arm. Against the white linen, there seemed to be a lot of blood.

Cabal looked straight at Marechal. 'You wouldn't accept my offer, Marechal. Now let me tell you one thing you couldn't know. I won't let you kill me. There's more at stake than you can possibly imagine in your blinkered little world. I don't have time for your stupid games.' All the fear was leaving him. The doubts and uncertainties that had blurred his vision were going now and the world was coalescing into a beautifully clear picture of what needed to be done and why. What remained was a single motivation that glowed within him like white fire. His soul, his poor mistreated soul, tended him and directed him. Marechal stopped being the only thing in the world and became a rather pathetic man with a silly moustache who believed his puerile plans for grabbing a few useless square inches on the map actually mattered. 'I am leaving here. If you attempt to stop me, I shall kill you. Is that understood?'

Marechal's opinion of Cabal might have changed in that moment but it certainly didn't improve.

'You insolent cur!' he roared and launched a terrifying attack culminating with a *mollinaro* that could have cored a rhinoceros. They found themselves momentarily *corps-a-corps*, Marechal called him a lowborn bastard and back-handed him so hard Cabal spun away and rolled on to the table.

Cabal blinked, saw Marechal appear above him with his sabre held high like a meat cleaver and rolled to his left, dodging the blade that swept past him like a guillotine. He quickly climbed to his feet as Marechal pulled the sword from the ruined surface and, as they seemed to be extemporising and as the table gave him a substantial height advantage, he kicked the count in the face and broke his nose.

The Count Marechal staggered back, rallied, and ran to the far end of the table where he could mount it, using a chair as a step, without opposition. Cabal and Marechal faced each other along its length, blood on both of them. They paused: Cabal expressionless and cold; Marechal with teeth bared.

Now they knew one another. Now there would be no more

talking. Marechal saluted, but this time it finished with a slash of the blade that left an almost tangible cut hanging in the air. Cabal saluted, and it was a staccato, precise thing. His sword tip travelled to precise points, his wrist moved through exact angles.

Then they fought.

Chapter 3

IN WHICH NAMES ARE CALLED AND A
FUGITIVE TAKES FLIGHT

'Of course I have a reservation. A government reservation. Here is my authorisation.' Gerhard Meissner was a low-ranking member of the Mirkarvian civil service and, as is sometimes the case, he had hugely inflated ideas as to his importance. If he didn't arrive in Katamenia on schedule with the incredibly important 'Agricultural Land Remittance Discussion Papers (Third Draft)' – currently safely tucked away in his documents folder – well, it hardly bore thinking about. Unable to have the latest draft of the papers, civilisation would be at a loss to discuss the remittance of agricultural lands. The results . . . catastrophic. Thus, he had been issued with the necessary documentation to bypass the lesser folk at Emperor Boniface VIII Aeroport customs and pick up his ticket. He examined it now and was pleased to discover that he had a berth aboard the *Princess Hortense*, a brand spanking new aeroship of the Mirkarvian civil aeroforce, MirkAir.

'You're a lucky man, sir,' said the woman at the counter. 'The *Hortense* was only commissioned a week ago – this is her maiden flight.'

Meissner sniffed – he wasn't lucky, he was a civil servant and this was no more than was due to a corpuscle of the body politic. Instead, he asked, 'Why are all these people milling around? It's like race day in here.'

'Some trouble in the city, sir. People panic. It's only human.'

A well-dressed man, sweating and frantic, pushed by Meissner who glared at him fiercely. 'Please!' said the man. 'Have you got any more berths available? Any at all?'

'I'm sorry, sir. All places aboard the *Princess Hortense* were booked up in advance.'

'What?' The sweating man saw the ticket in Meissner's hand. 'Please, sir. Would you be willing to sell that billet? My daughter . . . There's rioting in the city. I simply want her to get to safe—'

'Sell my ticket?' snapped Meissner. 'The impertinence, sir! Even if I were at liberty to sell this ticket – which I am not, it being government property – I very much doubt that I should feel disposed to . . .' But the man had more urgent matters to attend to than listening to how important Meissner was, and had already gone. Meissner pulled himself up to his full height, a little over six feet tall, and looked dignified, an expression lesser mortals could only assume with the aid of lemon juice and alum. The woman on the desk thought that he could almost have been attractive if it wasn't for what his personality did to his face. He noticed her attention and she smiled, politely but without warmth. 'When does the ship depart?' he demanded.

'In two hours, sir. If you'd care to check your luggage in now, then you'll have some time to relax aboard before she lifts.'

'Relax?' he snorted. 'I shall work!'

Having emphasised his innate superiority to the herd, he walked away.

Meissner went to the handling building – a capacious hangar split into many small bays with padlocked gates – to check his luggage in. On his way back out, he was accosted by a serious-looking man dressed in black and white. 'Excuse me, sir,' said the man. 'Might I have a word?'

'If you're trying to buy my ticket, my good man, I must . . .'

The man looked around, leaned closer, and said, 'State security, sir. It *is* a matter of some urgency. The wellbeing of Mirkarvia may be at stake.'

Meissner blinked and swallowed. He hadn't lost that paperwork, he assured himself, he'd only misfiled it. It would turn up, eventually. He'd been intending to look for it the very day he got back. It wasn't even important. Or, at least, it had seemed unimportant to him. Perhaps it was important to *somebody*. They wouldn't send security after somebody for that, would they? *Would* they? 'You . . . have identification?' he stammered, trying for time.

The man smiled grimly. 'I'm with intelligence, sir. We don't tend to carry papers to say that we're spies. I do, however, have this.' He showed Meissner a signet ring, its face turned in towards the palm. He turned it on his finger and showed Meissner the crest there.

'The crest of Count Marechal!' gasped Meissner, who had seen it on enough execution warrants to recognise it instantly.

'The same, sir. If you think you could keep your voice down?'

'Yes . . . yes, of course, I'm very, very sorry.'

'I understand that you're a government official, sir? I overheard you at the departures desk.'

'Yes, Gerhard Meissner – docket clerk first class, Department of Administrative Coordination. I'm a loyal citizen!'

'Precisely, sir. That's why I need your help. A first-class docket clerk? Excellent. I need a man of your calibre. There is a certain . . . situation developing here at the aeroport that concerns me greatly. By the time my colleagues arrive, it may well be too late. In short, Herr Meissner, I need your assistance.'

'Of course! Of course! I am at your disposal. How can I help?'

'This way, sir.' The secret agent directed Meissner to an empty and unlocked bay. 'Just in here.'

Meissner blinked in the gloom. 'Now what?'

'If you'd be so kind as to give me your papers,' said the agent, extending his hand.

'I . . . um . . . well, yes, I don't see why not.' He handed over his passport, visa and other documentation in a neat bundle.

The man rifled quickly through them. 'I shall need your ticket as well.'

'My ticket? But why?'

'So that I can escape the country, of course,' said Johannes Cabal.

Meissner bridled. 'What? But . . . you *are* from Count Marechal, aren't you?'

'I come directly from the count,' replied Cabal. 'In fact, I borrowed this from him.'

He drew the count's handgun and levelled it at Meissner. 'Now, time is pressing. Your ticket, Herr Meissner.'

Later, in the departure lounge – heaving with people running from tales of massacre and riot in the capital city of Krenz – Cabal studied Meissner's documents. They were of a height, both blond, both lean. The photograph wasn't very good either. If Meissner had tried looking like a person instead of a civil servant, there might have been more of a problem. As it was, Cabal had only to purse his lips and give the impression that everybody he spoke to was dung on legs and

43

he wouldn't have any difficulties. He practised his impersonation on several small children and, when he'd got it to such a
pitch that any child beneath five burst into tears at the sight
of him, he relaxed, satisfied.

He'd left the unfortunate Meissner tied up and gagged in
the bay and hoped and trusted that he wouldn't be found
until the *Princess Hortense* was well on her way. Since the
conclusion of his year with the Carnival of Discord he'd
found himself prey to strange twinges that, after some book
research, he had discovered was his conscience. This
unwelcome quality took exception to many of the perfectly
logical actions that he had previously committed with the
regularity of habit. In the present case, however, Cabal's
conscience had apparently taken account of Herr Meissner's
occupation as a civil servant and had remained as quiet as a
church mouse while Cabal had stuffed a dirty rag in
Meissner's mouth and trussed him up with little concern for
his comfort. Even a conscience knows its limits. There might
have been a slight moral tremor when he injected Meissner
with a variant on the same antideteriorant that he had used
on the emperor. It caused a deep comatose state for perhaps
a week in four cases out of seven. The other three would be
as dead as Sanskrit long before that week was out. It was a
considered risk on Cabal's part but, after all, he wasn't the
one who'd be dead if it didn't work properly. These were
odds he could live with.

As for the gun, he had regretfully dumped it in a drum of
waste oil in a supply shed. He doubted the customs and
excise officials would recognise his sword cane for what it was
and would hardly care if they did, Mirkarvia being
Mirkarvia. He had found his switchblade tucked unmolested
into the corner of his Gladstone and had transferred it to the
roll of surgical instruments for safety. It and they would
barely raise an eyebrow. A revolver, however, might excite

comment. Especially one with the Marechal coat of arms inlaid into the butt. There was no easy way he could explain its presence so he didn't even intend to try, and the gun ended up under three feet of filthy waste. Besides, it only had one round in it.

He roused himself and went to the dispatch desk to check on the details of the flight, and also to make sure that his Mirkarvian accent was as convincing as he believed it to be. He was basing it on Marechal's own aristocratic drawl, the effect he was reaching for being that of a third son to landed gentry having been dumped into civil service after his elder brothers got the plum jobs.

The woman there checked his ticket and, despite having dealt with Herr Meissner earlier, had managed to expunge the event from her mind in enough detail to accept one supercilious, tall, blond man for another. She also seemed entirely at ease with his accent, which was comforting. 'The flight takes two days to reach Senza, sir, where there will be a pleasant evening stopover. You will arrive in Katamenia around noon the following day. I can't be more accurate than that, I'm afraid; the meteorological bureau reports changeable headwinds.'

'Senza, you say?' Cabal stirred around in his memory for anything relating to the place. He seemed to recall some ugly border squall a few years ago.

'It's quite safe, sir. The state of détente remains secure.'

Did it? wondered Cabal. He remembered something about export controls between Mirkarvia and their allies in Katamenia. He doubted it was just some 'pleasant evening stopover' that was their reason for touching down in Senzan territory. More like a fine-tooth-comb search by the local authorities to make sure no military aid was making it through their territory. As if he cared. Still, it was a handsome bit of serendipity; he didn't really wanted to end up in

45

the hands of the Katamenian secret police who would, no doubt, send him straight back to their cousins in Krenz. In Senza, he could disappear into the shadows, sneak over a neutral border and be home in time for tea, metaphorically speaking. Splendid, things were finally starting to look up.

He thanked the woman with civility but without warmth and moved on. A step away he paused and asked, 'Is it permissible for me to join the *Hortense*? The lounge bores me and I would prefer to be settling in.'

She checked the time and the departures board and nodded pleasantly. Cabal almost forgot himself and smiled but managed to turn it into a frown of self-importance, nodded curtly and headed for the field apron. The further away he was from the police agents that cluttered the concourse, the happier he would be.

Lieutenant Hasso was Karstetz's replacement and was already demonstrating himself to have the charismatic flair of his predecessor. 'So, this Cabal wallah beat you? And now he's loose? Is that it?'

'He did *not* beat me,' grated Marechal in a patently dangerous voice that Hasso blithely failed to detect. The Count Marechal was rubbing feeling back into his recently freed hands, the pieces of bell-pull rope that had bound him now lying severed upon the floor.

'You *are* the finest swordsman in all Mirkarvia, aren't you?' asked Hasso, trying to get his facts straight.

'Forget about swordsmanship. Cabal cheated.'

'Ahhh.'

Marechal looked furiously at him. 'What do you mean, "ahhh"?'

'Oh. You know.' Hasso shrugged. It was obvious he didn't. "Ahhh". As in . . . "O ho!" I should think.'

'O ho?'

'I should think.'

'Yes, you should.' Marechal decided there were more important things to do right that moment than murdering new adjutants. 'Is there any word of Cabal?'

'The chap who beat you?' Hasso finally caught the count's look. 'Or should I say, *didn't* beat you,' he added hastily. He winked conspiratorially. 'Ahhh. O ho!'

'Is there?' demanded the count.

'No. Nobody's seen him. As soon as he beat . . . as soon as he'd finished here, he just vanished into thin air. Some sort of magician, isn't he? Izzy wizzy, wands and all that? Rabbits?'

'He's a necromancer, you idiot, not a children's entertainer. He can no more vanish in a puff of smoke than you can. Regrettably. Are all the ports being monitored? The borders? Mountain passes?'

'There *is* a rebellion going on out there, old man. Our chaps are terribly, terribly busy crushing the proletariat. But fear not, the orders have been sent out. Just have to hope that he shows his face.'

'Business or pleasure?' asked the customs man.

'Pleasure,' replied Cabal. 'The pure animal pleasure of presenting these government documents to my counterparts in Katamenia.' The officer looked at him blankly and Cabal decided that this wasn't going to be a meeting of minds. 'A little joke. A very little joke. I'm on government business.'

'Oh? Pertaining to what?'

'Agricultural policy. I'm not permitted to say more.'

'Very fortuitous timing, if you don't mind me saying so, sir,' said the officer, riffling through the stolen papers for the fourth time. Cabal wasn't worried. The man obviously wasn't reading them. 'What, with all this trouble? You just *happen* to be leaving the country. Very fortuitous.'

'Yes,' said Cabal pleasantly. The customs man was clearly

trying to imply that Cabal was some sort of moral coward for abandoning his country in its hour of need. Cabal didn't mind implying exactly the same thing back. Anything to annoy the hirelings. 'Isn't it? Aboard a beautiful new ship like the *Princess Hortense*, too. Lucky old me, hmm?'

'Yes. Very, *very* lucky. *Fortuitously* lucky.' The officer seemed to believe that it was possible to win some sort of implication prize if he kept it up long enough.

'You have it there in a nutshell. Are you finished with my hand baggage?'

The officer waggled his moustache and looked in Cabal's Gladstone. 'What's this?' he asked when he found the roll of surgical tools.

Cabal quickly undid the knot and unrolled it. Sitting in a spare pocket, the switchblade looked like it belonged. 'Surgical equipment. My job sometimes includes pathological examinations of sick animals.'

'You're a veterinarian?' The officer was suddenly interested.

'In a manner . . .'

'Do you do parrots?'

'Not by choice.'

'What's scales and falling feathers?'

Cabal paused. 'Is this a riddle?'

'Great scales, like . . . sort of . . . dandruff.'

'Is this a test?'

'No, no.' The officer shook his head urgently. 'My Liese's got mange.'

'Liese being your parrot?'

'I thought I'd said that? Or at least as much?'

'So you did, eventually. I'm only licensed to dissect cows and sheep,' lied Cabal, having to use more inventiveness than seemed necessary or fair after all he'd been through. 'I'm afraid I know nothing of . . .' he endeavoured to sound knowledgeable, 'exotics.'

The customs officer looked at him askance and sniffed. 'Well, that's a shame. Thank you, Herr Meissner. I'm sorry to have troubled you.'

'Not at all. We do what we do for the good of the state, yes?'

'Of course. The good of the state. Enjoy your trip, sir.'

'Thank you.' As Cabal walked out of the customs building, he had the feeling that could have gone a lot better. Then he saw the *Princess Hortense* and forgot all about the customs officer.

The customs officer, however, hadn't forgotten all about him.

Lieutenant Hasso stamped into Marechal's presence and performed a salute that was a lot of everything but brief. 'He's been spotted, sir! A customs officer at the port got suspicious and checked the wanted list.'

'Trying to leave the country, eh?' It always paid to state the obvious when dealing with men like Hasso – it would save a lot of explanation later. 'We've got him now. I want a patrol of the household guard ready in five minutes, understood?'

Unaware of the excitement at the palace, Cabal took a long minute to gaze up in appreciative silence at the *Princess Hortense*. She sat in her cradle, a huge basket of pylons and girders that supported the hull where it was designed to bear it. Despite appearances when airborne, aeroships like the *Hortense* were not lighter-than-air dirigibles. Instead, they nullified their weight with banks of Laithwaite gyroscopic levitators and pulled themselves through the air using magneto-etheric line guides that located and attached the vessel to the Earth's own magnetic line fields. The gyroscopes were out of sight within the aeroship's upper hull but the line guides – four massive aerodynamically smoothed nacelles twenty feet in length and ten square – were held at a distance from the ship's skin by pylons a little below the lateral midline, fore and aft port, fore and aft starboard. Although these provided both propulsion and steering, there were also four great rudders set wide to aft, two thrusting downwards and two – bearing the MirkAir colours and the crest of the Imperial Warrant – up. Along her sides were the rectangular cabin portholes and, to aft, the wide picture windows of the salon. At her prow, the nose was constructed almost entirely of glass panels exposing the bridge, its command stations, control linkages and aluminium mesh floor plates. Members of the bridge crew were visible moving around and looking out at the field. Cabal nodded slightly with satisfaction; he respected good engineering for its purity of thought and the *Princess Hortense* was clearly that.

Passengers were embarking from a balcony that extended directly from the side of the departure lounge and he belatedly realised that he had come out of the wrong entrance. Rather than walk all the way back round again, he noticed an iron spiral staircase within the cradle itself that seemed to be the crew entrance. Deciding not to stand on ceremony, he hefted his bag and made his way to the base of the stairs. His footsteps clanged harshly as he stepped up the iron helix and the shadows the metalwork made in the low light of the dying day swept around and around him as he rose spiralling twenty, thirty, forty feet above the field. He paused as the gloom of the aeroship's underside enveloped him and looked back at the port buildings.

Past the sweep of the customs house, he thought he saw mounted soldiers but a girder interrupted his view and he couldn't be sure. He sniffed; there was no point getting paranoid at this juncture. He'd done what he could. Now, he could only hope it had been enough.

*

Hasso had ridden his horse into the customs area, scattering nervous refugees. His horse, disappointed at not being allowed to ride down the common people – a favourite pastime of both rider and steed – was consoling itself by stepping surreptitiously on non-military feet. Muffled shrieks marked its progress.

Hasso stood up in his stirrups. 'Where's the cove who called the secret police?' he roared before adding conversationally, 'That's us, y'know.'

Marechal, who had taken a moment to dismount, walked past him. 'Have you ever heard of "discretion", Lieutenant?' he asked as he went by. Both Hasso and his horse looked equally bereft of a clue.

A hatchet-faced customs official, who looked like he might have been turned down by the secret police at some point in an attempt to improve their image, strode up to Marechal having instantly discriminated between the monkey and the organ-grinder. 'One of my juniors became suspicious of the subject,' he said without preamble. 'Passing himself off as an official. Didn't look much like his passport photograph. Checked lists, called you.'

Marechal waited for a moment; the words the official's statement seemed to be missing might be turning up late. They did not. 'Good,' said Marechal finally. 'Excellent work. Where is the man now?'

'Aboard. But the vessel will not get permission to leave until we are satisfied.'

Marechal's nostrils flared. The savoury aroma of hot vengeance was wafting through the air. The Italians might prefer it cold, but they had girlie sabres too so what the Hell did they know? 'Excellent,' he said again. 'Hold it until I've had a chance to talk to this *official*.' He turned his head to one side and barked, 'Hasso! Come on! We've got him! Bring up the guards.' He waited for the inevitable clip-clopping to begin before adding, 'And do it on foot, you bloody moron.'

Cabal saw the uniforms and stopped. Then he took a studied moment to recover his breath and reached the top of the spiral stairway. He'd entered the *Hortense* in a corner of the salon and the uniforms belonged to officers of the crew: civilian officers, not military. Even so, they *looked* very military. A man in his late forties with a lot of gold braid on the epaulettes of his white uniform – Cabal guessed he was the captain – was talking to a subordinate. The subordinate listened attentively and, when he was dismissed, threw a salute and clicked his heels before leaving. Cabal sighed. What was it about this country that bred toy soldiers both inside and outside the army? The captain turned, and was surprised to see Cabal there. His brow darkened momentarily and then cleared as he walked over.

'Forgive my astonishment, sir,' said the captain, thrusting his hand out. Cabal shook it politely and without grimacing as the captain ground his metacarpals together. 'Passengers usually embark through the aft gangway. Those stairs you've just come up are intended for the crew, Herr . . .?'

'Meissner,' said Cabal without hesitation, producing his stolen travel documents.

The captain smiled a little tautly and waved them away. 'Not my job, sir. The purser deals with that end of things. If you were to go aft, I'm sure he'd be delighted to deal with you.'

Cabal wasn't a man given to apologising, but he could see he'd got off on the wrong foot here and was drawing attention to himself. He leafed quickly through his memory until he found an image of somebody smiling apologetically, and then mimicked it. 'I'm terribly sorry,' he said, being nothing of the sort. 'I'm making a dreadful nuisance of myself. I went out on to the edge of the field to get a breath of fresh air and then I saw the *Hortense* was boarding. I really couldn't face going all the way back through the departure lounge.' He balled his hands together in what he sincerely believed to be a contrite posture and simpered slightly. Facial muscles that had never been used previously for anything other than stony implacability and the occasional sneer screamed under the strain. 'I saw the steps and just thought it wouldn't be any bother. I can see, however, I've broken your routine. I'm in the government so I know how important order and procedure are. Why, my whole job is *about* order and procedure. I'm carrying the documents for the forthcoming agricultural land remittance discussions and, believe you me, what a sad shambles they would be without a sense of order and procedure. For example, if we look at the first programme . . .' Cabal reached for his case.

The glazed look that had been settling on the captain's face was replaced by one of terror on the instant. Nobody wants to be buttonholed by an evangelising civil servant. It won't last for the rest of one's life, but can certainly feel that way. 'That won't be necessary, Herr Meissner,' said the captain quickly with a little too much emphasis on the first word. 'No harm done, eh? Just see the purser and everything will be shipshape.'

Cabal pointed around the salon. 'Shipshape? Oh, very good, Captain!' He knew damn well the captain hadn't been making a joke but it was too good an opportunity to miss. Cabal knew from past experience the peculiar horror that is the weak punster.

The captain looked blankly at him for a moment and then, finally spying the humour – such as it was – laughed faintly. Cabal hefted his bag and made to leave. 'Well, thank you, you've been very kind. I'll see you around no doubt, Captain . . . ?'

'Schten,' supplied the captain distantly, his mind filled with dreadful visions of being trapped in a confined space with 'Herr Meissner' for the next few days. Cabal left the salon with a sense of achievement. His work here was done.

Cabal arrived in the salon to find the process of boarding was already well underway. The *Hortense* was a large vessel but designed to carry relatively few passengers in the absolute lap of luxury. Extrapolating from the number of cabin doors he'd passed en route, it seemed unlikely she had more than twenty staterooms at most and so probably only about thirty passengers or so. Those less wealthy could travel in fat steerage ships like the *Bellerophon* or take several days to do the trip on the winding and inefficient railways that spiralled up and down and around the mountains. Even so, he wondered at the economic viability of running a ship of the *Princess Hortense*'s size with so few passengers. There had to be some other source of revenue, perhaps transporting airmail or some such.

The lounge was already thinning as the passengers were shown to their cabins. The covered boarding bridge was still open but unoccupied and it seemed likely from the crewmen standing around the ship end, trying to look patient while checking their watches, that it would soon be disengaged. It couldn't happen soon enough for Cabal.

He walked over to a man he assumed, from his air of harassed complication overlaid with a thin patina of unctuousness – and his clipboard – was the purser. 'Good afternoon,' said Cabal and offered his papers.

The purser flicked carefully through them, tore off a couple of perforated sections, initialled a box and ran a line through another before handing the majority of them back. 'Good afternoon, Herr Meissner,' he said, smiling. The smile firmed up slightly when he looked around and realised he'd just about finished. 'If you'll wait a moment, I'll ask a steward to carry your bag to your stateroom.'

'That won't be necessary,' replied Cabal, picking up his Gladstone and patting it with his wad of papers. 'Government documents. I feel nervous when they're out of my sight. I'll find my own way there. S6? Starboard six?'

The purser's smile turned yet more honest confronted with somebody who didn't need everything doing for them. 'Quite right, sir.' He reached into a compartmentalised case that sat open on a low table by him and took out a key. 'Your key.' Cabal took it, they exchanged farewells for the moment, and then both turned at the distinctive sound of military boots walking determinedly up the gangway.

Cabal's heart sank.

Approaching them was an officer in what, Cabal recognised with a deep sense of foreboding, was the uniform of the Household Guard, the imperial elite. 'I'll be getting on,' said Cabal to the purser, who was looking at the approaching soldier with open astonishment, and set off nonchalantly towards the starboard corridor.

'You!' barked the officer making everybody, Cabal included, freeze. The officer marched up to the purser, stamped to attention, and saluted. Even at this extreme, the purser returned the salute and even clicked his heels. The household guardsman opened his sabretache and produced an official-looking piece of paper. 'I'm looking for somebody,' he snapped, holding the piece of paper up to the purser's eyes to read. 'Do you have this man aboard?'

It could be anybody, thought Cabal. *A country like this, Marechal's people must be constantly hunting down enemies of the state. There's no need to worry. Just remain calm and await developments.*

The purser read the piece of paper twice before turning and pointing directly at Cabal.

55

All right, thought Cabal. *I may be in trouble after all.*

The officer wheeled, the purser being dropped from his attention like a leprous dog, and he looked at Cabal with a steady intensity that boded badly. Cabal began to regret not transferring his switchblade to his pocket earlier while he had the chance. He didn't fancy his chances in another fencing duel against a man in a gleaming metal breastplate. Tactically, sticking four inches of blade in the guardsman's throat as he approached would have worked much better.

The room seemed much darker with the guardsman standing over him. 'Can I help you, Lieutenant?' he asked.

In a single quick motion, the guardsman thrust the piece of paper in his face. 'Fourth draft, Herr Meissner!'

'I beg your pardon?'

'The agricultural land remittance discussion papers, fourth draft. I'm here on the personal orders of Baron Mitracht of the Agricultural Ministry. The papers you are carrying are to be redrafted while you are en route according to these criteria.' He leaned closer until he was nose to nose with Cabal. 'DO YOU UNDERSTAND?' he bellowed.

Cabal took a step back, realised he wasn't going to be dragged off in chains after all and nodded curtly. 'Of course I understand,' he snapped back. 'Tell the baron his orders will be carried out to the letter.' He twitched the paper out of the guardsman's fingers. 'You are dismissed.'

The soldier went very white and Cabal wondered if he'd overstepped the mark there. Then, with a wheel-about and stamp, the officer marched back to the gangway, snarling 'Bastard civvies!' to the purser, a comrade in uniform. His bootsteps, sharp with fury, echoed down the covered bridge until they were gone.

The purser looked over at Cabal. Cabal waved the piece of paper before putting it away in his breast pocket. 'A civil servant's work is never done,' he commented, picked up his bag, and went to stateroom starboard six.

The steamer packet *Heimlin* had been held up just as she was about to leave the lakeside port, and the passengers and crew made to wait until the Count Marechal and his troops had arrived. Lieutenant Hasso had stormed on board, thankfully not on horseback, and made a lot of fuss over a simple job. Finally, three-quarters of an hour later, Johannes Cabal, beaten and bleeding, had been dragged across the gangway and dumped on the quayside.

Except, of course, that it wasn't Johannes Cabal.

'It's not him, Hasso,' said Marechal, pleased that fate was at least being consistent in its unkindness.

Hasso kicked the groaning man another couple of times before asking, 'Are you sure?'

'I've spent some time in Cabal's company. I think I'd recognise him. This man is of about the same age and appearance but, no, it is not him.'

'Oh,' pouted Hasso. The man groaned. Hasso kicked him again. '*Do* shut up. We've just had a bit of bad news.'

'I . . . I'm Duke Aachel's nephew, you bastards,' moaned the man. 'I know . . . I know you, Marechal. Uncle Günter will . . . will have your miserable hide nailed to the gatepost for this.'

Marechal, sitting on a mooring bollard, listened and considered. 'Rough with the smooth, eh, Hasso?' Hasso grunted noncommittally. 'We may have lost Cabal but at least we located a dangerous spy and saboteur.' He drove his boot under the prone man's stomach and used his instep to lever him over the edge of the quay. There was a cry, a splash, weak struggling, and silence. 'Shame he died whilst attempting to escape.'

Hasso walked to the edge and looked down. 'What about Cabal, sir? Are we giving up on him?'

Marechal looked out across the waters of the Gallaco Sea. 'He could be anywhere by now. No, Lieutenant, we have other fish to fry. If he crosses my path again then that's different; he will not live to regret it. But life's too short for vendettas.' He paled slightly as he said it and even Hasso wasn't fooled. From the direction of the city square, there was the crackle of gunfire. Marechal stood up and dusted off his seat. 'Come on, we've got peasants to kill.'

Exactly on schedule, the gyroscopic levitators whirred up to speed and the *Princess Hortense* began, in a very real sense, to ignore gravity. The huge suspension springs in her landing cradle extended gently as the aeroship started to lift. Deciding that it would be suspicious if he were not on deck for the departure, Cabal checked the forward lounge-cum-dining room and found it too heavily populated for discretion. Instead, he went back to the salon and leaned on the starboard rails there, the windows that would seal them in flight having been slid aside for the occasion. The great line guide assembly was above and off to one side of him and he watched it with interest as it angled, twisting on its mount slightly, seeking out the magnetic lines that the *Hortense* would pull herself along like a great spider on an ethereal thread. With a sharp electrical crack that filled that air with ozone and a shower of blue sparks that drew delighted cries from the spectators in the aeroport and on the field apron, it found and latched upon a likely candidate. Almost immediately, the fore starboard nacelle found one too; Cabal couldn't quite see it but the flash of blue light was clearly visible on the grass around the cradle in the dying light of the day. There was an acoustic thudding through the public announcement speakers in the lounge and then the captain spoke to the passengers. 'Ladies and gentlemen, please brace yourselves. We are about to disengage from the landing cradle and there may be some slight disturbance. Once we are clear, we shall perform one circuit of the field and then begin our journey. Thank you.' The speaker clicked into silence.

For the few people in the lounge with Cabal, 'bracing themselves' seemed to mainly consist of gripping their drinks with both hands. As it happened, the disengagement was smooth and untroubled. The *Princess Hortense* rose in near silence but for the cheers of the passengers, the answering ones of the ground spectators, the click and crackle of one of the line guide nacelles abandoning its first setting in favour of a stronger one and the constant hum of the gyroscopes that sang through the decks and into the inner ear. At three hundred feet, she slowed her ascent and started to move forwards, swinging her tail out to perform the tight circuit of the field. Below them, the city was starting to light up with lamps in windows and angry red bonfires of houses burning as the riots spread. I suppose that's my fault, really, thought Cabal as he watched the fires and the dimly seen crowds amongst the smoke and the flicker of rifle fire. Then he looked up into the sky and tried to make out the early stars. Politics had always bored him.

The *Hortense* completed her circuit and set course for Senza, beyond the mountains. She accelerated and climbed gently until the lights of the city were little more than speckles, like fireflies, and then they were gone altogether.

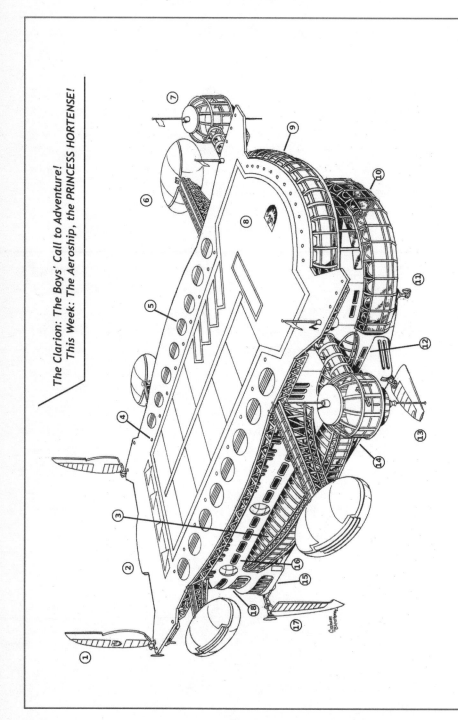

The Clarion: The Boys' Call to Adventure!
This Week: The Aeroship, the PRINCESS HORTENSE!

This week we take a look at the pride of the MirkAir aeroship fleet – the *Princess Hortense*! Commissioned only recently, the *Hortense* is due to make her maiden flight in the next few weeks, once fitting-out has been completed. She will be flying from Emperor Boniface VIII Aeroport, in the Mirkarvian capital of Krenz, to Memorial Field, in Katamenia, via Parila, in the neighbouring state of Senza. Many important people are expected to travel on this first voyage aboard the 'Princess of the Skies'!

KEY:

1. **Dorsal rudder:** The dorsal rudders are set wide apart to stay out of the way of the approach path to the flight deck. Still looks pretty scary to us!

2. **Flight-deck approach:** Entomopters coming into land approach from the rear of the aeroship, while she runs into the wind. The large arrows at the runway threshold can be illuminated for night-time landings.

3. **Starboard promenade,** accessible only from the first-class deck, Deck A.

4. **Landing lights,** showing the edge of the landing area.

5. **Gyroscopic levitator ventilator cover:** Beneath each cover is a shaft housing one of the *Princess Hortense*'s levitators, built to the Laithwaite engineering patent.

6. **Etheric line guide and converter housing:** Each of the aeroship's four lineguide nacelles is mounted on a steerable gimble, allowing them to detect and attach to the earth's etheric field.

7. **Flying bridge:** The aeroship has two such flying bridges, used during docking and lift-off to steer the ship in or out of her landing cradle. Nail biting stuff!

8. **Flight deck:** Visitors to the *Princess Hortense* need not wait for her to land to drop in! She carries a miniature airfield on her back so guests can come and go as they please, provided they own an entomopter!

9. **Bridge:** The aeroship's nerve centre. The bridge houses steering, engineering, and navigation positions. Imagine being the captain! The bridge is on the topmost deck – Deck D – which also contains the engineering section and most of the crew quarters.

10. **First-class dining room:** Broad windows offer a startling panorama of the world below as the passengers eat.

11. **Weather station:** A combination anemometer and wind vane gives relative wind speed and direction.

12. **Galley:** This one creates meals for the first-class passengers. Others aboard provide for second passengers class and the crew.

13. **Trim plane:** The trim planes are adjusted to keep the *Princess Hortense* flying steady and level.

14. **Deck A:** First-class accommodation. The best cabins aboard are on the lowest deck, because that's where the best views are!

15. **Salon:** At the rear of Deck A is the plush salon. When the aeroship is in her landing cradle, doors at the salon's rear are opened so that it can double as an embarkation/disembarkation lounge.

16. **Deck C:** Second-class accommodation. Even second class is pretty posh in a flying palace like the *Princess Hortense*! Deck B contains the stewards' quarters, storage, and the first-class promenades and galley.

17. **Ventral rudder:** One of a pair, making – with the dorsal rudders – four massive, rigid steering sails. A ship like the *Princess Hortense* certainly takes a lot of steering!

18. **Stewards' cabins:** Just above the salon and handy for Deck A. We hope the great view makes up for those early-morning room-service calls, chaps!

Next Week in *The Clarion* ... A Super Cutaway Picture of a Carnival Train!

Chapter 4

Five minutes later, Cabal was politely shooed away from the windows while the glass was slid back into place and locked. As he watched the procedure with limited interest, a steward appeared at his elbow. 'Good evening, sir,' he said and smilingly handed Cabal a menu.

'What's this?' asked Cabal, suspicious.

'The menu for the departure dinner, sir,' replied the steward. Cabal looked blank.

'It's in the itinerary,' added the steward.

Cabal pulled Meissner's little bundle of documents from his inside pocket and quickly sorted through them. Now he thought of it, there had been some sort of ship's timetable but he'd assumed it was for general meals, not for anything specific as a 'departure dinner'. But there it was, the captain's table, dinner dress mandatory. Cabal gritted his teeth very slightly; he couldn't really worm out of it without drawing attention to himself. He just hoped Meissner had seen fit to pack a dinner jacket.

*

Cabal let himself into cabin starboard six, locked the door behind him and sat heavily on his bed. He despised acting; the whole conceit of concealing his personality was distasteful in the extreme and he could hardly wait until these few days were over and behind him. In the meantime, however . . .

He opened Meissner's steamer trunk and had a swift sortie around its contents. Minor Meissner's role in government may have been, but the salary must have been quite impressive. Either that or Meissner's father was a rich man with plenty of strings to pull for his son. Somehow, the latter seemed more likely. Cabal found no fewer than three dinner jackets, one of which could only possibly be worn as a bet. He consigned it to the bottom of the trunk and looked at the others; they were both black and acceptable but one was cut less fashionably than the other and this was the one Cabal hung up in the small wardrobe for wear that evening. Next, he found a pair of trousers and measured them against his leg – yes, he and Gerhard Meissner were of a height. The shirts were also suitable. The underwear, Cabal was profoundly relieved to discover, was brand new and still in its shop wrappings. With no idea of whether Meissner was still alive or not, Cabal had few qualms about wearing a dead man's shoes but he drew the line at a dead man's knickers.

His ensemble for the evening decided, Cabal sat on his bed, picked up the thin bundle of documents from his bedside, and leafed through them to make sure there were no more unpleasant surprises. It seemed fairly quiet after the first evening; mainly optional events until a mandatory dinner the evening before journey's end in Katamenia. There was also a pamphlet about what a wonderful ship the *Princess Hortense* was, with a short and patronising section on the miracles of modern science she carried, whose very first

63

sentence – a lurching edifice of ill-applied technical babble made still more asinine by the addition of the ignorant hyperbole employed by the worst sort of feature writers – irked him so much that he read no more. Instead he tore a strip from it to leave him with a square of light card, and this he proceeded to fold into an origami swan.

When he was finished and the swan was in residence on the cabin's small writing desk, he turned off the bedside light, and sat in near darkness. Outside his porthole, there was nothing to see but stars. The Earth below lay in night without even the light of a cottage to break it. Cabal watched the world – or at least what little he could make out of the horizon – go by for a few minutes. He felt deeply, profoundly miserable.

He really, *really* didn't want to attend the dinner. On the one hand, he would have to spend the whole evening pretending to be something he wasn't and the forfeit for failing to be convincing was death: it simply wasn't conducive to having a good time. On the other hand, he disliked the company of others at the best of times and being forcibly surrounded by the well-to-do and very smug burghers and spouses of Mirkarvia intensified that dislike by a comfortable magnitude or two. Perhaps he could plead airsickness and retire early? Then he considered well-meaning matrons pestering him for the rest of the voyage with patented gippy stomach remedies, many of which would involve raw eggs. No, he'd just have to tough it out and be distant, offhand and generally unfriendly.

He perked up slightly; the evening was looking more interesting already.

The dinner was to be preceded by a champagne reception. Cabal allowed himself to be fashionably late in arriving only to discover that the fashion had become more exaggerated without anybody telling him. There were few passengers in the aft lounge, only just outnumbering the stewards. He was offered a bumper of champagne in a wide-mouthed glass rather than the flute glasses he thought were becoming the norm. Looking around, he noted that the women were receiving half-filled flutes and realised it was the male prerogative in Mirkarvian society to get very drunk very quickly. Somehow, he couldn't see the Temperance League making any great inroads into Mirkarvia any time soon. He looked dubiously at his glass – it had to have the best part of a quarter of a pint in it – before walking carefully over to one of the aft bay windows that sandwiched the closed and locked gangway hatch. There he sipped slowly, endeavouring to look both aloof and unapproachable.

It seemed to work. Nobody came over to talk to him except a steward who hovered by every few minutes to be silently appalled that Cabal was still only his first glass, not his third or fourth. In the rest of the slowly filling lounge, the men drank and drank and the women wittered. It was not humanity at its best and Cabal was not very interested in observing them. Instead he looked out of the window at the vault of Heaven. The cloud cover had thinned to the point that only a few ragged rolls of stratocumulus were moving slowly across the sky, glowing blue by the light of a gibbous moon. The stars were clearer and sharper than he ever remembered seeing them before; an effect of their altitude he assumed. Astronomy had exerted a brief fascination for him in his adolescence and he amused himself making out the constellations. Ursa Major was, as always, childishly simple to spot and he felt a small frisson of childish delight in doing so. He traced the line from the top of the Plough to find Polaris and watched it for a long time. He experienced a less pleasant frisson when it started to shift across the sky and he realised the ship was turning. A few difficult seconds later,

65

however, and it stopped; the *Princess Hortense* was merely making a small course adjustment, not returning to the aeroport. Cabal just wished the damnable meal would start, the sooner to be done with.

Despite himself, he felt he was settling into the rôle. He'd pulled together everything he knew about agriculture and was moderately sure he could impress a layman on the subject of scrapie. Especially if the layman was quite paralytically drunk. Abruptly, he became aware of somebody standing by his right shoulder a mere moment before he smelled perfume. He'd allowed his concentration to slip and, in those few moments when he wasn't being aloof and unapproachable, he'd been approached.

'Beautiful, aren't they?' said a young woman's voice. There was little intonation and it took Cabal a moment to realise what she was talking about.

'The stars? Yes, I suppose they are. I'm not a poet or a painter though, so that's just hearsay.'

The woman made a small noise that was probably a laugh, as if he'd said something witty or profound. In a sense, he had. Then she said, 'What do you think of when you look at the stars?'

He considered quickly. He'd heard about this sort of thing. If his understanding was correct, he could well be in the process of being 'picked up', currently at the 'small talk' stage. This could be useful. Keeping one – ideally fairly stupid – woman entertained for the length of the voyage would go a long way towards avoiding the company of others. Nobody, as the saying goes, wants to be a gooseberry. It might be as well to cultivate her acquaintance.

Looking steadfastly up at the stars and assuming an expression he had reason to believe was dreamy and romantic, he said, 'Once upon a time, it was believed that our futures were, literally, written in the stars. It was called *stelliscript*. It was said that you should read them West to East if you wanted to know the good things in your future.'

'And North-South for the evil things?' asked his companion, ingenuously.

'Of course, it's all nonsense; the stars are set in their paths,' said Cabal, wondering if that was a lucky shot on her part. 'The future remains unknown to us, no matter how you might try to read it. There was another technique called gyromancy, for example. A practitioner of this piece of flummery would spin around on the spot until they got dizzy and fell over. The manner of the falling over told the future of whoever had hired the gyromancer. I should think,' he added with an artful chuckle, 'that the true reading would invariably be, "You will soon be gulled by a confidence trickster."'

There was silence for a few moments and Cabal wondered if this would be a good time to turn and look as handsome as possible. Before he could commit himself, however, his companion spoke again.

'Gyromancy . . . I would have thought *necromancy* was more your style, Johannes Cabal.'

It went very quiet in the lounge.

Then somebody laughed, the chatter started up again and Cabal realised it had simply been a natural silence in a dozen conversations occurring simultaneously, the merest fluke. Or at least, nobody had stuck a gun in his back yet, so that was probably the reason. He stopped looking at the stars, his throat tightening and his head feeling a little gyromantic in itself, refocused on the reflections in the glass, and just for a moment saw a face he knew to be dead. His heart jolted. He took a sharp breath, looked again, and saw he was mistaken, but that the truth was just as shocking. Cabal was not a man given to gasping, usually, and did not do so again. Standing beside his right shoulder, her gaze balefully meeting his, was Leonie Barrow.

It can be said of a necromancer that, given their profession, there are few people that they can ever truly be sure of never seeing again, not even the ones they bury in shallow graves in the woods. Johannes Cabal, however, could have said in any second up to this that the last person he expected to see aboard the *Princess Hortense* was Leonie Barrow, a woman he'd previously encountered many months ago and a considerable number of international borders away.

Cabal had on that occasion held stewardship of a diabolical carnival, committed to wandering the railway network for a year, scooping up the souls of the disaffected as it went. It was all done at the whim of a bored and capricious Satan, who had made a wager with Cabal: Cabal's own soul would be returned to him on receipt of a hundred others, with one year to do it in and the carnival to help him bring in the harvest.

He had loathed that year, even though he really had only himself to blame for it. It had been a ramshackle period of travel, perfunctory damnations, and tawdry knick-knacks during which he had experienced much and enjoyed little. At the time he thought the end had justified the means, but – a final, bitter irony on top of a year full of them – the end had made him question those means, making his small victory seem petty and ignoble.

He had met Miss Barrow and her father towards the end of the year, when things had become unexpectedly desperate. Mr Frank Barrow, a retired policeman and redoubtable nuisance, had descended upon Cabal like Nemesis, but in the end it was Leonie Barrow who had proved the cleverer foe. Considered as a whole, it had not been a happy meeting, and they had not parted on the best of terms. In fact, if Miss Barrow had murdered him on that occasion, the prosecution would have had a hard time finding a jury to hang her.

Cabal turned to face her, needing the proof of direct sight. She was still tall, still crowned with the tawny blond hair that matched her name so well, still very striking in a Pre-Raphaelite sort of way and, judging by her expression, still deeply pissed off with him. He tried to speak but his vocabulary had studied the situation and taken the evening off. 'Accch,' he grated slowly, for once speechless. His thumb twitched involuntarily and the cup of his glass snapped off, dumping the remains of the champagne at their feet.

A steward was at his side in an instant, mopping up and apologising for the inferior quality of the glasses, the company would certainly complain to the manufacturers for their shoddiness. 'Can I get you another drink, Herr Meissner?' he asked as he gathered up the remains of the glass.

Meissner? mouthed Miss Barrow at Cabal. He barely responded, his mind finally getting up to whirring pace as the frost of surprise thawed. If she denounced him, they'd turn right round and take him back to the waiting arms of the Count Marechal. He couldn't let that happen. But he couldn't see a way around it either. He calculated possible schemes. Plan A consisted of punching her in the stomach and heaving her through the window. It was direct and effective but it had certain practical drawbacks that militated against its use. He didn't have a Plan B.

'Fräulein Barrow, perhaps you would like a freshener?' asked the steward, indicating her glass.

'No, thank you,' she replied, smiling for his benefit. 'I'm replete for the moment. I'm sure if I need any more, Herr Meissner will be kind enough . . . ?' This last directed at Cabal, who almost missed it.

'Of course, Fräulein, it would be my privilege,' he replied, nodding and clicking his heels as appeared to be de rigueur.

'A military man, sir?' said the steward, impressed.

Cabal blinked. He couldn't wipe his nose around here without committing some sort of social gaffe or telegraphing the wrong thing. 'Not really,' he prevaricated. 'I was at the academy in my youth but my horse . . .' *What do horses do that is bad for their riders?* he wondered. 'Fell on me.' That sounded more than a good enough reason for a medical discharge. He touched the imaginary shoulder wound the horse had caused and accidentally prodded the sabre cut that Marechal had left in him. His unfeigned grimace of pain seemed to do the trick. The steward nodded sympathetically and moved on.

Leonie Barrow watched Cabal as he watched the steward go. He was leaning back with studied nonchalance as he let his gaze wander around the room but she knew he simply didn't want anybody else walking up behind him unexpectedly, especially not when they started talking about what she knew they had to talk about. She waited. Finally, Cabal found words.

'Why didn't you denounce me?' he asked, not looking at her.

She smiled as if making small talk but her voice was cold. 'Because they'd have taken you back to Krenz and strung you up. That's if they didn't throw you overboard here and now. Your breed isn't popular among the Mirkarvians.' His gaze slid to look at her. 'Or anywhere,' she added with a certain emphasis.

Cabal narrowed his eyes, nettled. 'So you're preserving my life for humanitarian reasons. How very kind of you. I feel redeemed already.' She still had the power to send him to his death but, somehow, that was preferable to being patronised.

'Save your sarcasm, Cabal. When we reach Senza, I'll see you put under arrest. They don't have capital punishment for the likes of you. It will be life imprisonment but that's no more than you deserve.' She spoke with a cold certainty.

Cabal wished he had a drink just to give his hands something to do. Currently they were keen on carrying out Plan A and damn the consequences. 'You're your father's daughter,' said Cabal finally. 'Speaking of whom, how is he?'

'As well as can be expected after what you put us through.'

'I don't suppose your opinion of me would be moderated at all if . . .'

'No.'

'*If* I told you I was hardly a free agent.' He looked at her. 'No, I don't suppose it would. Not in your little world of moral certainties.'

'You really do think that you're superior to everybody else, don't you?'

'Don't be absurd,' he answered while trying hard to think of somebody he looked up to. There didn't seem to be anybody.

They stood in awkward silence for a few moments. 'So,' said Cabal, fractionally less irritated by the presence of words than their absence. 'What brought you to a pit like Mirkarvia?'

'My degree,' replied Miss Barrow grudgingly. She volunteered no more.

'Your degree? What sort of degree, precisely?'

'Criminal psychology,' she replied and looked squarely at him.

Cabal sighed. 'You really *are* your father's daughter. What is your intended career? A plodding police officer or the proprietor of an asylum for the criminally insane? I'd suggest you plump for the latter; the hours are better.'

In reply, she simply tilted her head and looked more keenly at him. It was a look he realised closely mirrored his own when a likely corpse happened his way. Usually under a tarpaulin on the back of a cart at three in the morning.

'Tch'ah,' he tutted. 'You think I'm a criminal, don't you? One of your grubby little perpetrators from a troubled family background who commits outrages because a cousin told him horses have five legs when he was an infant and it scarred him for life. Is that it?'

'You *are* a criminal, Cabal. But there's nothing common or garden about you. Do you know I decided on taking this degree in the first place after meeting you?' Cabal frowned. 'If you're trying to endear yourself to me, you've chosen an odd way of setting about it.'

'Your behaviour was criminal but your motivation . . . I didn't understand your motivation at all. Most of your colleagues—'

'I don't have colleagues. It is not a profession that encourages union activity or glee clubs.'

'Are a bunch of shallow megalomaniacs. They're easy – I can spot a power-crazy, corpse-raising nutcase . . .'

'Ah, now you're trying to lose me with jargon.'

'Stop interrupting me. I can spot one of those pathetic creatures at ten paces.'

'You must have met dozens,' muttered Cabal.

'I've met a couple,' she said. Cabal looked at her with surprise. Having secured his attention for the moment, she continued more sedately. 'In an asylum for the criminally insane, as it happens. Sad, lonely men, they took up necromancy in the same way madmen might take up knives to revenge themselves on a society that they don't understand and that makes no effort to understand them. You, though. You can fit in. It's no mean feat to pass yourself off as one of this bunch.' She indicated the gathered Mirkarvians with a nod of her head. 'I don't see you leading an army of zombies into the fray.'

'Zombies are so passé.'

'Don't be flippant with me, Cabal. Your life's mine. I want to do the right thing but, my God, it wouldn't take much provocation . . . Not much at all.'

Cabal scowled. 'What's this? Psychoanalysis by coercion? "Tell me about your childhood, or else?" I didn't realise psychiatry had become so two-fisted.' He smiled at her for appearance's sake but his eyes were sharp and dangerous. 'Don't think you can quantify me and put me in a thesis. A census taker once tried to test me. I let my front garden eat him.'

'Your front garden?'

He wrinkled his nose. 'You didn't expect *me* to do it, did you?'

Miss Barrow's eyes flickered to one side, and suddenly she smiled broadly and became the very spirit of vivacity. 'You told your gardener he could eat it! Oh! That's simply too precious!' She laughed full-throatedly.

Cabal was caught off-guard, but only for a moment. He looked to his side and pretended to realise that they had company. 'Well,' he said with ersatz joviality, 'you just can't get the staff these days, can you?'

The couple to which he spoke allowed a moment's bewilderment before laughing politely. 'No, no, you can't . . .' said the man, plainly wondering with what he was agreeing.

There was a short embarrassed pause during which Cabal wondered why they wouldn't go away, and the couple desperately tried to formulate a polite plan for getting away.

'I'm Roborovski,' said the man, having run out of ideas. 'Linus Roborovski. And this is my wife, Lisabet.'

They did not seem to be an especially well-suited couple.

He was in his late thirties to mid forties, careworn and starting to bald, who exuded an air of being in a state of permanent harassment. He wore a good but not very good bespoke suit in brown-green twill that he looked forced into despite it being made to measure. Cabal decided he was a small businessman who had unexpectedly become successful and wasn't quite sure how to deal with the trimmings that came with it.

His wife had a good six inches on him and was younger, no more than thirty. She was wan rather than simply pale, and she wore her loosely coiled strawberry-blond hair like an affliction. She had an unlovely dress in mustard yellow hanging about her that in no way complimented her complexion. Standing beside and a little behind her husband, they looked like the makings of a poultice. They served to remind Cabal – should a reminder ever be necessary – why his social skills were so poor; people were loathsome and not worth the practise.

'Meissner,' he said, shaking hands with Roborovski. 'Gerhard Meissner.' He hadn't even let Roborovski's hand go before his wife was offering hers, palm down. Hoping he successfully suppressed the weary note that would surely colour his voice should he let it, he clicked his heels and kissed her hand. 'Enchanté,' he added, for want of anything sensible to say. In his experience it was possible to talk any sort of rubbish in a foreign language and so sound sophisticated.

As he looked up in straightening, he noticed a glimmer in her eye that he didn't altogether like. There was something calculating there, and the fact that he had no idea what she was calculating caused him a twinge to his sense of self-preservation. In an instant, the glimmer was gone, and she was looking at him with the glassy expression of a bourgeois hausfrau, or a head of livestock.

Herr Roborovski was looking enquiringly at Miss Barrow. 'And your friend is . . . ?' he asked Cabal.

Miss Barrow, however, was not going to be spoken for, no matter what passed for etiquette in Mirkarvia. 'Leonie Barrow,' she said, and held out her hand. That she held it out thumb upwards, for shaking, may have been lost on the Roborovskis for they both shook her hand with polite smiles and the ghost of a curtsy from Frau Roborovski.

'You're English, aren't you?' she asked Miss Barrow. 'I've always wanted to visit England, but Linus is so busy, we never seem to get the chance to have a holiday.'

'Oh? Why, what do you do?'

She spoke the question directly to Herr Roborovski, but he just looked blankly at her like a rep actor who was considering what to have for supper instead of watching for his cue. After a moment, Frau Roborovski said, 'He's a cabinetmaker.' Her husband jumped slightly, like a rep actor who has finally decided to have Welsh rabbit for supper, and returns to the here-and-now to discover a whole stage-full of his fellow actors glaring daggers at him.

'Oh, yes,' he said, as if the statement was so astounding that it required confirmation. 'I'm a cabinetmaker.'

'And that keeps you busy, does it?' asked Cabal, seeking to reconcile cabinetmaking, extreme busyness, and journeys on luxury aeroships to his satisfaction.

'Ah, um. Yes?'

'Linus,' interjected his wife with the mildly acidic tone of someone who suspects that they're being made sport of, but isn't quite sure, 'is very successful. He runs one of the most respected workshops in the country!' The end of the sentence was punctuated with a sharp nod of the *and don't you forget it, buster* variety.

'Running a cabinet manufactory.' Cabal triggered the muscles that careful research had revealed would create a

75

supercilious smile. It was one of his more convincing ones. 'How fascinating.'

Herr Roborovski beamed, a happy hamster. His wife did not. 'What do you do, Herr Meissner?'

'Me? Oh, I'm just a cog in the Mirkarvian civil service, I'm afraid. I neither sow, nor do I reap, in all but the most figurative way. Making things with your hands, though, that's something to be proud of.' To illustrate the point, he held out his own hands, palms upwards. They hadn't seen any serious manual work in the last four months, at which time they had been callused from unofficial nocturnal exhumations, the necessity of bludgeoning several recalcitrant revenants back into an inanimate state, and then the resulting unofficial nocturnal cremations. Now they looked like the hands of a pencil-pushing administrator who might occasionally do a little gardening in a window box.

Herr Roborovski unconsciously mimicked Cabal's action, holding up his hands. Cabal noted that they showed some signs of labour, but like his own, not recently. While coming to the conclusion that, boringly enough, the little man and his irritating wife were just what they appeared to be, Cabal distractedly added, 'I mean, all that arcane business with G-clamps, shellac, dovecote joints, lathes, and suchlike. Always nice to actually make things with your hands.'

'It is nice,' he agreed, a little mournfully.

'In your own time, of course.' The wan Frau Roborovski seemed to take exception to building anything that was not for profit. 'You have your company to think of.' Deciding that her husband was clinically incapable of self-promotion, she said to Cabal and Miss Barrow, 'We are hoping to expand into Katamenia. Linus's designs are popular there, but having to transport things through Senza when those brutes insist on dismantling everything – as if one is likely to hide a cannon in a credenza – is costing us money. The intention is to open a workshop in Katamenia and cut out all that Senzan nonsense entirely.'

'Why would you . . . why would one want to hide a cannon in a credenza?' asked Miss Barrow.

'Military aid. The Katamenians are barbarians of course, but they are our historical allies. The Senzans fear a war on two fronts and use some silly treaty or another to prevent Katamenia rearming.'

'Rearming? How did they lose their last lot of weapons?'

The Roborovskis looked uncomfortable. 'I'm sure Herr Meissner can . . .'

'No, no,' Cabal assured Frau Roborovski. 'You're doing a good job.'

Cornered, she admitted, 'There was a war. More of a border dispute really . . .' Cabal, listening, thought of the many invasions that had started with a trifling 'border dispute' to provide a *casus belli*. . . . 'that the Senzans blew out of all proportion. The next thing you know, the Katamenians are expected to demobilise all their armed forces and melt down their weapons. Just enough for police actions, that's all they were allowed. A disgraceful affront to a nation's sovereignty! A calculated insult to a proud martial tradition!'

Or a wise victor drawing the teeth of a mad dog, thought Cabal, accurately if uncharitably.

'Those Senzans think *so* much of themselves, going around, behaving like they own the whole region! They'll even check the records of everybody not blessed to be born Senzan who travels through their precious territory to make sure they aren't a threat to national security. They'll search this ship when we reach Parila, you know? To check we're not desperate anarchists and that none of the crew has been in the military, since they've decided to make *that* illegal too! Because, obviously, we're going to invade them with a luxury passenger vessel, and we're carrying a load of deadly explosive potatoes that we're going to drop on them. They are so *stupid!*'

Cabal felt obliged to raise both eyebrows. 'Potatoes?'

'Calm yourself, my dear,' said Herr Roborovski, dismayed at his wife's outburst. Indeed, such was the depth of her passion that a very, very faint pink the shade and intensity of a drop of blood on crushed ice had coloured her cheeks.

'Yes. Yes, of course.' She reined herself in from the towering heights of faintly annoyed to a simmering peevishness. Eager to change the subject, she said to Miss Barrow, 'What part of England do you come from, Miss Barrow? The north?'

'Yes,' Miss Barrow laughed. 'I know, it is a distinctive accent, isn't it? I'm from the north-west, to be exact.'

The tension broken, the four made small talk (strictly, only three made small talk, Cabal containing himself to the occasional grunt) until the Roborovskis made their apologies and went off to make more new acquaintances.

Cabal watched them go, the polite smile he had been keeping on his face by sheer force of will finally allowed to lapse into a faint sneer. Miss Barrow, noticing it, murmured, 'Now *that's* more like the Johannes Cabal I know.'

'You know, by conspiring to conceal my identity from the Mirkarvians, you're probably committing some heinous crime, according to the comedic document they call a judicial code.'

'Is that concern for my welfare I hear?'

'It isn't, no. It is a suggestion that, since we both have a lot to lose if my real name is exposed, then it might be wise if you could stop blabbing it every few minutes.'

Stung, she glanced at him. 'Why couldn't you have decided to be something a bit less troublesome, Herr *Meissner*? A butcher, or a doctor, for example.'

'There's a difference?'

'Or a children's entertainer or . . . just something else. For God's sake . . . Mr Meissner, why *do* you do what you do?'

'That,' said Cabal, 'is my business.' At which point, with the sharp ringing of a small gong, dinner was announced.

Chapter 5

IN WHICH DINNER IS SERVED AND
ACQUAINTANCES ARE MADE

The same steward that had cleared up Cabal's spilled drink also seated him. The dinner was being held in the dining room at the ship's bow, the room that Cabal had first entered when boarding. 'Oh, there are so many more gentlemen than ladies on this voyage,' he confided. 'I'm afraid we're having to seat the men in twos, but at least every gentleman will have a lady to chat to.' To Cabal's dismay, he realised that he was being placed next to Leonie Barrow. He sat down in silence and looked pointedly off into the middle distance. The steward, however, had not quite fulfilled his quota of mischief for the day. As he leaned over Cabal's shoulder to pour the wine, he whispered, 'I took the liberty of seating you with *this* young lady.'

Cabal looked at him. The expression 'if looks could kill' does not begin to describe the pure corrosive abhorrence that he put into the glance. If, however, the steward had suddenly found himself transported far away and nailed, through his genitals, to the steeple of a church in the middle of a violent electrical storm, a more exact impression may be gained.

The steward winked conspiratorially and moved along, pleased with his work. Cabal turned reluctantly to find Miss Barrow smiling not altogether pleasantly at him.

'I think we're the ship's official lovebirds,' she murmured.

Cabal, stony-faced, took his napkin, flicked it out, and placed it on his lap. 'Imagine my delight,' he said, apparently to his place setting. Miss Barrow tapped his elbow and indicated the rest of the diners with a surreptitious gesture. Looking around, he realised that every single man there was tucking his napkin in his collar. Moving smoothly to avoid attracting attention, he picked his up and followed suit.

'Don't bother thanking me,' she whispered. Cabal growled slightly and ignored her. He was mentally kicking himself; he'd learned about this particular piece of etiquette during his stay in Krenz prior to the attempt at burglary that had ended in dog drool and disappointment. Now he'd allowed himself to get rattled and it had slipped his mind. Johannes Cabal hated being rattled. It was so . . . human.

The first course was soup. Mirkarvian tastes predictably eschewed consommé in favour of something a little more masculine. Miss Barrow filled a spoon but found she couldn't bring it to her mouth without the spectre of a gag reflex. 'What is this stuff?' she asked Cabal. 'Oxtail?'

'I'm not sure.' He sniffed cautiously. They didn't seem to have stopped with the ox's tail. 'Possibly boiled bull's blood.' He fished around in the dark depths with his spoon. 'With croutons.'

The next course was more acceptable – poached fish – and Cabal took the opportunity to study some of his fellow passengers. The 'Captain's Table' was actually a construct of all the dining tables in the room unbolted from the deck, rearranged into a squat oval and bolted down again. Captain Schten held court from the middle of the forward long side and very uncomfortable he looked in the rôle too. With

Leonie Barrow to his left, Cabal was almost opposite the Captain. Cabal watched without sympathy as Schten tried to look interested in what a self-made, self-satisfied, self-aggrandising businessman was telling him about pork scratchings, the *bierkeller* snack of the future.

To Cabal's right sat a man in his mid to late forties. His face seemed lived-in to the point of being second-hand, perhaps third. He was prodding his fish fitfully with the end of his knife and it was hard to tell who was unhappier with the situation. The man noticed Cabal looking at him. 'Poached,' he said in a tone of defeated disgust. 'Flippin' Nora, it would be poached. I thought, "Oh, your luck's in here, Alexei m'boy. Fish."' He patted his stomach. 'I'm a martyr to my guts. They ought to open an institute dedicated to the study of my guts. The Alexei Aloysius Cacon Memorial Institute.'

'It's traditional to be dead before having a memorial institution named after you,' observed Cabal.

'And how long can it be, eh? Murdered by me own internals.' Cabal thought they would have to go to the back of a long queue. 'Still, if they're the death of me, perhaps medical science can study them and find a cure for my ills so that future generations can say, "His sacrifice was not in vain."'

Cabal watched him carefully for any flicker of irony and found none. 'Ills?'

'Plural.' Cacon prodded his fish again. 'That would have gone nice with a bit of batter. Oh, yes. I've got a regular compendium of complaints, I have. Me doctor's baffled, baffled. Well, I say "doctor". I go to him and he just sends me home with the milk of magnesia and tells me not to worry about it.' His lip curled and he sighed deeply, disgusted at the way of the world. 'The quack.'

Despite himself, Cabal was fascinated. He'd never met

anybody so profoundly ... *wrong* before. 'I was under the impression that poached fish was supposed to be good for the digestion?'

'Oh, well,' said Cacon with the wearied yet supercilious air of somebody who's put down *that* specious argument before. 'They'd like you to think that, wouldn't they?' No further indication of who the mysterious conspiracy of 'they' might be was forthcoming.

The woman at Cacon's other side started talking about how lovely it was to be away from that tiresome trouble back home, and Cacon had opinions on that too. Cabal was unsurprised to discover that Cacon had been a tiger in his youth, a sergeant with the grenadiers. 'Clickety-snitch,' he kept saying, to represent the pin being pulled and the spoon springing clear of an armed grenade. Cabal found something almost touching in the man's self-belief, a faint tremor of empathy. Cacon seemed to live in his own little world and where the real one impinged upon his, it was always ... disappointing.

Cabal looked around for other distractions. As the steward had intimated, the men outnumbered the women by a ratio of more than two to one. From his own place and running clockwise, he let his gaze slide from diner to diner, as a second hand sweeps a path around a watch.

To his immediate left was Miss Leonie Barrow, and he regarded her with an outer dispassion and an inner sourness for a few seconds before moving on.

On Miss Barrow's left was sitting an old soldier, a brilliant deduction Cabal based upon the man no longer being young, and his wearing an impressive collection of medal ribbons on the breast pocket of his dinner jacket. The fact that the captain had called him 'Colonel Konstantin' also helped. The dinner jacket in question was rather old-fashioned in style, featuring the sort of high collar normally only seen in regimental histories in these days of loud ties and ill-considered cufflinks. The colonel was also old-fashioned in his manners; attentive to the ladies, and sober to the gentlemen. He nursed his wine slowly, waving away an increasingly distressed steward who seemed to regard topping up glasses as a religious duty. Cabal was pleased that Konstantin avoided war stories, and intrigued that he also avoided current affairs.

'Is this your first flight, Colonel?' Captain Schten asked.

'In an aeroship, yes. I've been up in the observer's seat of a few entomopters, though.' He gestured vaguely with his fork. 'This is a great deal more comfortable, captain. She's a fine vessel.'

'You've flown in an entomopter?' said Miss Barrow. Konstantin turned to her and, as he did so, his demeanour shifted slightly from that of a professional speaking to a professional to the pleasantly avuncular.

'Indeed I have, Fräulein, and trust me when I say that this is a far more pleasant way to fly. I have had need to see the land from above on some occasions, and an entomopter reconnaissance was the best way of doing it. I am an infantryman through and through, though – I cannot tell you what a relief it was to set foot on terra firma once more.'

'Herr Meissner here used to be a cavalryman,' said Miss Barrow. Cabal's fork stopped en route to his mouth.

'Really?' Konstantin regarded Cabal with a neutral stare. Then he smiled. 'You would have broken your lances on one of my squares, sir, let me assure you.'

Cabal smiled too, a purely technical exercise. 'I do not doubt it, Colonel,' he replied without the faintest idea what Konstantin was talking about.

Next to the colonel was a floppy-haired youth, which is to say, he was perhaps five or so years younger than Cabal. Cabal had, however, worked hard to cram such grotesque quantities of responsibility, activity, and learning both theoretical and practical into every one of his days that his years became akin to dog years. This youth, who – after muttering into his chest when questioned by the colonel – Cabal had finally been able to name as one Gabriel Zoruk, swung from moodiness to airs of unwarranted moral superiority depending on how out of his conversational depth he found himself. Cabal disliked him instinctively, having identified him as a man still prey to his hormones while his intellect puttered around in the background like an embarrassed parent. He was dressed simply, but not cheaply, judging by the tailoring, and it seemed safe to assume that he had decided to be a political activist somewhere along the line without regard for his painfully apparent lack of competence, knowledge, or acuity. Nice hair and the eyes of a cherub had doubtless gained him attentions that he had construed as somehow inspired by his political thoughts. In this he was mistaken, an error of the sort commonly found among millionaires who believe that they are charismatic.

Beyond Zoruk sat Frau Roborovski, sitting apart from her husband presumably as part of the etiquette of 'mixing'. He was to Cabal's right, two places beyond Cacon, and apparently not enjoying his liberty to chat with strangers. This may well have been because of the proprietary glances she would occasionally shoot him if he showed any sign of coming out of his shell. Marriage, it seemed, was truly an institution; in this case something along the lines of a prison or an asylum. Cabal avoided any eye contact with Frau Roborovski that might result in conversation, and moved on.

Captain Schten had managed to settle into a far more interesting conversation with the next man along; a gentle-man in his sixties whose taste in clothing was a trifle fusty but whose eyes and manner were bright. 'It's a fascinating vessel,

85

Captain,' he said, a piece of fish falling unnoticed from his fork back to the plate, 'a fascinating vessel. I've been out of the job for a while but you always keep your interest.'

'This isn't your first trip aboard an aeroship, then?' said Schten, helping himself to more potatoes.

'Oh, good heavens, no,' the man laughed in the indulgent manner of one about to make a revelation. 'I used to design the things.'

'Really? You astonish me, Herr DeGarre.'

'Ah, please, *Monsieur* DeGarre, if you would. "Herr DeGarre" sounds a little too much like "hurdygurdy".'

'Hurdy . . .?'

'One of those ghastly boxes that the English imagine is a musical instrument. Yes, I retired from aeronaval architecture, cah, it must be seven years ago. You've heard of the *Destrier* class? That was one of mine.'

'*Destrier*?' Schten looked uncertain. 'But that was a warship, was it not, M'sieur?'

'It was.' DeGarre took a sip of wine. 'Three were built. The *Bucephalus* was sold off for scrap about five years ago, the *Marengo* is now the entire aerial navy for some little republic in the tropics and the *Destrier* herself, she ploughed into a mountainside in bad weather.' A few people listening into the conversation showed mild signs of discomfort; nobody likes to hear tales of aeroship disasters while travelling in one. 'I told them not to use that type of altimeter but you know military contractors, anything to save a few francs.' He shook his head and picked up the piece of fish again. This time there was no escape for it.

'And all three were used in the Desolée Suppression, were they not, M'sieur?' said a clear voice, cutting across all other conversations. Heads turned to look at the interjector. It was Gabriel Zoruk, all dark-haired, clean-jawed, handsome, and probably riding for a fall. He looked, Cabal thought on further consideration, like the sort of man who does all the wrong things for all the right reasons.

Cabal leaned back in his seat and, inclining his head towards her, asked Miss Barrow quietly, 'What is the "Desolée Suppression"?'

She looked at him, suspicious with disbelief. 'You're joking?'

'Not at this exact moment, no.'

'You've never heard of the Desolée Suppression?'

Cabal bit his lip and sought patience. 'If I knew, I'd hardly be asking, would I?'

He received no useful reply. She was no longer listening to him but to the exchange between DeGarre and Zoruk. 'I'll tell you later,' she said offhandedly to Cabal, leaving him to stew.

'Yes,' said DeGarre, evenly and without rancour. 'They were used in the Suppression.'

'Your gleaming death machines,' said the young man, showing an entirely unconscious attachment to the melodramatic turn of phrase. Another mark of his breed, Cabal observed. 'Against women and children. Does that make you proud?'

'Mein Herr—' began the Captain, beginning to heat at this discourtesy. DeGarre interrupted him.

'Monsieur, you are a romantic, *non*?'

Zoruk frowned, uncertain.

'I was young once, too,' continued DeGarre. 'Things are pleasantly *blanc et noir*, are they not? All morality is a matter of certainty.'

Cabal glanced significantly at Miss Barrow but she was listening attentively to the exchange.

'The ships I built were intended for aerial warfare. Their every line proclaims it. Warship against warship. That was my brief and that was my design. The Suppression, as has been repeatedly shown and famously proclaimed, was the decision of an aeroflotilla commodore straying far, far beyond his orders. When he took those ships into a low-level attack against the villages of the Guasoir Valley, he did so out of a rage of frustration. He had been sent to fight the partisans. They, awkwardly, did not wear uniforms. They did not simply vanish among the villagers. They *were* the villagers. They slaughtered patrols and then vanished amongst their kindred. It was an impossible situation and should never have been given to an aeroship flotilla to resolve. A case for the infantry. Von Falks should have deployed his marines to prove as much and then reported it to his superiors. As we all know, he did not. It was regrettable.'

'Regrettable?' spat Zoruk, but DeGarre hadn't finished.

'The *Destrier* and her sisters were built to fight a good war, by the rules of war, to the honour of war. Commodore von Falks sullied those rules, his family and, to my chagrin, the reputation of my ships. Direct your ire elsewhere, Monsieur. It is wasted here.' He reached for his wine glass and took a calm sip amid a light patter of applause from other passengers who preferred war crimes not to be discussed at dinner. Zoruk glared at him, picked up his cutlery, made as if to start eating again but, after a moment's wavering, slammed them on to his plate, stood up and walked out with less dignity than he supposed. Cabal watched him go with approval: anything that distracted attention away from, say, a fugitive necromancer travelling aboard under the alias of a comatose civil servant was to be encouraged.

'Stone the crows, what a berk,' observed Cacon. 'Things were different when I was a boy. Respect for your elders, oh yes. Always the same though, isn't it? When you're young, you *had* to show respect for your elders or you'd get a right lathering. Now I *am* an elder, you have to treat the youth of today with kid gloves or they'll give *you* a right lathering. Doesn't matter which side of the generation gap I'm on, it's the wrong side.' He breathed a deep breath so he could sigh a deep sigh. 'Typical. Abso-lutely flipping typical.' He shoved his plate of disrupted fish away from him. 'Oi, garkon! Give this to the cat. What's for pudding?'

Pudding, however, still lay a little way off into the future. The main course came next, steak cooked in the Mirkarvian fashion – so rare as to be just this side of stationary. Miss Barrow looked at her plate as red juices oozed from the flesh. 'What am I supposed to do with this?' she asked Cabal in an aside. 'Eat it or resuscitate it?'

'Thank your stars that you asked for it well done,' he replied. He'd asked for his to be cooked medium rare, which in Mirkarvian cuisine meant it had been shown a picture of an oven for a moment and then served. A very brief moment, mind.

As his fellow diners had their full attentions upon their plates as they laboriously sawed away at their meals – less fine dining, more like a bayonet charge – Cabal took the opportunity to study them in more detail. Sitting on the captain's left hand was a young woman, expensively yet, unusually for the Mirkarvian aesthetic, tastefully dressed in burgundy silks and velvet. This, it transpired, was the Lady Ninuka, yet another of Mirkarvia's serried ranks of nobles. Apparently however she was quite senior, based on her place at table and Schten's great and careful civility towards her. For her part, she was polite but disengaged. The businessman with his major breakthrough in bar snacks, a Herr Harlmann, was on her left and had talked through her to Schten. She had disregarded him as easily as she might a small fly; a notable feat, in particular when Harlmann had gone on to the intricacies of manufacture.

In her early twenties, and beautiful in an obvious 'flawless complexion, perfect bone structure, glistering eyes of russet

89

brown, wine-dark hair' sort of way, there was a slight down-turn at the edges of her mouth that implied a dissatisfaction with life. It left her with a mild pout, but Cabal doubted there was much of the child left in her. Her gaze ranged around the table and he found himself the subject of it more than once, her eyes switching between him and Miss Barrow as if gauging the nature of their relationship, before moving on. When her eyes met his, there was no sudden looking away, or even glances laden with meaning. She looked dispassionately into his eyes as she might those of a statue, or of an animal at the zoo. He noticed she also looked occasionally at the door through which that singularly ineffectual rabble-rouser Gabriel Zoruk had left earlier, as if expecting him to return. That he didn't seemed not to concern her greatly.

To Cabal's left, Miss Barrow took a rest from her knife work. 'This isn't a meal,' she muttered to him, 'it's a cow's post-mortem. I think I'll stick with the potatoes and carrots.' She waved over a steward and asked for some more vegetables.

The woman on the far side of Cacon overheard her, and said, 'Ah, well, that's one thing we won't be short of on this voyage, my dear,' and laughed a curious laugh, *Muh'heh!* The *muh* was low and slightly distressed, as if she was expressing illness, but the *heh!* was higher and girlish. The overall effect was thus: 'Muh, I don't feel well . . . Heh! Fooled you!'

Cabal turned to look at the woman if only in curiosity as to what sort of creature would produce such a noise. She was approximately forty, he gauged, and exhibited that interesting combination of dour propriety overlaying an inappropriate coltishness for a lady of her age that was a peculiarity distinctive in women who have been to an English public school. Such schools begin the process of inculcating eccentricity right from the moment it is understood that English public schools are not meant for the public; the name is not merely inaccurate, it is actively misleading. Any other country would call them 'private', but where's the fun in that? She wore a dress that would be considered frumpy by most grandparents, a brown affair with a palpable air of spinster-hood. Her hair was very nearly the same shade, arranged in harsh shingles about a sharp, pale face. She had made an attempt at make-up, but the rouge sat on her cheeks like red paint on a white wall.

'Why so?' he asked.

'You don't know?' butted in Cacon, whose tales of military ferocity had gained some verisimilitude in light of the horrible wounds he was inflicting on his food. 'Blimey, mate, 'ave you been living under a rock? This is a mission of mercy we're on 'ere.'

Cabal said nothing, but his expression indicated that he had seen more likely angels than Cacon.

'The Katamenian famine, Herr Meissner,' supplied Miss Barrow. 'The crop failure?'

Cabal may have had many faults, but difficulty in rapidly absorbing, reviewing, and extrapolating from new data was not among them. 'Of course,' he said nonchalantly. 'My ministry has been working towards logistical relief pro-grammes, but I was not aware this ship was involved.'

'It's why there are so few passengers aboard this vessel, sir,' added the woman with the aggravating laugh. 'Herr . . . Meissner, was it?'

Cacon paused with a chunk of meat speared alongside a fragment of boiled new potato on his fork hovering before his open mouth. It was not a pleasing *tableau vivant*. 'Miss Ambersleigh, this is Herr Meissner of the Mirkarvian civil service. Herr Meissner, Miss Ambersleigh, 'er ladyship's companion.' It looked as though he was introducing the meat and potato to one another. As an afterthought, he leaned slightly towards Cabal, and said in a conspiratorial whisper,

91

'She's English.' This bombshell delivered, and etiquette satisfied, he dumped the food into his mouth with all the delicacy of a steam engine's fireman shovelling coal into the firebox. Cabal turned his attention towards Miss Ambersleigh quickly, that he might spare himself the sight of Cacon chewing.

'I'm sorry, you were saying, Miss Ambersleigh?' he prompted her.

'I said it's the reason why there are so few passengers aboard. This is the only occupied passenger deck. I'm told that above us is storage, and above that is the second class deck, but that it is entirely unoccupied. All the staterooms, you see, are full of food. Vegetables, mainly. Imagine! Tons and tons of potatoes, and carrots, and turnips, just above our heads!' Her eyes glittered at the prospect of so many root vegetables. Cabal sensed there was not going to be a meeting of the minds here. At least it explained Frau Roborovski's obscure reference to exploding potatoes.

'So, only the first class deck is occupied? And the crew deck, of course.'

Harlmann raised an interrogative hand. 'I say, the crew deck's at the top, isn't it? Along with engineering and such-like? Doesn't that make the old bird a bit . . . top-heavy?'

Schten had obviously fielded questions like this before. He had his glass to his lips, however, and by the time he could lower it, DeGarre had leaped into the breach.

'Yes, Monsieur, it does make the vessel top-heavy, but you see, that is the intention. It is an easy error to fall into, that an aeroship is much like a nautical ship, and in many respects, especially in how they are run, that is true.' He cupped his hand. 'An aeroship does not float in a sea of air, however.' He twisted his wrist so that his fingers dangled downwards. 'It hangs, like a chandelier in the heavens. Thus, may the Good Lord forfend, should any of the levitators fail, then it may lean over a little. If they were at the bottom and the same thing happened . . .' He shrugged. 'It would fall over. *Pouf!*'

Cabal did not recall ever having heard an apocalyptic disaster resulting in death and horror characterised as *pouf!* A disciple of understatement himself, he warmed slightly to DeGarre.

Captain Schten nodded benevolently. 'Couldn't have put it better myself.' Which was probably true.

'How many levitators does a vessel like this carry, Captain?' asked DeGarre.

'Or, strictly speaking, how many levitators carry a ship like this?' replied Schten. Delighted with his wit, he reached once again for his glass.

'As you say,' said DeGarre with the sort of smile normally employed in the patronisation of idiot children. 'How many?'

Schten paused, glass halfway to his lips. 'Eh?' His eyes wandered in their orbits as he re-engaged his attention. 'The levitators? Oh, there're two batteries of eight.'

'Parallel or cross-linked?'

'Ah . . . cross-linked. Much safer.'

'Much more expensive, too.'

Schten opened his arms in about as expansive a gesture as he dared without knocking DeGarre and Lady Ninuka off their chairs. 'She's not exactly a scow, mein Herr.'

DeGarre nodded. 'She is impressive. I wonder, may I see more of her, please?'

'I'm sorry?'

'May I see a little of her beyond the doors marked *Crew Only*?'

Schten paused, uncertain. 'Well, it's not company policy to give guided tours. The bridge is not spacious . . .'

'Please, Captain. I would be deeply obliged. As for the bridge, you need not concern yourself on that. One bridge is much like another. No, I'd much rather take a look at your engineering section, if I may. Just to see how the art has moved on since I retired.'

Schten wavered. Company rules and reasonable behaviour were doing battle within him. The impetus to make his decision one way or another was provided, unexpectedly, by Alexei Cacon. 'Oh, you might as well, Captain,' he said as he chased the last of his peas around the plate. 'The whole boat's going to be full of greasy Senzans getting their mucky finger-prints over everything, and they won't be saying *please*. Herr DeGarre's a gentleman at least. Why should they do anything they like, and he can't even have five minutes looking at your spinny things upstairs?'

Schten ignored the reference to his ship as a 'boat' and said, 'It's not that easy, I'm afraid, Herr Cacon. I don't want to set a precedent.'

'Give him his guided tour, Captain,' said Lady Ninuka, in a voice that might have been gifted to her by the Lorelei and a very good elocution teacher. 'I, for one, promise not to ask for a similar privilege.'

'Nor I,' added Miss Ambersleigh, which earned a disdainful glance from Lady Ninuka that seemed to say, *As if that were likely.*

'Nor me neither,' said Cacon, finally cornering the errant peas and spearing them on his fork amid a pizzicato of dinner silver on china.

There was a general round of muttered agreements. Captain Schten gave in with good grace, and arrangements were made for the following afternoon. For his part, Cabal slightly regretted that he wouldn't get a chance to see the engineering deck for himself. He had an interest in machinery of the metallic as well as the fleshly form.

Cacon's long-awaited pudding – *dessert* seemed like an altogether too feminine term – turned up as the next course. There was a limited choice between the famous Mirkarvian dish, *tschun*, which not only sounds like a sneeze but looks like it, or cheese and biscuits. Almost everybody, even the Mirkarvians, opted for cheese and biscuits. The cheese was fierce enough to strip a layer of tissue from the palate, but it was still preferable to the alternative. Cabal, however, had an unlooked-for opportunity to see *tschun* at close quarters, as Cacon was the only one to order it. Served in a long shallow dish, it looked and smelled like partially fermented milk, with an island of something slightly too large grained to be sago sitting in the middle of it. Scattered across this island was a red stain of blended cinnamon and pepper. Cacon tucked into it with noisy enthusiasm. 'Put hairs on your chest this will, old son,' he commented to Cabal. Cabal failed to see how this could be regarded as an advertisement, particularly in regard to female diners.

Finally, they reached the time for coffee, cognac, and cigars. The ladies retired, Miss Barrow giving him a meaningful look as she did so, and the gentlemen wandered down towards the salon. Cabal felt constrained to attend the ritual, but first made his apologies that he would be a few minutes. The same interfering steward who had placed him beside Miss Barrow now directed him to the nearest 'head', which Cabal understood to be a slang or technical term for the toilet. He thanked the steward, though he had no intention of using it; he just wanted a little time to himself to gather his wits. He made his way instead to the starboard promenade, the better to find some fresh air filtering through the external vents there.

The promenades ran down either side of the ship on Deck B, the storage and supply deck. No passengers bunked on this level, so the rooms had no portholes, only thin windows set high in their walls to let in light from the promenades. These were accessible only via stairs from Deck A – first class – at both their fore and aft ends, and ran most of the length of the vessel. Wide glazed windows angled out slightly to allow walkers to lean over the rail and gaze down at the hoi polloi without having their hair unduly disturbed. It was a far more scenic route from the dining room to the salon than going via the internal corridor on Deck A, but not nearly as expeditious, and Cabal was unsurprised that none of the other men climbed the stair with him, such was the lure of coffee, brandy, and tobacco.

He was hoping for a few minutes of solitude, but here he was to be disappointed. The petulant Herr Zoruk was there, hands on the rail by the windows, deep in thought, though more probably self-pity. He looked up when he heard Cabal turn the corner, denying Cabal the chance to withdraw unseen. It was an awkward situation where neither man wanted to be in the presence of the other, yet manners insisted they must. Cabal found a place perhaps a metre away from Zoruk at the rail, and looked out into the night.

There was silence for some moments, then Zoruk said, 'I suppose I made rather a damn fool of myself tonight.'

'Yes,' said Cabal.

Zoruk shot him a slightly startled look. 'You call a spade a spade, don't you?'

'It saves time. I am not noted for my diplomatic skills.'

'But you're a civil servant?'

'Not one in the diplomatic service. I deal in facts, Herr Zoruk, and the fact is, yes, you made a fool of yourself tonight.'

Zoruk started to say something, but the will to do so left him in a defeated sigh. He turned back to the window. 'I know he's right, that's the worst of it. You can't blame a man for making a bullet if that bullet is later used to kill a saint. I knew that, or I would have if I'd taken a minute to think. I was just so angry. The Desolée Suppression . . . words cannot . . .' He shook his head. 'I'm being a fool again.'

'I . . . am not very politically aware,' said Cabal, choosing his words carefully. 'In my post, I deal with figures, disbursements, quotas, and reports. Sometimes, things happen in the broader world,' he gestured at the dark Earth beneath them, 'and I remain ignorant of them, often to my shame. Herr Zoruk, what exactly *is* the Desolée Suppression? What did this von Falk do?'

Zoruk looked at him, an odd look of mild suspicion and surprise, and Cabal wondered if his curiosity was going to cost him dearly. 'You live in a sterile, isolated little world, Herr Meissner,' said Zoruk. 'I almost envy you. Very well . . . the Desolée Suppression; history lesson. You probably picked up most of the story from the dinner table. The Guasoir Valley was Priskian by right of the Treaty of Hollsberg, but the locals have always regarded themselves as culturally Dulkine. They complained about it, and especially the Priskian policy of forcible relocation and the shipping in of Priskian settlers, but nobody was listening. So, they started with civil disobedience, but all that got them was a few broken heads and some unjustifiably heavy prison sentences.'

Cabal frowned. 'So, this isn't a Mirkarvian affair at all?'

Zoruk shook his head. 'Politically, no. But we are all brothers against injustice, Herr Meissner, are we not?' Herr Meissner declined to comment, so Zoruk continued. 'Civil disobedience escalated to attacks on property, and finally to the derailing of a Priskian troop train. There were a handful of injuries, and one death. The Priskians responded by sending in Commodore von Falks's aerosquadron. He was supposed to monitor activity in the valley only, and lend support to ground troops should they request it.' He looked in the direction of the dining room and his humiliation. 'DeGarre was wrong about one thing. I should have pointed it out, small victory that it was. He said the locals slaughtered patrols. That's not true; they attacked one patrol when the Priskians started enforcing a curfew, and killed two men, at the cost of four of their own. Farmers against soldiers . . . hardly a fair fight. But one of the dead Priskians was an officer of von Falk's squadron who had been liaising with the ground troops.

'The commodore was furious. Insane with anger. Quite literally, insane. He located the three villages that were most likely the source of the "terrorists" who had killed his officer, and then . . .' He closed his eyes, and did not speak for several seconds. When he opened them again, he said, 'They eradicated all three villages. Bombed them and bombarded them. Strafed the streets with Gatling fire. Dropped liquid fire upon the homes and the farms and the churches. They burned the houses, and shot the people when they ran from the flames. By the time he received orders to cease immediately and withdraw, it was too late. Twenty-four hundred people were dead or dying.'

There was silence for a dozen heartbeats. 'Twenty-four hundred?' Cabal's voice was hollow.

Zoruk nodded. 'It was a disaster in many ways. Priskia had little choice but to cede the Guasoir back to Dulkis under international pressure. Von Falk was given a revolver with one bullet and a quiet room for ten minutes to give him the opportunity to do the decent thing, which he did. And, when the world saw what DeGarre's machines had done to those poor people,' he looked Cabal in the eye, 'orders went up by eight hundred per cent. I accept his argument that he didn't design his ships to kill civilians, but that doesn't excuse him getting rich from it.' He shrugged. 'Or am I still being a damned fool?'

'Yes,' said Cabal. 'I'm expected in the salon, Herr Zoruk. Good evening.' He made to go, but at the corner he paused and looked back. 'Humanity is a despicable mass, Herr

Zoruk, and ill-suited to the compassion of romantics. Sometimes it requires culling.'

'Oh?' said Zoruk. He sounded worn out and depressed. 'And who would choose who lives and who dies?'

I would, ideally, thought Cabal. *I'd make a more informed job of it than most.* But instead he said, 'Who indeed, Herr Zoruk?' and took his leave.

Walking into the salon was like entering a fog bank, albeit a very Cuban one. Every man present had a cigar in his mouth and a snifter in his hand containing enough brandy to preserve a mouse. The coffee pots sat by unloved and unused as the men stood around in that peculiar chest-out-and-stomach-sucked-in way that men in dinner jackets feel obliged to stand after dinner. Cabal had suffered the misfortune to attend several such gatherings before and was quite aware that they laboured under a sense of ritual that eroded a great deal of any potential enjoyment to be had. The Mirkarvian variety, however, was almost a full-blown dominance display of the sort that gets anthropologists excited. A certain pecking order was already apparent: Captain Schten stood unassailable because he was, after all, the captain, and they were all on his territory; DeGarre had age, experience, fame, and a certain cachet of notoriety about him, and so stood at an only slightly less certain second place. After that, however, it was every man for himself, with the sole exception of Herr Roborovski who refused to play, and who stood off to one side, gazing mournfully into his brandy as if he really did expect a pickled mouse to surface.

Currently holding the floor was Bertram Harlmann, king of the bar snacks. He had moved on from exhaustive details of the all-conquering pork scratching, and was offering to let the gentlemen present in on the ground floor of the next breathtaking breakthrough in overpriced tidbits for the *bierkeller* market. This white-hot cutting edge was called 'mixed nuts', and apparently contained the secret weapon of dried fruit. 'Almonds,' he said in a significant tone to one half of the gathering. 'Raisins,' he said to the other. Cabal managed to reduce a full roll of the eyes to a momentary interest in the carpet's pattern, and entered the fray.

Chapter 6

Cabal slept lightly. This was as much a learned behaviour as a natural aspect; far too many people and other entities had trod lightly towards him as he slept with less kindly intentions than tucking him in and kissing his brow. He skimmed through the dreaming edges of deep sleep like a man on ice skates, standing rigid, arms crossed, and wearing a disapproving expression as his subconscious mind threw phantasms, childhood memories, and random elements of his recent past in his path with more optimism than expectation. He slid through them all with the humourless gravitas of an Old Testament prophet challenged to a magical duel by Uncle Mungo the children's conjuror. When he did finally reach the places of the mind too dark and motionless for dreams, he paused barely over the treeline and waited for his body and mind to recuperate, all the time listening to the distant call of his senses, singing like the wind over telegraph wires. If they suddenly cried with pattern and purpose, he could be up and out of the well of sleep faster than a rabbit from a trebuchet.

Tonight, he had taken almost an hour to even drift into a light slumber, and was just in the act of strapping on his figurative skates when something roused him back to full wakefulness in a moment. He did not sit bolt upright – there's nothing like visibly declaring oneself awake to precipitate an attack. Instead he lay, his eyes opening only slightly as he took in his surroundings, and listened carefully. The steady thrum of the levitators he had grown accustomed to, and this he ignored. There was something else, however. A dull battering sound running through the outer hull as if somebody was kicking the wall. After a moment more it ended and there were only the sounds of the ship's running.

Cabal rolled on to his back and looked at the ceiling as he wondered what had made the noises. It was, he knew, largely an exercise to bore himself back to sleep; he had no inkling of the workings of a vessel like the *Hortense*. For all he knew, the sound might be a common occurrence, one made by some necessary component doing its job. There had been something about it, though, something organic rather than mechanical. He had heard dying men drum a similar tattoo on the floorboards with their heels and this thought shooed sleep away.

Five minutes later there was a new sound, and at this one Cabal did sit bolt upright. It a dull roar that grew in a rapid crescendo to a climax that coincided with a sharp metallic thud. Cabal had heard a sound very similar to it earlier in the evening when the sliding windows in the salon had been drawn back. But then they had been flying lower and slower. The window in one of the nearby cabins had been opened, he was sure of it, and this raised two objections in his mind. First, that the cabin would now be bitterly cold as the wind blew harshly around it. Second, that when he had been looking from his own window earlier in the evening, he had noted in passing that the sliding frame was locked shut by a bolt that would require a specialist tool to release. These two factors seemed to indicate that whoever had opened their window, had not done so purely for a breath of fresh air.

Cabal sat in the darkness, his hands clasped, his index fingers extended and tapping rapidly together as he fought his curiosity. It was an anomalous sound, and – as a scientist – anomalies intrigued him. Warring with his curiosity, however, was his instinct for self-preservation. If something was awry, and he was strongly inclined to think so, then wandering the ship's corridors might provoke suspicion, which was to be vigorously avoided. Then again, if he *didn't* investigate a noise that should have induced him to wander about in Meissner's unforgivably gaudy Chinese dressing gown, then wouldn't that also be cause for questions?

'Why didn't you go out to discover the source of this strange sound, Herr Meissner, as any true-blooded son of Mirkarvia would?' he imagined the captain asking him.

'Because I slept though it,' he imagined himself replying and, pleased with this simple but effective excuse, he settled back down to sleep.

Whereupon there was a commotion in the corridor, talking for a minute, and the sound of one of the neighbouring doors being knocked upon, apparently without effect. A few moments later, it was joined by a light but insistent knock at his own door. Cabal wandered whether he could reasonably say he'd slept through this too, when it was repeated with more vigour and he knew he was going to have to show his face.

'Good grief,' said Leonie Barrow when he answered the door. 'Where on Earth did you get that dressing gown?' She herself was wearing a red and blue tartan gown over a white winceyette nightdress. In purely aesthetic terms, her nighttime apparel made Cabal wonder how the English ever managed to find sufficient motivation to breed.

'How may I help you, Fräulein?' he said, ignoring her question.

'Didn't you hear anything?'

He drew breath to say he had slept through it, but changed his mind. 'I heard something.' He looked out into the corridor and saw Colonel Konstantin, the Roborovskis, and – inevitably – Cacon milling around outside DeGarre's door. 'What's happening?'

'I heard some sort of commotion coming from M. DeGarre's cabin. Well, we all did,' she waved at the other passengers. 'Now it sounds like he's got his window open somehow.'

'Has anybody called for the officer of the watch?' He was answered by the arrival of Captain Schten himself, still buttoning his uniform collar.

'Ladies. Gentlemen. Kindly step back. I am sure there is nothing amiss.'

He made to knock on the door, but Cacon said, 'You're wasting your time there, Captain. I've been knocking on that until my knuckles are red raw.' Cabal noted that they plainly were not. 'There's no answer. Just the wind, *whooooooo*. Y'know what? I bet 'e's done 'imself in.' He crossed his arms and looked both pleased and expectant, as if he anticipated everybody would applaud his deduction and go back to bed, mystery solved.

The captain gave him a look that was on the edge of hostility, and knocked sharply on the door. 'M. DeGarre? This is the captain. Are you all right, sir?'

'You won't get an answer, Capitano,' said Cacon. Irritatingly, he was right. Captain Schten listened for a moment, but all any of them could hear was the moaning wind beyond the door. Schten grasped the door handle and tried it; it did not yield. He took a master key from his jacket pocket, unlocked the door, turned the handle and started to open it while beginning an apology for the intrusion. Both the opening and the apology came up short as the door stopped abruptly in its travel.

''Is body's probably in the way,' said Cacon, apparently knowledgeable in such things.

'*Herr* Cacon,' began Schten, his temper almost visibly fraying. Whatever he was about to say was thankfully lost when Colonel Konstantin interrupted.

'Herr Cacon,' the colonel said evenly. 'Please return to your cabin. You are not helping affairs.'

'Eh?' The possibility of being less than vital in unfolding events seemed not to have occurred to Cacon. 'Eh? Me? You can't order me about, matey! I'm not in the army, y'know!'

'Sir,' said Schten, his temper reined back in the respite Konstantin had bought him. 'As the captain of this vessel, you are under my authority. Please return to your cabin.'

'Oi, oi, oi!' Cacon was outraged by this attack on his dignity. 'I 'ave as much right to be 'ere as anyone!'

'No,' said Captain Schten. 'You don't.' He summoned over the purser and a steward who had arrived and were standing uncertainly at the back of the group. 'Take Herr Cacon back to his cabin, steward. Make sure he stays there.'

Cacon was escorted away, still complaining. 'This is a blinkin' outrage! I'll write a letter!'

'As you wish,' said the captain wearily. He waited until Cacon was gone before trying the door again. There was a distinct 'clunk' against the handle after the first inch or so, and he could open it no further. He regarded it grimly. 'There's a chair under the handle. M. DeGarre,' he called through the gap, 'if you can hear me, please move away from the door.' He stepped back to give himself space and kicked the door hard with the flat of his boot, just under the handle. They heard the chair bounce across the cabin floor, Schten already moving in to follow it.

Cabal was slightly surprised to find himself in the doorway a moment after Schten. His curiosity had, not for the first time, overridden his sense of self-preservation. Still, now he was there, it would be more suspicious for him to suddenly become all backwards about coming forward. So he stood just inside the door and looked around officiously, as if inspecting mysteriously empty aeroship cabins in which a chill wind whipped around his naked knees was all part of a Mirkarvian civil servant's duties. Schten was already by the window, which was slid back along its track as far as it would go. He looked out into the darkness.

'He's gone,' he said, his words almost lost in the howling wind. He shook his head. 'Stupid, stupid man.' He slid the window shut with an angry slam. The sudden silence was almost shocking.

'How,' said Cabal, wondering how far he could let the uncomfortable persona of Herr Meissner slip in safety. Every degree was a relief. 'How did he open the window? If it's like mine, it's fixed with a screw.'

The thought hadn't occurred to Schten. He looked at the window again and seemed nonplussed. He started to cast his gaze around the room. 'I don't know, Herr Meissner. The windows can be opened when we are at anchor and low-level flight, but my crew would have been round all the cabins and secured the windows when we began to climb.'

On the bed, he found the answer to this small mystery. A tool wallet lay open, its elasticated straps holding in place the sort of small spanners, screwdrivers, and other devices a man with an interest in the mechancal might well carry in his luggage. One screwdriver was out of its place, lying across its fellows. By it was the missing window screw. He picked it up and showed it to Cabal. 'It was never foreseen that a passenger would have both the desire to open a cabin window at high altitude, and the means by which to do it.' He sighed as he looked at the window. 'A tragedy.'

'Why did he do it?' Konstantin walked past Cabal to stand in the rapidly cluttering cabin. 'He seemed at perfect equilibrium at dinner. Why would he return here with every appearance of good humour and then coldly and methodically put an end to himself?'

Schten shrugged. 'Dinner was several hours ago. Perhaps he spent that time brooding over something. The man who undid that window may have been of very different composure to the man to whom we bid good night.'

Konstantin was unimpressed. 'Brooding over what?'

'The boy was right. I have dedicated my life to science, and all it has brought is death. The victims of my machines cry out for justice. I shall give it to them.'

Konstantin and Schten turned to Cabal in astonishment. They found him leaning over a portable typewriter on the small writing desk. He was reading from a sheet still in place between platen and paper bail.

Cabal turned and looked at the two men. 'He typed his suicide note. How very modern of him.'

Schten glared at him. 'For God's sake, Meissner! A man's dead.' He made to remove the sheet from the typewriter. Before he could reach it, however, Cabal tapped a lever on the typewriter carriage twice smartly and then struck a key. He pulled the sheet from the machine himself and regarded it sharply for a moment before handing it over.

'The inevitable investigation into M. DeGarre's death will no doubt wish you to preserve this as evidence, Captain,' he said.

Schten was coming to the conclusion that he really didn't like the meddlesome Herr Meissner. 'What was the point of that, sir?'

'To give the police a comparison. I have repeated the last *m* of the message, as you can see. We are all witnesses that I typed it on this machine and, even to the naked eye, the two letters seem identical. Believe me, Captain, a thorough investigation would leave no stone unturned and no hypothesis unconsidered, including the possibility that this note was typed on another machine and left here to divert suspicion.'

'What? *What?* Are you serious, man? The door was locked and barred from the inside. Are you suggesting the poor man was murdered, the murderer threw the body out of the window, and then himself to follow?'

'I am suggesting it, yes, but not as a serious theory, only a possibility. There are such things as parachutes, after all.'

'Parachutes? This is a civil vessel, sir; it has no need of parachutes. And before you suggest this remarkable murderer of yours brought his own aboard, you should understand that we are travelling in near total darkness over wooded mountains. No one but a lunatic would attempt such a jump.'

'There are such things as lunatics, Captain.' Cabal held up his hands to forestall Schten's increasing wrath. 'Peace, sir. I do not believe for a second that this is the case. While there are certain religious and political groups that encourage a degree of fanaticism in some of their members that they may be used as expendable assassins, they are rarely subtle. I see no reason why any such organisation should want to kill M. DeGarre and then disguise it as suicide. Miss Barrow,' he turned to Leonie as did Schten and Konstantin, both in some surprise that a woman would want to hang around the scene of a death. She, in her turn, demonstrated some discomfort that her silence had not rendered her entirely invisible. 'I understand from our conversation earlier that you have some interest in psychology. What do you make of all this? The apparent equanimity of the M. DeGarre this evening? The abrupt nature of this note?'

That Cabal did not mention that her 'interest' in such matters was formal and criminological was not lost on her, and so she spoke as an unthreatening dilettante.

'Well,' she started uncertainly, 'from what I've read on cases like . . .' she gestured vaguely at the cabin and its window, 'this, there is no standard form. Sometimes there are notes, but . . . well, there's no rule that says there has to be. And when there is a note, it can be anything from pages and pages long to less than you'd leave in a note for the milkman. I understand Herr Meissner wishing to be thorough, but there is nothing here to say this is anything but what it appears to be. And that is very regrettable. I liked M. DeGarre.'

'As did I, my dear,' said Konstantin. 'I think we all did. This isn't the place for a young lady. Please, may I accompany you—'

'That won't be necessary, Colonel,' interrupted Cabal. 'I have said my piece and perhaps demonstrated my incompetence for such an investigation. I shall leave this in the captain's hands, who will surely do a better job of it than I. Good night, gentlemen. I am, of course, at your service if you should need me for a statement or suchlike.' He nodded curtly, to which the colonel clicked his heels, while the captain distractedly bid them farewell.

On the way to Leonie Barrow's cabin, Cabal stared at the carpet the whole way, his hands behind his back, thinking. She looked at him, mildly amused. 'If anybody saw you like that, they'd forget all about us being the ship's lovebirds. You're taking me, unchaperoned, to my cabin but you look like a man with acute dyspepsia.'

Cabal was not in the mood for verbal fencing. 'DeGarre, missing and, in all reasonable probability, dead.'

'Yes?'

'A suicide note. Typed.'

'Yes.'

'Brooding over a few feather-light jibes from some boy who's barely started shaving, he types a note, removes a securing bolt from his window, and throws himself into the void.'

'Yes.'

Cabal walked in silence for another few paces. 'Do you believe a word of it?'

'No. No, I don't. That business with the typewriter, what were you up to?'

'I told the captain. A letter from that typewriter for comparison.'

'That's something else I didn't believe a word of. You should be careful; I don't think the captain believed you either.'

Cabal stopped and looked at her. 'What's this?' he said, a bitter mockery evident in his tone. 'Concerned for my safety?'

'I've explained that once.' She kept walking and after a moment Cabal admitted defeat in this small conflict and followed. 'All I'm saying is that you should keep your head down. If you want to keep it at all. So, the typewriter.'

'The typewriter. I backspaced twice and typed the last letter in DeGarre's note, the *m* in *them*.'

'What use is that for comparison? It would have come down in the same place as the original.'

'No. It *should* have come down in the same place as the original.'

'But it didn't?'

'No. About half a millimetre to the right and a little higher.'

'Which means what, exactly? That the note was typed, removed, and then replaced? Why would DeGarre do that?'

'If DeGarre did it at all. And even if he did not, why would this hypothetical expendable assassin do it?'

They had reached Leonie's cabin and paused by the door, speaking in hushed tones.

'We believe he was murdered, then?' she whispered. 'I don't believe in hypothetical expendable assassins, with or without parachutes. Unless we can come up with a reasonable explanation as to how a murderer got out of a locked and barricaded room, we're just going to have to accept it was suicide, no matter how wrong that seems.'

There was something of the caged animal about Cabal, she thought, as she waited for a reply. He was angry and frustrated that he had been presented with a problem which intrigued him, but that engaging that problem might lead to his exposure, arrest, and execution. She could almost feel sorry for him. But this was Johannes Cabal, a man she knew from bitter experience was more than capable of monstrous acts of violence and cruelty when necessary. Then again, he was also the man who had sent her a letter and document of such astonishing and liberating power that it had made her father – a man of great imperturbability – sit down and repeat, 'Well, I'll be buggered' for the better part of a minute.

Whatever was going on inside Cabal's mind currently, he did not seem in the mood to share. 'Good night, Miss Barrow,' he said finally, and walked away, drawing his ridiculous Oriental dressing gown tight. Leonie watched him go through narrowed eyes, shook her head, and retired for what was left of the night.

Cabal got back to his cabin, closed the door heavily, dumped the horrendous dressing gown on the floor, and threw himself into his bed with a muttered expression of irritation with the world. He just wanted to go back to sleep. He did not want to become any more involved in the curious case of the defenestrated DeGarre than he already was. Indeed, if he could avoid any further entanglements, he would be a happy man. A happier man, at least. He was determined to roll over, make himself comfortable, forget all about the night's events, and go to sleep.

He managed exactly half of this list. After rolling over and making himself comfortable, he discovered that he was exactly comfortable enough to consider the night's events in detail, and in so doing drove away any hope of sleep. He was in that awkward place where rationality and logic don't quite match up, and the horrible squealing of misaligned mental cogs was driving him to distraction. Pure brute logic said the door was locked and barricaded, the window was open, the cabin offered no hiding places, therefore the occupant of the cabin had gone out of the window. Pure brute logic overruled any silly murder shenanigans by pointing out the suicide note, the locked room, and then proceeded to wave Ockham's razor around in a threatening manner.

Rationality, however, is a slightly different beast, or at least Cabal's was. It considered the curious facts of DeGarre's good humour at dinner, the curiosity of the misaligned suicide note, and . . . damn it! The chair! Cabal sat up in bed, thinking hard. Why had DeGarre barricaded his door at all? The door was already locked. Even if opening the window turned out to be a noisy operation, by the time a member of the crew bearing a master key arrived to open the door, he would have long completed his unsuccessful impersonation of Peter Pan and become an untidy mess in the Mirkarvian wilderness. To protect against or at least slow any attempt to kick the door down. Schten had dislodged the chair with a single well-placed kick, but the captain was a big man. Anybody else would have taken longer to get through, and that was what DeGarre had planned upon. There, it was satisfactorily explained. No, it wasn't. It was overplanned. Once the window was open, it was the work of a moment to climb out into eternity. Unless he ended up dithering before the jump? No, that wouldn't do either. That meant he had planned for time spent dithering, which meant he expected to be unsure or at least anticipated the possibility of being unsure, in which case he was unsure of committing suicide, in which case . . . Cabal growled with irritation. In which case, why had he committed suicide? People don't set out to kill themselves and make contingency plans lest they change their minds. It was a stupid, stupid circular argument. So, he returned to the point of departure. Why had DeGarre barricaded his door? Cabal looked around for a new path to follow that didn't curve so alarmingly, but was to be disappointed.

He slumped back down and tried to sleep. At first, his slowing conscious mind was naive enough to believe that his subconscious was helping him to drift off. It presented him with a vision of a limitless plain of tiles beneath a sterile white sky. The tiles were marked on each edge with a letter *a*, *b*, *c*, *d* to indicate orientation, and some mathematical symbols were scrawled across the centre. He half-heartedly attempted to read one, but the notations squirmed beneath his gaze and it seemed like too much work to force them to stay still. He was fairly sure they were something to do with topology, and that was enough for him. Topology was not one of his favourite branches of mathematics. Instead he went for a walk, feeling the reassuring touch of pure, warm, shag-pile scientific logic beneath his bare feet. There was little to look at except for the tiles, so he watched them pass beneath and by him as he strolled, enjoying the swirling patterns of notation on their surfaces, enjoying the regularity, and the . . .

Something stabbed his foot. He hopped sideways, swearing with surprise. One of the tiles was not flush with the others, and had gashed his foot. The tiles didn't feel warm and woolly any more, but cold and hostile. His blood was scattered in scarlet drops across the offending tile, shining like rubies. As he watched, the notation joined with his blood and made new shapes. Belatedly, he realised that the writing was not entirely topographical. It was too late now, though. All around him tiles were rising to reveal they were in fact the top faces of cubes. All but the one that had cut him; that one grew and expanded and he could see extra dimensionality within it, a tesseract. He tried to name its four dimensions, he felt he had to, but they came out wrong. This cube had the dimensions of height, length, width, and significance. It grew and grew until he was in its skeletal shadow, the white sky warped in its core.

Cabal awoke suddenly from a light slumber, sweating, angry, and with a phantom pain in his foot. He was angry at himself for looking and not seeing, angry at his unconscious mind's infuriating habit of telling him things in the most obscure way possible, and angry at circumstances for putting him in this wretched situation. He could investigate the potential clue he had just perceived, but he knew he shouldn't.

He managed to resist his curiosity for the best part of four minutes.

It was now over two hours since the discovery of DeGarre's disappearance and likely death. The corridors were quiet again, and the muttered conferences from his fellow passengers speculating about the night's events had long since died away. Cabal wrapped the dressing gown round himself again and, his phantasmically injured foot still fresh in his memory, put on Meissner's slippers.

He looked up and down the corridor, but it was silent and empty. Satisfied that he was alone for the moment, he turned his attention downwards, and started walking towards DeGarre's cabin.

The dark red carpet marked with a black pattern was not

made up of a single roll at all. Instead, the ingenious Mirkarvians has used individual squares of carpet. The practicality of being able to easily replace damaged or stained sections without the necessity of re-carpeting great lengths of corridor was not lost on him. Nor, now, was the significance of his dream. *Tesseract* sounds a great deal like *tessellate*, at least to an overactive unconscious mind. There are seventeen groups of tessellation with translational symmetry in two dimensions; the pattern woven into the identical carpet squares used group *pmg*, which only reflects in one direction. Therefore, if a tile is placed incorrectly, it breaks the pattern. The pattern was a complex one, wrought in one dark colour upon another, if one regards black as a colour. In the normal run of things, it could have been months before an error was noticed, if ever.

Between Cabal's eye for order and the analytical qualities of his unusual mind, it had been discovered within a few hours. A few hours, because Cabal was positive the carpeting had been perfect before. Yet now – he stopped and knelt just round the corner from DeGarre's cabin – one square had been lifted and replaced incorrectly. Why was that? The pattern was evidently disrupted if only one took a few moments to examine it properly. The obvious conclusion was that it had been replaced in a hurry, and there had been no time to check.

The square was well tamped down, and Cabal was frustrated to find that he couldn't lift it. A brief trip back to his cabin and he returned with his switchblade. It was the work of seconds to insert the tip of the knife beneath the square's edge and lift it out.

Beneath was a bed of underlay. Unlike the carpet, this seemed to be continuous. Yet he could make out a neat cut running through it close to the edge of the exposed area. Cabal lifted more carpet squares and revealed a square section of underlay, perhaps seventy centimetres along an edge, had been cut. It didn't look to be a hurried job and, when he lifted the loose square of underlay, Cabal saw that it had probably been done when the flooring had originally been laid. A maintenance hatch lay in the area he had cleared, a ring in its surface ingeniously flush with only a small space to insert a fingertip and flip the ring up so the hatch could be lifted. Without a second thought, Cabal did so.

He disliked extemporised activities, not least because going without preparation usually meant being unprepared. As he lowered himself into the darkness of the ducting that lay beneath the open hatch, he reflected that there were better ways to explore a mysterious dark place than without a torch and naked but for a Chinese dressing gown and a pair of slippers. Giving himself the assurance that he would not go far, he shuffled along on all fours.

The duct almost immediately reached a T-junction. He gauged that turning left would take him beneath the corridor on which DeGarre's cabin lay, so that was the way he went. The light filtering down through the open hatch behind him dimmed sharply as he took the corner, and he crawled forward the next two or three metres in deep gloom. Thus, he felt something unusual in the duct rather than seeing it. The slightly flexible sheet metal became suddenly rigid and, feeling around, he realised that he had discovered yet another hatch, locked shut at its four corners by rotating catches connected to small handles. He gripped one of the handles, gave it an experimental turn, and felt a catch disengage. He did the same to one of its neighbours, and felt that side of the hatch drop slightly until it came to rest on something. He guessed the hatch would have a lip running round its edge to prevent the hatch simply falling through once all four catches were opened, because unless he was much mistaken he had a good idea what was on the other side of it, and dropping the hatch would be inconvenient at the very least.

He released the last catch, lifted the far edge of the hatch, and pushed it away from him so it was lying on the duct floor on the far side of the opening. Then he crawled back a little and gingerly pushed the near edge of the hatch away from him to reveal what lay beneath.

It was Mirkarvia, some four thousand feet below him, and barely visible in the early-morning darkness. A cold wind blew up through the hatch and made him shiver, suddenly very aware of how ridiculously unprepared he was. Extemporisation! Pah! He spat, mentally, on the concept. Here he was, woefully underequipped to carry out any sort of detailed investigation, without light or notebook. And cold. Very, very cold. Still, he was here now, so he should make the most of it, although he had little idea what he hoped to find. The duct didn't run beneath DeGarre's cabin with a convenient hatch to give the hypothetical assassin an escape route. He felt around for anything suspicious, but there was nothing. The duct's main function seemed to be carrying assorted cables and pipes around the ship, with ventilation possibly a secondary task. There were a couple of sturdy metal handles mounted on either side of the opening, although they struck him as being more likely to be used as mounting for ladders during maintenance rather than rungs to hold when engineers climbed through here.

He reached down and felt around on the outer skin of the *Princess Hortense*, but found little to excite his attention. Well, it had seemed like an interesting avenue of enquiry when it had all been dreamscapes and hypercubes, but now that it had been reduced to freezing in a tin tunnel, Cabal decided it had lost some of its allure. He pulled his arm back inside and backed up a little to allow himself room to pull the hatch back into position. Except he couldn't back up a little;

something was in the way, and by the time he had realised that 'something' was actually 'somebody', it was much too late.

His knees squealing against the steel floor of the duct, he was shoved forward. He tried to scramble across to the other side of the open hatchway, but a hand came down in the small of his back and pushed him forcefully down. As he fumbled, looking for some way to pull himself clear, one knee dropped over the edge of the gap and Johannes Cabal fell out of the hatch.

Chapter 7

Johannes Cabal disliked many things, despised fewer, loathed fewer still, and reserved true hatred for only a handful. Understanding how intense his personal definition of 'dislike' was, however, this gives some impression of how hot ran his hatreds. This is a man who had, after all, shot men dead for making him faintly peeved.

Johannes Cabal hated people trying to kill him. He hated it, and he hated them. Certainly, most people aren't keen on it, but few have actually experienced it, and fewer still on the regular basis with which Cabal was familiar. Already, within this single narrative, we have seen how the Mirkarvian judicial system had salted him away for execution and then, more personally, how the Count Marechal had intended to skewer him upon a cavalry sabre. By degrees Cabal had grown more inured to the actual event of an attempt upon his life, but he never could gird himself effectively against the intent. It wasn't so much that he found it hurtful, as ignorant. To kill him would be either be the work of a Luddite, fearful of his necromantic studies, or a vandal who tried to destroy him

119

simply because that's what vandals do. Thus, for Johannes Cabal, was the world arranged: Luddites, vandals, and a vast chorus of the undecided.

His first thought, as his legs preceded him towards a likely doom, was that at least this settled the question of DeGarre's death. Unless there was some sort of recluse who lived in the ducting and took very unkindly to strangers, then the person who had just thrown him out was DeGarre's killer. Not suicide, then. Good. The numerous anomalies would have bothered him forever if it had been suicide. 'Forever', though, currently seemed to equate to the time it would take him to hit the ground.

Fortunately for him, the animal part of his brain that so irritated him with such base desires as eating and sleeping had different priorities. To expedite these, the uppermost of which was 'Don't die,' it had dumped a large quantity of adrenalin into Cabal's bloodstream, and had – after locating one of the rungs by the hatch edge during a panicked fumble – affixed his right hand with a grip of stone to it. Thus, Cabal did not tumble to a lonely death on an unseen mountainside. At least, not immediately.

Instead he hung by one hand like an apple from the bough, and wondered, with a degree of objectivity that surprised him even at the time, whether panicking might help. Despite received wisdom in such events being 'don't look down', he looked down, and regretted it terribly. Not because of the great height – he could barely see anything in the darkness and might have been a few metres above a mound of mattresses for all he knew – but because his dressing gown had come undone and he had neglected to put on anything beneath it, such had been the alacrity with which he had left his cabin. No, this view was not especially what he wanted for his last memory.

A slipper fell from one foot and whirled into the void and

out of sight. That settled it. The thought of his corpse being found largely naked but for one slipper (should it stay on during the fall) and a dressing gown that was a definite crime against aesthetics spurred him into action. He looked up and started to swing his free hand to grab on to the handle. As he almost reached the edge of the hatch, a gloved hand reached down and slapped his away. *Oh yes,* thought Cabal. *Somebody's trying to kill me. I'd almost forgotten.* His assailant, hidden in the shadows of the conduit, gripped the little finger of Cabal's right hand and started to very deliberately bend it back.

This was really too much. There was nothing for it; his attacker had to die.

Currently, however, Cabal was at a great disadvantage: in fact several. Yet even as his shadowy attacker worked on loosening Cabal's grip on the rung in particular and life in general, Cabal was quickly cataloguing his situation and assets. He had one hand free, he had one slipper, he had one dressing gown, and – he remembered with a pleasurable frisson – he had a switchblade knife in on of the dressing-gown pockets. Yes, between the free hand and the switchblade, he felt sure he would be able to formulate a robust response.

Preparation is everything. Cabal was very aware that to lose the knife was to lose his life, so he was careful to grip the knife firmly when he finally got his left hand into his right-hand pocket, the dressing gown having grown frolicsome in the aeroship's slipstream. He found the release, and the blade snicked out between the gap he had left between his fingertips and thumb. Closing his fingers and thumb to re-establish a good grip, he concluded the preparatory step of his plan. It had taken perhaps three seconds.

What the plan itself lacked in subtlety, it more than made up for in brutality. As his attacker, who seemed to be wearing coarse leather gloves, finally got a good grip on Cabal's little finger, Cabal reached up and stabbed, aiming at the attacker's wrist. Anatomically, you can really spoil somebody's day with even a shallow cut there, and Cabal was very much in the mood to cause as much misery as possible. There was a cry, and Cabal's finger was released.

He knew he had a moment's grace. If the attacker was only scratched, the attack would resume with a great deal more violence in a moment. Looking to his reserves, Cabal put the knife in his mouth and grabbed the other side of the hatch with his free hand. In his teens, he would have been able to pull himself up with little difficulty, but he was now in his late twenties and exercised but little. He steeled himself and pulled. He didn't care how many muscles he tore and how much agony he put himself through. Falling was not an option. Dying was not an option. There was too much to be done.

No muscles tore, but he knew they would be complaining bitterly in a few hours as he clambered gracelessly into the secure darkness of the conduit. His attacker was nowhere to be seen. He waited in silence for almost three minutes before he was convinced he was alone. Then he allowed himself the luxury of flopping forward, exhausted and half frozen, to lie on his front. Under his breath he mumbled, 'Too much to be done. Too much to be done. Too much to be done . . .'

Leonie Barrow found Cabal at breakfast. The long dining table of the evening before had been broken into individual tables and bolted down in their customary positions. Each also had the addition of a four-headed lamp; four iron swans' necks that rose from a central mounting curved down and then up to conclude with the swans' heads, beaks agape with light bulbs stuck in their gullets. It was a typical

Mirkarvian conceit; exquisite engineering merged with a barbaric aesthetic. She noticed that Cabal was sitting, probably deliberately, at one of the few tables that had no lamp. The rest of the room was almost empty, but for Herr Harlmann who it seemed had struck up a relationship with Lady Ninuka's companion, Miss Ambersleigh. He was presumably boring her with business anecdotes, though she was maintaining an air of interest that might even have been real. Whatever they were talking about, it was in a low tone that would have seemed conspiratorial but for the change in atmosphere brought on by the events of the previous night. The disappearance and presumed suicide of M. DeGarre had cast a pall on the ship, and the jollity of the previous evening had entirely evaporated. Even the crew seemed subdued beyond professional impassiveness.

Leonie ordered poached eggs and toast from a steward, who seemed perplexed that anybody would want such a combination for a meal when they weren't ill, and sat uninvited at Cabal's table. He paused for a moment in cutting his steak – a far more Mirkarvian choice for breakfast – to eye her suspiciously. 'Good morning, Miss Barrow,' he said in a perfunctory tone, immediately forking a neat square of meat into his mouth to forestall any more speech.

'Good morning, Herr Meissner,' she replied. She had momentarily considered teasing him with almost using his real name, but she was not in the mood and she was positive that he wasn't either. He looked tired and somewhat distracted. 'Any further thoughts about last night?' she asked when there was nobody near.

Cabal slowed his chewing for a moment. Then he took a sip of black coffee, swallowed, and said, as if it were a common subject for conversation, 'Last night, somebody tried to kill me.'

The steward's arrival with her food and a pot of tea

covered her surprise. When they could speak again, she whispered, 'Tried to kill you? Who did?'

Cabal regarded her with mild amusement. 'Smile when you whisper,' he advised her. 'You're supposed to be flirting with me, if you recall?'

She stared at him icily. The suddenly her expression thawed and she smiled winsomely, her eyes dewy with romantic love. 'Oh, sweetheart . . . somebody tried to kill you? Whosoever would do such a thing to my nimpty-bimpty snookums?'

Cabal could not have been more horrified if she'd pulled off her face to reveal a gaping chasm of eternal night from which glistening tentacles coiled and groped. That had already happened to him once in his life, and he wasn't keen to repeat the experience.

'What?' he managed in a dry whisper.

'Smile when you whisper,' she said, her expression fixed and bloodcurdlingly coquettish. 'You're supposed to be flirting with me, remember?'

'Please don't do that.' He wasn't sure if he wouldn't prefer to be dangling from the underside of the *Princess Hortense* again rather than endure another second of Miss Barrow's unnerving countenance. He certainly found it a great relief when she allowed the expression to slip and be replaced by one of wry amusement.

'So, I've discovered what it takes to frighten a man who deals with devils.'

'Not frightened, Fräulein. More . . . discomforted.' He took a moment to compose himself. 'Now, are you really all that blasé about somebody trying to kill me?'

She looked at him seriously. 'Of course not. Tell me what happened.' She ate her breakfast as Cabal concisely related the events of the night before. When he had finished, and was taking the opportunity to dispatch the remainder of his steak, Leonie drank her tea and considered.

'There are two possibilities, I suppose. The misarranged carpet really does have something to do with DeGarre's death. Or . . .' She studied him carefully before proceeding. 'Or, an enemy of yours has followed you on to the ship or has recognised you.'

Cabal stopped sawing up his last bit of meat. 'You're not serious?'

'You must have dozens of enemies . . .' She almost said his name, but controlled herself in time. 'Herr Meissner. Importantly, you probably don't even know a few of them on sight.'

'Explain.'

'You leave a trail of destruction through people's lives.' Cabal started to argue, but she talked through him. 'Even if the ones you affect directly either will not or cannot come after you, that still leaves family and friends. You provoke hatred and revenge. You know it.'

Cabal hadn't really thought about it in those terms, but he could see the truth in her words. He never went out of his way to damage people's lives – not except in some very deliberate cases, anyway – but people would insist in getting in the way. Now he considered it more carefully, he began to appreciate just why quite so many bullets, knives, and the occasional crossbow quarrel had whistled past his frantically dodging head down the years.

'Rufus Maleficarus,' he said in quiet contemplation.

'What about him?' Leonie had heard the name before: a notorious warlock who had to her knowledge crossed swords with Cabal on at least one occasion. 'I thought he was dead?'

'He is. I killed him thoroughly. That was the second time that I met him, though. The first time, it wasn't just happenstance. He blamed me for what happened to his father.'

'Was he justified in that?'

'Yes. Yes, he was. But, really, his father was a monster. I had no choice.'

'With your history, I don't think you're in any position to call anybody else a monster,' she said sharply.

Cabal's expression was unreadable. 'No, I am being entirely literal, in the non-metaphorical, purest dictionary sense of the word. His father was a *monster*. He was trying to kill me, just as he'd killed others. It was self-defence. Surely that's a reasonable justification even in your morally polarised world, Miss Barrow?'

The brief spark of warmth they had struck in the earlier part of their conversation was entirely dead now. The air between them was cold enough to condense dew.

'No,' he said finally. 'It has to be something to do with DeGarre's death.' Leonie noticed he'd dropped the *disappearance and probable death* formula. 'If it were somebody that I had . . . upset in the past for whatever reason, why would they go to all the trouble of sneaking after me, gloves at the ready, on the small chance that I would find a hatch in the ship's underside, open it, and then obligingly hang halfway out of it?'

'Why weren't they armed, you mean?'

'Not even that. You yourself, Miss Barrow, have already threatened me with exactly the same weapon that anybody with the slightest whiff of intelligence would use.' He looked around to confirm there were no prying eyes or ears before leaning forward and whispering, 'You know who I am.'

Leonie Barrow hated to admit it, but Cabal's point was solid. Unless he was being stalked by somebody who was absolutely determined to kill Cabal with his or her own hands, then the safest and surest way of seeing him die was simply to use the Mirkarvian state as the instrument of death. They would simply denounce him to the captain, and that would be that. The alternative – that this putative revenger wanted to kill Cabal him or herself – would presuppose that somebody who was organised enough to locate and then shadow Cabal on to the *Princess Hortense* would then absent-mindedly forget to pack a pistol, knife, garrotte, or other weapon with which to actually do the deed.

The form 'him or her' made her think of Cabal's story of his narrow escape. 'In the conduit, this person who tried to kill you, was it definitely a man?'

Cabal waited a moment while a steward came over and cleared away their plates. He poured himself another coffee. 'I've wondered about that myself. I couldn't see, and the thick leather gloves meant I don't even know what kind of fingers my attacker had. When they cried out, it was high, but I've heard men in great pain sound quite literally like a child, so that proves little.'

'I'm not even going to ask how you have heard such sounds, Herr Meissner.'

'No? You know so little of the world. You should get out more, Miss Barrow.'

Leonie made an offhand gesture that took in the aeroship. 'I would say this is fairly "out". Your definition probably involves more time spent in graveyards.'

Cabal reined in his habitual desire to argue. He had an unpleasant mental image of things getting so heated that Miss Barrow would end up standing on the table, pointing at him, and screaming 'Necromancer!' repeatedly. Instead, he raised his hand slightly in a conciliatory gesture. '*Pace*, Miss Barrow. This is not an ideal venue to air your views on my profession.' In the silence that followed, he realised that he had little left to talk about, so to give himself thinking time, he said, 'I wonder why this table doesn't have a lamp?'

The change of tack caught Leonie by surprise. 'A lamp? I thought you'd sat here to avoid having to look at one of the horrible things. It's the only table without one.'

'No. There's one over there without one as well.' He gestured carelessly over his shoulder without looking, and she saw he was indeed right; another table on the far side of the room was also lampless. 'I sat here because it was less cluttered. I wonder . . .' He lifted the plate in the middle of the table on which lay the butter dish and some small pots of preserve. Beneath it was a small neat hole in the tablecloth, its edge hemmed to avoid fraying. 'It's meant to have a lamp. That's where it would be screwed into place and the electrical cable connected.'

Leonie watched his investigation with an impatient frown. 'So? What do the table lamps have to do with anything?'

'Not the table lamps themselves. It's the absence of two table lamps. Probably not relevant.' He said this with an air of deep distraction.

Leonie Barrow knew enough about real criminal invest- igations to know full well that cases rarely if ever hinged upon an encyclopaedic knowledge of tobacco ash or the curious incident of the butler's allergy to spinach. Cabal's musings seemed self-indulgent and immaterial, and she belatedly realised that he wasn't truly talking to her at all. She was merely a sounding board for him to reflect his own ideas back to him in a slightly different light. Her irritation showed in her voice. 'To bring your attention back to the matter in hand, are you going to report the attack on you last night?'

Cabal blinked slightly, startled out of his reverie. 'I haven't made up my mind about that yet. I shouldn't draw attention to myself.'

'I think the time for that is passed. Let's just say that the captain's own enquiries turn up whoever attacked you and, under interrogation, they mention they'd try to throw you out of the ship in your dressing gown and slippers? The captain comes to you and asks the obvious question. "Why didn't you tell me that somebody tried to kill you, Herr

Meissner?"" What would you say? You didn't want any fuss?'

Cabal looked sourly at her, but he couldn't refute her argument. His first instinct was always to keep his business to himself, not least because his business frequently carried a death sentence. 'That *would* be an awkward interview, wouldn't it?' He got to his feet.

'You'll find him in his office,' said Leonie, studying the dregs in her cup.

Cabal paused in the act of straightening his jacket. 'And how would you know that, Miss Barrow?'

'I had . . . a letter to drop off with him, to put in his safe.'

'A letter?'

'Yes.' She looked up at him. 'It's for insurance purposes. I'm sure you understand.' By his narrowing eyes, it appeared that he did. Quickly changing the subject, she asked, 'What will you tell the captain?'

Cabal finished straightening his jacket in a stony silence Finally, he said, 'The truth Mostly.'

Captain Schten listened with the expression of a man who goes into a striptease parlour and finds himself attending a lecture on quantum mechanics, expectation giving way to bafflement. He had particular problems with 'Herr Meissner's' motives for wishing to take up a section of the corridor's carpeting.

'You excavated beneath the carpet because you had a dream that told you to?'

'No. The dream was just my subconscious mind's way of drawing attention to something I'd seen but had not perceived the significance of.'

'A square of carpet?'

'A misaligned square of carpet. Yes. Which had not been so misaligned earlier in the evening when I walked by.'

The captain pursued his point with the determination of a

man after the last pea on the plate. 'So you *had* noticed it was not misaligned earlier?'

'Yes, but not consciously. Captain, I have a problematical relationship with the inner workings of my mind. Why, I could tell you . . .' He almost said he could tell of times when such submerged ideations had saved his life while dealing with supernatural entities that had come from whichever blighted netherworld they called home with the express intention of swallowing his soul, eating his brains, and using his giblets for gravy. Then he decided not to, in much the same way he might decide not to say, 'Incidentally, Captain, I'm a necromancer. It would be best to shoot me now.'

Instead he said, 'I could tell you of the silliest things that lead to useful concepts, like displacement . . . vulcanisation . . .' He tried to think of a third thing, and failed. 'Jam. But this is all digression. The important point is that I knew the carpet had been interfered with, and I investigated.'

'And somebody tried to throw you out. Yes, I understood that part. You took a terrible risk, Herr Meissner.'

'How was I to know somebody was going to kill me?' protested Cabal. 'It was hardly the most obvious course of events.'

'I'm not talking about some phantom assailant, sir. I am talking about how ill-advised it is to go wandering around the bowels of a great machine of which you know nothing. You could have been incinerated, or electrocuted, or crushed. Worse yet, you might have interfered with the operation of this vessel and brought it crashing down! Did you ever pause to consider that?'

Cabal had not, and inwardly rebuked himself. He wasn't about to let the reference to a 'phantom assailant' go unchallenged though.

'Such catastrophic scenarios aside, Captain, I repeat: somebody tried to kill me. I did not imagine that.'

'So you said, and they just vanished. Hardly the actions of a determined attacker.'

'Only after I stabbed them!' There was sudden silence. Cabal searched the captain's face. 'I *did* mention that I'd stabbed them, didn't I?'

'You did not.' The captain looked suspiciously at Cabal. 'How came you to be wandering the corridors in the early hours in your nightwear and carrying a knife, sir?'

'I needed something to lift the corner of the carpet square. I had a pocket knife in my luggage, and went back for it. I do not habitually go to bed armed, if that is what you are implying.'

The captain didn't seem mollified by this explanation, but let it pass. 'So this individual is injured, yes?'

'In the wrist. It was all I could reach.'

The captain seemed satisfied for the first time. He was a practical man and – while talk of hallucinatory tesseracts and shadowy assassins might irk him – a wound was altogether more concrete an entity. 'Finally! Some real evidence. Very well, Herr Meissner. I shall start questioning every single person aboard ship, both passengers and crew, with the specific aim of finding a wounded wrist. Then, we shall see.'

Cabal was caught between conflicting emotions. On the one hand he was pleased that his attacker would soon be identified. On the other, he was being drawn in too close to official scrutiny for comfort. He would have to arrange jumping ship in Senza to a nicety when the time came. Previously he had only had to worry about the tenacious Miss Barrow handing him over to the Senzan authorities. An awkward bit of evasion would have been necessary, but nothing he felt he couldn't handle. Now he had Schten to worry about too. This was getting complicated, and complications could get him killed.

*

In a curious way, it was perhaps fortunate that there had been a probable murder and an attempted murder aboard (Cabal's nocturnal adventure soon became common currency), or else the trip would have been stunningly dull. Low cloud choked the valleys below and the *Princess* had climbed to avoid any mountain peaks. As a result, there was very little to see from the salon windows, and the passengers were thrown back on reading and conversation to pass the time. It was easy to imagine that under normal circumstances and in the absence of current newspapers, the ship's small library would be heavily patronised. Instead, however, the salon was party to little groups of two or three people sitting together and muttering to one another in conspiratorial tones, that died into watchful silence whenever anybody new entered.

Well, not quite anybody. Cabal himself was a topic of conversation already, based on what little was known about the night before, so when he came in, he was fastened upon to add meat to the thin stew of rumour. The Roborovskis were first out of the slips; specifically Frau Roborovski with her reluctant husband pulled along in her wake.

'Herr Meissner! You must tell us everything!' she demanded as soon as they'd finished the dance of courteous rising to one's feet and offering a seat. She then sat in silence, gazing owlishly at him with an air of attentive anticipation, like somebody who once came across the word 'excitement' while reading a dictionary, and is interested to know what it looks like in the wild.

Cabal wasn't inclined to for a variety of reasons, the least of which was he felt sure Captain Schten would not appreciate the detail of his attacker's incriminating wound becoming public knowledge. Instead, he limited himself to saying that he had noticed something amiss with the carpet, had investigated, discovered the conduit, opened the ventral hatch, and then somebody had thrown him out. It bored him to have to retell it, but it was almost worth the effort simply for the way Frau Roborovski went pale and seemed likely to faint when he got to the murder attempt itself.

'Dangling by one hand!' she managed when her attack of the vapours had attenuated slightly.

'Yes,' replied Cabal. And then, for sheer devilment, added, 'Largely naked.' He had been hoping for her to faint outright, or rush off in horror, or do almost anything rather than what she did do, which was to widen her eyes a little further still and look at him in such a way that he suddenly realised she was imagining it in far too much detail to be seemly.

'Fortunately,' he said quickly and a little too loudly, 'I was able to climb back aboard.'

'If you were just hanging there . . .' began Herr Roborovski, but the thought mired him down and he said nothing more.

'Yes?' asked Cabal.

'If you were just hanging there,' continued Herr Roborovski with renewed inertia, 'why didn't this blackguard who attacked you finish the job? You couldn't really defend yourself, could you?'

'He must have though I had fallen immediately, and was already scurrying away like a rat,' said Cabal, steering round the fact that he had, indeed, defended himself.

Herr Roborovski considered this for a moment. 'That was lucky,' he said finally, but Cabal thought he heard a note of suspicion in his voice.

Cabal inwardly admitted that it certainly sounded that way. Some economy in veracity seemed called for. 'Not lucky at all. Only a coward would have attacked me like that in the first place. It seems hardly surprising that he would want to be away from the scene of the crime as quickly as possible.'

'Herr Meissner has a point.' It was Colonel Konstantin, who had been listening from the next table. 'It was a craven assault. Any man worthy of the name would have struck from the front. Pushing people out of hatches . . . It's un-Mirkarvian.'

From Cabal's admittedly limited contact with the modern face of Mirkarvia, a sneak attack seemed entirely in character. Then again, he had only been dealing with the ophidian Count Marechal, a bargain-basement Machiavelli if ever there was. Konstantin, for example, struck him as an officer and a gentleman of the old school. He wondered how a man like that would fit into Marechal's vision of a new, resurgent Mirkarvia that embraced deceit and devious doings to achieve its ends.

'You have high standards, Colonel,' said Frau Roborovski. 'Not everybody else has them. No. Some of the things I read of in the newspaper. Shocking! Shocking!'

'A criminal is a criminal,' agreed her husband with a very Gallic shrug. 'If they had any honour they wouldn't be criminals, after all.'

Cabal assumed they took the *Daily Obvious*, and perhaps the *Sunday Truism* of a weekend.

'Do you think your experience has anything to do with DeGarre's death?' Konstantin asked Cabal.

Cabal decided to be noncommittal in the face of no definite evidence. 'M. DeGarre is only missing, Colonel.'

'Oh, for heaven's sake, man,' replied Konstantin dismissively. 'You think he's lurking in the hold with the potatoes? Of course he's dead. Somebody did him in, came up with a half-arsed attempt at a suicide note, and threw him out of the window.' He ruminated for a moment. 'Not necessarily *exactly* in that order, but I'm certain that's the gist of it.'

'And then escaped from a locked and barricaded room?'

'Well, I'm not pretending to know all the facts, Herr Meissner. I have to admit I have no idea how that was done, but I must also admit that it does not concern or worry me. Y'see, in my experience, the cleverer somebody tries to be, the more likely they are to come a cropper.' Cabal worked hard to maintain his composure, but the colonel had already moved on. 'How a killer escapes from a locked room, that's for a detective to work out. It's a little wrinkle that I'm sure will become clear after the captain's investigation is complete.'

Cabal wished that he could share the colonel's sang-froid about the affair, but he could not, not after having been unceremoniously dumped out of the aeroship's belly. His hackles were raised, and he wanted – he didn't even pause inwardly to find some euphemistic way to call it 'justice' – revenge. Nice, hot, juicy revenge. He and Count Marechal might have been miles apart in most aspects of their personalities, but this thing at least they had in common.

Furthermore, after his own interview with the captain earlier, he had received the distinct impression that Schten remained convinced, whatever his protestations about keeping an open mind, that DeGarre had committed suicide. The attack on Herr Meissner was something else again, and he seemed intent on turning all his enquiries in that direction. Cabal, in contrast, was convinced that DeGarre had been murdered, and that the killer had escaped from the room by some means that involved the underfloor ducting. The curious case of the defenestrated DeGarre and the adventure of the ersatz civil servant were inextricably linked and it seemed that, if he didn't get to the bottom of them, the likelihood was that they would remain unsolved. Therefore he would prosecute his own investigation, and so justice would be served, albeit in passing. The important thing was that Cabal would have discovered the perpetrator, and so be ahead of the field when it came to killing them.

In all fairness, Cabal's vengefulness was a product of his

lifestyle as much as his humours; in his career to date he had long since discovered that rivals and enemies rarely simply shook their heads and wandered out of his life, older and wiser. Instead, they were inclined to go off to a dark corner and fester away on new plots and schemes that would explode all over his life like acidic pus. Johannes Cabal had much better things to do with his time than spend it dodging acidic pus, so he had realised early on that the best way to avoid assorted blowhards and rapscallions bursting through the door declaiming 'We meet again, Mr Cabal!' or some similar nonsense, was simply to kill them the first time around while they were handy and vulnerable. It wasn't a perfect solution, he had to admit, his rivals and enemies tended to have access to the same sorts of forbidden arcane arts and unwholesome sciences that he did, so having them sometimes come crawling out of their graves, intent on inflicting a messy post-mortem revenge, was not unknown.

Still, as a working practice, it had a great deal to recommend it. Even the trail of murder it left was of little import since – first – most of his victims were already under sentence of death for crimes against God, Nature, and Humanity, and – second – Cabal himself was already under sentence of death for crimes against God, Nature, and Humanity, so another few corpses on the tally sheet was hardly going to concern him unduly. They could only hang him once.

He did not however even hint that he meant to carry on his own investigation. Somewhere on this vessel was somebody who wished him harm, and he had no intention of handing out any bulletins as to his plans that might reach unfriendly ears. He would move slowly and methodically, drawing together the facts until he had his attacker's identity in his hand, and when he did . . .

Cabal was just considering the best way he would isolate

and kill his prey when Leonie Barrow spoiled it all by approaching the little group at a fast walk and saying to him, but loud enough for everyone to hear, 'Herr Meissner! They've caught the man who tried to kill you!'

Chapter 8

It is a nuisance to be pre-empted. All Cabal's playful little plans to shove his hog-tied assailant out of the *Princess Hortense*'s ventral hatch to see how *he* liked it had now come to nothing, and all because the captain had done exactly what he had said he would, and carried out a thorough investigation. He had fastened upon the single most solid and therefore useful fact from the testament of 'Herr Meissner', and pursued it through every deck of the ship. Now, in a spare cabin in the second-class section that had been pressed into service as an impromptu brig and interrogation room, Schten and – after some bull-headed arguing on the basis that he was the only government official aboard and therefore a necessary witness, allied with some creative quotations from imaginary governmental directives – Johannes Cabal sat opposite the freshly arrested attempted murder suspect.

Gabriel Zoruk did not look pleased to be there. He was tousled and unshaven, his shirt was without tie or cravat, and his jacket was creased. He actually looked more like a revolutionary now than when he had been spouting ill-considered politicisms the previous evening yet now, contrariwise, he was silent. He simply sat with his hands in his lap and glowered at Schten and, occasionally, at Cabal who was sitting off to Schten's right and a little behind him.

For Schten's part, he sat reading some notes from a sheet of foolscap on a clipboard in silence and pointedly ignored Zoruk's glare. Unusually for the captain, his jacket was open, but this may have been to draw attention to the holster and revolver he wore, dark tan leather and acid-blacked steel against the white shirt and trousers. Zoruk could not have failed to notice it when Schten had sat down.

When he judged that Zoruk had stewed enough, the captain deigned to look up from his notes. 'Your hands, Herr Zoruk. Would you show me your hands, please?'

Zoruk kept his hands in his lap and replied quietly, 'Am I under arrest?'

'Yes,' replied Schten without hesitation. 'You are under arrest.'

'I haven't been read my rights.'

'I am not obliged to read you your rights, Herr Zoruk. I am not a policeman. You are being held under the provisions of the Aeolatime Act pertaining to the safety of aerial vessels, crew, passengers, and cargo. You can have a copy to read later if you doubt it. Now . . . Your hands, sir.'

Zoruk's gaze flickered from Schten to Cabal and quickly back again. 'Why?'

Schten made a deep rumbling sound. To forestall the captain's rising temper, Cabal said, 'To be blunt, Herr Zoruk, you are suspected of attempting to murder me. I succeeded in wounding my attacker in the hand or the wrist. Therefore, if you have such an injury, we would be very interested in hearing how you came by it. It is a simple thing. If you are uninjured, you may go. If you are injured and can provide a reasonable explanation, ideally with some corroboration, you will in all likelihood also be allowed to go. Truly, sir, if you are an innocent man, you have nothing to lose by helping the captain in his enquiries.'

Schten allowed Cabal's words to sink in before repeating, 'So . . . would you show me your hands, please?'

Zoruk was plainly nervous, and it took him a full five tortuous seconds before he finally placed both hands, fisted, on the tabletop. Cabal saw a bandage across the back of his right hand, about where the switchblade would have struck. Zoruk started talking the instant his hands hit the wooden surface.

'I can explain. I know what it looks like, but I can explain.'

Schten raised his own hand to signal silence, his gaze on the bandage. 'Explanations come later, Herr Zoruk. First, I should be obliged if you would remove that dressing.'

With obvious reluctance, Zoruk undid the gauze that held the bandage in place. When he had finished he carefully peeled it off, wincing as the wound beneath was exposed. Cabal leaned forward in his seat to get a better look, and sat back in disappointment. He had been hoping that the injury would clearly be a knife wound, but this was a shallow if bloody affair. It could easily be the result of a blade wielded with desperation rather than technique causing an ugly scoring instead of a clean cut. He couldn't be sure if his knife had or had not been the cause. It was very frustrating.

'Does that look like a knife wound to you, Herr Meissner?' asked the captain.

Cabal regretfully shook his head. 'It may be. I just struck upwards; I don't even know if the blade cut on its sharp edge or was dragged. It's not conclusive.'

Schten humphed. He had clearly been hoping for the examination to close the case immediately. He signalled to Zoruk to cover the wound again. 'So, mein Herr,' he said as

Zoruk started wrapping the gauze back round his hand, 'we are listening. How came you by that wound?'

'It was an accident, just a stupid accident. And I have a witness! I was in the corridor this morning and one of the stewards was just ahead of me. He reached the double doors leading into the dining room first and held it open for me. As I was reaching for the handle so he could move on, he lost his grip or thought I was already holding the door or something. In any event, the door closed on my hand. They're pretty heavy you know. Powerful springs on them. It made quite a mess of my hand. The steward was full of apologies and got me off to the doctor's . . . what do you call it? The clinic? The sickbay, that's it. It was cleaned up and bandaged and that was that. Well, I thought that was that, but now everybody's very interested in it.'

The captain had made a few notes and nodded. 'Very well, Herr Zoruk. I shall make some enquiries. In the meantime, you will have to remain in custody.' Zoruk started to protest, but Schten talked over him. 'Please remember, you are suspected of a serious crime. I would be failing in my duty if I did not complete my investigation before acting on its findings. If the steward and the ship's medic confirm your story, you will be released shortly. All I ask is a little patience.'

He rose and stood by the door, ushering Cabal out ahead of him. A burly engineer was keeping guard outside, and he locked the door once Zoruk was alone. Schten took the keys. 'Thank you, Kleine. You may return to your section.' The engineer saluted crisply and left them. Schten looked pensively at the locked door before walking slowly away, Cabal by his side.

'Do you believe him?' asked Cabal.

'It's irrelevant what I believe,' said Schten. 'Facts are all that matter.'

'You have a scientist's mind,' said Cabal approvingly. 'Yes, facts are paramount, clearly. But you must have an opinion? Even scientists use a degree of educated intuition to guide their research.'

'An opinion . . . I do not wish to prejudge, Herr Meissner. But, I will admit to some disbelief that you can injure a man in the hand in the early hours of the morning and, a few hours later, a suspect manages to injure himself in the same place in an innocent accident.'

'Your meaning being?'

'My meaning being, is it an innocent accident, or is it an apparently innocent accident?'

'My thoughts exactly. It is a long coincidence if the former, but an engineered alibi if the latter.'

Schten stopped at the head of the circular staircase that led down to the first-class deck. 'Just promise me that you made no mistake about injuring your attacker, mein Herr. I don't want to take a man's liberty because of a mistake made in the excitement of a struggle.'

Cabal drew his switchblade from his jacket pocket and snapped the blade out. Schten raised an eyebrow. 'Hardly a penknife, Herr Meissner. You carry that with you?'

'From last night, yes, Captain. I do. You can hardly blame me. Look, I haven't cleaned the blade since then. You can see blood has worked its way down to the pivot.'

Schten watched with evident disapproval as Cabal closed the knife and put it away. 'That knife is material evidence. It should be held in the ship's safe until official investigators have seen it.'

Cabal looked him in the eye and said, 'You may have it with my blessings the very moment that you supply me with a replacement of equal or greater lethality. A pistol would be nice.'

'Impossible.'

'Then I shall keep my knife.' The captain frowned, and

then shrugged. Cabal guessed it was unMirkarvian to disarm a law-abiding citizen. 'Now, Captain; who is next for questioning?'

The ship's sickbay was surprisingly large, a fact Cabal commented upon when they first entered. It was a long room with four beds out, but room for more. The rows of lockers at head height and the large glass-fronted pharmacy cabinet indicated that the bay was as well equipped as it was spacious. Dr Huber looked just as capable as his environment; despite only being in his mid-twenties and having a mop of wavy black hair whose exuberance no pomade could hope to quell. He blinked at them over ill-advised half-moon glasses, and seemed so friendly and competent that Cabal's usual dislike of doctors was hardly provoked at all.

Dr Huber smiled. 'You might be surprised at how quickly an infection can travel through a ship, mein Herr. Days from medical assistance, and people have to be isolated from the rest of the crew and passengers.'

'Can't they be confined to their cabins instead?'

'If the problem is mild, yes, but even something mild is debilitating, and the crew does not have individual cabins. Would you feel safe aboard a ship where some otherwise mild gastrointestinal illness had laid the crew low?'

Cabal had a momentary mental image of the crew fighting to use the heads while the bridge stood abandoned, the ship's wheel rolling gently this way and that as the *Princess Hortense* wandered whimsically into the nearest hillside. No, he had to admit. He would not feel safe.

'Besides which, 'continued Huber, 'serious illnesses and even, God forbid, serious accidents happen, despite our best efforts. The patients would require constant supervision. I cannot organise that if they are in their cabins.' He appeared not to have noticed his captain wince when he spoke of accidents. Some maritime superstitions had clearly made their way from the seas to the skies, and tempting fate was one of them. With hindsight, it also seemed likely this was why the doctor had not attended the meal that first evening; thirteen at table would be considered inauspicious. As things had turned out, twelve was not such a lucky number either. Cabal watched with quiet amusement from the corner of his eye as Schten surreptitiously looked around for some wood to touch.

'To business, Doctor,' said Schten, after tapping the edge of the doctor's desk with palpable relief. 'Earlier today, Gabriel Zoruk came to you with an injury.'

The doctor thought for a moment and nodded. 'The young man who came in this morning with an cut to his hand? Yes, a straightforward case. I just cleaned the wound and bandaged it. Asked him to come back tomorrow to make sure there were no signs of infection. What about him?'

Cabal recalled that there was some directive somewhere, probably a part of the Hippocratic Oath, about patient confidentiality. It seemed from Huber's blithe ignorance of such niceties that Hippocrates was regarded as some sort of dangerous liberal in Mirkarvia.

'In your considered opinion, Doctor, what do you think caused the injury?'

'He caught it in a door.' Huber looked at the other men's faces and frowned at their silence. Grudgingly he added, 'Well, he said he caught it in a door. I had no reason to think he was lying. What's this all about, Captain?'

'Was the cut consistent with being caught in a door, would you say?'

Huber bridled. 'I'm no criminologist, Captain. The forensic sciences are not my field. I would regard it as a courtesy if I were not forced to make a judgement in a discipline of which I have only a passing knowledge.'

Schten nodded unhappily. He had wanted a nice black and white piece of information, but he knew enough of life to realise that such things are a rarity. There was no point in trying to wring a certainty from the doctor; it seemed Zoruk would benefit from the assumption of innocence that even Mirkarvian justice used, providing the defendant wasn't a necromancer.

Muttering a thanks to Dr Huber, he and Cabal made to leave. As they reached the door, however, Huber spoke up, his tone grudging. 'I will say this much, gentlemen. When I was cleaning the wound, I remember thinking how remarkably sharp the door that cut him must have been.'

Muttering with dissatisfaction, Schten next sought out the other witness to Zoruk's accident. Cross-referencing the time against the location of the door (when a Swiss watchmaker wishes to say things are going precisely to schedule, he will say they are running like a Mirkarvian duty rota), he was able to locate the right man with ease.

Steward Dorffman had none of Dr Huber's tiresome caveats about objectivity and even-handedness.

'I was closing the door, and he sticks his hand right in it. I thought I hardly touched him, but next thing he's dancing around, saying I've broken his bones and there's loads of blood, and so on.' Dorffman then underlined his views on Gabriel Zoruk with a short and insulting impersonation that involved a downturned mouth that would not have looked out of place on a tragedian's mask, a wobbling lower lip, and holding up a dangling hand like a puppy with a sore paw. He kept this up for almost thirty seconds, despite his captain and Cabal staring stonily at him.

'So,' said Schten in an effort to stop Dorffman before he decided to base a comic monologue upon this show-stopping piece of mimicry, 'you felt that Herr Zoruk was exaggerating?'

'Yes, sir. I hate to speak badly of the passengers,' he said with the supercilious air of a man who very much enjoyed speaking badly of the passengers, 'but that door barely touched him. It was like this . . .' He tapped himself very lightly on the back of his right hand and instantly returned to his Zoruk impersonation, now with added whimpering.

Schten finally boiled over, leaving Cabal to lean against the corridor wall and examine his nails while Dorffman was left in no doubt about the necessary level of respect to show both passengers and senior crew.

Afterwards, as they descended to the first-class deck, the captain managed to choke down his anger far enough to ask Cabal what he thought of the two witness statements.

'Unhelpful,' said Cabal. 'The doctor doesn't wish to commit beyond a vague belief that Zoruk's explanation for his cut may possibly be a little unlikely. As for Steward Dorffman, I wouldn't trust him to tell me if it were day or night. He certainly thinks the accident with the door was a very petty one, and from our perspective we may infer that Zoruk may have engineered it to explain his damaged hand. As far as building a case against him goes, it is all circumstantial.'

'So this morning has been a waste of time.'

'No, not entirely. At the very least, we are left with the basis of a deductive argument of Zoruk's guilt.' Cabal looked at his own hand. 'I *know* that I injured my attacker's right hand. I have no idea how badly, but I certainly drew blood. Therefore, my attacker has a recent cut to his or – just possibly – her hand.'

'So we go back to checking everybody,' said Schten, and sighed.

'Both passengers and crew, as per your original orders. Absolutely everybody must be checked if the investigation is to have validity. No exceptions. We are lucky that this is a

146

relatively small pool of potential suspects, and that the pool is sealed. Nobody comes in and nobody goes out, except via the windows or maintenance ducts, and such people are unlikely to be guilty in any event.'

'True,' said Schten, letting the latter barb go unremarked. He clearly wasn't happy with the image of his ship dropping bodies like an oak drops leaves in October, but it was not an entirely unfair charge, especially coming from a near victim. 'The only survivable way on or off over this terrain is via entomopter.'

'Entomopter?' said Cabal. He would have soon as trusted his life to a cotton loom pushed off a cliff as flying in an entomopter. While himself a scientist and a great proponent of progress, there was something about the whirling wings of the flying machines that brought the word 'newfangled' un-bidden to his lips. The sheer complexity of the clutch assembly that controlled the two pairs of closely mounted wings as they beat in figures of eight so rapidly that they were barely visible was a sticking point for him. Anything *that* finicky and moving *that* quickly was simply asking for trouble.

'Yes.' Schten nodded upwards. 'There's an entomopter deck up top. I think the idea is that patrons can join and leave the journey en route, rather than having to go to an aeroport.' He shrugged. 'Extra weight for nothing, in my opinion. If they're mad enough to have their own machine, then they're mad enough to fly the whole way by themselves.'

'But not in comfort,' added Cabal. Schten grudgingly nodded, but Cabal was already thinking of something else. 'Are there any machines up there at the moment?'

'No. They tested the deck during the commissioning trials. The arrestor lines work well, and the deck is more than strong enough to stand a heavy landing. I've seen six machines parked and lashed down for heavy weather on that

147

deck, which was the benchmark for signing off that particular trial; an impressive sight. It's typical, though. They go to all that trouble to add a feature to the ship yet, once she's commissioned and taking paying passengers, not a single enquiry about using it. Not one! Utter waste of time, money, and effort.'

'Perhaps that will change. How prominently was it advertised?'

'Not very. It's all been very hurried, because of the food supply mission. Yes, between that and the civil trouble at departure, this hasn't been the most glorious of maiden voyages, has it, really?' He sighed heavily, and Cabal guessed he was thinking about DeGarre and the Zoruk problem. 'Not very glorious at all.'

Cabal felt tired and depressed all afternoon. He had eaten – sausage and some form of pickled vegetable, washed down with white wine served in another ludicrously capacious glass – by himself, glad that at least he didn't have to pretend to play at detectives with Miss Barrow. He had been slightly surprised that the captain's initial investigation leading to the arrest of Gabriel Zoruk had not been the detailed and thorough procedure he had at first believed. It had, in fact, consisted of little more than the captain telling his senior staff they were looking for somebody with an injured hand and one of his officers saying he'd seen somebody with a new bandage on their hand that very morning. So much for methodical police work.

In the face of the flimsy case against Zoruk, the captain had finally got round to following Cabal's suggestion and doing what he should have done in the first place. His officers were making the rounds of every cabin, every workstation, and every bunk and, in a flurry of unctuous apologies, checking every hand aboard. It was the logical and correct thing to do, which would make it all the more painful when it was all for nothing.

Even if they did demonstrate beyond any doubt that Zoruk was the only person on the *Princess Hortense* who carried the damning injury, it would founder in court because the prosecution's star witness, the redoubtable Herr Meissner, would be nowhere to be found. As soon as they arrived in Senza, he would be away like a particularly skittish and chemically enhanced rabbit, dumping the persona of the hapless Meissner in the nearest dustbin, and heading for freedom. All, of course, assuming that he managed to dodge the police reception that Miss Barrow would be quick to arrange at the aeroport.

He felt the heft of the switchblade in his pocket and considered the quickest and surest way to make sure that didn't happen.

But it was a hollow thought. He was just weighing options, and he knew it. Things would have to be a great deal more desperate before he would be obliged to kill her. There were certainly more elegant if less quick and less sure ways of dealing with Miss Barrow's moralistic intransigence. That he was having trouble thinking of any that were also practical was one source of his depression.

Abruptly, a new source presented himself. Without so much as a 'by your leave', Herr Cacon appeared in the dining room, looked around, ignored any number of empty tables, and sat down at Cabal's. Some imperious finger-snapping later, he had gained the attention of the waiter, made his order for lunch, and was settling down to the serious business of being boorish.

'So!' he began with ghoulish glee. 'What's all this about somebody tryin' to do you in, Meissner, me ol' mate?'

Cabal tried to think of an excuse to leave immediately, but apart from a convincing but undignified lie about having an urgent appointment in a water closet, nothing occurred to him. With heavy heart, he began to tell Cacon about the attack.

Only when he was almost finished did it strike him as mildly surprising that Cacon had only interrupted him twice, and on both occasions with intelligent questions. As he completed the story, Cacon's intent expression smoothly relaxed and once more he became the oafish poseur he had previously seemed to be.

Astaroth's tears, thought Cabal. *Why is nothing plain and simple in my life?*

An unsympathetic observer might have said that when one embarks on a career as a necromancer – consorting with demons, digging up the dead and bringing them back to life, or at least something resembling it – one can hardly complain when things become complicated. Even by those standards, however, it seemed a little unfair that the perfectly simple theft of a book had turned into a great tumbling chaos of politics, murder, deceit, and mystery.

He wouldn't have minded so much if he just had the faintest idea what was going on. No, that was untrue. He would have minded just as much even if in possession of a concise document entitled 'What Is Going On'. He would probably have minded it even more, because then the motives for what was going on would have been clearly listed as bullet points, and their weak, pettifogging, infantile nature would be revealed. Cabal, famously not a gambling man, would have put money on there being politics involved. Politics frequently was involved in so much that was weak, pettifogging, and infantile, and Mirkarvia seemed to sweat the filthy stuff.

And where there is politics, there is lying and deception. Cabal felt strangely let down that Cacon might not be Cacon, and that the transcendentally irritating man might not have been formed as other men by pressures of life and peers, but as an exercise in creative writing for some clerk in an intelligence or security bureau. If he had to make a guess, he would say that 'Cacon' was actually a member of Mirkarvian intelligence.

Marechal handled security, and Cabal could not believe that that such a polished performer would find much satisfaction working for a kick-the-door-down-and-shoot-them-in-their-beds merchant like the count.

Cabal reined in his hypothesising with difficulty. From a momentary change in Cacon's expression, he had transformed the aggravating little man from an exasperant at the dinner table to a super-spy at large. The weight of probability remained firmly on the side of Cacon being exactly what he appeared to be, albeit with an unexpected and intelligent interest in true crime. This latter thought amused him slightly; if Miss Barrow caused him any trouble he need only tell Cacon that she was a criminologist in training, and she would never be free of him for the rest of the voyage.

No, that wasn't quite true. The rest of the voyage was all the way to Katamenia. He was planning to jump ship in Senza, which was also Leonie Barrow's destination. From what little he knew Katamenia was not much of a holiday destination. He wondered how many of the other passengers were also going all the way there.

Mirkarvia, Senza, Katamenia. These little countries always seemed to have such long histories, usually full of extraordinary characters with horrible personalities. One would expect small places to breed small people, yet so many world changers had walked out of their minor nations, unblinking on to the great global stage where – as often as not – they messed it all up for everybody. These people . . . these great people, building empires out of blood that collapse into cinders as soon as the inevitable reversals of fortune begin.

Cabal loathed their every atom. If he had his way, a single scientific meritocracy would govern the world. Politics and economics were plainly too complex for the fuddled minds of politicians to take in.

He had been thinking all this as a preferable alternative to listening to whatever Cacon had to say. In this at least, it really didn't matter if Cacon was a phenomenally boring man or some variety of secret agent pretending to be a phenomenally boring man. The overall effect was still that of being talked at by a phenomenally boring man. Cabal found that he was phenomenally bored by him. Currently he was detailing the denouements of a long list.

'I'm sorry, Herr Cacon, but I have work to attend to,' said Cabal, rising from the table. 'I have some agricultural land remittance discussion papers to work up to a fourth draft, and all this business with M. DeGarre and suchlike has put me behind schedule. If you will excuse me?'

He walked off immediately before Cacon had any chance to excuse him or not. Back in his cabin, he sat down to plan how he was going to escape from the aeroport tomorrow in Senza. His understanding was that the vessel would be laid up for some time while the Senzans went through her with a fine-tooth comb looking for anything that might be construed as military aid for Katamenia. Miss Barrow would be sure to inform the Senzan authorities as soon as she could, and he would be arrested immediately.

Cabal played the likely sequence of events out in his mind. Miss Barrow leaves the ship as soon as she possibly can and denounces him to the Senzan authorities. The customs men or a police squad boards and arrests him. He is taken into custody, put on trial, and sent to prison for a period of, allowing for good behaviour, forever. This was a poor result.

Alternatively, she denounces him, the Senzan authorities attempt to arrest him, but are confronted by Captain Schten arguing that Herr Meissner is a Mirkarvian citizen and they can keep their stinking Senzan paws off him. Cabal liked this version. His liking for it deteriorated when he ran on the train of events a little further. The Senzans demand proof. Schten then wires to Krenz for corroborating evidence. Krenz wires back to say they've discovered Civil Servant Meissner in a vegetative state at the aeroport, oh and, incidentally, has Schten got an infamous necromancer called Cabal aboard who happens to look a little like Meissner and is wanted for crimes against the state?

Cabal spent the next hour running through further alternatives and variants on the alternatives; each and every one of them resulted in life imprisonment or death. The only way out of this ring of fire was to move back a step and do something about, 'Miss Barrow leaves the ship as soon as she possibly can and denounces him to the Senzan authorities.'

He took out his switchblade and opened it. The pivot still smelled of blood, and he doubted the moisture was doing the steel any favours. He took a handkerchief from Meissner's luggage and started to clean the blade carefully.

He could try and be off the ship and through customs before Miss Barrow had a chance to warn them, but this was fraught with difficulties given that she would be intent on beating him to it. Or, he could stop her being a problem now. She wouldn't have to die; he was reasonably confident that he could injure her badly enough that she would be in no state to tell anybody anything about him until he was free and clear.

But . . . she had hinted at leaving a letter with the captain to be opened in case anything happened to her. No, then – too risky. It was not even worth considering if he could somehow steal it from the captain's safe. For all his other accomplishments, Cabal had never attempted safecracking.

So, he had only one real option, which was to delay Miss

Barrow in some non-lethal way at the very moment of disembarkation, and then scurry through Senzan customs and excise with sufficient dignity to avoid suspicion. Simplicity itself.

Cabal had problems with simple things. His was a complex life, and when something simple was called for he generally had to sidle up to it in a long serious of lateral steps, circling it like a crab of the intellect. After some minutes of mental scuttling, his face was transformed by a smile. It was not a nice smile. It was the smile of a criminal mastermind who, on capturing his nemesis, decides to forego the circular saws and piranhas, and just shoots the man.

It was a good, elegant plan. He would spend a few hours using the official stationary Meissner had brought along to rustle up some convincing documentation to support the gross deception he would spin for the Senzan officials. It wouldn't stand up to close scrutiny, but it didn't need to. All he needed was a few minutes of confusion.

Chortling darkly, he unpacked Meissner's travel type-writer, and began drafting a governmental agencies bulletin concerning a wanted criminal.

A necromancer called Cabal.

Chapter 9

IN WHICH CABAL DISCOVERS THE FUTURE OF BAR
SNACKS AND TRIFLES WITH THE NOBILITY

An hour or two later, the false documents completed to his satisfaction, and with an unaccustomed song in his heart and a spring in his step inspired by anticipation of the dirty deed to come, Cabal entered the ship's salon in something as close to a good mood as he was ever likely to experience. Usually such mischief was not in his character, and it was partially the novelty as much as the sense of relief at having a workable plan that had raised his spirits so.

He sat at the bar and slapped his open palm on the wooden counter to attract the attention of the barman. The barman came over, polishing an already pristine glass, and smiled at Cabal's evident good humour. 'You seem in a very good mood, sir. What can I get for you?'

'I am, thank you. I shall have,' he started, and paused. He belatedly realised that he barely drank. He also realised that the Mirkarvians put a great deal of store by what a man put in his glass. Asking for the wrong thing might well put suspicions in people's heads. Sparkling water with a slice of lime, for example, would probably see him thrown overboard

155

for crimes against masculinity. What was safe? He plunged for the manliest thing he could think of. 'I shall have a beer, please.'

The barman looked at him with poorly concealed astonishment. 'A beer, sir? You'd like a beer?'

Cabal's heart sank. Why was it so damnably difficult to do anything around Mirkarvians without some ridiculous social more or another causing complications? He could try back-pedalling, but that would seem even more suspicious. He decided to plough ahead and try for 'mildly eccentric' in the barman's eyes, rather than 'highly dubious'.

'Yes. Beer. Why, don't you have any?'

The barman leaned forward confidentially, reaching under the bar as he did so. *If that hand comes up holding a gun,* thought Cabal, *I'm sunk. If he's holding half a billiard cue, however, I'm in with a chance.*

'I knew you weren't stuck up, sir,' he said quietly. 'Lot of the civils, they look down on beer. Not good enough for them. But you, sir, you're all right.

As the barman's hand rose from beneath the bar, Cabal was filled with a presentiment and strange foreboding that he hadn't felt since the last time he'd watched the nightmare corpse city of R'lyeh rise, effulgent with the ineffable and fetid with fish, from the depths of the Pacific.

In the barman's hand was the largest stein Cabal had ever seen. One could have drowned a sackful of kittens in it, and the drinker wouldn't even know about it until he reached the dregs. The barman held it beneath a beer pump and started to fill the stein. It took quite a while. When it was finally done, he placed it carefully before Cabal, winked conspiratorially, said, 'I'll put it on your chit. Good health to you, sir!' and went back to his duties, whistling jauntily.

Cabal looked cautiously into his drink. There was a great deal of slightly tan foam on top of the beer that, when he excavated down to it with a pencil, he discovered to be as black as treacle and only slightly less viscous. He sucked experimentally at the drops on the pencil and discovered the beer to be some form of porter, probably brewed from dark malts, fast fermenting yeast, and slightly coagulated dragon's blood. It seemed likely the dragon was very drunk when it died.

He noticed the barman looking at him, so he lifted the stein and took a good gulp, giving himself an undignified if manly foam moustache in the process. He wiped the moustache away with his handkerchief and nodded in a comradely way to the barman, who nodded back and got back to his work. The gulp had barely touched the level of the beer and Cabal realised he would have to engineer some ruse to be called away so as to avoid drinking it all. If he had to finish the whole stein he would probably be drunk for two days, and heaven alone knew what he might say in his cups.

That said, it was actually a pleasant enough drink. It coated his throat all the way down in such an assured and thorough manner that it felt like it might last for some weeks. On the other hand, he had spent more than enough time in laboratories to know all about organic chemistry and, without resort to a hydrometer, he could still make a fairly accurate guess from the faint scent of ethyl alcohol that the beer had an alcoholic content by volume of somewhere in the region of ten per cent, possibly a few points more. Given the cavernous dimensions of the stein, this meant there was enough alcohol in it to burn down a mid-size bonded warehouse. Cabal was only an occasional drinker and knew that he would be singing about goblins before he was even a quarter of his way through it.

He was just thinking how he could abandon it before then without having his essential Mirkarvianness called into question, when a small bag made of greaseproof paper filled with strange brown shavings appeared under his nose.

Cabal looked sharply to his right to discover that the bag was being held by Bertram Harlmann. He was smiling widely, apparently of the opinion that Cabal should be glad to have a collection of strange brown shavings appear beneath his nose. 'I know what you're thinking,' said Harlmann.

Cabal was confident that, no, he didn't.

Harlmann continued, 'You're thinking, "That's a lot of beer to drink with no solid sustenance to complement it. What I could really do with is a lovely bar snack". But what? Beer nuts? Beer nuts are a bit tired, aren't they? Pretzels? You can choke on pretzels. Meat sticks? Bits always end up floating around your beer. No, no, no, no. You don't want any of that old rubbish.'

Cabal said nothing, but watched him levelly, not even slightly agog to hear what new rubbish Harlmann was peddling.

'You want . . .' Harlmann nodded at the bag with an encouraging smile, and shook it temptingly.

'I'm not letting one of those anonymous . . . objects pass my lips without a full description and, ideally, an analytical chemist's report,' said Cabal.

'Save yourself the trouble, sport,' said Harlmann, a man difficult to put off his stride. In contrast, Cabal had never been called 'sport' before in his life and was inwardly reeling at such effrontery. 'I can tell you exactly what you're getting here. Zero carbohydrates, sixty per cent protein, thirty-two per cent fat, all of which is unsaturated, mostly oleic acid, which is good for you, and most of the rest is stearic acid, which is harmless. Bit of salt for flavour, but a little goes a long way. Go on! Try one!'

He still had misgivings, but the breakdown of the snack's chemical makings sounded reassuring enough. In fact, it sounded vaguely familiar. He took one of the puffy brown shavings and chewed slowly on it. It wasn't bad, and he said so.

'Y'see? Y'see?' Harlmann regarded the greaseproof paper bag as if it contained the Philosopher's Stone. 'The bar snack of the future, these little babies.'

'What exactly are they?' asked Cabal, taking another. He'd heard Harlmann use that phrase at the embarkation dinner, but Cabal hadn't been paying much attention on that occasion. What had Harlmann called them? Cabal suddenly remembered, and stopped chewing.

'Pork scratchings,' said Harlmann proudly.

'Pork scratchings,' echoed Cabal, his voice empty of expression. The name suggested that where there were pork scratchings, there were pork itchings, and mental images of pigs with terrible skin diseases filled his mind. Had he just been chewing on hog scabs?

'It's the skin, you see. Basically, cold crackling for the casual peckish market.'

'Pig skin,' said Cabal, starting to chew again. That didn't sound so bad; after all, pork crackling and rinds were all part and parcel of eating pork. 'What process do you use to get rid of the hairs?'

'Just burn them off. What do you think?'

'You may have to do something about the name, but that's not bad at all, Herr Harlmann.'

'Thank you, Herr Meissner. I respect your opinion. Please, have the bag with my compliments.' He waited until Cabal had taken it from him, before saying in a casual tone, 'You're something in the government, aren't you?'

So that was it. 'A very minor cog in the great Mirkarvian machine, Herr Harlmann. Specifically, a docket clerk, first class in the Department of Administrative Coordination.'

If Harlmann was disappointed with the rank, he didn't

show it. The department, however, seemed grounds for optimism. 'Administrative Coordination, eh? Why, that means you have contact with all other departments, including Military Logistics, doesn't it?'

Cabal had no idea, but it seemed likely. 'We have dealings with most other departments, that's true. Why do you ask?'

'Those little wonders,' he answered, gesturing at the bag in Cabal's hand. 'High energy food, gives you pep right when you need it! Perfect for troops on the march, eh?'

'It's an interesting idea, certainly,' said Cabal, for whom war was already such a ludicrous idea that the addition of thousands of soldiers marching off to butcher one another while chewing on slightly salted deep-fried chunks of pig skin added not a jot of absurdity. 'I could mention it to my superiors on my return.'

Harlmann smiled patiently and shook his head. 'No, no, no, no, my boy. You're getting this all wrong.' He sat on the next stool and then, to Cabal's profound discomfort, put his arm round his shoulder. 'Your bosses will just take all the credit. That's not the way to do it at all. You have to present it as a fait accompli, with your name all over it. Look, you can get at the SCF, can't you?'

Could he? Cabal tried to look noncommittal while working hard to guess what the SCF could possibly be. To buy himself some time, he attempted to turn the conversation around. 'You seem to know a great deal about it, sir.'

'Well, of course I do. It's my business. I'll not lie to you, Herr Meissner. A government contract for my scratchings would be a great boon for my business, and . . . it could do you a lot of good, too.'

If this was the way Mirkarvia usually operated, thought Cabal, no wonder it was a shambles. As for the SCF, civil services always seemed to be full of committees, and Harlmann was after funding. Therefore, he would guess that it was something along the lines of the Special or even the Secret Committee for Funding. When Harlmann said he wanted Cabal – or more accurately, Meissner – to 'get at' the committee, it seemed evident that he meant for some palms to be greased.

'Well, I can't *get at* anyone while I'm aboard the *Princess Hortense*, sir. We shall have to talk about this in greater detail when we're both back in Krenz.'

Harlmann frowned. 'Why wait? You can wire when we reach Senza.'

Bribery by telegram was new one on Cabal, especially from a telegraph office in an unfriendly country. 'It's not quite that simple. I'm involved in agricultural remittances. I can't just telegraph them out of the blue like that.'

'Them?' Harlmann looked at him very closely, and Cabal realised that he might have made a serious error.

He was saved by Miss Ambersleigh, who appeared at his elbow like an English djinn, which is to say suddenly but without a lot of flash and smoke and bother. 'Excuse me, gentlemen,' she said. 'Herr Meissner? Lady Ninuka wonders if we might have the pleasure of your company.'

The force of Cabal's desire for any escape from Harlmann might in a different man have manifested itself in bear-hugging and kissing Miss Ambersleigh before conducting her in an impromptu polka around the salon. In Cabal, it was ruthlessly subjugated while he inclined his head in a curt nod. 'I should be delighted, Fräulein.' He rose and bowed to Harlmann. 'If you would excuse me, mein Herr?'

Harlmann nodded and, somewhat to Cabal's surprise, smiled in a warm and fraternal manner. 'No problem, old man. My best wishes to her ladyship.' He stood, bowed and turned to go, but, as he turned, he caught Cabal's eye, and very deliberately winked. Then he was gone, taking his pork scratchings with him.

Inwardly perturbed by Harlmann's behaviour, Cabal took his drink, and walked over to go through the pleasantries with Lady Ninuka. As they sat, he noticed Miss Ambersleigh regarding the stein with icy disapproval. Cabal could almost have thanked her for it, because it gave him an excuse to have it taken away and replaced by tea and cakes. Usually Cabal had little time for the English way of life – or indeed anybody else's way of life – but at some point he had developed a weakness for afternoon tea, and the pleasure he expressed when the tray arrived was entirely genuine.

'I'll be mother,' said Miss Ambersleigh, taking up the teapot. Lady Ninuka's caught Cabal's eye, and smiled slightly at the comment. Cabal took her meaning; this seemed likely to be the only way the censorious Miss Ambersleigh would ever be a mother, unless she unexpectedly entered a convent.

Cabal took his tea with lemon and no sugar, and confined himself to a yellow French Fancy. They chatted politely enough about the weather, the ship, the view, and Cabal was just beginning to think that he was on safe ground, when Lady Ninuka said, 'I hear you're involved in the investigation into poor M. DeGarre's disappearance. Is that so, Herr Meissner?'

Miss Ambersleigh tutted. 'Really, Orfilia! I'm sure we don't want to hear about such a horrid event.' She turned to Cabal. 'I'm sure I shan't sleep a wink tonight! And as for poor Orfilia, she has trouble sleeping at the best of times. You must not excite her with such talk!'

'You have trouble sleeping?' Cabal asked Lady Ninuka. 'You should ask the ship's doctor for a sleeping draught.'

'She did,' cut in Miss Ambersleigh as Lady Ninuka was drawing breath to reply, 'but it's not good for you to take them too much, my dear. You cannot depend on chemicals.' She turned earnestly to Cabal. 'You're an educated man,

JOHANNES CABAL the Detective

Herr Meissner. You tell her. It simply isn't wise to depend on chemicals.'

Cabal, whose work involved a large quantity of chemicals, resisted the desire to highlight Miss Ambersleigh's appalling ignorance of scientific matters by telling her that she was entirely constructed from chemicals, and that she ate chemicals, drank chemicals, breathed chemicals, and that this was all completely natural. Instead he said, 'Insomnia can be a terrible burden on your well-being, my lady, both physiologically and psychically. Medication is all very well in the short term, but you should try to discover the root of it and deal with it.' That said, he thought she looked remarkably well on it. It was probably the glamour that women create with paints and powders, but she didn't look like somebody who went without regular rest. In vulgar terms, she was bright-eyed and bushy-tailed. He briefly entertained the idea that she might be depending on some much less innocent chemical than a mild sedative, but it didn't sit well with her behaviour or appearance; she didn't seem to be exhibiting any of the telltale signs associated with common stimulants.

'Thank you, Herr Meissner. I truly appreciate your concern. May you talk of your investigation, though? It seems very interesting.'

Speaking quickly to head off the interruption that Miss Ambersleigh had ready in the slips, Cabal said, 'I really cannot speak of the investigation, Lady Ninuka. You understand, of course. It could prove damaging to any findings if they were to be publicised prematurely.'

'Oh, I wouldn't tell a soul,' she replied, the very picture of innocent propriety, although the way she laid hand upon her décolletage as she spoke could just as easily have been due to coquettishness as to expressiveness. 'I am the very epitome of discretion.'

'Herr Meissner has made it quite clear that he cannot

discuss such things, my dear,' persisted Miss Ambersleigh. In her mind, subjects suitable for civilised discussion frolicked happily in a great green pasture of loveliness surrounded by a ha-ha filled with spikes and acid, beyond which lay the Frightful. Violent death and suicide were very much of this congregation of the unspeakable, and for every word spoken on such subjects, an angel shed a tear, or a fairy died, or a bunny was blinded. Miss Ambersleigh, who was fond of angels, fairies, and bunnies (despite having met only the latter), was therefore very keen to confine her conversation to the lovely pasture.

Lady Ninuka was not.

'Well, there must be some aspects you can explain to me,' she asked Cabal. 'Your methods, your strategy to get to the bottom of all this?'

He was flattered that she thought there was any strategy involved in the investigation at all, given that its only solid piece of evidence was an injury sustained during a murder attempt. If real police officers relied on such methods, precious few would ever draw their pensions.

'My lady, you make too much of my humble abilities. I am no detective; I am merely an instrument of the state attempting in my poor way to help the captain find the truth.'

'Can't you see he doesn't want to talk about it, Orfilia? Come, now! Let us speak of happier things.'

Cabal was beginning to find that Miss Ambersleigh's shrill interjections were grating on his nerves. If he had been himself, he would have said as much, but Gerhard Meissner – or at least his rendition of Gerhard Meissner – was a more patient man. His true mind flickered on his face for a second, but he brought it under control with a steely flex of his will.

It seemed that Ninuka shared his opinion, though, as the very next moment she said, 'Oh, for pity's sake, Miss Ambersleigh! Can't you see that every time the poor man tries to say something, you tell him that we don't wish to hear it? Of course he's keeping quiet. He's being polite!'

Miss Ambersleigh was momentarily speechless. Only for a moment, though. 'Well!' she said. 'Well, I never!' Which was probably true.

She rose to her feet, and speaking in short bursts coloured with repressed emotion, said, 'I see my company is not appreciated here. I'm very sorry. I shall take myself away. Herr Meissner.' Cabal, who had also risen to his feet, nodded, and muttered in a fair impersonation of an embarrassed man. Miss Ambersleigh turned to Ninuka. 'My lady.' And then, like a schooner swept along on winds of decorum, she walked quickly to the other side of the salon and sat alone.

Cabal sat down again. 'That's even more embarrassing,' he said to Lady Ninuka. 'I thought she was going to leave, but she's just sitting there watching us.'

Lady Ninuka didn't even deign to look, settling back in her chair. 'She has no choice. She's not just my companion; she's my chaperone. My father hired her to keep an eye on me.' She looked at Cabal over her teacup as she took a sip. 'She's very conscientious.'

Abruptly, and with the sensation of being the last one in the theatre of getting the joke, Cabal realised that Lady Ninuka was not so much interested in the progress of the investigation as in the investigator.

The French Fancy turned to ashes in his mouth. The last thing he needed was some new complication in his life, a life that was already built almost entirely of complications. Quite apart from the necromancy, the assumed identity, the mysterious disappearance, the attempted murder, and the Mirkarvian noble after his neck, now he had another Mirkarvian noble after one or more other parts of his anatomy.

Or possibly not. While he knew he was presentable

enough, his vanity was not physical, and he had never noticed women swooning in his path before. Perhaps she was just one of those strange souls who derived a sordid, vicarious excitement from crime and death? The sort of young woman he had observed attending public executions, while he himself had been there to spread bribes and so secure the cadaver as fresh experimental material.

He found this thought a great relief. The idea that she might derive some perverse pleasure from tales of vile crime and ugly death rather than something more amatory involving him was deeply reassuring. It was one less complication to worry about, and for that he was very grateful.

For her part, Lady Ninuka was disappointed when Herr Meissner's eyes widened with surprise when she finally dropped a hint broad enough for the insensitive nincompoop to detect, but then he seemed to relax and she knew that they had an understanding. She wasn't sure what she found attractive about him; physically he was good enough, if not extraordinary. She thought it might be those eyes; those blue, intelligent eyes, behind which an earnest if unenterprising mind whirled with whatever it was that civil servants found to dwell upon. Yet he had defied expectations by going around exploring in the middle of the night and, when attacked, had defended himself successfully. There was more to Herr Meissner than met the eye, and Lady Orfilia Ninuka intended to split him open like an oyster and discover what lay within.

So with the lines drawn, albeit on entirely different battlefields, the conversation continued.

'Is it true that somebody tried to kill you last night?' she asked, eyes wide and expectant.

Cabal winced inwardly. His efforts to fade into the scenery had only succeeded in making him a font of sensation. Next time he wanted to evade notice, he decided, he should dress as a clown and hope for a converse effect.

'Where did you hear that?'

'On a ship, with only a few people aboard? If I hadn't heard about it, *that* would have been the marvel. So, it is true, then?'

'Yes,' admitted Cabal, sensing that to squirm any further would be pointless as well as undignified, and told her the story excepting the detail of the assailant's wounded wrist.

Lady Ninuka hung on his every word, and Cabal interpreted this as an unhealthy appetite for the lurid. At least, he did at first, but as the tale wound to its conclusion, it occurred to him that the last person who had shown such a close interest in his little adventure – Captain Schten excluded, as it was his job to be interested – was Cacon. On that occasion, Cabal had been quick to suspect the irksome little man of being an agent of some hue. What, he wondered, was rationally preventing him from suspecting the same of Orfilia Ninuka? Neither her sex nor her title precluded her in the slightest. Then again, he had only the most vague grounds to suspect Cacon, so was fearing the same of Ninuka merely rational caution or the shallows of paranoia?

Paranoia is an occupational hazard common amongst necromancers. When the whole world really is out to get you, one has to set the hurdle of unreasonable fears that much higher. Generally, necromancers who last that long discover quite early on in their careers that all threats, no matter how nebulous, should be acted upon. In populated areas this is patently impractical as every single person who comes within a mile of a necromancer may mean harm. Thus they move away from cities and towns and even villages, and set up on barren mountain tops, or reclaimed chthonic subterranean redoubts, or as in Cabal's case, a nice three-storey townhouse moved, by methods that do not concern us here, from the middle of a respectable suburban terrace and placed, front garden and back yard intact, on a grassy hillside miles from anyone. There he was pleased to conduct experiments that would have made Victor Frankenstein wrinkle his nose, safely away from prying eyes, and there he dearly wished he was now, feet up in front of an open fire, drinking tea and reading the *Principia Necromantica*. That he was doing none of these things, apart from drinking tea, distressed him. The realisation that his own sense of nurtured and measured paranoia was now so sensitive as to be useless distressed him too.

He concluded his narrative and reached for the teapot. Lady Ninuka was positively aflutter.

'You brave man,' she said, her face full of hero worship. She leaned forward as she spoke and Cabal was struck again by how very cleverly her wardrobe was cut. In this case a short jacket offset the modish neckline of the dress to create an overall effect of virginal sensuality. He had no idea where he stood with her; their relative positions were entirely at her whim. It was all very confusing for a man who was much happier at a dissection slab than a soirée.

'It was nothing, really.' He had meant it as a statement; there is nothing intrinsically brave about fighting for your life. It was only after he had said it that he realised how heroically modest it sounded, and the fact that he had said it without affectation had merely inadvertently served to compound the effect.

'Of course it was,' said Ninuka. 'In such a situation, I should have been frozen with fear. You are so much more capable than I, Herr Meissner.'

Cabal briefly considered telling her that it would have been the slipstream freezing her, but that snapped a vision of her dangling by one hand in Meissner's dreadful silk gown – which looked a lot better on her – and then there was the detail of the gown falling open. The surface effect of these thoughts was to make the start of the sentence he was about to make dribble to an untidy halt and leave him gawping, as if he'd just remembered something important.

'Have you remembered something important?' she asked.

He felt vaguely ashamed, as if she'd read his mind. 'No. No, I was just . . . reliving the events of last night. It was . . .'

'Exciting?'

'Traumatic, I was going to say, but exciting? Yes, it was that, I suppose.'

Lady Ninuka leaned back into her chair and regarded him. She didn't quite fling herself around in abandon and pant animalistically, but a sense of flinging and panting still pervaded her far more conservative posture and attitude. In fact, to an uninvolved bystander, she would have seemed the very model of decorum and respectability. Cabal wasn't sure how she was doing it, but he was sure she was doing something. This was an entirely new field of human endeavour for which he had no familiarity and no understanding.

He did, however, have the distinct impression that he was enjoying it. It made him feel warm and important in a way that had never especially occurred nor seemed pertinent to him before. He was just going to explain, in the most roundabout and circumspect way, that he *had* actually been very brave and it *had* actually been very exciting, when Leonie Barrow appeared at his elbow and said, 'Lady Ninuka! How delightful!'

She sat down with them without being invited, and started talking about the theatre in Krenz. Considering that he'd been doing most of the talking up until then, Lady Ninuka seemed unaccountably put off her stride. She smiled politely, but barely responded to the new subject of conversation at all and the polite smile quickly became forced, as if masking some other emotion that was trying to rear its head. Finally, she made a big show of realising the time, made her apologies, and left the salon with the wretched Miss Ambersleigh scurrying along in her wake.

As soon as she had gone, Leonie stopped her monologue and smiled, broadly and not without some malevolence.

'What,' said Cabal, somewhat testily, 'is going on? What was all that about?'

'Did she ask you about what happened last night?'

'Yes, but she's hardly the first one to do that.'

'Ah, but did she ask any questions, or just listen very closely?'

'She just listened. What are you getting at?'

'Did she congratulate you on how you handled things?'

Cabal nodded, still confused.

'Did she lean forward a lot? Like this?' She demonstrated, and Cabal had to admit that it was a good impersonation. 'Did she touch you lightly on the knee at any point? No? Well, she was certainly working up to it.'

Cabal looked at her, his bafflement lifting. 'A witch?' he said, lowering his voice. It wasn't too surprising, now he stopped to consider it. The upper classes were the embodiment of discretion, and he had certainly heard of members of the nobility who dabbled in practices that would get a commoner drowned in the village pond by her neighbours. 'She's a witch? She needed some sort of direct contact to cast a spell? But, why me? What was she after?'

He noticed Miss Barrow's shoulders were shuddering with the effort of holding in her laughter. This did nothing to improve his mood.

When she managed to damp down her hilarity a little, she said, 'For a clever man, you can be such an idiot. She's no witch. Not the way you mean it, anyway.' She leaned forward and gestured him closer. 'She was seducing you, you blockhead,' she whispered, then sat back, unable to contain her laughter any more.

'She was . . .' Cabal wasn't at all sure he'd heard correctly. 'She was *what?*'

She brought herself rapidly back under control, sobering up with a deep breath. 'You heard. And it's *excellent.*'

Chapter 10

IN WHICH THE LIGHT OF TRUTH IS ENCIRCLED
BY DARKNESS

Science and mathematics are wonderful things. They cut like an arc light of truth through the cobwebbed depths of supposition, superstition, instinct, and guile. For the scientific mind, it can sometimes become too easy to ignore these thin, insubstantial threads as irrelevant, but this can be a serious mistake.

'But why?' he asked her as they dined together that evening, his animosity towards her erased by the realisation that in matters of social interplay he was as innocent as a babe in the woods. 'What possible reason could she have to want to . . . you know. Why?'

'Why?' Miss Barrow paused in cutting a morsel from her Spanish omelette, her first victory in the search for something Mirkarvian chefs wouldn't undercook. She was about to tell him, but then decided she would be interested in learning a little more about this huge and unexpected area of Cabal's ignorance. 'Why do you think?'

'Well, she wants something.'

'Clearly,' she said, a little archly.

'But what? Money? Information? She's not really a Senzan agent, is she?'

'Money? She's an aristocrat who spends more on an everyday dress, than you – Herr Meissner – would see in your monthly pay packet. I really don't think she's after your money. Information? Bloody hell, you see agents everywhere. I strongly doubt she represent anybody's interests other than her own. No, you're putting far too much thought into this. It's all much simpler. Our Lady Ninuka has a hobby. Whenever she sees a man who interests her in a certain way, she isn't happy until that man has joined her for an evening of sport.' It was obvious from Cabal's face that he was working down a list of possible sports. The slight expression of consternation indicated that he had arrived at cricket. Leonie decided to put him out of his misery. 'She's a bike. A tart. A slut. She'll be buried in a Y-shaped coffin. A baggage. A hussy. She's the good time that was had by all. A wanton floozy.' She looked closely at him, but he still seemed to be stuck on cricket. 'A nymphomaniac.'

The use of a technical term shook him from his paralysis. Realisation flooded his face and a silent 'Oh!' filled his mouth.

'Not that she is, of course. Well, maybe the last one, but all the other terms, the ugly ones, were invented by men. A man sleeps around, he's just being a man. Not really very fair, is it? Do shut your mouth; you'll catch flies sitting there like that.'

Cabal shut his mouth somewhat shamefacedly. He'd been prepared to consider almost any eventuality except the one that was evidently true. In his defence, it was a situation entirely alien to him. He could honestly say he'd never had an elegant and attractive woman of high breeding set her cap at him in this fashion. In fact, he'd never had any woman of any demeanour, appearance, or birth do so. He was not unattractive, and his attention to detail extended to how he presented himself, so at first glance it was not so odd that he should be in such a situation. In the normal run of things, however, he kept himself fastidiously to himself and furthermore usually carried a faint scent of formaldehyde around with him, which had the effect of depressing any amorous intent of any woman with a working nose. The combination of his long absence from a laboratory, the stolen clothing, and the enforced socialising had conspired to place him neatly in the sights of Lady Ninuka, and he had not realised it for a second.

'So, let me see if I understand this. You're saying that I was intended to be a diverting interval for her ladyship, to lighten a dull voyage? What's the matter with her? Isn't a death and an attempted murder enough to keep the woman amused?'

Leonie shook her head as she finished her omelette. 'No, no. You don't see the whole picture here at all. Yes, you were supposed to be a diverting interval, but note the indefinite article.'

Cabal frowned. 'There was supposed to be somebody else?'

'Wrong again. There *was* somebody else. Nothing supposed about it.' She smiled not altogether charitably. 'Sorry, sweetheart, but you weren't her first choice.'

Cabal fumed. 'Just because you're in a position that currently allows you the liberty of taunting me, you would be ill-advised to actually do so. Nor should you present a lot of half-formed conjecture as somehow significant, when it likely has no more importance than those missing candelabras at breakfast that— Oh.' He looked around and noticed that every table now carried one. Quickly dropping the subject, he said, 'You are being obscure for no better reason than your own amusement, just like your magical appearance this afternoon when I was talking to her ladyship. You can be so very . . .' He paused, a sudden thought filling him first with realisation, then dismay, and then anger. 'You knew this was going to happen.'

'Ah,' said Miss Barrow, and took a sip of wine.

'You were lurking around somewhere waiting for this to happen. I was *bait!*'

'*Lurking?* Oh, poor you. How awful to be manipulated. Yes, I could see Ninuka's had her eye on you. It was just a case of seeing if she was going to do anything about it. And she did. That's brilliant. Brilliant.' She finished her wine and looked at him. 'I have no idea what you're so upset about. I saved you before the naughty woman could besmirch your precious virtue, didn't I? To be serious, I really needed to know what she would do. It is very important.'

'Important? Important how, exactly?' Cabal was having difficulty keeping both his temper and his voice down. He was pining badly for his laboratory. Things were so much simpler there. If something proved problematical, he could just drop it in the waste bin and start again. Sometimes, admittedly, whatever proved problematical didn't especially want to go into the bin and he might have to smite it several times with a retort stand or perhaps shoot it before it would behave, but these were procedures he understood, and used. This great social laboratory within which Leonie Barrow seemed so at home was a horrible mystery to him, and he especially despised being used as an experimental subject.

'You're a scientist . . . sort of. You know how important it is to follow a hypothesis with a practical experiment. I thought I knew what kind of person Lady Ninuka was, but I needed to be sure. That's where you came in. Thank you for that. Your look of gormless incomprehension as the tigress circled you will keep me amused for many years to come, I'm sure.'

Cabal ignored the slight with difficulty. 'Are you saying

she's the killer? Or involved somehow?' Ninuka had been wearing long sleeves and gloves, the skin of her arms and hands being far more thoroughly covered than other parts of her body. Could she have been wearing a bandage beneath the material?

'No, of course not. She's a bored aristo, not Lucrezia Borgia. All she wants in life is new dresses, exciting parties, and to go for the occasional gallop on an obliging member of the bourgeoisie.' She ignored Cabal's glower. 'Just think what she may be instead of a killer.'

Cabal couldn't. If she wasn't directly involved in DeGarre's disappearance or the attack in the vent, then Lady Ninuka seemed entirely irrelevant. Leonie watched his mental wheels spin haplessly until she took pity on him. 'She could be a witness.'

'A witness? But DeGarre vanished from a locked room, and there was nobody else in that vent except my attacker and me. How could she have seen anything?'

Miss Barrow looked agonisingly sage, not to say smug. 'Ah, there's more than one type of witness. It's not what she saw, it's what she didn't see.'

And she would say no more, not even when Cabal made several veiled threats of physical violence.

Miss Ambersleigh answered the knock at Lady Ninuka's stateroom door. If she was perplexed to find Leonie Barrow there, or dismayed to find Cabal, she made no sign of it. She only asked them for a moment to see if her ladyship was receiving visitors. When she returned, she ushered them inside.

Lady Ninuka was waiting to receive them in the sitting room of her suite, a far cry from the small if well-appointed cabins of Cabal, Miss Barrow, and the late M. DeGarre. She was the very embodiment of reserved politeness, but she plainly expected the interview to go one way, and an awkward way at that. She ordered tea and made small talk until it arrived. When it did, she tactfully dismissed Miss Ambersleigh who left without rancour, saying that she hoped the young people had a pleasant chat.

Lady Ninuka waited until the door had closed quietly behind Miss Ambersleigh before speaking. 'You are doubtless here to discuss my talking with Herr Meissner without proper supervision?' she said in a reasonable tone carrying the message that there was nothing here about which they could not come to agreement.

'Doubtless,' said Miss Barrow, smiling. It was the smile of a large predator just prior to driving its fangs into its prey's cervical vertebrae. 'Actually, no. We're here to talk about Gabriel Zoruk.'

Cabal endeavoured not to look surprised. Were they?

Lady Ninuka blanched slightly. 'I don't really know the gentleman . . .'

'Please, please, please. Don't start off by making statements that you later come to regret.' Miss Barrow shook her head like a governess who has caught a small child out in a transparent lie.

Lady Ninuka was having none of it. 'I spoke to him at dinner last night. That is the limit of my association with the man.'

'Oh. Oh, dear,' said Miss Barrow regretfully.

'You see? I'm afraid you've wasted your time coming here.'

'Hmmm? Oh, no. That's not what I'm sorry for. I was just feeling sorry for poor Herr Zoruk, thrown into the brig, all alone, and under suspicion of murdering M. DeGarre.'

'Well, of course we're all sorry—'

'I hadn't quite finished,' interrupted Miss Barrow, looking steadily at Lady Ninuka. Ninuka shifted awkwardly in her chair. Despite himself, Cabal couldn't help but admire Leonie

Barrow's handling of the interview. She had found a chink in her ladyship's armour, driven a stiletto deep into it, and was now slowly turning the blade. 'What I was about to say was that I feel so very sorry for Herr Zoruk being in such a dreadful situation when he is entirely innocent.'

Lady Ninuka sat very still, hardly breathing.

'Entirely innocent, yet unable to prove it. Because proving it depends on an alibi, and it's an alibi that the poor, stupid, chivalrous boy refuses to use.'

Lady Ninuka, deciding that outraged morality would provide a suitable high ground, retorted, 'What are you implying?'

Miss Barrow laughed, still pleasant, as if they were discussing hats. 'I'm not implying anything, your ladyship. I'm stating it. You are Gabriel Zoruk's alibi. While he was supposed to be off engineering a disappearance and attacking Herr Meissner here, he was in fact . . . shall I use a euphemism? He was providing you with company through the dark hours. That seems like a gallant way of putting it. I could be far more specific, of course, if you'd prefer?'

It was clear that Lady Ninuka did not prefer. Standing slightly unsteadily on her dignity, she said, 'This is an outrage, Miss Barrow. It is a libel in front of a witness. You will regret this vile slur.'

'No, I shan't. You're quite wrong, on two counts. First, you mean *slander*, not *libel*. Secondly, it is only a slander if it isn't true. We both know it is. Let us not quibble, Lady Ninuka. There is a man in serious trouble, all it requires is a word from you, and the inquiry will discreetly redirect its attentions elsewhere. Isn't that so, Herr Meissner?'

Somehow Cabal managed not to look around. He'd been so attentive to what was being said that he had momentarily forgotten he was incognito.

'Of course. My lady, we are not journalists looking for

something to amuse the hoi polloi. Nor do we travel in your circles. We simply wish to clarify the events of last night. The search for my attacker has stopped because Captain Schten believes he has him in custody.' He decided not to tell her that the search had restarted, not when he could see a way to bring Ninuka's self-interest into play. 'If he is wrong, that means the real criminal is still at large, walking these very corridors. We have no inkling as to why I was attacked or whether M. DeGarre's disappearance truly was suicide; it is not inconceivable that the perpetrator has not yet finished his or her plan, whatever it may be. In which case, nobody aboard is safe.' He looked significantly at Ninuka. 'Nobody.'

Ninuka considered. Then she said, 'There is not an iota of truth in what you say. You understand that? I have a chaperone to guard my honour. How do you propose that I led this ridiculous *demi-mondaine* existence you hint at under the very nose of Miss Ambersleigh? Does she strike you as being so laissez-faire?'

Leonie Barrow did not flicker an eyelid, but nor did she speak, and Cabal knew that she had no answer. He, on the other hand, did. Once he had got over the initial shock of being selected as a bedpost notch, he had been thinking events and conversations through again in the light of this revelation, and had made a deduction or two of his own. Miss Barrow might be his superior in matters of the human mind, but when it came to raw data, he was the master of synthesis.

'No,' he admitted, pleased to be adding something concrete to the arena. 'She does not. Nor is she. Then again, you don't strike me as a woman with insomnia.'

Miss Barrow looked sideways at him, and he met her glance. There was something like satisfaction and perhaps a tic of respect there. He felt childishly pleased for a moment, before reminding himself that this was the same woman who intended to hand him over the Senzan authorities on the morrow.

'What nonsense is this?' demanded Lady Ninuka. It was bluster, and weak bluster at that.

'You are not an insomniac. You claim to be, but only so your doctor will prescribe you sleeping powders. These you squirrel away until such time as they are required. Specifically, when a conscious Miss Ambersleigh would just get in the way.'

Lady Ninuka said nothing, but simply looked at her gloved hands lying in her lap. It seemed that she had finally realised that denying everything is simply undignified.

'Finally,' said Miss Barrow. 'Now we can move on. Herr Meissner will inform the captain that there is a witness who can state that Herr Zoruk was nowhere near DeGarre's cabin or the vent last night. The captain will want a name.' Lady Ninuka coloured slightly. 'Herr Meissner will have to provide it, but he will also underline the need for discretion. The captain is no fool. The matter will go no further, and Herr Zoruk will be released, free of suspicion. You need have no part of any discussions, although you may depend on the captain paying you a visit to confirm these facts. He will probably also wish to know why you did not come forward earlier.' Miss Barrow's voice hardened. 'Which is an excellent question that I would like answering myself.'

There were several seconds of silence. 'Must I say?' whispered Lady Ninuka.

'Yes,' said Cabal. 'You must.'

She looked up. The confident young woman of only a few minutes before had gone. Now she had trouble meeting their eyes. When she finally managed it she said only one thing.

'It was romantic.'

*

'Romantic?' said Captain Schten after Cabal had taken him to one side and told him the state of affairs.

'I couldn't say,' admitted Cabal. 'I believe the idea of a man prepared to fritter away his liberty in defence of her honour occurring outside of a novel was a profound shock to her.' He coughed and added in a confidential tone, 'I fear the young lady is becoming jaded well before her time.'

'Good God,' said the captain. He shook his head and brought himself back to the matters in hand. 'I'll have to talk to her, of course, but I'll have a word with Zoruk first.'

'He won't say anything.'

'I know, I know, but at least we can let him know that *we* know, and that his release is imminent. Should be a weight off his mind. Come along, mein Herr. Let us give the unhappy chevalier some cause for joy.'

They walked down the silent corridor to Zoruk's temporary cabin. As they approached, Cabal commented, 'I notice you do not have a guard posted, Captain.'

'A guard? It's not a military ship. Besides, you've seen that cabin; there are no windows, and the lock is secure enough. I don't think we have anything to fear, especially in the light of Herr Zoruk's apparent innocence.' He took out his key wallet, and moved to unlock the door.

'That seems like very few keys for a vessel with so many doors, Captain,' said Cabal.

Schten held up the key he had selected. 'Most of these are for my house.' He smiled. 'This is a master key.' He inserted it into the lock and opened the door.

Cabal looked into the room as the door swung open, swore a short and bitter oath, and was through before the captain had even taken his hand off the handle. Cabal's switchblade was in his hand in a thrice and the blade out by the time he reached Zoruk's dangling body. He climbed quickly on to the interview table, noted instantly that it

181

would take too long to try and release Zoruk's belt from either the light fitting at the ceiling or from round the hanging man's neck, and instead sawed quickly through the taut leather. He kept the blade very keen for a variety of reasons, and was glad of it now. The belt parted quickly and Zoruk dropped to the floor, where he was caught and slowly lowered by Schten who had quickly overcome his own paralysis of shock.

Cabal checked Zoruk's pulse at his throat and wrist, but the already cool skin told him it was a vain effort. He rocked back on to his heels, glaring angrily at the corpse. 'Stupid!' he spat. Schten thought Cabal was talking to, him for a moment, but then realised Cabal was addressing the dead man. 'Stupid! Stupid! Stupid! Life is such a precious gift! To squander it . . . And for what? For some idiotic concept of honour? You fool! You utter, utter . . .' Words failed him, and he paced up and down, breathing hard with fury.

Schten perched on the edge of the table, and looked at Zoruk. Hanging without much of a drop was a hard way to go. The young man's face was mottled dark, his eyes bulged, his tongue pushed out of his mouth. The room stank; *in extremis* Zoruk had voided his bowels.

'This whole voyage is cursed,' he murmured. 'I've never heard the like. A disappearance, an attempted murder, a suicide. We can't tell the other passengers of this, not yet. It will put the women in a panic, and then when the Senzans board . . .' He shook his head. 'This must remain confidential until then. Just what is happening aboard my ship, Herr Meissner?'

Cabal ceased his pacing, and looked down at the body. Schten noticed that he didn't even flinch at such an awful sight. Civil servants were supposed to have iced water for blood, but surely even their sang-froid had limits?

'A murder, an attempted murder, and a suicide. I'm sure of

it. I doubt we shall ever see M. DeGarre again.' Cabal held his chin in his hand and thought for a moment longer. 'Possibly two murders.'

Schten looked up sharply at him. 'What?'

'How secure is this room, Captain? There was no guard on the door; anybody could have walked in here and done away with Zoruk.'

'It was locked!'

'There are master keys.'

'Only three. The first mate's, the purser's, and mine. Mine has never been out of my sight since I boarded, and I can guarantee that the purser and the first mate can say the same about theirs. Bearing a master key is a serious responsibility, Herr Meissner. I can assure you that they have never been left lying around. As for the characters of First Mate Veidt and Purser Johansson, I would trust my life to them. Unless,' he said, his brow clouding, 'you suspect me also?'

'Yes, Captain, I do, but only for the purposes of keeping an open mind, in exactly the same way that you should suspect me. As for serious suspects, well. Zoruk was all we had, and then only because of his wrist injury. Means, motivation, and opportunity eluded us. No, they *continue* to elude us.' A thought occurred to Cabal. 'Tell me, Captain, did you ever complete your checks for similar wounds on anybody else aboard?'

Schten nodded. 'Nobody. Zoruk here was the only one. You know, even if you're right and DeGarre was murdered, it doesn't necessarily mean that Zoruk did it, but he may still have been your attacker. His . . .' He coughed. 'His companion for the evening could have fallen asleep for some time. Not long, but long enough for him to find the vent open and go in to investigate.'

'Is that likely?'

'Not if the two events are unrelated, but what if Zoruk was

183

in cahoots with somebody else? He allows himself to fall for . . .' He coughed again. He did not seem able to mention Lady Ninuka's name in direct reference to such sordid activities, as if it were somehow treasonable. 'For his companion's wiles, and that provides him with an alibi.'

'Which he doesn't use.'

'Which he doesn't need to use for the moment. He can hold off naming names until it is convenient for him, and will be regarded all the more as a gentleman for being so reticent until he had no choice.'

'It's an interesting thought, but I perceive a problem.'

Schten was very taken by his hypothesis, and frowned at Cabal. 'What problem?'

'The problem lying at our feet. If this was all part of his plan, why did he hang himself?'

Schten had no answer, and shrugged.

'Sorry, Captain,' said Cabal. 'The only reason I can think of was that he did not commit suicide, but was murdered by this accomplice that you imagine, presumably to make sure Zoruk has no opportunity to turn coat. You tell me, however, that this room could not have been entered. If you are right, your theory founders.'

Schten stood up and looked across at the door, arms crossed. 'Locks can be picked.'

Cabal nodded. 'Indeed they can,' he said heavily, and a little ruefully as if this was an unpleasant occurrence he had experienced. He went to the door and examined first the lock itself, then the bolt and striking plate, and then the lock again. I can see no trace of pick scratches or anything else unexpected. But that doesn't preclude the possibility that it was picked by an expert.'

'An assassin,' said Schten slowly. Cabal looked at him with a raised eyebrow. 'An assassin!' repeated Schten, warming to the idea. 'A trained killer! He, or possibly she, was working with Zoruk. Zoruk makes himself the obvious suspect and then draws off the heat. But, he doesn't realise that he's expendable!'

'You,' said Cabal severely, 'should cut down on the caffeine and reading Pfennig Dreadfuls. Highly trained assassins, indeed. No, we should hearken to Friar William of Ockham and his *entia non sunt multiplicanda praeter necessitatem*. This appears to be a suicide and, if the only alternative involves bizarre orders of wraith-like assassins haunting the corridors of the *Princess Hortense*, then a suicide it certainly is. A young fool doing the decent thing, if you can dignify it thus. The only mystery extant in this corner of the affair is the wounded wrist. That remains puzzling.

'Come, let us leave this room before the stink settles in our clothing, captain. You should inform your medical officer immediately, and then decide exactly what you are going to tell the Senzan authorities. There is little time left.'

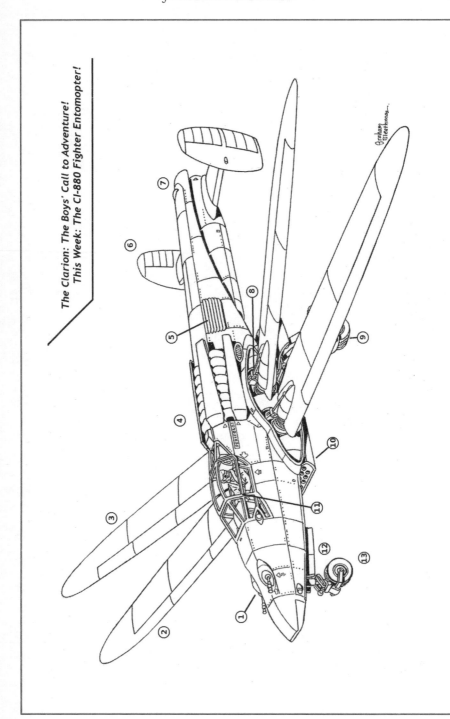

The Clarion: The Boys' Call to Adventure!
This Week: The CI-880 Fighter Entomopter!

This week we present a look at those big cats of the Senzan skies, the CI-880 Ghepardo ('Cheetah') entomopters, which are every bit as fast and ferocious as their namesake! Entering service for the first time two years ago, the CI-880 (the 'CI' prefix marks it as a fighter-interceptor) has patrolled the Senzan borders, rapidly becoming a favourite amongst pilots for its speed, manoeuvrability, and reliability, as well as for packing a powerful punch! Let's take a look at what makes it so special.

KEY

1. Twin 15 mm Martello Mini-Cannon: Each gun holds 275 rounds, usually a mixture of tracers and Armour-Piercing High Explosive (APHE). A deadly cocktail!

2. Forward starboard wing: The forward wings on each side perform more of the lifting than the aft wings, and are therefore of a slightly heavier construction.

3. Aft starboard wing: The aft wings have an important role to play, too, though. These are the 'manoeuvre wings', responsible for the entomopter's nippy handling!

4. Engine unit (intake manifolds and radiators visible): The Ghepardo gets its power from an Alessa two-row radial engine developing a fierce 950 hp, which allows this cat to strike at 250 mph!

5. Vertical exhaust vents: Normally, the engine exhaust vents to the rear (see No. 7), but the CI-880 has a clever trick up its sleeve. During takeoff and landing, the exhaust can be diverted to these secondary vents to jet downwards, giving extra lift when the pilot needs it most.

6. Rudder: The CI-880 has a double-rudder assembly that provides better control at high speeds.

7. Tail boom: The rear boom not only provides a mounting for the rudders; it's hollow, and contains the main exhaust tube, which vents directly backwards to give the entomopter a little extra push. In emergencies, fuel can even be sprayed directly into the hot exhaust vents, making her go – quite literally – like a rocket. Rather them than us, we say!

8. Clutch assembly: Ask any entomopter engineer what the most complicated part is, and he will point you straight at the clutch assembly. This mechanical miracle allows the wings to beat with the same complex motion used by a flying insect, and to do it at incredible speeds.

9. Rear landing gear: The two rear pieces of landing gear are useful even in flight. Once in the air, the gear is swung up sideways, allowing the wheel support's aerodynamic fairing to provide extra lift. Pretty clever, those Senzans!

10. Zeus rocket launcher: The Zeus comes with a whole quiver full of thunderbolts to rain down on ground targets – twenty-one 60 mm rockets, each packing a 3 kg warhead. Depending on the mission, however, this equipment mount can, instead, be loaded with a clutch of four 50 kg bombs, one large 250 kg bomb, or even a drop tank for extra range.

11. Cockpit: The pilot sits within a canopy of bulletproof glass.

12. Nose wheel bay doors: Unlike he rear landing gear, the nose wheel is retracted into its own snug little bay during flight.

13. Nose wheel: First thing off the ground and the last thing down. The nose wheel is also steerable, making it that much easier to get around the airfield!

Next Week in *The Clarion* . . . A Super Cutaway Picture of Hell!

Chapter 11

IN WHICH CABAL BEHAVES DESPICABLY
AND INQUISITIVELY

Cabal, for his part, knew exactly what he was going to tell the Senzan authorities.

The *Princess Hortense*'s entry into the skies of Senza was marked by the appearance of a flight of military entomopters. As the passengers gathered in the salon to watch the machines zoom by in a whirl of metallic wings, Captain Schten was at pains to announce that the aircraft were there as an honour guard, come to escort them in style to Parila Aeroport in the long promontory of land that split Mirkarvia and Katamenia. Nobody believed it for a second. They all knew, or were told quickly enough by their fellows, that the escort was there to keep an eye on them. Nobody said what would happen if the aeroship deviated on its approach path to Parila, but nobody needed to. The guns and rockets the entomopters carried were not there simply for show. Perhaps oddly, it was that the pilots did not return the waves of the passengers, but remained grim and cold, that caused a greater sense of foreboding than all the weaponry.

'Bloody Senzans,' sniffed Cacon, making one of his

occasional but always unpopular appearances. 'Wouldn't kill them to crack a smile now and then.' That this was the most rank hypocrisy, coming from a man who looked like cracking a smile himself would probably prove fatal, was silently noted by his listeners. None, however, commented on it; that would have meant possibly provoking a conversation with him, and this was too great a price to bear.

The captain's description of the fighter aircraft as an 'honour guard' was therefore believed by no one, nor was his additional announcement that there would be a stopover of a full day at Parila to allow the passengers to stretch their legs a little and take in the sights. In reality, all knew that Senzan officials would be going through the ship's every nook and cranny in search of possible military supplies intended for Katamenia. On this particular occasion, it would mean searching the tons of food supplies intended for disaster relief, which could only lengthen the search process. There are only so many bags of potatoes that can be bayoneted in a working day.

The final approach to the mooring cradle was slow but sure, the tone of the manoeuvre being 'no sudden moves' writ large. The fighter aircraft had stacked into a formation high and astern of the *Hortense*, all the better to stoop down and strafe her into wreckage if she did anything the squadron leader considered suspicious or threatening. Captain Schten intended to provide no such excuse, clearly signalling every turn and alteration in speed right down into the cradle itself. It was not just the relief of completing the difficult landing that caused the passengers and, it was reasonable to assume, the crew to sigh, but also the lifting of the threat of machine-gun bullets and rocket explosions.

Cabal stood at one of the long salon windows. He had watched the approach with a lively interest, specifically the arrangement of the aeroport itself. Around the field stood a high wire fence and without that a ditch or possibly an overgrown ha-ha. Alongside the wire ran a long strip of carefully maintained tarmacadam, near the end of which were two hangars. One seemed to be for civilian aircraft, but the other was divided off by another fence and gates, and was presumably the hangar from which the military ran their aerial patrols. Between the runway and the two aeroship cradles (the other standing empty) was a clear green swathe of short cut grass perhaps three hundred metres wide. The cradles stood much closer to the aeroport buildings than the hangars, and it was clear that entomopters were the lesser part of the facility's traffic, in status if not quantity. It seemed all very efficient. Rather too efficient for Cabal's liking. To be sure, he had a Plan A to get him out of the aeroport, away and clear before anybody was any the wiser about the truth of 'Herr Meissner'. He didn't like the plan much, though. It involved close dealings with the Senzan authorities and if they failed to react the way that he'd predicted, they would only have to reach out to arrest him. He had hoped for a less complex Plan B to present itself – something along the lines of sneaking through the aeroport's perimeter under cover of darkness – but the high fences and military presence had snuffed out that hope. There was no choice then; Plan A, with all its attendant opportunities for unwanted complication, was his only option. Filled with conflicting emotions, none of them pleasant, he retired to his cabin to prepare.

Even after the ship had settled on to the cradle, the etheric line guides had disengaged, the gyroscopic levitators had been allowed to wind down to a halt and the passenger ramp had been lowered, nobody was allowed to disembark. Instead, there was a long and humiliating wait while Senzan customs prepared. The passengers hung around in the salon, impatient but speaking little. Only Leonie Barrow was actually scheduled to leave the journey here, but everybody wanted to stretch their legs and see a little of Parila, a city noted for its history, art, and architecture throughout the civilised world. Even the most fervent Mirkarvian patriot would not like to be regarded as a barbarian – though most were – and so they were prepared to wander the streets, guidebook in hand, and pretend that they appreciated what they saw.

It was necessary for Herr Meissner to lead the crowd, however, and he couldn't do that via the salon. Instead he took advantage of the crew hatch down through the dining room and found himself on the top of a steel spiral staircase leading down one of the support stanchions, the very cousin of the one by which he had first boarded the *Princess Hortense* at Emperor Boniface VIII Aeroport in Krenz. He was thankful that they all seemed to be built to a standard pattern; the alternative might have involved him dangling from the aeroship's underside by his fingertips, and he'd done quite enough of that for one voyage.

He descended quickly, carrying no luggage but for his case and his cane. Meissner's could stay aboard the *Hortense* and be divided up amongst the crew by lots as far as he was concerned. He was almost done with the petty civil servant whose persona he had been forced to estimate and assume. He had only met the real Meissner briefly and had not sufficient time on that occasion to properly foment a real dislike for the man. He had, however, by a combination of going through Meissner's luggage, personal effects, and work papers, got his measure and could not wait to shrug the lowly and loathly civil servant from him as a serpent might slough a particularly irritating skin.

His progress was noted and acted upon by the Senzans, which was fine and predicted, and so he was unsurprised to be met a few metres from the base of the steps by a small cortege of serious and concerned customs officers. Their leader made as if to say something officious and obvious, but

Cabal pre-empted him with an impatient wag of his finger. 'Not here!' he snapped at the surprised officer. 'Not now!' He moved through them with such a sense of purposeful intent that the customs men found themselves falling into twin columns as he headed for the main aeroport buildings, the cortege becoming an entourage.

On arrival at the customs shed, he glared significantly at the junior officers until they wilted. Taking the hint, their senior dismissed them with a wave, as if shooing off flies. Once again, the officer drew breath to demand of Cabal an explanation and, once again, Cabal pre-empted him. He drew a long white envelope from an inner pocket quickly enough to make a small *krak* like a tiny whip. The customs man looked curiously at it, and raised his eyebrows when he saw the Mirkarvian State Seal in red wax upon the flap. Cabal ran his thumb under it and broke the wax before the officer had a chance to see that it was a low priority variant of the seal such as a docket clerk (first class) might carry with him.

'I was given this when I embarked upon the *Princess Hortense*,' Cabal told the officer in a conspiratorial tone. 'You will understand that there are . . . politics in play, even within my government? Factions and suchlike. One of these has taken to dabbling with certain . . . procedures that are not acceptable to civilised persons, no matter what their nationality.' He took the two folded sheets of paper from the envelope that he had placed there less than an hour before and passed them over. If the customs officer had been startled by events so far, that was as nothing to his expression when he read the first paragraph of the letter.

He looked up from the letter and stared at Cabal with wide eyes. 'A necromancer?' he said, nearly in a whisper.

'Indeed so,' confirmed Cabal. 'Read on, read on.'

The officer did so, and his discomfort increased with every

line. 'This is dreadful,' he said when he had finished, this time in a definite whisper.

Cabal hoped and trusted that he was referring to the document's content and not that it was a forgery. 'Yes, it is. I am ashamed that I have to turn to you for help, instead of concluding this affair in Mirkarvia. The people who first employed this . . . monster made that impossible. This is my last chance to prevent their plan reaching fruition.'

The customs officer was out of his depth. He kept rereading the document, or at least one part of it. Cabal suspected it was the phrases 'mass resurrection' and 'army of the dead' that had fixed his attention so admirably, which was gratifying as that was exactly the reason he had included them. The vision they provoked was of the victims of the Katamenian famine being so ill-bred as to not only be Katamenian and dead, but brain-eating Katamenian zombies stumbling over the border into Senza to suck the cerebellums of the Senzan citizenry, all under the domination of a mercenary necromancer backed by Mirkarvian money. To an officer whose usual workaday routine consisted of saying 'Anything to declare?' repeatedly, it was all a bit much to grasp.

Cabal allowed him another few seconds of grasping time, then said, 'You have to inform your superiors immediately! This plot has to be exposed and stopped, for the sake of your people and for the very soul of mine! Do you understand how important this is?'

'But who?' asked the customs officer, almost pleading. 'Who should I go to?'

This foxed Cabal for a second. He'd expected the Senzan customs to be rather more thorough in their preparedness for the ghastly plots of their neighbours. 'You're going to be overseeing the search of the *Princess Hortense*, are you not?'

The customs man shook his head. 'No, no. The military

handle that. We always expect trouble from those Mirkarvian bast— from Mirkarvian vessels, so the military are used to discourage anything, y'know, a bit dodgy.'

The military. Of course. 'Then take this report to the officer of the watch at the military hangar immediately! Now! Time is wasting!' The customs man took a couple of uncertain steps towards the door and then stopped, dithering. Cabal allowed a little of his impatience to boil over. It was a realistic reaction under the circumstances and, besides, it made him feel better. 'What in Heaven's name is it?'

'Would you come with me?' asked the customs officer. 'Please?' The customs and the military did not always see eye-to-eye, and it would help his case to have an actual Mirkarvian agent with him when he tried to explain to a hardboiled wing commander that the Katamenians and an element of the Mirkarvian elite were planning a mass illegal immigration into Senza of undead cannibals.

'Come with you? Impossible! I have to get back to the aeroship before I'm missed.' A happy bit of invention occurred to him, and he added, 'They've already murdered two other agents during this trip. I don't want them to make it three. You understand me?'

The officer didn't, not really, but at the mention of murder the tide of responsibility rose past his chin and up to his nose. He was desperate to pass it on to somebody senior to himself who might actually know what to do with the information. Ideally, somebody in the military. Then if they messed up, and voracious zombies overran Senza, he would be in the delightful position of being able to mutter, 'Typical bloody military. Can't get anything right,' shortly before ingestion.

So, after the mysterious man from Mirkarvia had gone out of the exit and was presumably sneaking back aboard the

Princess Hortense, the customs officer girded his loins and set off for the military compound. A minute after he had left, the mysterious man from Mirkarvia stealthily re-entered the customs shed and, discovering it to be as empty as he had hoped, became nonchalant and strolled out through the arrivals hall.

Finally, after the wait had exceeded calculated rudeness and was now simply boring, the Senzans finally deigned to board the *Princess Hortense*. Captain Schten was disturbed to note that instead of it being primarily a customs operation backed up by the military, only troops boarded and took up positions with their rifles unshouldered and ready.

A lieutenant marched up to Schten and saluted crisply. Schten returned the salute more slowly, frowning at the unexpectedly threatening presence. 'Why do these men have their weapons ready, Lieutenant?' he asked quietly enough to avoid the passengers present from overhearing.

The lieutenant drew a couple of sheets of paper from his peacock-green jacket and held them up so Schten could read the first. Schten saw the heading and demanded, 'Where did you get this? This is an official Mirkarvian document!'

The lieutenant was unimpressed. 'Read it, sir,' he said with the carefully controlled inflection of a junior officer who has authority over a senior officer on a different chain of command; a sterile sort of respect. Holding his anger in with a grimace, Schten read on. A few lines in, his anger turned to astonishment.

'That's impossible! I don't believe it! I can't believe it! I *refuse* to believe it!'

The lieutenant was enjoying himself, albeit inwardly. He folded the sheets and replaced them. 'Then you don't believe your own government, Captain. As you said, this is an official Mirkarvian document.' He turned to a soldier who was reading a copy of the ship's manifest. 'Sergeant, have you found the suspect yet?'

'Just about, sir.' He looked around the salon, and asked the captain, 'Are these all your passengers, sir?'

'Yes,' snapped Schten. 'You can see yourself. Oh, actually, no. We're a couple short. I was meaning to speak to . . .'

'We know about the deaths, Captain,' said the lieutenant. He took the manifest and passenger list from his sergeant and started matching names to likely faces, ignoring Schten's thunderstruck expression. He walked slowly through the passengers who, uncertain what was going on, but certain that something *was*, moved slightly away from him as if he had a contagious disease or was about to rope them into a party game. He stopped. 'You are Signor Cacon, no?'

It was not. It was Signor Harlmann, who was visibly relieved that he wasn't. He pointed out Cacon, who in turn shrivelled up a little beneath the lieutenant's cold stare. The lieutenant slowly walked towards him, but paused halfway there to check his list again. He turned to his right and looked at Lady Ninuka. 'You are . . . Signorina Barrow?'

Ninuka didn't get a chance to answer, as an outraged Miss Ambersleigh fluttered in front of her like a combative chicken. 'She most certainly is not, young man!' she said in her severest tones. 'This is the Lady Orfilia Ninuka, and I shall thank you to show her the proper respect! That,' she nodded at Leonie Barrow, 'is Miss Barrow.'

The lieutenant looked over at her with mild interest.

For her part, Miss Barrow was wondering what all this head counting was in aid of. She was wondering how the Senzans had learned of the deaths aboard, especially as it was evident that the captain clearly hadn't been the one to tell them. Perhaps Cabal had been right with his belief that there were agents aboard, just not Mirkarvian ones. And speaking of Cabal, where was he? It struck her that she hadn't seen him since the approach to the aeroport.

'Signorina Barrow?' asked the lieutenant.

'Hmm?' she said, thinking hard. Perhaps this wasn't about the mysterious happenings aboard at all. Perhaps this was all about Cabal. 'Yes. Yes, I'm Leonie Barrow.'

'*Splendido*,' said the lieutenant, snapped his fingers, and lazily pointed at her. At the sound, his soldiers stood smartly to attention. At the gesture, Miss Barrow found herself ringed by six rifles.

'What?' She fought an impulse to jump with surprise as the rational part of her feared, with reasonable grounds, that the soldiers might regard that as an excuse to fire. This left her up on the balls of her feet, from where she slowly descended back on to her heels in an effort to appear unthreatening.

'I still don't believe it,' rumbled Captain Schten.

'What . . . what is the meaning of this?' Miss Ambersleigh was even more a-flutter than a few moments before. 'You can't point your horrid guns at her! She's . . . she's English!'

The lieutenant ignored her. He marched up to Miss Barrow and took a moment to curl his lip and sneer at her properly so that she was in no doubt at all that she was being sneered at. 'Signorina . . . *Leonie* . . . *Barrow* . . .' He said the latter words as though they were patent and obvious lies. 'Or should I say . . .' He let the seconds linger, taking pleasure in the tension, knowing his civilian onlookers – poor ignorant fools that they were – were craning forward, hanging on his words. He let them squirm for a moment longer, and then delivered the denouement. 'Johanna Cabal . . . Necromancer!'

There was a collective gasp, including one from the freshly unmasked necromancatrix.

'You have got this *so* wrong,' she managed to say eventually.

He was aware that he could not push the sneer any further without it just looking silly, so he waggled his head a little for emphasis instead. 'Oh, have I indeed? We shall see. You are under arrest for crimes against humanity, nature, and God. Specifically, the proscribed practice of necromancy. You do not have to say anything, but anything you do say will be taken down in evidence and may be used at trial. You have the right to legal counsel during questioning, and during any subsequent trial. Do you understand these rights?'

Miss Barrow's throat was very dry. The initial disbelief had gone now, and been replaced with the certain knowledge that she was in deep trouble. *Johanna* Cabal? It seemed evident that they were after Johannes Cabal and somehow lines of communication had become tangled and they thought their man was actually a woman. But, why her? She wasn't the only woman aboard. And where was Cabal anyway? She was having trouble thinking, and being badgered by some coxcomb in army uniform was not helping. Did she understand these rights, he kept asking. Did she understand? She started to stumble through what might have been an agreement, when Miss Ambersleigh was suddenly between them.

'She's ENGLISH!' the tiny Miss Ambersleigh screamed in the lieutenant's face. 'How dare you suggest such a foul calumny upon an English lady, you . . . you . . . *foreigner!*'

The lieutenant looked down upon the incandescent woman, and raised an unbearably superior eyebrow. 'Ah, signora. Here, *you* are the foreigner.'

There is possibly no insult so calculated to sting the English as the suggestion that they may at any time be considered foreign, as this flies in the face of the obvious truth

198

that the whole of Creation actually belongs to the English, and they are just allowing everybody else to camp on bits of it out of a national sense of *noblesse oblige*.

If looks could kill, the lieutenant would surely have been turned to gritty dust in an instant, and his entire family tree dating back seven generations retrospectively stricken from history. Looks, however, do not. He remained alive and smug, despite Miss Ambersleigh's very best efforts.

'You vile man,' she said slowly, managing to make even 'you' sound like a dreadful slur. She pointedly turned her back to him and spoke urgently to Miss Barrow. 'You mustn't worry about a thing, my dear,' she said, taking Miss Barrow's hands in hers. 'This ridiculous toy soldier has obviously made a stupid mistake. I shall go straight to the British Consulate and inform them of what has happened. You mustn't worry, please. Help is on its way. Chin up, Miss Barrow. You show 'em, eh?'

Leonie Barrow had not had much time for the twittering antics of Miss Ambersleigh on the journey, but there was something very affecting about the little woman's faith in her innocence, and in the certainty that the truth would out, that made a lump grow in Miss Barrow's throat. No matter what, she could be sure of one ally in this ordeal.

'Thank you,' she managed to say. 'Thank you, Miss Ambersleigh. I shall.'

'Tcha,' muttered the lieutenant dismissively. The thrill of doing something out of the ordinary was wearing off. He'd been hoping for a gunfight, or a pitched battle against zombies. Two Englishwomen being unutterably English at one another was just boring. He gave an order to the sergeant, and Signorina Johanna Cabal, a necromancer of some little infamy apparently, was escorted off the aeroship, and into custody.

*

Herr Johannes Cabal meanwhile, an actual necromancer of some little infamy (and even smaller scruples), was wandering the streets of Parila and considering his next move. His original plan had been to get out of the town with as much alacrity as he could muster. The reason for such haste was based upon the least helpful chain of events that he could hypothesise: to wit, that Miss Barrow proclaimed, 'I am innocent! That document is a forgery! You are actually looking for Johannes Cabal, who has been masquerading as Gerhard Meissner, a Mirkarvian civil servant!' and the Senzans replied, 'So you are! So it is! After him!' In this dire case, the whole town would have a hue and cry up in minutes and he would be arrested very shortly thereafter. This was an unpleasant hypothesis, and he didn't care to think about it for too long, not least because it was not very likely. The document was not a bad forgery, and would maintain a thread of doubt in the mind of the authorities no matter how convincingly Miss Barrow proclaimed her innocence. They might believe her, but it would be gross incompetence to release her without definite proof of her bona fides. It was, after all, far better to detain an innocent person for a day or so and then apologise, rather than to let a necromancer go free. A day or so, then. That was all the leeway he had. Trying to leave town with undue haste would draw attention, so he would spend a little time making life difficult for the pursuers who would inevitably try to pick up his trail when the authorities wearied of the little joke he had played upon them. Miss Barrow, also.

He had an uncomfortable feeling in his chest that he believed was probably the prickling of a guilty conscience. He was glad to have his soul back, but the whole 'conscience' business that had come with it was very wearying. How dare this irksome inner voice torment him for doing what was necessary? Furthermore, it kept bubbling up another unfamiliar sentiment – that he hoped she *was all right*. He couldn't begin to imagine why he should care. She had been mildly discommoded, that was all. Good grief, he had shot people for being less of a nuisance than her. She should be grateful. He felt the faint flickering of a resentful anger at her, and this alarmed him too, with its base irrationality. Finally, he drove all such thoughts from his mind by forcefully reminding himself that he was on borrowed time, and that she would soon be free – if rather cross with him – and the hounds would be on his trail.

So, Cabal made his plans. The first thing to do was to draw a line between himself and the discarded 'Meissner' persona. The first part of that was to lose the Mirkarvian accent he had adopted – very successfully, it seemed, judging from how not a single native Mirkarvian had commented on it. Instead he would exaggerate what was left of his own Hessen pronunciation and claim to be a tourist from the Germanies. A casual stroll into a bookshop and a perusal of their geography section gave him the details he needed to fill out his story. He was staying in an inn at Escalti, a small town some fifteen kilometres away. He had found the place a little dull (a point intended to play to the locals, who maintained a friendly rivalry with Escalti), and cadged a lift to Parila, on the understanding that he make his own way back. Thus, could you direct me to the Stazione Ferroviaria Parila, *bitte?*

Of course, he had no intention of going to a provincial little dump like Escalti. Instead he would lose himself in a city like Genin until he could find a way to get over the border. That shouldn't be too difficult, he thought; it was its eastern borders with untrustworthy neighbours like Mirkarvia and Katamenia that Senza guarded closely. The west was a different thing altogether.

He would also have to undergo a physical transformation, and this he was not looking forward to in the slightest. He would change clothes when he reached the city, but in the meantime he would locate the necessary chemicals to make himself a quantity of impromptu hair dye. He certainly didn't want to just buy the stuff ready made; a single police enquiry in the right place and the fact he was disguising his hair colour and the shade used would be known. Far better to make his own. The necessary knowledge to synthesise hair dye from common chemicals was something he had developed some years before when it had become apparent that it might very well come in handy. To Cabal's mind it had been worth a few days then and a few hours a year subsequently to brush up on his notes to avoid the possibility of ending up on a gallows simply because he looked so very much like himself. His most obvious physical feature, after all, was that he was very blond indeed. Once he changed that, descriptions lost a lot of their usefulness. He had thus developed a simple dye, synthesised from common chemicals, which rendered his hair a convincing brown. Furthermore, the stuff washed out again after four or five washings using warm water, a strong shampoo, and a lot of white pickling vinegar. It left him smelling like a gherkin with hair the consistency of straw, but that passed quickly after a further wash in more sympathetic substances. Beer and raw egg worked well.

After a visit to the bank to change some of the British notes he had concealed in the lining of his case for Senzan lira ('I'm touring,' he told the cashier, almost truthfully), he found a dispensing chemist's and a very well-stocked hardware shop that between them sold everything he needed for his hair dye. He had no intention of actually making it while in Parila; the plan was to mix it in the train's lavatory en route to Genin so he would step down to the platform a different man. For the moment, he stored his purchases away in his bag, and wondered if it would be advisable to buy a change of clothes before travelling too. No, the chance of police enquiries revealing the purchases and so updating his description was too great. On the other hand, he could always buy something gaudy and memorable, and then dump it at the first opportunity. Should the police discover the purchase, they would certainly regard it as an attempt to radically alter his appearance and therefore report it in their police bulletins, rendering them even more inaccurate. This seemed like a desirable state of affairs to Cabal. He was just wandering the streets looking for somewhere that might sell orange ruffled shirts, when he paused to look in a shop window. In the reflection, he saw a familiar figure across the avenue behind him, but only a flash and then it disappeared up an alleyway. Cabal's heart sank.

All that paranoia aboard ship had just been mellowing into an acceptance that there weren't armies of agents and masses of interlocking conspiracies at all, and he had been enjoying being able to forget all that to concentrate on simply avoiding the police. As a necromancer, this was very much part of the job requirements, and he flattered himself that he was quite practised and professional at it. Now, however, all those fears that something terribly complex that killed people in passing was going on and he had no idea what it was came back to him with sobering intensity. The man he had seen reflected in the glass was Alexei Aloysius Cacon, and he was positive that Cacon had been watching him.

Cabal turned, but just caught a glimpse of Cacon's coat as he scurried up the alley and out of sight. This complicated things; Cabal needed at least another half an hour to complete his arrangements before catching the train. If Cacon ran off to find a police officer, flight would become dramatically more difficult. The railway station would immediately become off limits, and he could be sure that the main thoroughfares out of Parila would be watched. There was nothing for it. Cabal would have to take what mealier-mouthed governmental types might call 'executive action'. Cabal's term was much shorter and involved sticking his switchblade between Cacon's ribs. Sighing heavily, for he disliked violence generally and murder in particular, Cabal set off to commit violent murder.

His earlier walk around this district of Parila had already formed a reliable map in Cabal's well-ordered memory, and he knew that Cacon's alley would bring him out on to the Viale Ogrilla, a leafy avenue bounded by clothes shops and cafés. He set off at a fast trot down the road he was on, a long narrow street with an uncommonly high frequency of bookshops upon it called the Via Vortis, to intercept Cacon as he emerged from the end of the dog-legged alleyway.

At the corner, however, he had reason to slow down abruptly and affect a grand show of mannered nonchalance. Directly opposite the end of the alleyway, an officer of the *Polizia di Quartiere* was chatting up a waitress at a roadside café. Cabal could only watch and inwardly plan a rapid retreat as he watched Cacon emerge from the alley and head directly for the policeman. After he crossed the road and was a mere couple of metres from the café, however, he turned to his left and started walking away from Cabal and, indeed, the policeman. Cabal dropped his plans for immediate flight and watched perplexed as Cacon wandered off. No, that wasn't accurate. Cacon was emphatically not wandering. Rather, he was walking with definite intent up the Viale Ogrilla in the direction of its junction with the Via Pace. This was all very mysterious.

Cabal checked his watch to see how long he had until he had to be at the railway station, but his interest in running was being chipped away by pure curiosity. What on Earth did Cacon think he was up to? He checked his watch again, just to give him a moment to think. He had time to follow Cacon for perhaps five minutes before the need to complete his purchases and get to the station became overriding. It probably wouldn't be very difficult to follow him undetected; the sun was almost down and the pale stone of the buildings was already glowing a darkening blue. Very well then, he decided. Five minutes, and no more. Walking like a man enjoying a stroll on the way home from work, Cabal set off after Cacon.

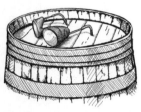

Chapter 12

IN WHICH THE GLOVES COME OFF

Cacon was evidently not in the mood for window-shopping. He moved up the Viale Ogrilla like a man with a mission, moving from the right-hand side of the avenue back over to the left as he reached the junction with the Via Pace. Cabal had no trouble shadowing him; he had no interest at all in watching his own back, his attention being focused entirely to his forward quarter. Cabal watched him vanish round the corner, then dog-trotted in pursuit, in a semi-casual 'If I'm late home for dinner again, my wife will kill me' sort of way. He still took the corner cautiously himself. He had half an idea that Cacon really was a Mirkarvian agent after all and might be waiting in ambush, but this proved fallacious. Cacon was already fifty metres away, on the kerbside of the pavement, walking at a fast pace and sometimes craning his head to the right as if looking for something or somebody that was just obscured by the line of buildings. Curioser and curioser.

Opposite the Church of San Giovanni Decollato was the western end of the Via Vortis, where Cabal had first espied Cacon, and it was on to this road that Cacon turned. Cabal followed to the corner and looked round it more than a little suspiciously. The only reason he could imagine anybody walking so fixatedly around the same buildings was to see if he was being pursued. That would depend on Cacon actually checking his back, but he never did. An alternative occurred to him. Perhaps Cacon was shadowing somebody else? But, in that case, whoever this third member of the chain was, why were they circling the buildings too? Perhaps Cabal was doing the wrong thing; perhaps instead of following Cacon widdershins round the triangle of buildings until boredom set in or shoe leather gave out, he should reverse his path and discover of whom Cacon was in such single-minded pursuit.

No, he realised after a brief second, that was a bad idea as it would mean walking straight into the unknown prey, if prey they were and not hunted predator. Instead, he would wait in ambush. Cacon had already passed the end of the alleyway he had originally used between the Via Vortis and the Viale Ogrilla, apparently intending to go at least as far as the junction where the two met on the edge of the Piazza Bior. That was good enough for Cabal; he would wait in the alleyway working on the hypothesis that the third man would circle the route at least once more. The dusk was gathering rapidly, for which he was grateful as it allowed him to lurk with an excellent chance of going unseen.

He found a dark corner between a drainpipe and a barrel half full of food wrappers, and was just turning to see how good a view of the Via Vortis it afforded him when he received a resounding slap across the face that snapped his head to one side and sent his dark spectacles flying. In the moment between impact and turning his head back to glare at his attacker, he realised two things. First, that the dusk wasn't quite as gloomy as it had seemed from behind smoked glass, and second, that Leonie Barrow had got out of custody with remarkable alacrity.

'*Guten abend*, Fräulein Barrow,' he said, watching her guardedly as he recovered his spectacles. It was obviously becoming too dark to wear them, so he slid them into his breast pocket instead. 'How pleasant to see you.'

Miss Leonie Barrow, for her part, called him something utterly frightful that she had never ever called anybody in her life before and that even her father – career policeman that he had been – had only ever heard a handful of times, and then kicked Cabal hard on the shin.

Cabal was a great fan of dignity in general and of his own in particular, and managed to keep the hopping down to two low springs before overcoming the sharp and penetrating pain.

'How bloody dare you? How could you? I gave you a chance and this is how you repay me?' she shouted at him. 'I could have handed you over right there! Right on the first night, as soon as I saw your pasty, smug face in the salon! I must have been demented not to! I need my bloody head examining!'

Cabal wasn't giving her his full consideration. He was mindful that the mysterious third man might be walking past on the Via Vortis in front of him, and that at the end of the alley behind him on the Viale Ogrilla there was a police constable who, if he could tear his attention away from the waitress at the café, might wonder what all the commotion was about down the alley. Cabal had an ugly intimation that Miss Barrow would tell him, too. She needed to be quiet . . . *he* needed her to be quiet, and quickly. To his small credit, he only considered stabbing her and dumping her body in the barrel for no more than a very few seconds, although he did get as far as targeting her solar plexus for the fatal incision (followed by angling the blade upwards to penetrate the diaphragm and aorta), and gripping the knife in his pocket before dissuading himself.

Instead, he put his left hand over her mouth, and forced her up against the wall. The suddenness of the move shocked her into compliance, her only reaction being an alarmed widening of her eyes. He locked his gaze to hers, raised his right index finger to his lips, and whispered with harsh impressiveness, 'Shush . . .'

Miss Barrow bit his palm. He snatched it from her mouth with a muffled curse that hadn't been sounded since the destruction of a pre-human species, much given to foul utterances that surpassed even man's aptitude for filthy imagery. Even to this long-vanished race, however, what Cabal said would have been considered a bit naughty.

He almost backhanded her, but with a massive effort of will, reining in a burning desire to create pain, he prevented himself. Instead, he stood glaring at her, hand raised. She flinched a little, but only a little. Finally, shaking with bubbling violence, he lowered his gloved hand and examined the palm.

'You've left teeth marks on the leather,' he said, for lack of anything else civil to say. She started to say something, but he raised a finger to her lips. 'Before you utter another syllable, ask yourself two questions. First, what would you have done in my place? And second, what am I doing hiding up an alleyway, anyway? And, no, it wasn't to get away from you, as should be evident by both my surprise at your liberty and by the fact that you found me so easily.'

'I wish I'd told the captain about you.'

'If wishes counted for anything, neither of us would be in our current situations, Miss Barrow. You concede that I had no choice, however?'

'No.'

'Close enough. Which brings us to my second question. If you would care to join me behind this barrel, I will explain.'

'Behind that barrel?' Now she was no longer looking at

him as if he were the very epitome of evil, but just rather mad.

'Yes. With some urgency, please. Time is short.'

'You're not going to stab me, are you?' she asked, mindful of the knife he'd used to defend himself when he was attacked aboard the *Princess Hortense*.

'I was, but it would have been impolite. Believe me, if I was going to kill you, you would already have breathed your last, instead of using said breath to yack tediously at me. Behind the barrel, please. *Now*.'

Shaken by Cabal's admission that her murder had crossed his mind, but been dispensed with for logical rather than moral or compassionate reasons, she allowed herself to be steered into hiding. From a cautious crouch, they surveyed the Via Vortis in the darkening twilight.

After a minute of boiling resentment slowly reducing to a simmer, Miss Barrow asked, 'What are we waiting for?'

'Not what,' answered Cabal in a whisper. 'Who.'

Miss Barrow analysed this reply in silence for a moment, found it lacking, and asked, 'Very well, then. For whom are we waiting?'

'I don't know. Let's wait and find out, shall we?' If he was aware of the filthy look that Miss Barrow gave him, he did nothing to indicate it.

'So,' she said with indignant sarcasm, 'We are hiding behind a barrel in a town that I believe neither of us have ever visited before, waiting for somebody that you don't know. From behind a barrel. I think the barrel aspect of this situation bears repeating.'

Cabal considered saying that if she would prefer to be dead as a doornail and head down in the barrel, it still wasn't too late for him to organise that for her, but he did not. Instead, he kept his attention on their view of the road and waited for somebody indefinably suspicious to walk by. Unfortunately, to Cabal's finely honed sense of paranoia, they all looked suspicious.

'That one looks dangerous,' he whispered, to which Miss Barrow replied, 'He's about nine.'

'That one is hanging around,' he whispered, to which Miss Barrow replied, 'He's sweeping the street.'

'That one is an obvious agent,' he whispered, to which Miss Barrow replied, 'He's a blind man, selling matches, pencils, and shoelaces.'

'That's what he wants you to think.'

'He's doing a brilliant job, in that case. Look, he's moving on.' She slapped Cabal's shoulder. 'I don't even know what I'm doing here. I should be pressing charges against you. Not waiting for God only knows who in some back alley in Parila. Behind a barrel. I'm mad. I must be. After all you've done, I must be mad. Not even *after all you've done* in general, but just *after all you've done* to me today.' She looked at Cabal, bewildered by herself. 'Why am I doing this?'

'Simplicity itself. Firstly, my ruse with the falsified bulletin must have been rapidly seen through.'

'No.' She shook her head wearily. 'You're too good a forger, it seems.'

'Oh?' A slow smile of wry amusement appeared on his face. 'Why, Miss Barrow . . . are you a *fugitive?*'

'No! Nothing so . . . you. They checked their files and couldn't find a "Johanna Cabal", only a "Johannes". So they decided there was no conspiracy, just a bureaucratic cock-up somewhere along the line. They're a very pragmatic bunch, the Senzans. The lieutenant who arrested me gave me his personal apology. Then he asked me out to dinner.'

Cabal grunted under his breath. 'Most pragmatic.'

'He was busily kissing my hand when Miss Ambersleigh turned up with half of the British Consulate in tow. Things were explained, and they asked if I wanted to make a formal complaint.'

'Did you?'

'Well, no.' She seemed a little embarrassed. 'It seemed a bit rude, what with him kissing my hand and everything.'

'And everything?' he echoed with disdain.

She shot him a dirty look. 'You like to pretend you're some sort of pure scientist without a human feeling in your body, but you're just a horrid little man really, aren't you, Cabal?'

Cabal had no answer, or at least no answer that he cared to make, so they crouched in silence for a minute longer.

Cabal checked his watch. 'I may have miscalculated,' he said. 'We should have seen something by now. In fact,' he looked up at the road as he replaced his pocket watch, 'we should have seen Cacon by now.'

'Cacon? From the aeroship? I thought you said you didn't know who you were waiting for?'

'I wasn't waiting for Cacon. I was waiting for the man Cacon was following.'

'Who's that?' Miss Barrow was growing more confused by the second.

'I don't know. I thought I'd already explained that?'

'You haven't explained anything. This is the first I've heard that Cacon is somehow mixed up in all this. Why is Cacon following somebody anyway?'

'I don't know,' said Cabal testily. 'That's why I was waiting for him to pass by.'

'I don't understand any of this.'

'Neither do I. Do you think I hide behind barrels in shadowy alleyways for fun? No, I don't,' he said to head off Miss Barrow, whom he felt sure was about to say that it wouldn't surprise her at all. 'There is something going on, and it has to do with the murders.'

'Probable murder and suicide, you mean?'

'Oh, please.' Cabal was splendidly dismissive. 'DeGarre is murdered for some reason, then when the suicide story falls flat, Zoruk is incriminated. The killer makes a hash job of it, and eliminates Zoruk before the shortcomings in the charade can be exposed, not realising that it's too late.'

'Lady Ninuka's alibi for him, you mean,' said Miss Barrow.

'Exactly so. I have an inkling as to how DeGarre was dealt with, but killing Zoruk is a different matter. The more that I think on the matter, the more solid Schten's ridiculous concept of a league of assassins becomes.'

'That makes me think of magicians and their stage illusions, you know. They pull off half their stuff because they are prepared to do the most incredible feats of engineering, far beyond what the audience thinks is reasonable for a small effect. Just because something seems ridiculous, doesn't mean it isn't true.'

Cabal considered her words, and said, 'You have a very good point, and one that undermines the basis of much of my logic to date. I told Schten that he was a fool – although not in so many words – because this conspiracy of shadows flew in the face of Ockham's Razor. When given the choice between a simple explanation and a complex one, the simpler is usually the truth. That's why I believed in Zoruk's suicide for an unconscionably long time. I've been an idiot, though. "Usually" is a long way indeed from "always". As with the whole "Johanna Cabal" nonsense – you may hate me for it now, but you will dine out on it for a year, I assure you – they preferred to believe in incompetence rather than a forged document. But, the document *was* forged.' He looked seriously at her. 'And there *are* conspiracies out there. I've stood too close to several to deny their existence. In a hotbed of intrigue like these little states, so small that you can drop a penny and it will roll over half a dozen international borders before coming to a halt, and where everyone hates their neighbours, plots and conspiracies are endemic.'

Leonie Barrow looked at him with a strange expression, her pale skin blue and shadowed by the failing light, her eyes dark and bottomless. 'Cabal . . .' she whispered.

'Yes?' he replied.

'How . . .' She paused, searching for the words. Her gaze fell, and then rose again, and she looked deep into his eyes. 'How did you ever become so very fucked up?'

Cabal sighed. He knew it wasn't even intended as an insult. It didn't matter; he had no answer. He looked back out on to the street. 'Cacon's gone,' he said, rising from his crouch. 'He didn't come back round this way again. You can stop hiding down there. Unless you've developed a taste for it, of course.'

She had not, and rose, patting the dust off her skirt. 'If anybody sees me coming out of a side street with you, and I'm even a bit dishevelled, I swear I will never live it down.'

'Nor I,' said Cabal offhandedly. 'I wonder where he went? Let's see if we can find him.' He walked out on to the Via Vortis, and looked both ways. There was no sign of Herr Cacon.

Miss Barrow joined him, albeit in a poor temper. 'Why? He's just an odd little man. Why are you so interested in him?'

'You didn't see him. He was like a man with a mission.' He started walking and Miss Barrow had to scuttle a little to catch up. 'Not the sort of man I would normally associate with missions. Would you? He was behaving curiously, and since recent events render that which is curious, suspicious, then I want to know what he was up to.'

'Oh, come on,' she laughed disbelievingly. 'Are you telling me that you suspect a pug in a bad suit like Cacon of crawling around the ship's vents and trying to throw you to your doom? You're kidding me.'

'I am kidding nobody,' he said icily, then reconsidered. 'Well, apart from everybody who thinks that I'm a Mirkarvian civil servant called Gerhard Meissner, obviously. Them, I am kidding. In this case, however, I am sincere. I do not believe he attacked me, true, but I suspect he may know who did.'

'Based on what? Masculine intuition?'

'Based,' said Cabal, beginning to chafe under all the unwarranted sarcasm, 'upon the weight of probabilities.' They had by this point reached the Piazza Bior with no sign of Cacon. Cabal looked up the Viale Ogrilla, and frowned when he remembered the policeman at the café. He turned to Miss Barrow and, with evident reluctance, offered her his arm.

She regarded it with equally evident suspicion. 'What's this?'

Cabal forbore to state the obvious and said, 'It would help us go unnoticed if we looked like people who can actually bear to be in one another's company.'

'I'm not a good enough actress for that, Cabal.'

'I'm not asking you to look as if you dote upon my every word and glow with happiness in my mere presence . . .'

'That's lucky.'

'I just need you to look as if you don't loathe me.'

'I'm *really* not a good enough actress for that. Why the sudden concern?'

'There's a café up there, where there is a police officer busily derelicting his duty . . .'

'Hold on. There's no such verb as *to derelict*.'

'There is now. Would you kindly stop interrupting? There is a police officer, and I do not wish to arouse his suspicions. Should he have eyes for anything other than the waitress, which I doubt. Therefore, it would help if we were to avoid obvious shows of animosity. Will you take my arm?'

Miss Barrow looked up the avenue, thinking. Then she

215

smiled at Cabal, and offered her arm. 'I should be delighted, Mr Cabal.'

Cabal took her arm, and they processed like old friends towards the café, or at least the sort of old friends in which the lady wears a somewhat smug smile while the gentleman scowls darkly. Cabal wasn't sure why she had suddenly consented to walk arm in arm with him, but he took it to be some sort of arch, feminine insult that he did not understand, nor did he care to try to understand. It was only when they were less than ten metres from the police officer that he realised how remarkably stupid he had been; so focused on looking for Cacon, he had regarded the policeman as nothing more than a trifling inconvenience that he could guard against by using Miss Barrow. Only now did he remember that using Miss Barrow in any ploy that involved being within calling-for-help range of an officer of the law while he stood right next to her was akin to searching for a gas leak with a flamethrower.

He thought he understood her well enough that she would be more interested in Cacon's activities than in just handing Cabal over to the police. But, that said, he *had* framed her as a necromancer and set the military on her, and she might still be a tad upset.

In any event, it was far too late to punch her and run. Instead, he had to touch his hat, smile as convincingly as he could, and say '*Guten Abend*, officer,' as the policeman noticed that he had company. The policeman's attention stayed on him so briefly that Cabal didn't know whether to be relieved or mortally insulted. He could have been wearing one of the more fetching 'Wanted' posters published in his wake* on a piece of string round his neck, and the officer

---

* He kept a collection, his favourite being the one with the decent wood-cut, the correct punctuation, and – a tiny bit of egotism here – the eye-wateringly large bounty on his head.

would not have noticed. Instead Cabal watched as his attention slid effortlessly across him like mercury in a pan to settle on Leonie Barrow.

'*Buona sera*, Signorina,' he said, failing to acknowledge Cabal altogether. If he had applied the same observational skills to crime scenes and suspects as he did to ascertaining Miss Barrow's marital status, he would have made *Capo della Polizia* before he was thirty. As it was, that seemed unlikely. At this precise moment, for example, he was far less interested in Cabal's awkward body language and rictus-like smile than in whether women were more interesting when they were dark and passionate like the waitress, or pale and interesting like the beautiful lady out walking with the undertaker or clerk or whatever he was.

Miss Barrow barely looked at him. 'Good evening, Constable,' she said, and walked on. Cabal gave her a sideways glance that she pointedly failed to acknowledge. A few paces on, an argument broke out between the policeman and the waitress.

When they were safely past the café, Cabal said, 'I am unsure whether to thank you or demand an explanation.'

Miss Barrow did not reply for several paces before replying, 'The former, I hope. As I'm not sure why I didn't just grass you up like the scum you are.'

'That's uncanny. Are you channelling your father at the moment?'

Miss Barrow raised a hand in admonition. 'Please, Cabal. Please don't mention my dad, or I'll feel guilty that I didn't just do the right thing and stitch you up like a kipper.' She put her hand to her mouth. 'Even my dad doesn't talk like that. He would have understood not giving you up to the Mirkarvians,' she continued, otherwise unabashed, 'he's not a great fan of capital punishment. But he'd never understand why I didn't just hand you over to Constable Don Juan back there.'

'No,' said Cabal, remembering the implacable Frank Barrow, 'I don't think he would.'

'Don't get any bright ideas that I didn't do it because I think you're anything other than the monster that you are, Cabal. Under different circumstances you'd be under arrest right now. But . . .' she stopped, and Cabal stopped too. She looked up at him, frowning slightly, and serious. 'There's something going on. Something . . . wrong. Something terribly, terribly wrong. Something wicked and cruel that ate DeGarre and Zoruk and would have killed you too if it had had its way. It's worse than you, Cabal. I've understood you better than I ever wanted to, and part of that is knowing that you don't go looking for trouble. It just seeks you out, but that's something else. Whoever or whatever is behind what has happened over the past couple of days *makes* trouble. The kind of trouble that makes corpses, and I think it's only just beginning. I want to stop it before it leaves anybody else dead.'

'And how do I fit into this monster hunt of yours?'

She smiled, but there was little humour in it. 'Set a monster to catch a monster, Cabal.' She took his arm and started walking again. Cabal allowed himself to be drawn along, his mind distracted and distant.

By the time they reached the end of the avenue, the night had truly fallen. A lamplighter was busily hurrying along, lighting the gas lamps as he went, clearly behind schedule. They stepped aside to let him trot past, and turned on to the Via Pace. There was almost nobody about, it being the hour of the evening meal.

'Where from here?' asked Miss Barrow as they passed into the shadow of the San Giovanni Decollato.

Cabal gestured loosely across the road to the end of the Via Vortis. 'We go down there as far as the alleyway where you spotted me, and then we give it up as hopeless. Cacon, or at least whoever he was following, obviously stopped pacing around this triangle of the town, and the pair of them are long gone. After that,' he checked his watch, and swore mildly, 'I don't know. I was intending to leave town, but I've missed my train. I assume if I attempt it in the morning without your permission, the police will be watching the stations along all routes from here just as soon as you can warn them?'

'You assume correctly. I think you're right about Cacon. We'll try the *Princess Hortense*, I think. He's probably there.' She took a step, but was pulled up short by her arm linked with Cabal. He wasn't moving at all. She looked at him curiously. He was staring off into the middle distance, his nostrils flared, hardly moving. After a moment, he relaxed a little and felt her gaze. He glanced at her, apparently embarrassed. 'What is it?' she asked.

'I don't want you to make any frivolous comments. You obviously enjoy calling me a monster, and I'm not inclined to give you any more ammunition. However . . .' He flared his nostrils again and inhaled. 'However . . . I can smell blood.'

She looked at him in astonishment for a moment, and then sniffed experimentally. Perhaps it was just his words playing on her imagination, but she thought she could scent something warm and metallic on the warm evening air. 'Oh, God. I think you're right. Where's it coming from?'

Cabal looked around, questing. 'I think it's coming from . . . Ah. Actually, you're standing in it.'

To her credit Miss Barrow reacted in no more melodramatic a fashion than stepping back to study the dark, wet patch that had formed between the cobbles at the end of a small shadowed pathway that led down beside the church before joining the road. It looked black and oily under the yellow glow of the warming gaslight mantles, high atop their lamp-posts.

'That's a lot of blood,' she said with more detachment than Cabal was expecting.

'Not necessarily. A little blood goes a long way,' he replied a little ruefully, the voice of experience.

For her answer she daintily dipped the toe of her shoe into the patch. It went in quite a way. It seemed that the patch was just the surface of a deep pool that had formed where a cobble was missing. 'That's a lot of blood,' she repeated, and Cabal couldn't argue with that. It had to be the best part of a litre, and people tend to get very distressed when they find themselves missing such a large portion of their vital bodily fluids. That, or dead.

'There's a trail,' he said. There was indeed, but not one made up of drops. The pool had formed by blood running down the pathway for a metre or so, but shortly beyond that there was a broad, smeared trail of the stuff. It didn't take a great forensic talent to realise that whoever was bleeding had collapsed, and dragged themselves away further up the path. 'Odd. If I were badly wounded right next to a thoroughfare, I would head towards it, try to get help. Admittedly, it's quiet at the moment, but it's still the best choice.'

'Would you be thinking that straight if you were so hurt?' Miss Barrow was walking slowly up the path, following the trail.

Cabal didn't know. He also didn't know if they should be getting involved. 'This has nothing to do with us. We should go.'

'No. There's somebody terribly injured. They need help.'

'Help? Look how much blood there is, woman. They're dead. So, I repeat; we should go.'

She stopped and turned to look at him. In the darkness, he couldn't make out her expression, but her stillness unnerved him strangely. When she spoke, the tone was tired and dismissive, but he thought he heard something else there that he couldn't quite identify. Perhaps it was disgust. Perhaps it was disappointment. 'Go then, Cabal. Just shoo. I'm done with you.' She turned her back on him and continued to follow the trail of blood.

He watched her, while he failed to do anything: he failed to come up with a witty retort; he failed to say anything very profound regarding their unusual relationship; he failed to walk away with dignity. He only succeeded in opening his mouth and closing it again, undecided, and – as her back was to him – she didn't even see that. He was still standing there impassively thirty seconds later when she became tired of being stared at. In that time she hadn't progressed very far, the blood becoming increasingly difficult to see in the shadows.

'Just bugger off, will you, Cabal? You're in my light. If you aren't going to—'

The groan that shuddered out of the darkness made her spin round with a small yelp of surprise. It was a barely human sound, deep and miserable, but Cabal – who had far too much experience in such things – realised that it definitely was human. It seemed he had been wrong to believe that the donor of the blood on the cobblestones was dead, although by the sounds of it that error would be moot in a few minutes. Checking his knife was easily accessible in his jacket pocket, he followed Miss Barrow as she walked as quickly as she dared into the shadows.

A few paces on, she paused. 'It wasn't far away,' she whispered, ready to be quiet immediately she heard anything else. 'There's a side door here.' Cabal heard a handle being tried. 'It's locked.'

He stood beside her. The shape of the door frame was just visible in the shadows. Further along the wall beside it was a shuttered window. 'Are you sure this is where that groan came from?' he asked, whispering too.

'Must be.' She squinted into the darkness beyond them. 'I don't think there's anywhere else it could have come from. It just looks like blank walls after this house.' She tapped experimentally at the ground past the door, and then turned back to him all business. 'The cobbles don't seem tacky past the door. I think the trail stops here. We need to get in somehow. Can you pick locks?'

'No,' said Cabal shortly, and kicked the door open. He stepped through and stood in the dark while checking his pockets. Miss Barrow heard a rattle and suddenly a match flared in Cabal's hand. He quickly held the match away from himself to save his eyes from the sudden light, and shielded it further with his free hand. In the reflected glow from the walls, they saw the door opened into a narrow hallway. At the end, a staircase ascended a few steps on to a landing before turning to the left. In the unsteady light, there seemed to be a widening in the hallway just before the stairs and the hint of another door leading further back into the house. To the right was a small dresser with a tray on which sat a candle in a holder. Finally, a door stood half open in the wall to their left. Cabal glanced down. The blood trail angled beneath his feet and through the door. A single smeared bloody handprint showed on the whitewashed plaster by the base of the frame.

He took a moment to light the candle, and lifted it. He stood before the half-open door and favoured Miss Barrow with a sideways glance in which only a grim necessity was decipherable. Then he turned his attention back to the door. With the fingertips of his gloved left hand, he gently pushed it open.

Chapter 13

IN WHICH CABAL PRACTISES NECROMANCY
AND WAYS ARE PARTED

Cacon had seen better days. To be precise, every day up to this one had been better, for today was the day that some unkind soul had stuck a long, thin-bladed knife into him and twisted it, and so murdered him.

He lay in a dark pool of his own blood in the middle of the barely furnished room. Cabal stood over him and noted the pallor, the slow drip of blood between the floorboards, and the slight quiver of Cacon's eyelids as he prepared to breathe his last.

'Dear God, Cabal!' Miss Barrow was past him, and kneeling by Cacon's supine body. 'Don't just stand there! He's still alive!'

Cabal was going to say, 'But not for long,' when he thought ahead and just knew that this would result in Miss Barrow doing a lot of moralistic shouting in his face that he could well do without. So instead, noting that the windows were already closed and shuttered, he set the gas going in the two mantles in the room and lit them cautiously from his candle. Now, at least, Cacon could die in decent visibility.

Miss Barrow had meanwhile, with an admirable disdain for ladylike decorum, opened Cacon's jacket, and torn open his shirt. The knife wound was instantly apparent despite the mass of venous blood around it. A blade-wide slit forced open by the twist of the blade, it lay in his skin like a single gill cover of a pale cave fish, his life pulsing weakly from it in time to his slowing heart. She tore a strip from his shirt, folded it into a thick wad, and held it over the wound, pressing down hard, trying to hold his soul to his body by the strength of her arms.

'Do something, Cabal! Do something! Get help!' She looked up at him and, suddenly, Cabal understood that she had never seen death at first hand. The realisation sent a cool shiver of remembrance through him, back to when this had been him, kneeling over somebody and willing them back to life. And failing. Now, he could only stand, and watch, and see the signs of imminent, inevitable death, and he felt nothing. Miss Barrow looked up at him, and she didn't even like Cacon, but there were tears in her eyes. 'Do something, Cabal. *Please!*'

He knelt to the other side of Cacon, unconsciously avoiding the blood, and leaned in close. 'Alexei. Alexei! Can you hear me?'

Cacon's eyelids flickered, but beneath them, his eyes rolled drunkenly in their sockets. Cabal gripped the side of Cacon's head and drew up one eyelid high using the pad of his thumb. It was rough treatment and Miss Barrow started to speak, but Cabal quenched it with a glance. She fell silent, finally understanding that the man was going to die, and that there was nothing either of them could do about it.

'Alexei Cacon! Listen!' Cabal spoke loudly and clearly into Cacon's face, demanding a response. 'Who did this to you? Who stabbed you? Cacon? Tell me!'

He tried. Cacon truly tried. He drew together what was

left of his consciousness and tried to force words out through his mouth, his garrulous mouth that had always seemed so eager to gabble on about nothing in particular. Now it wouldn't respond properly, and his jaw flapped and his tongue lay stubbornly still. He felt thirsty, terribly thirsty, but he couldn't ask for water, he couldn't ask for anything at all. The dark shapes above him that might have been people grew darker still. Cacon felt so thirsty and so tired. He would have a little sleep, and ask for water when he awoke, because we always wake up from sleep. And so Cacon died.

They stayed in tableau for some moments afterwards, Cabal deep in thought, and Miss Barrow uncertain as what to do. She rose awkwardly and sat on an upright chair near the window.

Cabal didn't seem to notice. He stayed silent for a little longer, then closed Cacon's eyes and laid his head down. 'Typical, Cacon. Not just of you, but of our whole unhappy race. Prattling importunately over nothing, but when you have your chance to say something important, silence. Typical.'

He stood up, brushing off his knees as he rose.

'Well, it won't do. We need to know who killed him.'

'We?' said Miss Barrow, too tired and sick at heart to speak with passion. 'Need?'

'Very well. *I* need. It seems unlikely that this isn't all associated with events on the aeroship, which means whoever stabbed Herr Cacon may well be whoever tried to kill me. I don't like leaving unknown enemies in the shadows. They have a habit of jumping out again. This business needs attending to, before I can move on.'

'Good. Good.' Miss Barrow seemed terribly weary all of a sudden. Cabal recognised a shock reaction when he saw one. He could have helped her, but it seemed too distracting when he had a murderer to find. 'We have to find the murderer. Good. How are we going to do it?'

'Your criminology degree doesn't suggest anything?' he said.

She didn't rise to the baiting. Indeed, it seemed unlikely she even noticed it. 'I'm still an undergraduate. I don't know what to do. I don't know.' She looked lethargically around the room as if noticing it for the first time. 'Dust for fingerprints? I don't know.'

'Fingerprints. Feh. Very useful in most circumstances but not when we know that he was stabbed outside and made his way here. I doubt his attacker even set foot inside the door.' He looked around the room. It was an odd house; sparsely furnished and with little sign of occupation. He frowned.

Miss Barrow was wondering the same thing. 'What is this place, anyway? Who lives here? I'm not sure anybody does. The air's stale, and there's a thin layer of dust.'

Cabal made no reply. Instead he took up the candleholder, relit the candle, and left the room. Miss Barrow found herself alone with the corpse. She felt she should be scared, or at least awed by the presence of death, the last great mystery. But the body was Cacon's, and he was as unimpressive in death as when he was alive. She sat staring at him and thinking how unlike a person a human body is, once the breath of life with all its pulses and beats and tics and movement are all gone. His corpse was pathetic – in that it inspired pathos – and pitiful – in that it aroused pity. She found herself feeling more sorry for Cacon than she had ever felt for anyone before. All hopes and dreams extinguished, all potential gone. If only she could wave a wand and make him breathe again, it would be the greatest gift that could be bestowed.

Cabal returned, shattering her reverie. 'I found this,' he said, and held up a key on a ring. 'It fits the lock. The one next to it is of the same pattern as the cabin keys aboard the *Princess Hortense*. It would be no surprise to discover it unlocks Cacon's stateroom.'

'So this is Cacon's place,' said Miss Barrow, with an apparent lack of interest. Cabal pursed his lips and was about to speak, when a spark of animation ran through her as her intellect stopped freewheeling in shock and started to re-engage her mind. 'But Cacon's Mirkarvian. Why would he have the keys to a house in Senza?'

Cabal wagged his finger at her tellingly. 'Exactly.'

'And the answer is?'

Cabal shrugged. 'I have no idea. But I know a man who does.'

She looked at him with eager interest. 'Who?' Infuriatingly, Cabal just raised his eyebrows and looked meaningfully at her. 'What? You? But you just said . . .' It took a second for her to understand him, but then her gaze fell to Cacon, and her mouth fell open in astonishment. Astonishment and horror. Definitely some horror. 'Oh, you have to be joking.'

'I never joke about my work,' he said, and was unable to suppress a malevolent smile at the end as the ramifications settled upon Miss Barrow.

'No! You can't. You absolutely must not, Cabal! It's . . . a monstrous crime. A terrible, terrible thing!'

'Is it? What is our alternative? Do you have a criminological department about your person to aid in the application of your towering forensic skills? You do not?' He simulated amazement, and did not trouble himself to simulate it well. 'Then we shall do things my way.' He made for the door.

'Where are you going?'

'For reagents. Not the ideal circumstances under which to gather them, but I think I can throw something together in a hurry that should give the hapless Herr Cacon one last shudder of animation.' Miss Barrow did not seem convinced. Impatient, for the first few minutes of a person's death are the most vitally important minutes of opportunity for a necromancer, Cabal added, 'Look, I have to go. Without the necessary chemicals, we'll lose whatever wits are still floating around his cooling brain. The only more immediate alternative that I can think of is a tantric ritual involving necrophiliac sodomy and, frankly, I don't think my back is up to it. So, if you will excuse me?'

And he left, inwardly treasuring Miss Barrow's expression.

The dispensing chemist and the general grocery stood next door to one another and both contained homes over the shops in which the chemist and the grocer respectively lived with their families, which was very convenient if you wanted to throw small pebbles at both sets of windows at much the same time.

The chemist was the first to respond. He swung open a window and looked down into the street through half-moon glasses. He was jacketless, his white hair slightly awry, and he had a napkin in his collar. 'Eh! What is it? Who are you? What do you want?'

Cabal finished writing a list in his notebook, tore out the page and held it up for the man to see. 'I need these supplies urgently.'

'What? What is that? Supplies?' Somebody said something behind him, and he turned away to reply, which involved a lot of arm-waving and extravagant shrugging. He returned his attention to Cabal. 'I'm having my dinner!'

'A man's life is at stake,' said Cabal, not entirely untruthfully.

'Eh?' The chemist looked him up and down. 'You're a doctor?'

Cabal's expression twisted in a way that seemed to suggest *If my gun hadn't been confiscated in Mirkarvia, I would currently be in the process of shooting you.*

'No,' he said with crystalline iciness, 'I am not a doctor, but these supplies are vitally important.'

As he spoke, the door of the general grocery swung open and the grocer, a man of middle years but bearing a surprisingly full and raven-black head of hair, appeared. He stood straightening his thoroughly askew collar as he looked around and saw Cabal. 'Signor? Did you cast stones upon my casement?'

'I did,' said Cabal. 'I have an urgent requirement from your shop.'

'Eh?' said the chemist. 'What is this? You are on an errand to collect vital medicine and yet you have time to bother Signor Bonacci? For what? Some nails, perhaps? A mop? I was having my dinner, Signor! Not so urgent, eh? Not so urgent!'

Cabal ignored him. To Signor Bonacci the grocer, he said, 'Dolly blue. Do you stock it?'

'Eh?' said the chemist. Cabal continued to ignore him.

'Dolly blue, you say?' said Signor Bonacci, clearly taken aback. 'What, the stuff housewives put in the last white rinse?'

'Specifically a mixture of indigo blue and starch. I need those chemicals.'

'Pah!' said the chemist. 'You're mad!' He started to close his window.

'I will pay double the price for a little alacrity, gentlemen,' Cabal said, loudly enough to be heard through the rapidly closing shutters. The shutters paused, and then reopened.

'Double?' said the chemist. 'Eh?'

*

Miss Barrow was sitting on the stairs in the house when Cabal returned. She had found and lit the gaslight in the hall and, judging by the muted glows, those towards the back of the house and upstairs. Cabal said nothing as he placed the paper bag containing his purchases on the dresser, and hung up his jacket and hat. Miss Barrow finally said, 'I've looked over the whole house. It's strange. Everything you could want to be comfortable is here: bedding, books, the larder is full of tinned and dried food. A lot of preserves in jars, too. But there isn't a single personal touch about the whole place. I can't see the personality of the owner. I don't understand why Cacon had a key for it. I would say it was rented, but I've never heard of food being supplied like that.'

Cabal kept his counsel. He had a theory about the house, but would wait to hear what Cacon had to say on the subject. Providing, of course, that the ad-hoc resurrection worked. He took up the paper bag and went into the room where Cacon lay, pausing at the doorway to ask Miss Barrow, 'Do you want to see this?' She looked at him, her eyes tired and haunted. Cabal tried again. 'You might find it . . . educational.' She didn't respond, just staring at him through the banisters.

Cabal went into the room alone. Miss Barrow sat silent and motionless on the stair. She heard the crackle of the paper bag being opened, and its contents removed and checked. Shortly thereafter, she heard the fizz of powders being tipped on to flames and smelled pungent chemical fumes drifting through the crack of the ajar door. Cabal started chanting under his breath, a strange singsong in a language she didn't recognise, that she doubted more than a handful of people in the world would recognise. Then, defying a reluctance that would have joyfully driven her from that house, that town, that very country, she climbed to her feet and walked slowly down the couple of steps to the boards of the hallway, and into the front room. Cabal's chanting paused, then continued.

Twelve minutes later, Alexei Cacon returned from the dead.

The room stank like a laboratory fire, and the thick chemical fug made Miss Barrow's eyes sting. Cabal ignored it all, his own eyes screwed shut as he chanted and chanted a seemingly endless litany of inhuman words from an inhuman religion. They were awful words, incomprehensible to her, but jagged, ugly things that he spat out like stones and razors. That he knew them by heart did not escape her, and she feared him for that, for it showed depths in him that opened into the abyss. Nor did he hesitate when Cacon's heels began to rattle on the floor, his legs spasming like the galvanised corpse of a frog on a school science bench. It was death, but it was in reverse, and the most obscene abrogation of the laws of nature she could ever imagine. Life did not return easily to the carcass, but was bullied and coerced, and what little dignity there is in death was torn and tattered by this sordid reversal. Cacon seemed to swell with something that was just close enough to life to serve, but equally, she sensed in her every fibre that it was a poor sort of stopgap and that it would leak away again soon enough. When Cacon started to shake and suck in ragged, dry breaths, she shuddered with revulsion, but she could not stop watching.

Cabal did not notice her reaction. He checked the second hand on his pocket watch and started a new, more urgent chant. The ritual as a whole would only give him a few seconds in which to interrogate Cacon, providing this last stage succeeded in nailing his soul back into his body, a relationship that would perforce prove to be a delicate one.

Cacon's eyes fluttered open. 'Oooh! Right in me guts, that was! Ruined me vest and that was fresh on this morning. Still, mustn't grumble.' His eyes managed to stop on Cabal's face and went most of the way towards focusing. 'Hullo, Herr Meissner! You found me then? Very good, very good. I thought, "Cacon, me old fruit bat, I would say you're just about stuffed. You've been left for dead, and that's what you'll be, oh, any minute now, I'd so, yes." Not dead, though, am I? Result! Alexei Cacon, one! Grim Reaper, nil!'

'Cacon, you're dying,' said Cabal bluntly, painfully aware of the vital seconds already wasted.

'Cabal!' said Miss Barrow, snapped from profound horror to mannered indignity at such rudeness. She already had her hand to her mouth when he shot her a furious look.

'What? How's that?' Cacon tried to look around, but his reanimation was barely enough to get him talking again, and his head was too heavy for his enervated neck to move. 'Who's there?' What Cabal had just said filtered through at about that moment, and he looked back at him with an expression of offended rectitude. 'Dying? What d'you mean, *dying*? I feel as right as rain, me ol' mucker. Just let me have a bit of a rest, and I'll be back up on me hind legs, hopping around like a kangaroo, full of rude health!'

'Of course you will,' said Cabal tersely, in what he believed was an acceptable bedside manner. He was mistaken in this. 'Now quickly, Cacon, tell me. This is urgent. Who stabbed you?'

'Stabbed me? Pshaw! A mere flesh wound. I've had worse shaving.'

'I doubt it . . .'

'It just bled a bit.' He considered, while Cabal – impatience rising – checked his watch again. 'It bled quite a bit, true. It . . .' The complacent expression turned to one of realisation, and then fear. It seemed Cacon had sped from denial to understanding with a rapidity that might have dismayed his circumlocutory mores had he been generally less gutted and exsanguinated. 'Oh, bloody hell! I remember now! I'm dying!'

'Quite so. Your time is short, Herr Cacon. Make these seconds count for something, I beg you. So, again . . . who stabbed you?'

Cacon's face bore a rictus of terror. 'Help me!'

'Then help me! *Who stabbed you?*'

Cacon's eyes swept from side to side, and their light was beginning to fade. Cacon's brief curtain call to the world's stage was already coming to an end.

Cabal took him by the lapels and shook him furiously. 'Cacon, you *verdammt* fool! If you don't tell me who did this to you, they will escape! Is that what you want? *Is it?*'

Cacon said something, but the words were lost as his head rolled back. 'What?' barked Cabal. 'What was that you said?' He held Cacon still and listened closely, his ear an inch from Cacon's mouth.

In the sudden stillness, Cacon's next words were perfectly audible even to Miss Barrow where she sat some feet away.

'I saw her . . . I saw her following you, Meissner.'

Cabal's astonishment could only have been greater if Cacon had told him he'd been stalked by an allosaurus in twinset and pearls. 'Her? A woman?'

Cacon rallied enough to say, 'Yes, a woman. Flamin' Nora, Meissner! It's a bad time to need lessons on the blinkin' objective form of the singular feminine nominative, isn't it?'

Cabal had been insulted by enough dead men not to concern himself. 'This woman, who was she?'

'Following you. I thought, "O-ho, what's this, Rovetta? Young love? Not with that viperess!" So I cut up the alley, went 'round. Get b'hind, see?'

Cacon had started slurring. Cabal knew his synapses were firing their last, but there was so much he needed to know.

'Rovetta?' said Miss Barrow. 'Who's Rovetta?' Cabal shot her a furious look, but Cacon answered all the same.

'Rovetta's me. 'S my name. Arturo Rovetta. 'Smee.' He frowned. 'Your voice has gone all high, Meissner, mate.'

Cabal could see that Cacon – or Rovetta so it seemed – had reached the stage where his brain was no longer capable of doing the complex work necessary to lie. *In morte veritas.*

'Went 'roun' an' 'roun' an' 'roun' 'til I los' 'er. Thought, "Ah, sod it." Wen' to safe 'ouse and there she wasss . . . "Ullo!" says I. "Bam!" she goes. Stiletto righ' in me gizzards. Don' hurt so much now. Don' hurt a' all. Goin' all dark. Goin' allllll dark . . .' His eyes lost focus and Cabal knew it was too late to ask him any more questions. There was a silence broken only by the rasp of Cacon's shallow breaths. 'Eh, Meissner, me ol' . . . me ol' . . . thingy. Guess wha'. You'll never . . . guess wha' . . .'

'What is it, Rovetta?' The bark had completely gone from Cabal's voice. Miss Barrow watched him, surprised and a little perturbed by how gentle he had become, how quietly he spoke.

'I 'ave . . . the oddest feelin' I've done this before . . . Déjà vu, isn't it, ol' son? Déjà vu . . .'

Then Alexei Cacon . . . Arturo Rovetta . . . died for the second and final time.

Ten minutes later, Cabal was sitting in the upright chair that Miss Barrow had been using. He could hear her pacing back and forth upstairs. When Cacon had died, she had made a sound in her throat somewhere between a gasp and a sob, and fled the room. Cacon lay still and cold on the floor, covered with a sheet from the bedding cupboard. Cabal sat with his hands in his lap, fingers interlaced, and he stared at the body, thinking. False names, safe houses, shadows, and murder; it seemed he had been right all along about Cacon being an agent, but with a true name like 'Rovetta', Cabal had evidently put him in the wrong camp.

All of which raised the question, why was Cacon – Cabal found it impossible to think of him as Rovetta – aboard the *Princess Hortense* in the first place? It was possible he was just leaving Mirkarvia at the completion of a mission, or a placement, or whatever it is that the less dynamic spies do. That idea didn't appeal to Cabal, though; with a potential revolution fomenting in Mirkarvia, it would certainly be in Senza's best interests to keep as many intelligence agents and agents provocateurs on the ground as possible, all the better to pour fuel on its enemy's troubles. So, the weight of probability was that he was aboard the *Princess Hortense* for a particular reason, that might or might not have something to do with DeGarre and Zoruk's deaths.

Cabal cupped his hands over his mouth and nose and sighed heavily. As a scientist, he was used to evolving his knowledge by developing a hypothesis and then building a bridge of experimental and evidential proof that got him from where he was to where his hypothesis suggested he could go. Sometimes the hypothesis was flawed and the bridge could not be completed, but even that failure was potentially useful in itself. Here, however, he lacked the most basic things; he had no hypothesis that linked everything together. He had a retired engineer, a feckless and naive student of politics, a Senzan secret agent – all dead – and himself, victim of an attempted murder. He could not escape the likelihood that politics was behind all these, and that each killing or attempted killing might have different motives, but that took him no further.

He was still sitting in a dismal brown study when Miss Barrow came quietly down the stairs and re-entered the room. She couldn't help but glance at the sheet-covered body on the floor, before saying to Cabal, 'Sorry.'

'Sorry?' Cabal lifted his head. 'Sorry for what, precisely?'

'For . . .' She tried to find words, failed, and gestured vaguely in the direction of upstairs. 'I was a little upset. I can't say why. I was upset the first time poor Mr Cacon . . . died. But the second time, that was so much worse. I don't know why.' She looked sideways at him, unhappy at confiding in the foul Herr Cabal, and unhappier still to ask him, 'Why would that be so?'

'Because you saw hope.' He got to his feet. 'We should go. His colleagues are bound to wonder where he is, and they will surely come here first. I do not think I care to explain all these interesting piles of burnt chemicals and chalk markings on the floor to them. They will doubtless show a lack of imagination as to my aims and a lack of sympathy as to my methods. And then torture and kill me.' He walked past her into the hall. She heard him putting on his jacket and hat as he added, 'It's only to be expected. Occupational hazard.' He reappeared in the doorway, straightening his cravat. 'I think we shall go out by the other exit. It's always nice not to have to traipse through a crime scene. Coming?'

To anybody who hadn't seen a man die twice in a room stinking of blood and burning dolly blue, it was a lovely evening. The sky was clear, the pavement cafés were doing a quickening trade as people came out to follow their evening meals with more evening meals, and lovers walked arm in arm, whispering secrets.

Miss Barrow, who had taken Cabal's arm for the purposes of blending in with the evening crowd, was whispering secrets in his ear, but of a nature that would have disappointed Cupid. They were murmurs of murder and murderers, daggers and death, necromancy and necessity.

'But you see the efficacy of my methods,' replied Cabal.

'Imagine if every murder victim had a chance to name his or her murderer. Think what a boon it would be.'

'No,' she said, quietly. 'It's monstrous. Dragging souls back into their bodies for the convenience of the living for a few muddled moments before sliding off into the shadows. Isn't dying once cruel enough?'

'Oh, you mustn't judge from that little display. That was just a party trick thrown together from easily available components and a few rarer items from my bag. If Cacon had died more quickly, or been poisoned, or a dozen other variables, it would not have worked at all. Even with a near-perfect subject to work with, there is only perhaps a one in three chance of the Asyrinth ritual you witnessed taking effect. We were lucky we got as much from him as we did.'

'Listen to yourself, Cabal. He wasn't a subject. He was a human being.'

Cabal's jaw tightened. 'I would ask you not to lecture me on morality. I don't take it kindly. Besides, you say "human being" as if it's something special. There are a lot of them about, you know, and few are worth the price of the calcium in their bones.'

'Most of us don't measure a person's worth in calcium!' she said, a little too hotly as she drew some confused glances from other walkers.

Cabal smiled quietly at suchlike, a smile he had spent painstaking minutes in front of the mirror bringing to a high finish, a smile that said *I will indulge your attention for a few seconds, but then you should really look away* with a pitch perfect subtext, barely discernible at a conscious level, that went *Or I shall run an open razor across your eyeball*. Everybody looked away.

Unperturbed, he murmured to Miss Barrow. 'And perhaps that's why there's so much wrong in the world. Calcium's quite my favourite alkaline earth metal. It should be more highly regarded.'

They walked in silence for a little while then, while Cabal wondered who Cacon's murderous 'viperess' might be, and Miss Barrow wondered if Cabal was serious about the ethical qualities of calcium. With anybody else it would have been a joke, but with Cabal, she couldn't be so sure.

'It's a small pool of suspects,' said Cabal, changing the subject from preferred elements. 'In the case of Cacon, at any rate. A woman, and I think given his comments, one from aboard the ship. Just four possibilities.'

'Lady Ninuka, Miss Ambersleigh, and – I suppose – Frau Roborovski. That's three. Who's the fourth?'

Cabal did not answer, but continued to promenade down the road, looking straight ahead. She finally understood, and it did not please her.

'Me? You suspect me? Oh, you're a piece of work, all right, Cabal.'

'There you go, thinking like a civilian, Miss Barrow,' Cabal chided her. 'Your father would be most upset to hear you talk like that.'

'Not nearly as upset as he would be to see me walking arm in arm with a bastard like you.'

Cabal nodded thoughtfully. 'That's a fair point. To return to the matter in hand, however, I cannot eliminate you as a subject, not least because you were in the area, and you did seem to be following me.'

'I just saw you lurking around that street! I followed you a hundred yards at most, and I didn't take a short break from following you to do in Cacon, the poor swine.'

'So you say.'

The suddenness with which Miss Barrow came to a halt jerked Cabal almost off his feet.

'Look, Cabal,' she glowered at him, 'I didn't do it. The

only criminal act I've committed to my knowledge on this trip was not handing you over to the authorities and, God knows, I'm regretting that.'

'It's not as if you're a prime suspect,' said Cabal, checking his shoulder for possible injury. 'But I cannot eliminate you; there simply isn't the evidence available that would allow me to do that. I do, however, admit that I think you're a less likely murderer than, say, Miss Ambersleigh, who is also low on my list.'

'Third place?' said Miss Barrow, somewhat mollified but working hard not to show it.

'Joint second, which puts you at fourth. She only makes second because I think she's as unlikely a candidate as Frau Roborovski. I can't draw a line between them.'

'Ah,' said Miss Barrow, starting to walk again. 'So you've plumped for the voyage's very own femme fatale, Lady Ninuka.'

'And you haven't?'

'I'm not even convinced Cacon was killed by a fellow passenger. The way he spoke, it could have been somebody he knew from elsewhere.'

'No,' said Cabal with finality. 'Remember he talked about "young love". That implies it was somebody known to me. Miss Ambersleigh is not young. Frau Roborovski is married. You . . .' He considered in silence for a moment. 'You, I may have to move up the rankings.' Then, quickly to quench her outrage, he added, 'Based purely on your age, but you are still a country mile behind the Lady Ninuka in my mind. Consider: she is demonstrably manipulative, mendacious, and self-centred to the point of sociopathy.' He noticed a faint smile on Miss Barrow's lips. 'What?'

'Nothing,' she said. 'I'm finding this very educational. Please, continue.'

'Furthermore, she is a member of the Mirkarvian gentry,

and they seem very political creatures. I'm sure they are read Machiavelli in the nursery, and practise by setting their dolls against one another. Nor are they above acting as their own agents. If you want a Senzan spy dead, sometimes you just have to do it yourself.'

'You might have something there,' she said, now sober. 'I heard that her father is somebody big in the government or the military.'

'It will be both. It's very hard to tell the two apart in Mirkarvia.'

'I overheard the purser gossiping with the chief steward, because she'd given one of the stewards a hard time over some stupid little thing she found to complain about. The purser said the steward should just grin and bear it, because if Lady Ninuka went running to her "daddy the count", things could get very sticky for him.'

This time it was Miss Barrow's turn to be jerked to a halt.

'This count,' said Cabal slowly. 'Would he have a name?'

'Yes, but I didn't remember it. I didn't think it was important.'

'Could it have been Marechal?'

'Yes! That was it. I remember thinking it was quite a French-sounding name for a Mirkarvian, but that's just the name of his fiefdom. Oh, that would be a *county*, wouldn't it? I'd never really thought about that before. Anyway, the land used to belong to a neighbouring state until some war ages and ages ago, and they kept the name for the title, but the family name is actually Ninuka. Thinking about it, I'm a bit surprised that a country that's so influenced by the German language doesn't use *Graf* instead of *Count*. "Graf Marechal." Hmmm.'

She looked closely at Cabal, but he had clearly stopped listening somewhere around 'Yes!'

'Ohhhhh,' she said, the smile coming back again. 'Friend of yours, is he?'

'Not in any recognised sense of the word, no. This puts a markedly different complexion upon matters.'

Miss Barrow's smile slipped. 'How?'

'My main interest in getting to the bottom of the affair has been part curiosity, but mainly a sense of reactive self-preservation.'

'What? Get them before they get you? Well, that's lovely. How about, to bring a murderer to justice?'

Cabal glanced at her, frowning slightly at such foolishness. 'What a quaint idea. No, I can honestly say that was never in my thoughts. The possibility of Marechal's involvement, however, puts a new emphasis on matters, which is to say, upon my life, and extending it beyond, say, tomorrow.'

Miss Barrow was taken aback. She had come to expect the unexpected with Cabal, but cowardice seemed out of joint with the architecture of his personality as she understood it. 'You're scared of him!'

Cabal raised an eyebrow at this impertinence. 'I would not characterise it as fear. Simply a desire not to be cut to bleeding chunks by a maniac with a cavalry sabre. More of a rational concern, really.'

'But the deaths . . .'

'Unfortunate, but we shall just have to congratulate the killer or – far more likely – killers on some murders well done, and bid him, her, or them a fond farewell. *Bon voyage, ma chère Hortense*, and try not to let your body count get any higher. We're well rid of the whole sordid affair.'

'Not *we*, Cabal.'

'Eh?'

'I'm rejoining the ship. I've decided to go all the way to Katamenia.'

'What? But why? Why rejoin the ship, that is. Any reason

for wanting to go to Katamenia is already beyond my understanding, but why put yourself in harm's way?'

'I can't just let whoever did this go, Cabal. I can't. To answer your question, because it's the right thing to do.'

Cabal's face tightened with ill-concealed anger. 'What your father would do, you mean.'

She smiled, a little wanly. 'It's the same thing. It usually is.'

'Your father's a busybody.'

'My father,' replied Miss Barrow, gently disengaging her arm from Cabal's, 'is a good man. But he's at home, back in Penlow on Thurse, so I shall have to do this.' She started to walk away, back towards the aeroport, but paused after a few steps. 'I doubt we'll meet again.'

'I doubt it too. You're playing Mirkarvian roulette, Miss Barrow. Much like the Russian version, but with only one empty chamber.'

They stood in the gaslit street alone, the other evening walkers already at their tables speaking of love and life and happier subjects than lowering death. Miss Barrow's face was difficult to make out in the shadow of her hat, but Cabal could see the skin of her cheek, pale and sickly in the flickering yellow light. She was scared, just as she was brave, just as she was doomed. He could almost see the chain of events that would surely follow: she would ask questions, she would make somebody nervous, and she would die.

'Miss Barrow, whatever else you think of me, know this. I abominate death. I deal in it, but I loathe it. Your intentions reek of it and, if you return to the ship, the path of your life will be a short one, I am sure.'

'You want me to stay here in Senza.'

'It would be wisest.'

'Whoever's behind these crimes would go free in that case. The captain seems a good man, but he's out of his depth. If Ninuka is behind all this, he can't do anything anyway. She could stand in front of him with blood on her hands and he'd trot off to get her a basin to wash them in. It's more than his career . . . it's more than his *life* is worth to do otherwise. I can make a fuss, because I'm a foreigner, and I have my country behind me.'

'If you imagine your country would go to war just because some silly girl gets herself killed, you are a fool.'

'Perhaps I am. But God looks after fools and little children, doesn't he? *Auf Wiedersehen*, Herr Cabal.' He stood and watched as she walked away.

'Goodbye, Miss Barrow,' he said to himself with a heavy finality.

CATALOGUE No.:   00153342

AUTHOR: UNKNOWN (vide infra)

TITLE: Principia Necromantica

EDITION: C. 1820, demy 4to. Printer &
                    publisher unknown.

GENERAL CLASS: Restricted (under absolute
                    interdiction)

NOTES:

Other known editions: John Rylands Library, Manchester,
                    Great Britain. Incunabulum, with
                    marginalia. Earliest known, C16.
                    Subsequent editions have textual
                    fidelity to this edition (c.f.
                    McCaffey).

                    Vatican Library. *Index Librorum
                    Prohibitorum* file copy, restricted
                    collection. C. 1860, French.

General: The *Principia Necromantica* is a rare
                    surviving artefact of the notorious
                    'Whitely Scandal' of the early
                    nineteenth century. Captain Horace
                    Whitely's initial attempts to publish
                    the *Principia* – presumably copied
                    from the volume that ultimately
                    came to reside at John Rylands
                    Library – resulted in the enactment

of byelaws to prevent its publication in three boroughs of London. He went on to the continent and brokered a deal with a French print shop known primarily for producing pornography. Only twenty copies had been produced when the master printer was made aware of the book's contents and ceased work, burning most (accounts suggest seventeen), and attacking Whitely. Whitely escaped with the surviving sheets, and returned to Britain, where he had them bound at a bindery where no one spoke Latin.

The cover is of black leather, assumed to be calfskin. It bears no title, author, or maker's mark. The front cover bears the motto *Fais ce que tu voudras* embossed in silver leaf.

The content of the book is understood to be a treatise on certain blasphemous studies represented in the form of fables, obscure metaphors, and Socratic dialogue. The text has proved impenetrable to scholars.

This copy of the Whitely Edition is believed to be the last surviving example. It was confiscated from the effects of an itinerant found wandering the northern forest, whose identity was never confirmed, and who died shortly thereafter in the asylum at Hamkar.

The book is *absolutely interdicted* without personal permission, by word and in writing, from the Librarian.

Chapter 14

IN WHICH VILLAINY IS REVEALED AND
LIVES ARE RISKED

Weighing up the pros and cons of his current situation, Johannes Cabal had to admit that he was definitely ahead in the game. The route had proved circuitous, and the clean lines of his original plan to steal the *Principia Necromantica* had long been trampled under the feet of any number of interested and interfering parties. There had been two very distinct attempts upon his life along the way, although such was the nature of his calling that if nobody had tried to kill him during such a project he would have regarded it as, at best, freakish or, at worse, highly suspicious.

Still, here he was with the *Principia* nestling happily in his Gladstone bag, with the murderous mess of bloody circumstance otherwise known as 'the maiden voyage of the aeroship *Princess Hortense*' due to fly away from him at dawn, taking the last vestiges of menace with it. He might even go down to the aeroport perimeter and wave to it from behind the wire as it dwindled into the distance and out of his life.

In the meantime, he would find a small, clean, discreet *locanda*, have a meal that was not subject to Mirkarvian standards of machismo in the kitchen, a long bath, and sleep the untroubled sleep of a man who is tolerably sure nobody is going to try and cut his throat in the wee small hours, which is to say, he would still lock his door and wedge a chair under the door handle.

And so it went. He found a quiet little inn just by the Via Dulcis, whose proprietor was friendly but incurious. He asked Cabal if he was on holiday, Cabal agreed he was, and that apparently fulfilled the landlord's entire expectations for gossip. He did not even much care that Cabal only had a single small bag, but blithely showed him up to a small, clean room that had a decent view of a municipal park over the low rooftop of its neighbour. The room shared a bathroom with the other three rooms on its landing, but these were all unoccupied, so Cabal enjoyed his long bath uninterrupted. Clean, shaven, and in his only change of fresh clothing until he would have the opportunity of buying more on the morrow, he sat down to a light meal of pasta and chicken in sauce accompanied by a glass of dry white wine from, the landlord explained, his family's own vineyard. Cabal admitted he was right to be proud of it; while not an extraordinary vintage, Cabal's spectrograph of a palate found much to admire in it, and so he went to bed tired, very slightly drunk, and – at least briefly – at peace with the world. This last he managed by assiduously avoiding any thought of the last few days and Miss Leonie Barrow's current circumstances. It was a mental trick that came easily to him, after so many opportunities to practise it in his past.

He slept through dawn, and therefore any chance to wave goodbye to the *Princess Hortense*, but this caused him little concern and less dismay. It was hardly his affair if Miss Barrow would insist upon sticking her head in a lion's mouth. That thought made him consider the coincidence of the leonine Leonie putting her head in any such place, and his thoughts went off in other directions, and had to be dragged back into line by the scruff of the neck and spoken harshly to.

He came down to breakfast, and enjoyed a light meal in the Continental manner with strong coffee and tart orange juice in a sparsely occupied dining room in which the other guests kept themselves, much to Cabal's satisfaction, to themselves. When he had finished, he had another coffee to drink while he skimmed the morning newspaper. This, he was further pleased to note, contained nothing about skies full of murder, or spies turning up cold and dead. He wouldn't be at all surprised if Senzan Intelligence had already found Cacon, but they would hardly be likely to advertise it. Any suspicions they had would be ranged upon the Mirkarvian aeroship now heading for their border with Katamenia, and there it could remain with his blessings. He, in the meantime, just needed to buy some travelling clothes, and then set off in entirely the other direction. He had suffered his fill of other people for the time being, and he missed his laboratory.

Thinking of his laboratory reminded him of other elements of his life, his real life and real business, away from all the alarums and excursions people seemed hell-bent upon imposing on him. Such nonsense, so distracting. He looked at the empty chair opposite him across the small table, and imagined it occupied. He sank into a brown study as he considered the vagaries of fate that had led him to this place and this time and breakfast by himself.

He would probably have been a solicitor. His father had connections with Hinks & Hinks in town, a small firm specialising in the bread and butter business of English solicitors – conveyancing, last wills and testaments, and bickering over property lines. His father had so wanted to be

English, for his sons to lose their accents and to conform. A whole trajectory for Cabal's life had been calculated that concluded in his sixty-fifth year when he was to retire as senior partner at Hinks, Hinks, & Cabal to a cottage with roses round the door, Sunday lunch with the grandchildren, and the autumn of his life spent with his wife.

Even at the time, it had been anathema to him. All but that last element. There he had plans himself. Plans that came to an abrupt halt with his brother Horst standing ashen-faced on the doorstep, the mindless run to the river's edge where a silent crowd stood by, gathered by her where she lay on the grass, her summer dress lank with river water. The doctor had delivered the formula then – that there was nothing that could be done, that all hope had gone, that he was sorry for Johannes Cabal's loss. He was vague with shock then, hearing without listening, but later when the priest came and had the damnable temerity to tell him that she was in a better place, then Cabal swore and raged and would have struck the man across his stupid sanctimonious face if Horst hadn't held him back.

That night he made his decision and, as was in his character, acted upon it immediately. That night, the baleful shade of Hinks, Hinks & Cabal winked out of existence and was replaced by a new arc, that led to here and now, sitting alone at a breakfast table under an assumed name. He noticed the landlord standing close at hand, an expression of concern on his face warring with a professional desire to avoid upsetting the customers. 'Mi scusi, Signor. But, you said something?'

'No,' said Cabal. He got up to leave. 'I said nothing. Nothing of import.'

Teeth brushed, bag packed, and bill paid, Cabal walked out into the clear Parilan morning. The sky was a brilliant blue, the buildings shone in the sun's reflected glory, and the air was fresh, just a hint of chill still lingering from the clear night. It was a good day to be alive and did much to lift his mood. He would have been a mite happier still if his Webley revolver had been snuggling safely in his bag, but the day was otherwise as good as any day without a large calibre handgun can reasonably be. Cabal stepped into the street busy with people going to work, and set off towards a gentleman's tailor he had spotted the previous evening that stocked a lot of black suits and white shirts in unenterprising styles. By his calculations, he would be able to buy some fresh clothes and still be able to reach the railway station towards the end of the morning rush. The crowds would offer him cover while he checked that nondescript men with bulges in their armpits were not monitoring departures. His acute sense for danger told him that he was probably in the clear, but, then again, his acute sense for danger had failed to tell him somebody was about to throw him out of the belly of the *Princess Hortense*, so he was not inclined to trust to it, at least not until it could prove to have recovered its edge.

The tailor was most accommodating, and – once he had got over his disappointment that the gentleman was only interested in items off the peg – bustled around fetching items as Cabal reeled off his measurements from memory. 'You are in a hurry, Signor?' he asked from the top of a stepladder from where he fetched down white shirts wrapped in tissue paper.

'I have to meet a boat arriving at Santa Keyna, and my train leaves in two hours,' explained Cabal, missing no opportunity to cover his tracks. Santa Keyna lay eastwards of Parila, while he would be travelling to the west. 'I shouldn't have left everything to the last minute, I know.' He shrugged.

*

Out on the street again with his new purchases wrapped in a neat brown paper bundle under his arm, he checked his watch. The timing was slightly off, he realised; the tailor had been more efficient than planned for and Cabal found himself slightly ahead of schedule. In an unexpected show of pleasantry, that he didn't even attempt to rationalise, he bought a red carnation from a woman on a street corner who had a basket full of them. Furthermore, he suffered her to place it upon his jacket's lapel, and for this he could offer no rationalisation. With the uncharacteristic splash of colour illuminating him, he strolled onwards.

As he entered the square whose northern side was dominated by the railway station's façade, he heard the happy shrieks of children, and the sound curdled his enjoyment of the day somewhat. He had once been forced by circumstances to be vaguely polite to children for a whole year when he had been running the carnival, and the experience had scarred him. When he saw that the source of their amusement was a puppet show, the day darkened still further. A detour was impossible, as the show had been mounted close by the pedestrian approach to the station entrance. Most of the commuters passing by smiled and tossed coins into the collection buckets, apparently unconcerned by the bottleneck created by the show's audience.

Cabal started to edge around the crowd, but paused, distracted by the nature of the show. It was not a simple tall booth with a stage in the upper third, beneath which lurked a glove puppeteer, like the 'professors' of the English Punch and Judy show. This was an altogether more massive construction of wood and canvas, the best part of two and a half metres along the front and deep enough to hold a floored stage and sufficient 'backstage' and space behind the proscenium to give the puppeteers room to stand and operate the marionettes that pranced upon the stage. The play currently being performed seemed to be an old story albeit lent a satirical edge for the adults present by passing references to local gossip and national politics. The tale's root was something like 'Hansel and Gretel', but instead of a witch's cottage, the pair had stumbled upon a secret military camp in the woods run by grotesquely caricatured Mirkarvian soldiers. The Mirkarvians – led by an idiotic captain that reminded Cabal strongly of Lieutenant Karstetz – were at a loss as to how to deal with the children, the captain having inadvisably used his orders as toilet paper in an earlier scene. Now they found themselves 'in a pickle', which led into a running joke about how the captain loved pickles, and what an extraordinarily wide variety of things the Mirkarvians enjoy pickled.

Cabal watched the soldiers whirling and dancing around, their wooden feet clacking across the boards of the little stage. He had to admire the skill of the puppeteers, even if the script played a little too strongly to the Senzan appetite for scatological humour. Still, it was easy enough to ignore the words and just watch the varnished arms wave and the varnished boots stamp.

The realisation came upon him suddenly and violently, not as a light of revelation, but as a dreadful hollowing. For a moment it seemed as if nothing existed within his chest but cold vacuum, freezing the inside of his ribcage.

It was so clear. It was all so clear. And it had always been so clear, right from the beginning, if he had only opened his eyes and ears, if he had not only looked but also seen, not only heard but listened.

It meant Leonie Barrow was in terrible danger. No phantasm of peril, but true, real, and immediate danger. It also meant that it was none of his concern. He could just walk away.

So he did.

*

Miss Leonie Barrow had not expected Johannes Cabal to see the *Princess Hortense* off on her final leg, so she had no grounds to feel disappointed when she was proved right. Being right, however, is not always the recipe for good humour, and she felt hers deteriorate as the aeroship cleared the landing cradle, realigned the etheric guides, and set course for Katamenia. Part of the reason was simple annoyance with herself. She felt somehow gulled, as if he had made a fool of her. Cabal had been entirely in her power right from the moment she'd laid eyes on him that first evening, and – despite great provocation – she had never used it. It had seemed that there was a greater, or at least a more immediate evil to contend with, and she had let him keep his liberty and his life. Yet when she needed his coldly analytical mind, he had turned his back at the first sign of trouble. Well, the second sign of trouble. Being shoved out of the ship while in flight could reasonably be regarded as the first.

The other part of the reason she didn't like to think about. Cabal had been very emphatic in his warning to her, that she was risking her life by rejoining the ship. She had to acknowledge that his was a career path littered with greater hazards than redundancy and insufficient pension contributions. Cabal had lived as long as he had by having a very keen sense for danger and a very simple strategy for dealing with it; turning a full 180 degrees and running. It was not a very valorous lifestyle, but he liked the way that it kept him off ducking stools, clear of bonfires, and safely away from nooses. Thus, it seemed likely that if Cabal said there was terrible danger before performing one of those turns and running, then there was very likely to be danger.

She had little idea how she would deal with it. Her father had taught her the bare essentials of self-defence – when in real unalloyed fear for your life, fight to maim and kill because you will get no second chance – but the assumption there was of an unplanned attack in the street. A calculating killer or, worse yet, killers, was not something she or her father had ever considered. Cabal must certainly have performed his 180-degree manoeuvre in the past and found himself facing a wall, but survived somehow. That was what he was, a survivor. Though she hated to even think it, a survivor was what she needed on her side right now. Somebody who could spot the dagger before it was drawn or the pistol before it was aimed, and find a way out.

But then, wasn't that exactly what he had done? Worse still, wasn't that exactly what he'd told her to do too?

So, between feeling like a fool for her kindness unrewarded and feeling like a fool for not running while she had the chance, it is unsurprising that Leonie Barrow watched the new day dawn with all the enthusiasm of a prisoner on the morning of execution.

'Ah, you poor dear. Left all alone, my poor sweet.'

The voice at her shoulder did not lighten her mood. In the normal run of things, Lady Ninuka would merely have been irritating. If Cabal's suspicions had any grounds, however, Ninuka was perfectly capable of walking up to somebody, sticking a dagger into their vitals, and looking them in the face the whole time as she twisted the steel. So Miss Barrow found herself in the unfamiliar territory that lies between peevishness and fear, an uncomfortable place filled figuratively with disease-carrying flies whose whining wings put one's teeth on edge, and brutal stranglers mispronouncing 'controversy'.

Unaware of her companion's inner conflict, Lady Ninuka continued, 'I heard that Herr Meissner was called away on urgent business at the embassy in Parila. He'll just have to catch up with his luggage in Katamenia, I suppose.'

'You heard that?' replied Miss Barrow in a neutral tone. It

didn't surprise her. Cabal wouldn't have jumped ship without some sort of story to prevent awkward questions.

'Yes. And dear Herr Cacon apparently has family in Parila, so he's gone too. I suppose he'll just have to make his own way onwards after he's said hello.'

Miss Barrow turned sharply and looked at Lady Ninuka. Apart from being slightly startled by the sudden movement, she looked very much like a monied and landed simpleton dispensing gossip might. Or, just possibly, a monied and landed stone-cold killer passing herself off as an ingénue.

'I thought the Senzans were going to spend a long time searching the ship? They waved it through very quickly, didn't they?'

Lady Ninuka shrugged. 'You should have seen them, my dear. The ship was absolutely heaving with Senzan soldiers. I think the captain was just expecting a few grubby little customs men. Instead we must have had a whole regiment tramping around the place!' Her animation suggested that she was very enamoured of large numbers of young men in uniform marching back and forth in front of her. She frowned unhappily. 'They were finished *so* quickly.'

'I beg your pardon?'

'Searching the ship. Military efficiency, I suppose.'

'Didn't the deaths aboard concern them?'

'Not as far as I know,' said Lady Ninuka a little tartly. 'I'm sure they were only too glad to leave poor Gabriel alone. The captain told us at the same time as he did the Senzan captain. Gabriel was Mirkarvian, aboard a Mirkarvian ship, who died within Mirkarvian borders. Poor Gabriel.' She dabbed quickly and delicately at her eyes with a lace handkerchief as if drying soap bubbles. 'Poor, stupid boy. Please, forgive me. I must . . .' And she fluttered away.

Miss Barrow watched her with mixed emotions, though

256

none were sympathy. Even if Lady Ninuka was all that she seemed, that just made her a callous sensualist who hadn't killed anyone, as opposed to a callous sensualist who had. In either case, it hardly made her a figure worth pitying.

From the salon window, she watched Parila dwindle into the distance until finally it was lost in cloud and haze as the *Princess Hortense* gained height. With it went Cabal and, unhappy circumstance, the only person she'd trusted in the game of death she'd rejoined. Despondent and perhaps a little scared, she ordered a pot of tea – a drink she enjoyed all the more so since realising that the Mirkarvians disliked it even conceptually as having too little alcohol or caffeine to be trustworthy.

An hour or so later, and on her third cup, she was reading a book on Mirkarvian history (a dismal study of a country that never learns from its mistakes, akin to watching a baby play with a revolver. Something dreadful is sure to happen and only the exact timing is in question), when there was some commotion.

Colonel Konstantin, still prickly after the Senzans had questioned him closely and been impudently thorough in searching his luggage on the basis that he was the most obvious manifestation of Mirkarvian militarism aboard, was looking out of the aft windows while smoking a foul cigar when he took it from his mouth with an expression of surprise and stared steadily through the glass. 'What's that fella doing, hmm?'

The Roborovskis came over to join him. 'It's one of those flying machines,' said Frau Roborovski.

It's an entomopter!' added her husband, in an enthusiastic tone at odds with his usual demeanour. 'How wonderful!' When the Senzans had sent a squadron of the machines to shadow the *Princess Hortense* towards Parila, he had been the only person aboard to regard them with anything but suspicion and trepidation. 'They must have sent one to escort us out of their skies.'

The colonel, always prepared in a way that many Boy Scouts frequently are not, had already pulled a set of small prismatic binoculars of the Daubresse pattern from his pocket, and was observing the distant aircraft. 'No,' he said definitely, 'it's nothing like the other ones. I don't see any weapons. I think it may be a reconnaissance model. Coming on damn quick.'

Miss Barrow joined them in squinting at the black dot against the white cloud. Amid the speculation that murmured around her, she had trouble keeping a straight face. It was difficult not to be a little smug; not for the first time, she had read Johannes Cabal better than he knew. For a man with a stated hatred of the dramatic, she knew he wouldn't be able to leave the mystery of the *Princess Hortense* alone, and here he was, riding to the rescue aboard a doubtless stolen entomopter. She didn't flatter herself for a second that he was doing this for anyone but himself, but the sense of knowing his mind before he did gave her a proprietorial sense of warm regard, like the owner of a well-trained dog.

After a few minutes, it was apparent to all with or without binoculars that the entomopter was of a different design to the Senzan fighters, and that it carried no obvious weapons. It gained height until it was some little distance above the aeroship, and the last they saw was it slowly vanishing overhead until the salon ceiling got in the way.

Colonel Konstantin put his binoculars away. 'That machine landed on us.' He looked towards the doors as if hoping a member of the crew would enter and make an explanatory announcement, but the crew was notable by its absence. Even the bar was unattended. 'Just what is going on here?' He marched off to find out.

*

Just what was going on there was not immediately forthcoming. Indeed, the remaining passengers gravitated to the salon and were eventually reduced to helping themselves to drinks from behind the bar. Colonel Konstantin returned in a bad humour, having been given short shrift by what few crew members he had been able to find. Apparently the arrival of their unexpected visitor had caused quite an upset, and the captain and all his senior officers were not available. Almost an hour passed before Captain Schten appeared in the door, just as Herr Roborovski was filling a stein.

'Ah,' Roborovski started apologetically, 'we've been keeping a record of what's been drunk, Captain,' but the captain just waved him to silence. It seemed that bar accounts were the least of his concerns at that moment.

'Exactly what has been going on, Captain?' asked Miss Ambersleigh. 'There's been a very queer atmosphere aboard this vessel ever since we arrived at Parila, and things just seem to be getting worse.' She would have expanded upon this theme, but Lady Ninuka shushed her sharply, and she sank into an aggrieved silence.

'The lady is correct,' said Konstantin, referring to Miss Ambersleigh and not Lady Ninuka, which is to say, *lady is as lady does*. 'What in blazes is wrong with this voyage?'

Captain Schten looked at them all unhappily. Then, at the sound of boots on the floor behind him, he stepped to one side.

The man who walked into the salon was an utter stranger to Leonie Barrow, but she disliked him instantly. Perhaps it was the way that he looked at the passengers with the disdain of a chess grandmaster faced with an opponent who refers to his pieces as 'prawns', 'castles', and 'horsies'. He was a lean man in a black uniform that, despite clearly denoting a high rank, bore few decorations, and was all the more impressive for it. In truth, since he wore the Imperial Star at his throat,

259

it could pretty much be taken for granted that he already had all the others.

He carried a shako under his left arm, while in his right hand he held a typewritten sheet of paper. Lady Ninuka started to say something, but he quelled her with a glance. Once he had silence he studied the paper, then slowly looked around the salon, checking every face. His brow clouded and Miss Barrow had the very distinct impression that this was a man inclined to violence with very little provocation.

'Where is he, Captain Schten?' he said in a voice low with threat.

'Sir?' Schten looked at the newcomer as if they had previously been rehearsing a drawing-room comedy yet he'd just been given a cue from *Macbeth*. 'I thought I explained. We . . .'

'Two . . . scheduled departures. One . . . *disappearance*,' grated the man. 'One . . . *suicide*. But there are five people missing here.' The violence in him was bubbling to the surface as surely as a geyser. '*Where is he?*'

The captain finally understood the specifics, if not the animosity, and quickly said, 'You mean Herr Meissner? He stayed behind in Parila, but – I assure you – he is a loyal servant of Mirk—'

'Herr . . . Gerhard . . . *Meissner* . . .' spat the man, 'is in Harslaus Military Hospital, Captain. In a *coma*.' As he said this last word, he spun on his heel to glare at Captain Schten. Schten had two inches in height and better than forty pounds on the stranger, but he quailed before the man's anger, and Miss Barrow saw that she wasn't at all overdramatising his power. Schten was terrified of him, and that terrified her.

'The man who so easily pulled the wool over your eyes, Captain, is called Johannes Cabal. He is an agent provocateur. A saboteur! He assassinated our glorious emperor! He is the despised enemy of *every* Mirkarvian!' He was bellowing in

Schten's face now, and Schten seemed to shrink with every shouted syllable, with every fleck of foam the raging man spat into his face. 'And you, "Captain" . . . *you* have allowed him to escape justice and run off into his rat hole! If I didn't need you, you moronic piece of garbage, I would kill you now.'

There was a horrible silence. Then, Lady Ninuka said in a very small voice, 'Hello, Daddy.'

'Hello, Orfilia,' said the man offhandedly, not turning his head.

Miss Barrow's eyes widened. This, then, was Count Marechal, of whom even the bloodless Johannes Cabal was wary. Now she understood his reluctance to continue the journey. Indeed, now she shared it.

The count spoke quickly and emphatically, his mind already planning ahead. 'How far are we from the Katamenian border?'

'About ninety minutes, sir.'

'At flank speed?'

'Less than an hour.'

Count Marechal grimaced. 'It will have to do. See to it.' Captain Schten saluted, clicking his heels, and left the salon, apparently very happy to do so.

'Excuse me?'

Marechal looked over at the passengers and saw a young woman with rather unruly blond hair had her hand up. 'Who are you?'

'Leonie Barrow. Would I be right in thinking you're Count Marechal?'

'You would. What do you want?'

'I was just wondering, really. What on Earth is going on?'

'What is going on is none of your concern, Fräulein. We shall be reaching our destination a little earlier than scheduled, you will all disembark, and that will be the end of your involvement in this affair.'

'Yes, but . . .'

'That,' he barked, unused to women doing anything other than answering when spoken to, 'will be the end of it.'

'Oh, I doubt that,' said a voice from behind Marechal.

Marechal spun round to face the speaker and was both astonished and delighted to see Johannes Cabal leaning nonchalantly against the wall by the door.

Chapter 15

IN WHICH CABAL SETS THE SCENE

'Cabal!' cried Count Marechal warmly. 'I cannot begin to tell you how very happy I am to see you!'

'Really?' said Cabal, his sang-froid slightly shaken.

'Really!' Marechal drew his revolver and levelled it at Cabal's head. 'Now I can finally kill you.'

Cabal rolled his eyes. 'For somebody who fancies himself as a great thinker, you don't tend to let it get in the way of doing something stupid, do you?'

'There's nothing stupid about shooting you, Cabal.'

'In front of witnesses? Oh, but of course, that's not really a problem, is it? There's not a person here who will ever tell.'

'Hold your fire, sir,' said Colonel Konstantin. 'This is not the place for an execution.'

'Oh, you're going to shoot him, Daddy?' Lady Ninuka stepped forward, face flushed with excitement and every inch her daddy's girl. She smiled. 'Good. He was *horrid* to me.'

Under different circumstances, Miss Barrow might have remonstrated with Lady Ninuka, but she had only just seen her ladyship for what she was. The vanity and solipsism, the lack of concern for others, the hunger for new amusements to titillate a palate that jaded too quickly – Miss Barrow could have kicked herself for not spotting a textbook case of psychopathy until now.

Count Marechal grunted with irritation. 'Will you please be quiet, child? One thing at a time.'

Cabal was growing irritated, too. He had been planning his grand entrance for the past few hours, and people kept chattering instead of letting him get on with it. He coughed loudly and a gratifying silence fell. 'You have the gun, Marechal, so you make the rules. I would, however, suggest that I know several things you don't and that these facts represent areas of ignorance in your knowledge which may – no – *will* prove very important soon. You can kill me now, but I guarantee that you will regret such precipitous action before very long.'

Marechal sighed heavily. 'Don't you ever shut up, Cabal?'

'In my laboratory, I may remain entirely mute for months on end. This is not a time for silence, however. I have a story to tell that will illuminate much for some, less for others, but everybody will learn at least one thing vital for their futures. Such as whether they have one.'

'Why did you come back, Cabal?' said Miss Barrow. There was an electricity in the air that she did not like, an approaching storm of violence that contained at least one thunderbolt specifically meant for him. What was worse was the building sense that Marechal was not intending to stop with one body at his feet. Cabal had been right all along about the deaths aboard having political roots, and politics can be a more ruthless killer than any number of wild-eyed maniacs.

'Now there's a funny thing,' replied Cabal. 'That is exactly the thing I would like to talk to you all about first. With your permission, Count?' and without waiting for a reply, he walked into the centre of the salon where he stood like an entertainer about to start his act. 'Please, sit down. You may as well hear this in comfort.'

Nobody moved for a moment, then Konstantin stepped over to Miss Ambersleigh and drew out a chair for her. 'Ma'am?' With a weak little noise of affirmation, Miss Ambersleigh sat. It was the catalyst, and the other passengers found chairs too. Marechal watched the proceedings with contempt, but realised that the perfect moment for shooting Cabal had come and gone, and he could no longer do it with panache, at least for the moment. He would have to wait for Cabal to finish his piece, and then kill him. This could represent his last wish, Marechal decided. It would have been more convenient if he had just asked for a cigarette and a blindfold like a normal person, but no matter. It would only serve to sharpen Marechal's anticipation. He'd arranged the execution of so many peasants while putting down the short-lived revolt that he had got quite bored with it. This, he hoped, would serve to clear his palate and restore the pleasure of revenge.

He strolled to the bar, helped himself to a glass and a bottle of Mirkarvian spirits that bore a similar chemical composition and taste to de-icing fluid, and settled himself on a bar stool. His revolver remained in his hand. 'Very well, Cabal. You have your few minutes' grace. Amuse us all with your intellect.'

Cabal bowed. It was possible that it wasn't meant to be mocking, but that was certainly the effect.

'To begin with,' he began with, 'it is important to understand how we come to be in this situation. I shall start with my own journey.'

Interludes

And so he did. It is unnecessary to recap much of what he said, but to emphasise that, for reasons best known to himself, he was entirely frank in all details. There are, however, two parts of his story that have not appeared in the narrative thus far. These sections we shall refer to as *How Cabal Defeated Count Marechal in a Duel* and *How Cabal Came to Change His Mind*.

How Cabal Defeated Count Marechal in a Duel

'I cheated,' said Cabal evenly.

'A-ha!' said Marechal. 'Finally! I should have you write that out and sign it, Cabal. Everybody from the generals to the sneeriest little *putzer* has decided that you're some sort of master swordsman, and that you bested me!'

'Well, technically, I did.'

Marechal's paper-thin patience was beginning to tear. He slammed his glass on the bar and tightened his grip on his revolver. 'You cheated! You just admitted it!'

'I am well aware of that,' replied Cabal, perfectly unperturbed. 'I bested you by cheating, but you were definitely bested. I was off and running while you remained behind, tied up. You could not have been much more bested.

Although, in hindsight, perhaps I should have killed you while I had the chance.' He was pensive for a moment. 'No, I should definitely have killed you. So much unpleasantness could have been avoided.'

'It was very easy to outwit the count,' said Cabal to his little audience, which by this time included Captain Schten, who had returned from the bridge and was standing by the door. 'He is a creature of pride, and as such prone to appeals to his vanity, in this case that of being a great swordsman. Which, in fairness, he is. And, my, doesn't he like to demonstrate the fact? In this case, he gave up his revolver, unloading it beforehand, dropping both revolver and bullets to the ground.'

'Go on then, Cabal,' growled Marechal. 'Tell them what your great party trick is.'

'I can load a revolver very quickly. I forced the fight to one side of the room, ran very quickly to where the revolver and bullets were, and had a round chambered before the count could reach me.'

'Damn your eyes,' said the count, emptied his glass and refilled it immediately, demonstrating one of his own party tricks in the process.

'Oh,' sighed his audience, disappointed.

'See?' said Cabal. 'This is why illusionists and conjurors never reveal their secrets. The sheer banality of it more than offsets any pleasure the feat may have created in the first place. You're sorry you asked now, aren't you?'

Indeed they were.

How Cabal Came to Change His Mind

It meant Leonie Barrow was in terrible danger. No phantasm of peril, but true, real, and immediate danger. It also meant that it was none of his concern. He could just walk away.

So he did.

He made his way into the railway station, enjoying the day, the blue skies – although clouds were beginning to drift in from the south-east – and the delicious sense of liberty born of shedding a heavy responsibility. Soon he would be free and clear of the whole mess, and he could get back to work.

The station was a neat, unfussy building clad in sandstone slabs, the mica, quartz, and feldspar it contained lightening its colour and creating the occasional spark of reflected light from the beaming sun. In the ticket hall, Cabal found time to admire its simple but elegant architecture as he surreptitiously glanced around the space for any signs of surveillance on departing passengers, suspicious figures, or a dangerous level of police presence. To his immense satisfaction he saw nothing of the sort, but for a single bored policeman looking at a poster for weekend breaks.

Cabal's inner contentment deepened. He was still a long way from home, but he saw grounds for quiet optimism that he would actually reach there. He was looking at the large mosaic rail map picked out on the wall for a likely station in Senza's western marches to head for when, most unwelcome of things, a voice sounded over his shoulder.

'Ah ha, ha, ha!' said a man's voice in a tone usually reserved for the detection of unauthorised hands in biscuit barrels. 'I knew it! I just knew it! "Civil servant" my maiden aunt's arse!'

Cabal turned to discover a man with large red sideburns, a rubicund complexion, and a strange little hat with a feather sticking out of it, regarding him as if they were long lost cousins. But the eyes . . . Cabal knew those eyes, though it took him a stunned moment to remember where exactly. 'Ach mein Gott!' he said finally. 'Herr Harlmann?'

Harlmann shushed him melodramatically with a lot of finger-waving, and steered him by the elbow to a café that occupied a corner of the ticket hall by a newsvendor's stall. He found a table, attracted the attention of the waiter with a few imperious snaps of his finger, and ordered two coffees, in – Cabal was astonished and perturbed to hear – a perfect Senzan accent.

Wonderful, he concluded. *Now I'm in the hands of Senzan Intelligence*. So much for quiet optimism. His hopes of showing a clean pair of heels vaporised like a martyr's spit upon a bonfire, and he gloomily reconciled himself to spending the foreseeable future in a cell somewhere. At least, he consoled himself, the food would be better this time.

'Well, Herr Harlmann,' said Cabal as he fitfully considered escape plans without any great enthusiasm. The whole concourse was surely dense with assorted secret policemen just itching for an excuse to kick his spleen into sausage meat. The fact that he was being treated to coffee rather than being bundled into the back of an unmarked van by several burly servants of the state armed with overactive thyroids and lengths of rubber hose implied that the covert machinations of Senza were handled with rather more civility than those of its neighbours, as well as subtlety. He could barely believe that he had so utterly failed to spot the trap. Therefore, he decided, he would wait for the scale of the operation he had wandered into to become apparent before giving any bright ideas for escape serious consideration. 'What happens now?'

Harlmann shushed him with the same unnecessary finger-wigglage as the waiter returned with their order. He waited until the waiter had gone again before whispering to Cabal, 'I'd appreciate it if you would call me "Signor Moretti", old man.'

Cabal looked at him curiously, and took a sip of his coffee to hide his surprise. '*Moretti?*'

'Guido Moretti. Guido means "wide one".' He smirked at some private joke and started on his own drink.

When dealing with devils, demons, and the ungrateful undead, hiding one's emotions is a survival skill. Cabal, being a well-practised necromancer of several years experience and still alive to boot, had long since nailed that particular talent down, and so gave no hint of his inner bewilderment. He had been expecting Harlmann, or Moretti, or whatever his name was, to be in control of their little tête-à-tête, secure in the knowledge that he had any number of goons within easy call to jump on Cabal should he prove intransigent. Instead, he was behaving as if he were on equally thin ice. *Guido means 'wide one'*, he thought. *What's that supposed to mean?* Wide one. Wide. A morsel of slang occurred to Cabal, and then he understood. *Wide boy.*

With calculated nonchalance, he tested the water. 'Profitable trip?'

Moretti (as Cabal decided to consider him, given that 'Harlmann' was no truer a name) grimaced over his cup, and shook his head slightly in answer until he had swallowed his coffee. 'No. Utter disaster. I was getting somewhere with Miss Ambersleigh on the first evening out, so the old girl could give me an "in" with her ladyship. Rolling in it, she is, the stuck-up little baggage. I had such plans.' He sighed regretfully. 'But then that Digger fella throws himself out of the window, and then somebody has a go at you, and suddenly everybody suspects everybody. Utter, utter disaster. Just getting aboard that flying hotel cost me a fair wad of seed money, I don't mind telling you. Well,' he added with a conspiratorial wink, 'I don't have to tell you, do I? Setting up as a civil servant, though. I have to hand it to you, that takes some neck. The Mirkies treat the civil service like the state religion. Is it true you can get executed for impersonating a pen-pusher?'

It sounded like the kind of thing the Mirkarvians would do, so Cabal affected additional sang-froid on top of his nonchalance, and nodded. To think, he had been an ice-cold master criminal all along and hadn't noticed. 'I believe so.'

'You're a cool one, Meissner,' said Moretti, chuckling. 'So, what's your real name?'

'I haven't decided yet,' replied Cabal. His instinct was towards evasiveness, but when he realised that this had furnished him with the sort of bon mot that real master criminals sit up all night devising, he was not displeased.

It certainly had the desired effect on Moretti. He grinned appreciatively and tapped the side of his nose. 'I hear what you're saying, *il mio amico*. I don't know what game you were playing, but I'm sure it was something big. Hey,' he leaned forward, 'so did you have that English girl?'

'I beg your pardon?' said Cabal, honestly perplexed.

'That sweet blonde,' Moretti insisted. 'C'mon, you must have, the amount of time you two spent together. What was she like?'

Something slipped inside Cabal's mind, like a gear slipping in a transmission, or a plate slipping from a shelf. It felt intrinsically wrong, and profoundly unpleasant. Here he was, pretending to be a criminal, which was all very well and good, but he was pretending to be a criminal to a criminal, and he was being all too convincing. Cabal knew that, technically, it was no more than the truth; he broke laws with such monotonous regularity that he no longer even noticed himself doing it. He stole books, he disinterred fresh corpses, and, when necessary, he killed people. He committed misdemeanours with the ease of breathing, and felonies were barely more challenging. In the strict legal sense – i.e. that committing crimes is the act of a criminal – then, yes, he was a criminal. He was good at it too. He was very rarely caught, and never successfully punished, which was just as well as most of the punishments for his acts involved nooses, axes, or immolation. All this, it was reasonable to suppose, made him a master criminal.

Yet here he was with a real criminal, a career confidence trickster, and the man made him sick. Every law Cabal broke, every crime he committed was dedicated to one, single, shining, glorious goal. To defeat death. That was all he desired. Money didn't matter to him. Power didn't matter to him. All he wanted was to be humanity's champion against its first, its last, and its greatest foe.

Money mattered to Moretti. Power mattered to Moretti. He would gorge and bloat himself as a parasite on humanity's flank, one of hundreds of thousands, perhaps millions of similar parasites in the world. Cabal saw a sea of filthy sucking things like Moretti, the unconscionable tide, and he saw himself there too, drowning and indistinguishable.

Moretti was waiting for him to speak through the long silence. 'That good, eh?' he said cheerfully.

Cabal ignored him. 'Who lies with dogs, shall rise with fleas,' he said in an undertone. Sometimes he wished he still lacked a soul. It hurt so much.

'What?' said Moretti, all mystified by the muttering.

'I have to go, Signor Moretti,' said Cabal, rising abruptly and gathering his things.

'On to greater things, eh? Look, old man, if it's a game that you've got in mind, I'm a reliable partner. Ask anyone.'

Cabal paused and glared down upon him. Moretti suddenly had a distinct sense that his offer had been rash. 'My *game*, Moretti, is not for the likes of you. In the next few hours I intend to lie and steal for no material gain. Then, I have little doubt, I shall kill some people for no better reason than that they dismay me with their activities and I have decided to prevent them ever doing anything similar again. In my experience, death is an excellent prophylactic measure.'

Moretti, who had only ever heard the term 'prophylactic' used in a single context, blanched. 'My God,' he exclaimed.

'Your God, Signor Moretti, is of no use whatsoever.' He touched the rim of his hat in mocking salute. 'Good day, sir.'

He marched out of the railway station and down the main road in the direction of the aeroport. He had purpose and he had a plan, and his soul sang within him. *Well, I'm glad one of us is happy*, he thought.

To anyone with the slightest sense of self-preservation, there is something unnerving about being in the presence of an entomopter that makes one think that going by train, or perhaps narrow boat, might be a better idea. Or walking. Or staying at home. Perhaps it's the lightweight construction, or perhaps the whirling wings that cut twin figures of eight on either side of the skeletal fuselage. It may even be the frequent and appalling accidents. In fact, it probably is the frequent and appalling accidents that put all but the most suicidal of thrill-seekers (and military pilots, which is to say much the same thing) off even standing near one at rest.

It should be no surprise, therefore, that finding students for an entomopter flying school was a very hard sell. Signor Bruno, of Bruno's Aviation College, was a man of lean and hungry aspect, at least financially. To show the slightest interest in the aircraft was to find Signor Bruno – a small muscular man with a thousand-yard stare – making himself at home in one's personal space and employing one of his many tried, tested, and usually futile sales spiels. He would appeal to potential students' sense of adventure, the possibilities of employment that a flying licence offered, their pride, their poetical spirit, their vanity, their patriotism and, as a last resort, telling them that they were a big girl's blouse if they didn't sign up right this minute.

When the tall pale man in the black suit strolled up to him

where he knelt by his entomopter checking the oil levels in the port wing clutch assembly, and asked to be taught to fly without so much as a 'Hello' or a 'That's a fine machine you have there,' Signor Bruno was momentarily nonplussed; where was all the foreplay? But, being a manly sort of man, he had a low opinion of foreplay in any case, and warmed quickly to the forthright Herr Meissner. He didn't even care that the man was Mirkarvian. There were no actual embargoes in place on training Mirkarvians, not least because they were quite capable of getting the same training in their own country. That the valuable Herr Meissner had decided to get his training here rather than there was of no import except to Signor Bruno and his thin-lipped bank manager.

They went through the necessary paperwork beforehand, and if Herr Meissner hesitated on some pieces of information that should have been at his fingertips, then Signor Bruno saw no reason to mention it. Indeed, he was otherwise engaged on counting the wad of notes that the estimable Meissner had paid him with, so how could he notice any such momentary indecisions?

Herr Meissner did not care to remove his jacket, but that was of no matter; Signor Bruno had a set of flying overalls that easily fitted over it. Besides, as Signor Bruno pointed out, it gets cold up there. Herr Meissner strapped on his flying helmet, and they were ready to go.

The entomopter that they were using – indeed, the only entomopter Signor Bruno had – was a two-seat Symphony trainer. Not the fastest machine, but stable and relatively forgiving, at least compared to its nimble if fractious military brethren, which would whirl into a hillside given the slightest inattention. Signor Bruno took the rear pilot's seat, while Herr Meissner obediently took the forward co-pilot's position.

Signor Bruno had a good feeling about Herr Meissner; he

had listened intently to the technical lecture Signor Bruno had given him in the hangar on the principles of insect-like flight, asking rare but trenchant questions. The man was undoubtedly a scientist, by inclination if not actual profession, and Signor Bruno was able to finish the lecture in record time without resorting to training aids like *Dino the Dragonfly* or *Bambalina the Bumblebee*.

A quick run-through of the controls did nothing to diminish the good feeling. Herr Meissner only needing telling anything once. Helmet intercom, loud and clear. Cyclic, check. Throttle, check. Collective, check. Torque pedals, check. Electrical systems on, check. Fuel and oil levels, check. Ignition.

There was a loud crack to the rear of the entomopter as the ignition cartridge in the Coffman starter fired. Signor Bruno was impressed that Herr Meissner did not jump with surprise. The radial engine turned over and quickly caught, barely spluttering at all before producing a powerful throaty roar. Signor Bruno smiled and patted his cockpit edge as he would a favoured dog or horse. Good girl. A quick check of the oil pressure and he told Herr Meissner they were ready to go. His student nodded, and laid hands on his controls. With more confidence than was usual at this stage, Signor Bruno slid forward the lever that deactivated his own controls and enabled the co-pilot's.

The man had the touch of a surgeon or a virtuoso. He gently engaged the drive shaft, until the entomopter's wings started moving in sluggish horizontal figures of eight, carving infinities into the air. He opened the throttle steadily without jerking, then simultaneously increased the collective to angle the whirling wings, making them bite. The suspension springs in the landing struts creaked, audible even over the engine, as the aircraft started to lift. A few seconds later they were airborne, holding their altitude at about ten metres in a hover.

Signor Bruno was delighted. Such a fine student! *Bravo! Meraviglioso!* But, he did not remove his hand from the control shift, because even prodigies make mistakes. From there, Herr Meissner brought her down to a gentle landing. Then up again, with translation into forward flight, to a halt, to another landing. Signor Bruno was full of happiness, although regretfully he knew that Herr Meissner would not be requiring very many lessons before he would qualify for his solo licence.

They flew up and down the field, Herr Meissner bringing the Symphony to gentle hovers and briefly experimenting with backward and even, to Signor Bruno's mild alarm and a tightening of his hand on the control shift, sideways flight.

After an hour the lesson was over, and Herr Meissner landed the entomopter with great precision from where he had first lifted off. They unstrapped and climbed out, Signor Bruno extolling his student's natural ability to the heavens. Herr Meissner said it was nothing, nothing but a good understanding of the principles at play and a calculated degree of handling with the controls, neither tremulous nor violent. Signor Bruno said such a balance was a rare thing in itself. Herr Meissner replied that it was the secret to how he lived his life.

They parted then, Herr Meissner bidding Sign Bruno a polite farewell and a promise of another lesson the following day, if Signor Bruno was available. Signor Bruno mentally reviewed his empty appointments book, and replied that he was sure he would be able to squeeze another lesson in somehow. He watched Herr Meissner walk away towards the administrative block with pleasure and a distinct sense of financial relief. Things were definitely looking up. He set off for the field exit, intent on having something nice for lunch.

A quarter of an hour later, Herr Meissner returned from the administrative block, where he had occupied his time by locking himself into a toilet cubicle and reviewing what he had learned. He wandered around Signor Bruno's hangar as if looking for him until he was sure he was alone. Pausing only to put on the same flying suit and helmet that he had so recently doffed, and to take a handful of cordite cartridges for the Coffman starter, he walked out to where the Symphony trainer sat patiently.

Then he stole it.

Chapter 16

IN WHICH MUCH IS EXPLAINED AND
DERRING IS DONE

'So now you're an ace entomopter pilot?' remarked Count Marechal with mannered incredulity. He lit his fourth cigarette in a row, and puffed smoke up into the thickening air of the salon.

'I wouldn't presume to such a thing,' said Cabal. 'Not least because I'm not sure what constitutes an "ace". I can take off, fly, manoeuvre a little, and land. I doubt that marks me out as a daring aeronaut, but if you say so.'

'And you managed a landing on a moving aeroship on your first attempt, did you?'

'In truth, I almost didn't,' admitted Cabal. 'I was very short of fuel on the final approach and I doubt that I would have been able to make a second attempt. The lines across the roof . . .'

'The arrestor cables on the flight deck,' Marechal corrected him with the testiness of the jargon martinet.

'Quite so. The lines on the roof were a nice innovation, but I think one really needs some sort of a hook on one's entomopter to make best use of them. The trainer I borrowed was not thus equipped. Or, if it was, I didn't know which lever to pull to extend it. Not to worry. I set down fairly lightly and the distinct possibility of falling off the front was happily curtailed by another entomopter that was parked up there. That would be yours I assume?' Marechal paused in mid-drag, his cigarette quivering in his lips, which gave Cabal all the answer he needed. 'I'd have them take a look at it before you use it again. I gave it a rather stiff wallop when I drove into it.'

'Oh, I've had enough of you, Cabal,' said Marechal, less languidly than he planned. He reached for his revolver.

'Don't do that,' said Cabal in light reproof. 'I haven't got up to the point of all this, including why I came back.'

'We already know that. To play the hero,' said Marechal, although his hand paused, the fleshy base of his thumb resting on the revolver's butt.

'I doubt that,' said Miss Barrow and then looked uncomfortable when everybody stared at her.

'Miss Barrow is correct. Unflattering, but correct,' said Cabal, once again becoming the centre of attention. 'I do almost everything for reasons that might be characterised as selfish. I regard my life as a vital thread in the ongoing march of humanity from protoplasm to . . . I don't know, to be honest. Something slightly better than protoplasm would be a start. Therefore, anything that threatens my life now or later has to be dealt with. Paradoxically, that often means risking my life to secure my safety. The difference is that I risk it on my own terms.'

Marechal looked at him as if he'd delivered his little speech via a sock puppet called Mr Mimsy. 'Dear God, Cabal. Just how mad are you?'

'It really isn't in your interests to kill me, Count, for reasons that will become apparent. That is, if I may be allowed to continue?' He took his pocket watch out and checked the time. Marechal took the gesture to be a melo-dramatic expression of impatience, and with an air of disgust waved him on to finish his story.

'Thank you,' said Cabal. 'Now, let me explain my understanding of the events that have occurred during this voyage. To be brief . . .'

'That would be delightful,' muttered the count.

'To be brief . . . any crime is definable by the classic trio of motive, method, and opportunity. The recent occurrences are no different, but – to my chagrin – I concentrated on the most mechanistic of the three: the method. I thought if I could penetrate the mystery of how M. DeGarre was murdered in a locked room, then the other details would become apparent and the murderer unmasked. Well, I worked out how it was done, and it didn't unmask anybody at all. The corollaries that it presented were suggestive, but I still could not focus on to the members of the conspiracy.'

'A cabal, in fact,' said the count, much to his own amusement.

Cabal ignored him. 'Opportunity is a difficult thing to make much of. With a police force to gather detailed state-ments and a timeline, perhaps something could be shaken out, but I doubt it. A large vessel with very few passengers, rattling around like peas in a coffee can. The periods that people are out of sight of one another are too great; any attempt to cross-reference alibis would be frustrated by the great blank areas.

'This leaves us with motive, and motive is critical here. Once I started to understand a few of the peculiarities of this journey, the reasons behind them weren't far away.' He started pacing up and down: four steps one way, four steps back. 'I had all manner of strange theories. The ship had Senzan agents aboard. No, it had Mirkarvian agents. Perhaps it had Katamenian agents. No, it had Senzan and Mirkarvian agents involved in some sort of shadowed battle aboard this ship. It became more and more ludicrous, and eventually I discarded these ideas. That was a mistake, because I was just one variant away from the truth.

'I shied away from such ideas because they continued to snowball in scale, and there comes a point where reasonable suspicion turns into paranoia. That was where I drew my figurative line in the sand, beyond which I would not go. What is paranoia to the rest of the world, however, is business as usual in this grubby little pressure cooker of penny-ante countries with overarching dreams.'

Colonel Konstantin sat upright, breathing heavily through his nose, but he said nothing.

'It was the silliest thing that made me realise it,' said Cabal. 'A marionette show on a street in Parila. It was a little play that wouldn't appeal to you, as it made light of the Mirkarvian fetish for matters military. It made me think of something I saw almost the first minute I set foot upon this vessel, and that made all else plain. Specifically, why DeGarre had to die.'

Miss Ambersleigh, who had read any number of novels involving the solving of nefarious crimes by sundry Walloons and landed gentry, was on the edge of her seat in bright-eyed excitement. 'Because he was a Senzan spy?' she blurted out, and quickly covered her mouth with her hand.

Cabal ceased his pacing long enough to look directly at her. 'No. No, Miss Ambersleigh. There is a Senzan spy involved in all this, but it wasn't DeGarre. No, DeGarre died for being DeGarre. For being exactly what he appeared to be: a respected and world-famous designer of aeroships.'

Now it was Miss Barrow's turn to be confused. 'What? He was going to build a ship for the Senzans?'

'No, he was going to inadvertently prevent the Katamenians

281

taking receipt of a dreadful weapon of war from the Mirkarvians.'

'But they searched the ship?'

'Yes, they did, and that was a masterful stroke of misdirection. All those tons of potatoes and turnips and other root vegetables too grimy to enumerate. Was that your idea, Count?'

Count Marechal smiled, and wafted his fifth cigarette in a casual salute of mocking acquiescence. In fact, the idea had come from a member of his junior staff, but it is the role of junior staff to make senior staff look good and take the blame for anything that might make the senior staff look bad.

'It was so obviously an attempt to hide something that the Senzans were all over those wretched piles of vegetables in a second,' continued Cabal. 'They were so focused on them that they only gave the rest of the ship a cursory inspection. Even if they hadn't been otherwise engaged in bayoneting carrots, they probably wouldn't have noticed anyway. Not like DeGarre; as soon as he was on the engineering deck, he would have been asking awkward questions. Why are the engines so overpowered? Why are the bulkheads so thick? Why is the flight deck – thank you for the correct term, Count – capable of holding so many entomopters?'

Konstantin was looking around himself with growing realisation and astonishment. 'Ach, *du lieber Himmel!*' he breathed, having just managed to suppress saying something a great deal stronger.

'What is it?' demanded Miss Ambersleigh of anyone handy. 'I don't understand all this engineering talk. What is he talking about?'

'He's saying,' answered Miss Barrow quietly, 'that this ship is not a passenger vessel. It's a warship.' Now she understood the delicacy of their position. DeGarre had been a nuisance, and had been eliminated with rapid efficiency. The fact that he was a foreigner and a man of some standing had not stayed the killer's hand for a second.

'A warship? You sent me on a trip in a warship, Daddy?' Lady Ninuka was scandalised. 'You told me the *Princess Hortense* was the finest ship in the skies!'

'And so she is. Just not a passenger ship. *Princess Hortense* . . .' Count Marechal cogitated upon the name for a moment. 'That name's going, I can tell you. The Katamenians will give it a proper name, something you can be proud to go to war in. The *Invincible*, or something. Or the *Stormcloud!*' He warmed to the name immediately. 'Raining death upon our enemies!'

Cabal raised an index finger in mild admonition. 'Pardon me,' he said. 'I was in mid-exposition.' Marechal made an exasperated face, but waved him on. Cabal checked his watch again, and continued. 'It was supposed to look like suicide, but mistakes were made and, from there on in, they multiplied. The attack on me was made in a panic – it would have been far wiser just to leave me to my own devices. I didn't actually find anything in the ventilation ducting; I was all set to go back to my cabin and forget about it. A murder attempt spoiled all that, and – more importantly – emphasised that DeGarre's disappearance was certainly not down to suicide. Now they needed a scapegoat that Zoruk, with his unseemly display at dinner, was perfectly suited to be.'

'I still don't understand,' said Miss Ambersleigh, quite bewildered by so much naughtiness in the world. 'Who are *they*? You cannot be referring to this gentleman?' She gestured at the count, although, being a lady by breeding if not entitlement, she was careful not to point. 'He has only recently joined us.'

'They?' Cabal looked at her with mild surprise. 'I'm very sorry, Miss Ambersleigh. I thought that was evident. *They* are very nearly everybody on this vessel. All the crew, and several of the passengers. They have all conspired in three murders. They also intend to kill, let's see, Miss Barrow, myself, and, I'm afraid, you.'

Miss Ambersleigh seemed to shrink into her chair, her eyes wide, and her mouth open with shock. This could not be. Ladies need only fear ruffians. Not gentlemen. Never gentlemen. She looked beseechingly at Schten. 'Captain?' she said in wavering tones, but he could only look at the floor, his shame apparent.

'You can't blame the captain,' said Cabal. 'Or not completely. The first two killings were carried out under his orders, which is why such a hash was made of them. The captain is not a natural murderer; all this cloak and dagger nonsense does not come easily to a military man, does it?'

Captain Schten managed to look Miss Ambersleigh in the eye. 'I'm sorry, ma'am. I didn't want any of this.'

'He was just obeying orders, you see.'

Miss Barrow looked at Count Marechal, but couldn't bear to speak to him directly. 'His orders?' she asked Cabal.

'Yes, but not directly. Marechal here had his cat's-paw aboard – the ship's very own Mirkarvian intelligence officer – here to make sure smuggling the *Princess Hortense* through Senzan skies went to plan. She was also the one who grew suspicious that Cacon and, I think, myself were not what we seemed. Cacon was the Senzan spy I alluded to earlier. She shadowed me in Parila, was spotted by Cacon, who shadowed her, I shadowed Cacon, and – after a bracing round of "Here we go round the mulberry bush" – she ducked out. Unhappily for Cacon, she took refuge in the very alleyway that led to the safe house where he was supposed to wait to be debriefed. He walked right into her, and she murdered him.'

Lady Ninuka became aware that a lot of eyes were on her. 'Me? I've never heard such slander!'

'No?' said Cabal, all innocence. 'There are probably men's toilets in Mirkarvia where slanderous comments about you are commonly aired. If you pause to read the walls, you will likely find much that is libellous, too. You remember the difference, yes? Oh, sit down,' he said to the count, who had risen from his bar stool to defend his daughter's honour, such as it was. 'You will get to your chance to kill me anon. In the meantime,' he turned his attention back to Lady Ninuka, 'yes, it would be slander, if I were talking about you. I have had brief but unpleasant dealings with Mirkarvian security. I understand that security and intelligence all fall under the same organisational heading in Mirkarvia – which is unusual – and go by the name of "Section A". Marechal here is the de facto head of it, but will the Section A field agent please stand up?' Nobody moved. Cabal tutted impatiently. 'Oh, come along, Frau Roborovski. We haven't got all day.'

Frau Roborovski folded her hands in her lap, but she said nothing. Nor did she need to; her lack of surprise and calm demeanour was all the reaction necessary.

'Hold on, Cabal,' said Miss Barrow, 'you said the killer was a single woman. Frau Roborovski's, well, she's a *Frau*. She's married.' She looked sideways at Frau Roborovski, who returned the glance coolly. Miss Barrow's conviction wavered. 'Isn't she?'

'No,' said Cabal, disappointed at such ignorance, 'Of course she isn't. She's an intelligence officer. Probably changes her identity six times before breakfast even when she doesn't need to, just to stay in trim. Incidentally,' Cabal addressed Frau Roborovski directly, 'what is your real name? There's not much point in maintaining your alias now, and I dislike calling you by a *nom de guerre*.'

'Special agent Lizabet Satunin,' she said in a clear voice.

The fussy hausfrau image had slipped away entirely. Now she sat there, calm and confident as a chess player one move from victory. 'At your service.'

'Not mine, unfortunately,' said Cabal, 'or I would already have set you on Marechal. Your "husband", though . . . You're no agent, sir. When we first met, I spoke of dovecote joints when, of course, the term is "dovetail". I was a little distracted at the time, and I can't even remember if I said it in jest or in honest error. I do know, however, that a real cabinetmaker – or even a spy passing himself off as such – would surely have reacted in some way. What is your role in all this?'

Herr Roborovski sat in embarrassed silence, unsure whether he was permitted to speak. Fräulein Satunin did it for him. 'His name really is Roborovski, but he's not a cabinetmaker. He is this vessel's architect. He oversaw its construction and he will be spending some time in Katamenia to assist them in making her ready for war.'

'I like this,' confided Cabal to Schten. 'I like being able to ask questions and getting the answers without being lied to. I like the truth.'

'You were lying as much as any of us. A necromancer!' replied Schten, with a sulkiness unseemly for a man of his stature, either physically or professionally.

'I lied to save my life. You lied to take others. If we're playing moral superiority, Captain, you'll find even necromancers further up the ladder than you. As it happened, you gave me the single point of data that revealed the whole sordid business to me.'

Captain Schten's face dropped. He glanced nervously at Marechal, who was lighting up his eighth cigarette. 'I did?'

'You did, though you didn't realise it. Nor, to be brutally frank, did I. Not until I saw those marionettes. You probably won't be very flattered to hear that the puppet masters were remarkably good at mimicking the actions of Mirkarvian soldiers. Actually, it is probably closer to the truth to say that Mirkarvian soldiers are a gift to puppeteers because they behave like marionettes. A great deal of wheeling on the spot, and walking in lines, and – significantly – clicking their heels. Only the military do that, don't they? It's considered ill mannered and slightly dangerous for civilians to do it. Yet the very first time I laid eyes upon Captain Schten and his senior officers, they thought they were unobserved, and were busily snapping salutes and clicking heels at one another. The salutes are explicable; the heel-clicking from a crew that pretends to contain no military officers, less so.'

Schten winced, as well he might.

Cabal continued. 'Once I was open to the idea that the conspiracy involved the crew, then everything that had happened more or less became self-explanatory. Zoruk never stood a chance. He was injured by having his wrist "accidentally"' caught in a door exactly as he claimed, but the steward then stated that Zoruk had engineered the accident, and that the door had closed on him with no great force. Why would we disbelieve the apparently disinterested and uninvolved steward? Well, because he's an ass, but otherwise there's no reason not to accept his account. All the time the real culprit, one of the bridge crew or possibly an engineer, was salted safely away on the top deck, he and his injured hand kept out of public sight while the captain continues the charade of checking everyone else.

'Once again, however, the ruse was flawed, the military mind turned to expedience rather than elegance to cover the lies, and Zoruk was hanged in an effort to create another suicide. One would have thought that after one dismal failure at staging a suicide, a different strategy would be attempted, but Mirkarvians seem to be great adherents of "if at first you don't succeed, then repeat your failure until nobody's left alive to comment.'"' He smiled with the benevolence of somebody watching an unlovable toddler walk under a table and bang their head painfully. 'My main error was believing that the deaths were attributable to a couple of daring and dastardly spies of some hue, when in fact the malefactors were more akin to a third-string comedic music hall troupe, led by a psychotic in a plaid skirt. There wasn't a single bit of cleverness in the whole enterprise; just desperation and violence.'

There was a pause, and Marechal perked up, believing that the talk was over and he could now get on with killing Cabal. Miss Barrow spoke, however, and Marechal slumped back on to his bar stool with an impatient grunt.

'There's one thing, though, Cabal,' she said. 'DeGarre was killed in a locked room with a chair stuck under the handle. How was that done?'

Cabal looked at her as if she were the slowest child in the class. 'Isn't that simplicity itself? Think, Miss Barrow. Was it truly a locked room? What about the misaligned tile in the corridor, and the missing candelabras on the dining tables?'

'The candelabras? You're kidding? Anyway, you said they were irrelevant, didn't you?'

'Yes, but I was wrong. At the time I thought they couldn't be involved because it was inconceivable that they could be taken and returned without being observed by one or more stewards. Once you appreciate that it was one or more stewards taking them in the first place, that cavil is removed and the trick to DeGarre's murder becomes apparent.'

Miss Barrow frowned, thinking. In her mind's eye she disassociated them from their proper purpose and saw them simply as objects. What, she thought, were their most important features? 'They were ugly, really ugly. Curved, stylised swans, S-shaped. Made from steel, so they're strong.'

'Ugliness,' said Cabal, feeling like a teacher with a brighter than average pupil, 'is in the eye of the beholder. Limit your thoughts to the objective factors. Nobody can deny those.'

Curved and strong, she thought. *Like steel hooks.* 'That's mad,' she said. Then, 'No. No, it isn't. That would work. I think I see it.'

'You probably do,' said Cabal, not nearly as condescendingly as he might. 'Well, then. Dazzle us with your deductions.'

Miss Barrow stood and, quite unconsciously, started to mimic Cabal's pacing up and down. 'It's the first evening after the dinner. The captain is very worried about DeGarre seeing the engineering section. He is sure to realise that the ship's not what it pretends to be. They need some way to . . . I think the captain would have just wanted to put him off somehow. Killing DeGarre, though . . .' She remembered Cacon breathing his last – twice – and how ruthlessly he had been put down. She looked at Fräulein Satunin, who returned her gaze dispassionately. 'I think that was your idea, faked suicide and all. You come up with the suicide note, but locking the door won't be enough. It might even draw attention to the ship's officers, who I'd guess have passkeys. So, it goes something like this: there's a discreet little tap at DeGarre's door in the night. He answers it and there's a steward there, probably two. They get in under some pretence. Then they kill him; they're both military and have probably killed before. No blood, so he was strangled or smothered. They lock the door while . . . No, better still, one leaves while the other locks the door and leaves the key in the lock on the inside. He puts the chair under the door handle. He puts the previously typed suicide note into the typewriter. I think the note was actually typed on DeGarre's own machine while he was in the salon after dinner in case anybody thought to check the typeface and wear patterns. It didn't matter if the note didn't exactly match up with its original position on the platen since the plan was probably to pull it from the machine as soon as possible to prevent such a comparison. Cabal got there first, though. Anyway, as I was saying. The man still in the cabin undoes the window, and pushes DeGarre's body out. How am I doing?'

'It was a steward and an engineer looking for a "pressure leak", and they chloroformed him,' said Fräulein Satunin, 'but otherwise not bad.'

Miss Barrow blanched and stepped away from her as if she were contagious.

'Chloroform?' interrupted Cabal, his professional curiosity piqued. 'I wonder why I didn't smell it. Oh, of course. The open window. It was blowing a gale in there.'

'Cabal!' cried Miss Barrow. 'He was alive when they threw him out!'

'But unconscious, probably all the way down. You're quibbling over niceties, Miss Barrow. However he died, it was murder. Anyway, do carry on; the comatose M. DeGarre has just tumbled into darkness, both literal and metaphorical. What happened next?'

Miss Barrow glared at him, and took a moment to marshal her thoughts. 'Then whoever is left locked in the cabin, presumably a small but strong man, feeds a rope out of the window. On the end of it is one of the candelabras. They're steel – very strong for what they are – and the arms are curved. Here it's used as a makeshift grappling hook. Meanwhile, some other member of the crew had lifted the carpet tiles and gone down into the ducting. The tiles are replaced once they're down there. In fact, they probably got into position before M. DeGarre was even woken. They open the hatch in the ship's underside and feed out another rope with the other candelabra on it. With enough line and – I'd guess – the ship slowing down a little to reduce the slipstream, it isn't long before the two lines meet and tangle.

The man in the duct pulls up the rope, ties it off, and tugs on it. The man locked in DeGarre's room ties his end of the rope around himself and then . . . he jumps.'

'Bravo,' said Fräulein Satunin simply.

'Then it's just a case of drawing him up into the ship's belly by brute strength,' finished Cabal. 'I think there were probably at least a couple of men to do that. They clear up their gear, and crawl back to the floor hatch to wait. When the corridors are quiet again, the carpet tiles are quickly lifted and the men allowed out. But in all the haste the tile is replaced incorrectly and . . . Well . . . Here we are.' He was thoughtful for a second. 'I think that's everything,' he said finally. Then, to Miss Barrow, he asked, 'How was that?'

She grimaced. 'Long-winded and smug.'

'Good . . . good,' he said complacently. As if remembering something, he pulled out his pocket watch and checked it again.

'Your time's up, Herr Cabal,' said Count Marechal, stubbing out his latest cigarette and sliding off the bar stool. He stretched. 'Now, you die.' He reached for his revolver.

Cabal didn't look up. 'Possibly,' he said distractedly, still looking at his watch and ruminating.

'There's no "possibly" about it, you jumped-up conjuror.' Marechal drew his pistol and pointed at it. 'I'm going to shoot you, certainly once, probably two or three times, and then you'll be dead and that will be that.'

'What about us?' said Miss Barrow. 'Are you going to kill us?'

'Oh, Daddy!' said Lady Ninuka petulantly. It is true that people display different personas dependent on company; the femme fatale had vanished in Marechal's presence, to be replaced by a schoolgirl. 'Don't kill Miss Ambersleigh! I like her. She's funny and drinks tea.'

Marechal rounded on them both angrily. 'Will you all just

291

shut up!' he barked. 'I have had a very trying few days, and I just want a little "me" time to relax and unwind and kill Cabal. Is that so much to ask? Stop being so bloody self-centred and let somebody else have a bit of fun, will you?'

'And what of me, sir?' Colonel Konstantin had risen from his chair. 'What part have I in this plan?'

'You?' Marechal was surprised. 'You'll be a soldier about it and maintain secrecy. Believe me, Colonel, you were never considered a potential leak. Your record speaks for itself. I know that you are a true son of Mirkarvia.'

'I have always tried to be so,' said Konstantin with slow dignity. 'By the values of the first empire of the Erzich dynasty, I have always stood. In its every hour of need back through five hundred years, Mirkarvia has always known it could depend on the Konstantins to fight, and bleed, and die for her.'

'Yes, quite so. I think that's what I just said, except more briefly,' said Marechal impatiently.

'You, sir,' snapped Konstantin, sticking out his jaw and looking down his nose at Marechal, 'are not Mirkarvia. You, sir, are a jumped-up jackanapes who plays politics with the lives of our citizenry, tramples our honour beneath boots that have never seen a battlefield, and whores us out to a cesspit of barbarism like Katamenia as if we are nothing but mercenaries! You, sir, are a disgrace to your uniform and your title, both of which, it gives me no pleasure to remind you, were bought for you by your father.' Konstantin crossed his arms. 'And he was a self-serving bastard, too.'

Marechal stood as if stunned. 'I cannot count on you to keep this business secret, Colonel? Even though it is for your own country?'

'My own country? This is all your doing, Marechal; do not besmirch my country's name with your dishonourable filth.'

The shot was very loud, and reverberated against the hard

surfaces of the salon; the tables, walls, windows. Konstantin fell back into his chair, and nobody knew if the first bullet killed him outright because Marechal advanced on him, firing twice more. The shooting was angry and inaccurate; the first bullet caught him square in the ribs just to the left of the sternum, the second was three inches higher, and the third went directly into Konstantin's face at almost point-blank range.

'I . . .!' Marechal made to say something, but was so angry that it caught in his throat. Finally, 'Traitor!' spluttered out, blackened with petulant rage, and he pointed the pistol at the corpse as if to fire again. Miss Ambersleigh, who had cried out at the first shot, but was now somewhere beyond belief, sobbed in horror at the gesture, and Marechal, grimacing like a thwarted schoolyard bully, turned away.

Cabal was very disappointed by this development; he had been hoping that Marechal would have emptied the gun in a furious ecstasy, making it much easier for Cabal to murder him quickly and efficiently before he had a chance to reload. *No, not murder*, he reminded himself. *It would be self-defence. Ah, the novelty of it.*

Marechal looked around the room, daring anybody to speak, before returning his full attention to Cabal. He levelled his revolver, but Cabal was studying his watch yet again, this time with some perplexity. 'What the hell are you gawping at, Cabal?' spat Marechal. He was already regretting shooting the colonel; he would have had to go, of course, but it could have been done less messily. It also meant that he couldn't just shoot Cabal immediately as he so urgently desired, without looking like an utter maniac. He made a conscious attempt to recover some dignity. 'I've got a gun here, and you can't drag your eyes off your watch. What is the matter with you?'

'Me? Well, apart from having a revolver aimed at me, very little. My watch, I fear, is running a little slow.' He finally looked at Marechal. 'You know,' he added, taking Marechal into his confidence, 'I had a feeling I should have dragged the explanations out for another minute or two.'

'They were quite long enough.'

'Well, I would have thought so, but without time to take proper titrations to make sure the concentrations were as advertised, and, of course this hardly represents standard laboratory conditions with respect to temperature and pressure, my calculations might have been a little off. So frustrating.'

There was a distant 'boom' like thunder, but it reverberated throughout the *Princess Hortense*'s hull like a lump hammer against a tin bath, the deck lurching sharply to starboard for a moment. There were cries in the salon, and swearing from some quarters.

'Ah,' said Cabal, happily. 'There we go.'

'What was that?' Marechal narrowed his eyes and aimed his revolver directly at Cabal's head. 'What have you done, Cabal?'

'Blown up No. 1 etheric line guide. That's the forward port one, isn't it, Captain?'

But Captain Schten had already left the salon at a run. Cabal watched the door swing to after him, then confided to Marechal, 'He's probably got a lot on his mind at the moment.'

'You've done what, Cabal?' Marechal, pale and suddenly sweating, looked at Cabal over his revolver. He wanted so very much to fire, but had an ugly feeling that he had been outmanoeuvred.

'I've outmanoeuvred you,' said Cabal, confirming those fears. 'That first one was on a timer. The others . . .'

'Others?'

'Of course there are others. Not much of a threat if there's no chance of escalation, is there? The others, as I was saying, are on long timers, but have a rather cunning anti-tempering device I came up with at short notice. It's wonderful what you can hash together with the contents of a general grocery store and a pharmaceutical chemist's shop. I suppose,' he said, stroking his chin thoughtfully, 'I should really have mentioned that to Captain Schten before he rushed off. The business about the anti-tamper devices, that is; I don't imagine grocers and chemists are very high on his agenda at present.'

Marechal was at the door in a few long strides. As he opened it, a steward almost ran into him from the other side. 'Find the captain!' snapped Marechal, gripping the man fiercely by the shoulders. 'Tell him not to disturb any devices he finds! Tell him Cabal has planted bombs and the slightest interference could set them off!' He released the man, who simply stood there wincing at his freshly bruised biceps. 'RUN, you idiot!' roared Marechal in his face. 'All our lives depend upon it!' That was sufficient, and the steward bolted back the way he came.

Marechal wheeled round to face Cabal. 'Very well, you whey-faced bastard. What do you hope to gain by this?'

Cabal, ignoring the slight, considered thoughtfully for a moment, calculated to irritate the count within the limits of his small temper. 'I desired to put you in a position where you or – more accurately – the captain and the homicidal Fräulein Satunin would feel restrained from killing me. That's one. I am also of the strong opinion that this aeroship should turn round and go back to Parila. That's two. I must admit, I was not expecting you to be here when I arrived, Count, but since you are, I think the Senzans should have a chance to chat with you. That's three, and final.'

Marechal stared at him; angrily, yes, but also rather sulkily. He shook his head heavily. 'Forlorn hopes all.' He returned to his bar stool, picking up an empty ashtray from a table in passing, lit a new cigarette, and regarded Cabal as a head-master near retirement might regard a troublesome school-boy who defies all attempts at discipline. 'I don't understand you, Cabal. You were free and clear. You don't give a damn about what happens in this part of the world. Why would you come back? Bombs or no bombs, you're not leaving this ship alive. I . . .' He shook his head again. 'I don't understand you.'

'I'm aware of that,' said Cabal. 'If you did, you would have gift-wrapped the *Principia Necromantica* for me, given me free passage out of your country right at the beginning of our acquaintance, and counted yourself lucky. I have dealt with greater forces than you, Count.'

'Don't give yourself airs, Cabal.'

'He isn't.' Leonie Barrow's voice was quiet, but clear. With Marechal's eyes upon her, she said, 'Cabal is more dangerous than you can believe, Count. Both the angels and the devils fear him. He's a monster, but an even-handed one. I know he is capable of the most appalling acts of evil.' Her glance moved to Cabal, who was listening dispassionately. 'I believe he is also capable of great good. But to predict which he will do next isn't easy or safe.'

Marechal grimaced. 'What is your relationship to this man? Public relations or something?'

'I loathe him,' she said with sudden venom. Then more quietly, 'And I admire him. You're right; he didn't have to come back. He's taken a big risk, but I know he's taken bigger. I can't tell you whether he's a monster or playing the hero right now, but I know one thing. You made the biggest mistake of your life when you made an enemy of him.'

Cabal raised an eyebrow and smiled a smile at Count Marechal so dry that you couldn't have dragged a molecule of water out of it with fuming sulphuric acid. 'I sound quite mythical, don't I, Marechal? What wonders shall I perform next?'

'You can perform them from beyond the grave, Cabal. You've made a mistake.'

'Oh?' said Cabal, mildly curious. He drew out his pocket watch and checked it. 'And what would that be?'

'You've told us that the other bombs have long timers. Very soon we shall be over the border. There are cleared areas there. We can set the ship down and the engineers can deal with your bombs without fear of crashing out of the sky. Not that you'll be there to see it. Checkmate, Cabal.' He drew back his pistol's hammer slowly, with every sign of enjoyment.

'You would have a point except you have made an assumption. That I told the truth about the bombs.'

Marechal narrowed his eyes. 'There are no more bombs, are there?'

'Oh, there are bombs. Just no anti-tampering fuses. I mean to say, as Miss Barrow so kindly intimated, I *am* terribly talented, but rustling up mercury switches out of thin air is beyond even my admittedly extraordinary abilities.'

'Even better,' smiled Marechal. 'My only concern was that a heavy landing might trigger them. Thank you for removing that last lingering anxiety.'

'Oh, my pleasure. Really. But . . . I also lied about the timed fuses.'

Marechal's smile slid off his face like a stunned monkey from a buttered banyan. 'What?'

'They're not actually very long.'

At which point, the second bomb exploded.

Chapter 17

IN WHICH THERE IS DANGER, DISASTER,
AND DEATH

The detonation was that much closer and that much more violent, throwing Cabal and Marechal from their feet. The large windows to the starboard side of the salon exploded inwards and suddenly the room was home to a howling gale and tumbling fragments of glass. The clouds outside seemed to buck backwards and forwards as the *Princess Hortense* yawed wildly. Miss Barrow and the other passengers were hurled from their seats, Lady Ninuka sent sprawling over Colonel Konstantin's body. Her screams mingled with the other cries of surprise and terror.

'Cabal!' bellowed Marechal, climbing to his feet and standing with his legs well apart, braced against the rolling deck. 'You're insane! You'll kill us all!' He looked around, and caught sight of Cabal taking refuge behind a sofa. It was no sort of cover; Marechal aimed and fired, the heavy slug tearing clean through it. The lurching deck had spoilt his aim, however, and the bullet hole went through the MirkAir antimacassar on the sofa top.

'Two bullets left,' called Cabal. 'This is one of the many

reasons you would make a bad ruler, Marechal: poor resource management. Also, you show appallingly weak anticipatory skills.'

'Oh? And how would anybody guess that you would be mad enough to do this?'

'Not this,' said Cabal, his tone dismissive. '*This.*' He leaned out suddenly. Marechal barely had time to register that Cabal had a gun in his hand before it fired. The swaying of the deck saved him too, the round going high and punching a hole in an aft window, and he ducked low and scuttled away. 'You think a city as close to a bunch of rabid dogs as Parila is to Mirkarvia wouldn't have a good supply of gunsmiths?' Cabal called after the scampering noble.

He weighed the gun in his hand; the man behind the counter had looked at him quizzically when he'd enquired whether they stocked the Webley .577 revolver. Thwarted, Cabal had settled on a Senzan revolver, but at least had the mild pleasure of finding one in an equally untidy calibre – 10.35 mm. His mind was usually quite pristine, but – O! secret sin – he had always taken a perverse joy in dangling decimals.

'The ship's going down and you two are having a gunfight?' shouted Herr Roborovski. 'You're both mad!'

'Sir, this may not be the best time for this,' agreed Fräulein Satunin, grimly holding on to the carpet. Behind her, the ground was briefly glimpsed through the aft windows as the ship's tail dipped and swung.

'Shut up!' spat Marechal, his black hair askew and his composure shattered, from the end of the bar furthest from Cabal. 'You, Satunin! You're supposed to be a trained killer! Get him!'

'Sir,' she replied forcefully, 'He has a gun. I have a knife. He has cover. I have open ground. Worst of all, you've told me in his hearing what you want me to do. Tactically, this is a very unsound proposition, sir!'

'I don't give a flying pfennig for your damned tactical propositions, you stupid bitch! Just kill him!'

'No! You're not listening to me!' interrupted Roborovski with urgent passion. 'We're all in dreadful danger!'

'Nice attempt, sir,' called Cabal from where he lay in moderate comfort behind the sofa. He was glad all the furniture was bolted down. With the *Princess Hortense*'s current perturbations, he would otherwise have been forced to chase his place of concealment around the salon. 'But the line guides only provide forward motion, not lift. As long as the gyroscopic levitators continue to spin, we will not crash. We will just drift. Shortly the Senzan airforce will come in pursuit of my stolen entomopter, and they will find us.'

'Oh, God,' said Miss Barrow, and Cabal had a sudden intimation that he might have made a miscalculation. 'Cabal, the line guides are the ship's main source of power! Didn't you know that? It's in the pamphlet!'

Cabal twitched. 'Pamphlet?'

'The one about the ship! The one you got with your travel documents and itinerary!'

Cabal thought of an origami swan, and swallowed.

'Not so mythical now, eh, Cabal!' Marechal started laughing; a coughing, barking laugh that contained little humour.

'She's right!' Herr Roborovski was hanging on to a table support for dear life as the deck pitched violently beneath him. 'With two of them destroyed, there's barely enough to keep the levitators running! We need to land! We need to land immediately before the reserves are depleted!' He was interrupted by a shuddering groan that juddered through the whole fabric of the vessel. It ran through their bodies and shook their hearts in their chests. Roborovski swore something in a Mirkarvian dialect, a desperate and pleading jumble of words. 'It's the ship's spine! She's not designed to be thrown around like this! If we don't set down soon, she'll break her back!'

But beneath them was nothing but forest and steep hillsides.

Johannes Cabal was, though it pained him sorely to admit it, only human, and it is human to err. In his chosen profession, however, to err was to risk lynching, immolation, or ingestion. Cabal had so far kept his errors mainly on the small side – a singed eyebrow here, a deranged imp with a meat cleaver there – but overlooking the intimate connection between the etheric line guides and the gyroscopic levitators was beginning to look one of the more final variety.

Furthermore, there was naught he could do about it while pinned down in the salon. While he and Marechal maintained their standoff, there was little chance of anybody getting out of there alive. He could bet that the crew were too busy trying to restore trim to the ship to bother him for the moment, but this was an imperfect state of affairs. They would either succeed, and then he would have a lot of angry Mirkarvians after him, or they would fail, and Cabal would finish his life and career cremated on some anonymous Senzan hillside.

He considered his options. How much of a threat was Marechal? Assuming he had the same sort of revolver that Cabal had stolen from him back in Harslaus, then it was a six-chamber design. Assuming further that he wasn't the cautious type and therefore carried a round under the hammer, that left him with two rounds. Might he have reloaded? Possible, but unlikely; given the softness of Cabal's cover, it would have been an obvious tactic to place three or four rounds in judiciously chosen points through the sofa with a guarantee of at least one hit. Even if not fatal or debilitating, it would give him an advantage. That he had not done so suggested that he had come out unprepared to shoot more than six peasants. Cabal had five rounds remaining, and was bitterly regretting not having brought some more with him. Like Marechal, however, he had not been anticipating a gunfight. So, he had a small advantage, but time was wasting. He risked a peep along the side of the sofa away from the bar and saw Miss Barrow and the others clinging to the furniture.

Not so long ago, he thought, *I would have been safe on a train at this point. Harlmann could have said what he liked, and I wouldn't have cared a fig.*

The ship pitched upwards amid shouts and screams. Everybody who could, clung on for their lives. Unattended, Konstantin rolled heavily back and up against the base of the bullet-damaged window in a half-sitting position. With a hollow musical tone, a great crack formed between the hole and the base of the window. It held for a second longer, then shattered, great shards of glass falling down to the treetops. Konstantin lolled like a rag doll with nothing to support him, and slipped backwards out of the window. Cabal watched the old soldier vanish, and ground his teeth together. *So, this is what a conscience does for one, is it?*

He'd had enough. Precipitate action would kill him just as surely as indecision, but at least he would be doing something. He quickly analysed his situation, recalled that almost everything aboard an aeroship is built to save weight, and decided that the wood panels of the bar could not be as substantial as they appeared. In the moment between the *Princess Hortense* swaying this way and that way, he stood up and put three judiciously aimed bullets through the side of the bar. The scream of rage from behind it told him his gamble had paid off, thus far at least.

Moving quickly towards the huddled group of passengers, he tried to get an angle on Count Marechal – a clear shot that would finish all this now. The roaring wind through the two broken windows whipped through his clothes and made his tie flutter like a black pennant as he strode forward, gun aimed at the bar edge, waiting to see his target.

He never heard the metallic hiss of the blade being drawn; there wasn't the faintest possibility that he ever could in that maelstrom of sound and whirling newspaper sheets and napkins. He would have died there and then, but for Miss Barrow calling, 'Cabal! Behind you!' He didn't look at her first, which saved his life too. He simply turned immediately, gun leading, and found Fräulein Satunin, standing behind him with a stiletto in her hand, the same blade she had used to kill Cacon. It wasn't raised dramatically high – she was a killer not an actress – but out to her right, blade pointing in, ready for her to step close behind Cabal and grab him with her free hand over his mouth or throat as the blade drove in just below the sternum and up into his heart. But even the coldest killer may baulk a second when her target turns and she finds herself facing a gun barrel at mouth level. In that second, Lizabet Satunin looked over the gun into Cabal's eyes and, in them, she saw . . . nothing at all.

Cabal fired, and turned away.

Marechal, believing he was being shot at again, leaned out of his bullet-riddled cover and fired at Cabal. It was an impulsive shot, but still a narrow miss, and Cabal shied to his left away from the path of the bullet. It was a sudden movement that caught him as much by surprise as it did Marechal, and that took him clear past the end of the bar, leaving both him and the count entirely without cover.

Suddenly, it was no longer a gunfight. They faced one another, both armed with heavy revolvers containing but a single round apiece and – in a shared thought that occurred to each man simultaneously – they realised that this was a duel. This was the same duel they had started with swords three days before, and this was where it would finally end. Their guns barked, a fraction of a second apart.

Count Marechal was fast, but Cabal was sure.

He turned away as Lady Ninuka threw herself wordlessly across her father's body

He reached down and took Miss Barrow by the upper arm. 'We should leave now,' he said in a terse undertone.

'No! Cabal, we can't. *I* can't.'

She was looking at the surviving passengers: Herr Roborovski pushed back up against a chair, unable to look away from Satunin's body; Miss Ambersleigh, hands to her mouth, trapped in incomprehension; Lady Ninuka, her dark lace cuffs darkened further by blood as she held her father tightly. 'What has happened?' she asked nobody in particular. 'What has happened?' For his part, Marechal lay with his eyes open and with the calmest expression Cabal had ever seen him wear, his brow now troubled only by a dark hole a mite over 10.35 mm wide, the brain behind it forever stilled by the addition of 179 grains of lead.

Cabal grimaced. 'They can look out for themselves. Come on. Every second wasted narrows our chances.' It seemed unnecessary to expound upon the fact that their chances were already as narrow as the leg of an emaciated giraffe.

Miss Barrow was having none of it. She shook off his hand. 'Why *did* you come back?' she demanded through taut lips.

'It wasn't for you, if that's what you're thinking. Are you coming or not?' They glared at one another.

Coming to a decision, she turned to the others. 'If we stay here, we'll die. Come on.'

Two of them looked at her with eyes like hunted animals, but Lady Ninuka's hunt was over. Her eyes were as glassy as a vixen's in a museum. 'Daddy,' she said with faint certainty. 'Daddy will make everything right.' She hugged

Marechal's corpse more tightly yet, a still point in a shattering world.

Miss Ambersleigh moved to follow her, but Miss Barrow stopped her. 'I have to go to her,' said Miss Ambersleigh. 'I have a duty.'

'Your duty is discharged. She's made her choice. Come with us.'

Miss Ambersleigh started to protest, but paused, looking regretfully at Ninuka. 'Orfilia?' she said querulously. Her voice was lost in the winds that were singing over the edges of broken glass. Then more firmly, 'Orfilia! You must come with me! Come at once!'

Lady Ninuka did not respond at all. She simply held her father and stared into nothingness.

'It would be kinder to leave her here,' said Cabal, noting that – just for once – it was possible for the best course of action also to be the most convenient.

'Such a wilful girl,' Miss Ambersleigh said in an undertone. Then, to Miss Barrow, 'Very well, I shall go with you.' She turned to Herr Roborovski. 'Sir? You must come too.'

He shook his head. 'This is all my fault. It was my idea to disguise the ship. I never expected all this to happen. I swear.' The words tumbled out him, thick with despair. 'DeGarre, he was a great man, a hero to me. I had no idea what they would do to him. It was barbaric. It's all my fault.'

'That's that settled then,' said Cabal. 'Can we go now?'

Miss Barrow waved him to silence, much to his irritation. 'Herr Roborovski, can you fly an entomopter?'

The unexpected question confused him out of his desolation. 'What? Yes. Yes, I can.'

Cabal understood immediately. 'Ideal. Both Marechal's machine and the trainer I stole are two-seaters. His isn't as damaged as I suggested; I just said that to aggravate him. Two pilots. Two passengers. This should work. We just need to get to the flight deck before impact.'

Ascending to the flight deck was both easier and harder to achieve than expected. Cabal had come down from there to the first-class deck via an access spiral stairwell that ran through all the decks. The doors from the circular well to each deck were secured by a door that opened easily going from the well to the deck, but which required a key to enter from all the passenger decks. Cabal had taken a minute to disable the lock when exiting the stairwell, and this foresight saved them a lot of time. The actual ascent, however, was accomplished in a claustrophobic metal tube standing several storeys high that was swinging violently, the bulkhead lights flickering on and off, sometimes leaving them in darkness for minutes at a time. Miss Ambersleigh faltered once, telling them to go on without her, but a remark from Cabal on the ephemeral nature of 'British pluck' caused her to suddenly start climbing again in a stony, uncomplaining silence. Miss Barrow was going to congratulate Cabal on his grasp of psychology when she realised that he'd meant it. At least they had not had to contend with crewmen running from deck to deck; everybody was already at their emergency stations, and it would take a direct order from a superior to make them leave. Besides, even though most probably knew the ship was doomed, there was nowhere to run to; Mirkarvia subscribed to the view that providing parachutes would only encourage indiscipline and the giving up of the ship when the situation was not yet irrecoverable. Even an experienced crew weighed less upon the balance sheet than a combat aeroship.

It was a relief to reach the small room at the top of the stairwell. In its narrow confines bad weather gear swung on coat hooks, and equipment clanged heavily against the inside of wall-mounted lockers. To one side, a shallow metal staircase rose to the ceiling, into which twin doors were set. Cabal climbed quickly up to them and undogged the handles, before pushing upwards hard. The doors swung open and clanged down on to the flight deck, leaving them with a great blue rectangle of sky above them.

They climbed out into a howling gale. The crew had managed to stabilise the *Princess Hortense*'s wild pitching and yawing, but the levitators were barely keeping the ship airborne. A crash landing on the forested slopes with who knew what exposed boulders and rocky outcrops beneath would be like driving a frigate on to a reef. She was a strong ship, but she had never been designed to suffer that sort of punishment. The only alternative was to run her for the Katamenian border in a headlong rush, hoping to clear the forest and put her down in the pasturelands beyond. Without full power, however, she was caught in a slow, blundering, onward wallow. The *Hortense* was drawing to disaster as surely as any storm-torn galleon caught with a rocky coast to leeward.

The view was magnificent, if terrifying. They had left the last few clouds behind them in the charge for the border, and the ship was lumbering through clear skies. The horizon seemed to be as high as them, as if the world was a great shallow bowl. Miss Barrow put this down to an optical illusion, and guessed that they were actually still several hundred feet up. This also turned out to be an illusion, punctured by the appearance of a hilltop, whose jagged crown was definitely above them, gliding past on the starboard side.

Roborovski was full of action, given new impetus by responsibility and perhaps the chance for some redemption, at least in his own eyes. He had been shepherding Miss Ambersleigh along as if she were a favoured aunt, checking that she was all right, and giving her assurances that he would get her out of there alive. Now in the access room, he was able to show his special knowledge of the functions of a military ship. He opened an equipment locker and pulled out a pair of binoculars that he used to look along the length of the flight deck to where the two entomopters stood. 'They look serviceable,' he said. 'Herr Meissner, did you remember to apply the parking brakes?'

Cabal, who liked things to be tidy, replied tartly that, yes, of course he had.

Thus reassured, Roborovski opened a cupboard set flush into the access room's wall. Inside was something like a railway signal lever; a great thing with a grip release at the end of the handle, and a great bolt at the hinge. He took the handle, squeezed the grip release closed, and then threw himself back. Vibrant twanging sounds as of cables under tension sounded through the wall.

'What are you doing?' asked Miss Barrow, but the diminutive Herr Roborovski was putting too much effort into it to be able to answer.

'I assume this is something important,' said Cabal, stepping past her and lending his strength too. The lever was dragged back, complaining in strident metallic clicks all the way, and locked in position.

Roborovski took a moment to recover his breath. 'It's . . .' He wheezed a couple of times and tried again. 'It's the arrestor . . . line lever. They should be back flush with . . . with the deck now. Shouldn't . . . get in the way.'

Cabal climbed halfway up the steps and stuck his head up out of the hatch; the arrestor cables had indeed been withdrawn into long slots running across the runway.

'Won't we need to bring the entomopters around so they can have a run-up?' asked Miss Barrow.

'Not necessary,' said Roborovski. 'They can take off vertically, if need be. They have lifting surfaces at the base of the wing stubs and the underside of the faring, so they do fly better at speed, but they don't need to get speed up for take-off.'

'Oh,' said Miss Barrow, uncomfortable with a depth of ignorance that would have been spared her if she'd only read more boys' comics. 'Why all the business with arrestor lines, then?'

'Taking off is easy, Fräulein. Landing . . . well, imagine it. You might be approaching a rocking ship, in high winds, driving rain, and possibly under ground fire,' he nodded sincerely, 'you need the biggest landing area you can get, and you won't be coming in slow and easy. The arrestor lines mean that you just have to set your machine down, without worrying about going over the edge.'

Cabal had turned to listen, but now sat heavily on the step. 'Fuel,' he said. 'The trainer's almost dry. How long will it take to refuel it?'

Roborovski put his hand to his mouth. 'With a deck crew, five minutes. With just us, double that. You'd even used your reserve?'

'Reserve?'

'Secondary tank. You switch over to it when you run low.' He took Cabal's blank expression as good news. 'Don't worry,' he said slapping Cabal on the arm. 'I'm sure you would have found out about it on your second lesson.'

They climbed up the steps and out on to the flat-top, linking arms for mutual support as much as safety. They had to almost close their eyes as the wind tore the moisture from their skins and bared teeth. It took almost three minutes to walk the length of the deck, and all were glad to take some respite from the gale behind the waiting entomopters.

Roborovski climbed up on the side of the trainer and checked inside the cockpit. He came down again holding a flying helmet he'd lifted from the seat. 'I'll take the

Symphony,' he bellowed in Cabal's ear. 'The reserve's full. We should make Parila without any problems.'

'Parila?' shouted Miss Barrow, huddling against the cold.

'Yes,' he replied. 'I don't want to go to Katamenia, and I don't think I want to go back to Mirkarvia, either. There's nothing there for me any more. I'll ask for political asylum. With what I can tell them, they'll grant it.'

'Isn't that treason?' asked Miss Ambersleigh, her reedy voice almost lost on the wind.

'My country right or wrong . . .' Roborovski shook his head. 'They killed my country when they killed DeGarre for the sake of convenience. They killed it when poor old Konstantin was put down like a dog for saying what was right. I'll go home one of these days, but not while it's being run by butchers like Marechal and the crooks that backed him.' He gave Miss Ambersleigh his hand, and helped her on to the inset rungs in the side of the entomopter's fuselage. 'Come along, ma'am. We're leaving.'

Miss Ambersleigh was commendably prompt under the circumstances, not even showing an unhelpful demureness in the face of the wind whirling her skirts around and the necessary loss of dignity imposed by clambering into a cockpit. Once he was assured she was getting along perfectly well without assistance, Roborovski climbed up into the aft cockpit of the tandem arrangement.

He was just strapping himself in when Cabal appeared at the cockpit edge. 'Herr Roborovski, when you reach Parila I would be obliged if . . .'

'I don't know any Johannes Cabal,' said Roborovski. He smiled. 'I've never heard of the man. I'm sure Miss Ambersleigh hasn't either.' Cabal said nothing more, but nodded once in thanks and farewell before climbing down again.

'You'd better get clear, 'Roborovski shouted to Cabal and

Miss Barrow. 'You don't want a love tap from the wings when they start up.'

They moved back as the starter banged and the engine turned over. It was still warm from its previous flight and caught immediately, growing to an eager snarl to be off, that became a crescendo of engineered fury as Roborovski opened the throttle. He shouted something forward to Miss Ambersleigh, who plainly didn't catch it. It was almost certainly something along the lines of 'Brace yourself!' because in a moment the entomopter flung itself off the front of the flight deck and dropped like a cannon ball from a leaning tower, immediately vanishing from sight.

'I wonder if he had enough altitude to do that,' said Cabal into Miss Barrow's ear in a tone of mild scientific interest. It wasn't even a question, but simply a remark. Despite which, it was promptly answered by the sight of the Symphony dashing up ahead of them in a steep climb, before banking to port, and sweeping by at speed on a reciprocal of the *Princess Hortense*'s course.

Cabal climbed up the rungs in the side of Marechal's entomopter. It was a very different machine from the Symphony trainer, and he was already regretting being left with it. Where the Symphony was designed to be friendly and forgiving, this one was lean and antagonistic. It had brackets on its side panels that were probably intended to act as gun mounts and the root of weapon-bearing wings. Its livery was a matt camouflage green with a discreet Marechal crest painted on to the fuselage below the edge of the pilot's cockpit. Cabal assumed it was a fighter that had been stripped down for a reconnaissance role, lending it the range and the speed to travel undetected over Senza. By flying low over the treetops and staying away from populated areas, it would be unlikely to be spotted from the land or the air. Also unlike the Symphony, the cockpits were fully enclosed; the aft

JONATHAN L. HOWARD

pilot's position set higher than the co-pilot's. He found a catch and tried to unfasten it. It proved recalcitrant, and he barked his knuckles sharply on it, drawing blood and expletives.

'We do *not* have time for this,' he muttered, trying to free the catch. He had momentarily feared that it was somehow locked, but now saw that it was just awkward by accident rather than design.

'Come on, Cabal!' shouted Miss Barrow. 'We don't have time for this!'

He favoured her with an old-fashioned look, and went back to wrestling with the mechanism. He had a further worry, one that he decided not to mention to her, as then she would become all recriminatory and the explanation combined with the inevitable theatrics would eat into the very time that they both knew they didn't have. As soon as the phrase 'third bomb' passed his lips, he knew she'd be impossible, so he kept that little piece of intelligence to himself, and congratulated himself on a wise calculation.

As is often the way with self-congratulation, it proved premature; unlike the bomb, which was grotesquely tardy. The intention, back in those happy halcyon days when Cabal still believed that the levitators were in no way dependent upon the etheric line guides, had been to destroy three of the four guides. Destroying all four would have been more thorough, as well as more aesthetically pleasing, but he had insufficient materials with which to engineer a fourth device. The plan had been for one to go off first, to distract the crew and to give him some bargaining time should it be necessary. Then the second and third bombs had been due to detonate within a minute or so of one another, crippling both starboard line guides and meaning that the ship would only have been capable of a slow clockwise circle, trapping it within the Senzan frontier. He had been displeased that only

312

one device had detonated, but not too concerned until the flaw in his plan – to wit, plunging out of the sky and everybody dying – had been exposed. Since then he had been hoping that some flaw in the reagents had rendered the third bomb entirely ineffective (the alternative, that he had made an error in its construction, had not occurred to him at all), rather than just slow. Hope, in the same manner as self-congratulation, all too often invites a good crushing.

The third bomb was mounted in No. 2 line guide at the ship's forward starboard quarter. This was also, incidentally, the line guide they were closest to. The explosive force was not great – it was not required to be – but it was loud, flamboyant, and unexpected even by its creator.

Miss Barrow leaped sideways to the deck with a scream of surprise, and so was in a good position to reach into one of the grooves running laterally across the deck and hang on to the arrestor cable that lay there. This was to prove advantageous when the ship dipped its prow thirty degrees.

Thirty degrees does not seem a great deal when drawn on paper during a geometry lesson. When hanging on to the side of an entomopter, the deck angles down by such an amount, and the entomopter – brakes or no – starts to slide forward, it seems a very great deal indeed. Cabal looked down and saw the entomopter's wheels *squeeeeing* urgently across the rubberised surface leaving white burrs as the machine slid sideways towards the deck edge. He ran rapidly through the different options: if he lost the entomopter, he lost the only way off the *Princess Hortense* before she belly-flopped into the forest. To use the entomopter, he needed to open the cockpit. The cockpit canopy was being difficult. Once inside, he needed to start the engine, and bring the wings up to operational speed before the entomopter fell, or very shortly after it started to fall. He was not familiar with the cockpit layout. The canopy was still being difficult. He was running out of deck to scrape across. The *verdammt* cockpit canopy was still . . .

It opened suddenly under his hand, just as he felt the machine angle up under him as it started to topple off the edge. He had no choice; he threw himself backwards and twisted partially in the air to land on his side. He flattened his hands across the deck surface in an attempt to stop sliding off himself as the entomopter flipped over the edge and plunged into the treetops a hundred metres below. He was only partially successful. He wasn't moving as rapidly as the entomopter had, but he was still sliding relentlessly towards the edge. He saw Miss Barrow some ten feet away, hanging on for her life with one hand. Her expression was fearful, but determined, and – astonishingly – she had her free hand reaching out towards Cabal as if somehow she could extend her grasp beyond the length of her arm by pure force of will. It was a hopeless endeavour, but Cabal appreciated the sentiment. He raised his eyebrows at her in a 'Heigh-ho, here we go again,' sort of way, as if plummeting from aeroships was something he did as a hobby.

Somebody at the helm presumably didn't appreciate the idea of the *Princess Hortense* ploughing into the forest quite so soon, either. Finding power from somewhere in the ship's dwindling resources, her prow was brought up vigorously. While Miss Barrow held on to her cable despite being hurled vertically as if performing a one-handed stand, Cabal was flipped into the air like an especially sociopathic pancake, only to crumple heavily on to the deck a moment later, driving the breath from him in an explosive exhalation.

He did not rise or react, but simply lay there on his back, his arms slowly moving from the elbow. Miss Barrow feared he might have been knocked unconscious, and half rising to walk in a crouch, her fingertips low in case the deck moved again, she went to him. 'Cabal! Cabal? Are you all right?' She saw his eyes were open, and he was looking straight up. He spoke quietly, and she half made out what he said, and managed to half translate that from what little German she knew. From the quarter-sense she thus derived, she made an educated guess that he was commenting on how blue the sky was and how pretty. When Cabal touched upon the purely aesthetic, it was time for extreme measures.

A few stinging slaps later, and he was more or less composed. 'Did I say anything?' he muttered, sweeping his hair back in a distracted fashion.

She considered Cabal's fiercely guarded dignity, and that it would be kind for her to preserve it. Then again . . .

'You were raving about how pretty and blue the sky was.' Then she wilfully added, 'I think you also said something about gathering flowers and dancing.'

Cabal's eyebrows rose with baffled astonishment before lowering again into a suspicious stare. 'I'm sure I didn't,' he said, albeit not quite as self-assuredly as usual. He climbed to his feet, and walked away from the ship's leading edge in a crouch; being quite that close to imminent extinction had lost its allure.

'Now what shall we do?' asked Miss Barrow, as he passed by her. He stopped and considered. They had only a few more minutes of flying time left before the inevitable crash, and every plan he could think of required more time, more materials, and a great deal more altitude. Meanwhile the ship was performing the wide clockwise circle he had predicted, which was currently bringing it into the mouth of a wide tree-lined valley. Through the trees he could make out rocky escapements that, while very scenic, boded ill for a painless crash-landing.

He drew in his attention closer, to the ship itself. Three of the line guides were blackened and smoking from the impromptu bombs he had planted inside convenient maintenance hatches. The devices had been small, merely intended to damage a few components and cripple the line guide. Instead, the great louvred casings were smoke-blacked and buckled. He *knew* the strength of the explosive mixture he had used, and there was no earthly way he had miscalculated to this degree. It was possible . . . No, it was probable that there was something inside the guides, some sort of coolant or oil reserve, that had proved unexpectedly excitable when blown up. The guide at the ship's forward starboard quarter had detonated so spectacularly that its pylon was bent, the guide itself waggling slowly a few feet back and forth in the slipstream like the tail of an uncertain dog, creaking ominously. Cabal looked at it and made a decision. It wasn't much of a plan, but assuming the rest of the ship carried the same flammable fluid then staying where they were and hoping for the best seemed even less likely as a strategy for survival.

'Follow me,' he ordered her peremptorily, and set off for the line guide.

'Where are we going?' asked Miss Barrow, carrying her shoes as she ran beside him.

'That thing,' replied Cabal with a nod of his head. 'It will probably come off as soon as we hit the valley wall. The plan, if I can dignify it so, is that we climb on to it, and hang on. With a little luck . . . I misspeak . . . with a great deal of luck it will take the majority of the impact, tear loose, and get us down to the ground relatively unscathed. Providing the impetus doesn't throw us off and dash us against the ground just before the line guide rolls over us. As you can see, the aft guide on this side is mounted closer to the hull, so at least we shall fall outside its path, and won't have to worry about being crushed into paste by it.'

Miss Barrow's pace faltered. 'It's one less thing to worry about,' he offered.

'This is your plan?'

'The alternative is staying aboard when the ship crashes and probably bursts into flames. Between the crew and all the vegetables aboard, I imagine the smell will be something akin to bacon pie.'

They had reached the base of the pylon. 'So,' Miss Barrow recapped, 'we can either die suddenly on that thing or be burned to death if we stay here. Is that it?'

'Yes. With a footling chance of survival if we go the former route.'

Miss Barrow grimaced, hitched her skirt up, and tested one foot on the base of the pylon. 'Cabal? If we should live through this, please, promise me . . .' She stepped forward, falling to all fours as she did so to grab the pylon edges.

'Yes?'

'Promise me that you'll never become a motivational speaker.' And, so saying, she crawled rapidly across the pylon in a few sharp, deliberate movements, her concentration completely on the metal beneath her and pointedly not on the hundred yards or so beneath it, all that separated them from perdition. The treetops ran by in a blur of hard greens variegated with black shadow, the lack of distinction in her peripheral vision giving the impression of a great sea, waiting to drown them. She reached the other side and used the louvred vents to hold on to as she climbed up on to the line guide's top, getting covered in carbon black in the process. Once she was more or less secure, she turned to see if Cabal was following.

He was, and exhibiting no sign of enjoying the experience. Down on all fours and with a face like the wrath of Jove, he crept slowly forwards on to the pylon, his gaze focused entirely upon it. Miss Barrow made one half-hearted and unconvincing attempt at saying something encouraging, but Cabal shot her such a testy glance that she decided to leave him to it. He was about a third of the way across when his unreliable luck failed him once again.

Somewhere in the labouring innards of the *Princess Hortense*, a tortured relay finally overloaded, and failed in a spray of sparks to a chorus of swearing engineers. Three gyroscopic levitators in the fore starboard array died, their constant reassuring hums diminishing *al niente*. Like a puppet with a string cut, the corner of the aeroship where Miss Barrow clung and Cabal crawled dipped sharply.

Anyone who has ever ridden quickly over a hump-backed bridge or experienced the first descent of a roller coaster will know the sudden sense of falling while the stomach seems to carry on rising. It is a thrilling sensation when enjoyed in safety, but as this was not the case with Cabal at that moment, the sudden horrid sense of helplessness created by the pylon moving quickly away from him leaving him momentarily falling made him cry out. The pylon stopped, even swung up a little, Cabal smashed heavily into it, and rolled off the edge.

For the second time in his life, he found himself dangling by one hand from an aeroship. Miss Barrow was shouting, no, screaming at him, telling him to hang on, to pull himself up, to do all the obvious things that he intended to do anyway if only he could. He looked down and was surprised to see the treetops so close below. He wondered briefly if a fall would be survivable, but then saw in a gap amongst the trees how tall they stood and decided against it. Then he realised that Miss Barrow was screaming about a tree, too. He was just thinking what a coincidence it was that they were both so concerned with trees when the particular example Miss Barrow was talking about – a monarch of the forest growing well above its neighbours – struck.

Cabal heard the collision at the same moment that he felt it, the tree hitting the pylon halfway along its length. Suddenly he was swung forwards to bang harshly against the pylon's underside as a mass of pine tree fronds whipped against his back. The *Hortense*, massive and imperturbable, was not to be slowed by such a thing and was in the process of shearing off as much of the treetop as possible, and bending back the rest. It was not a one-way act of destruction, however. Cabal grabbed a second handhold and hugged himself as close to the ship's hull as he could as the tree tore away the pylon's skin and much of the girder work beneath it. Miss Barrow cried out in terror as the line guide sagged on the pylon tip and lurched backwards on the ruined pivoting mechanism that connected it to the pylon.

With a loud *crack*, the tree was behind them, leaving only shredded fronds hanging from the ripped metal and a pleasantly fresh scent. The collision had done Cabal a little good; where before he had been able to reach nothing but smooth steel, now snapped and bent girders jutted out of the pylon just behind him. He tested one before trusting his weight to it, pushed his foot into the bend at the torn end, and slid back towards the upper surface and relative safety. Miss Barrow, fingers driven deep into the line guide's uppermost louvred slot, was surprised to see him emerge, and then even more surprised to feel relief. She watched him heave himself on to the pylon top and roll back on to the deck edge. He lay there, breathing heavily and watching the sky for several long seconds as he recovered his strength and his composure.

'Cabal?' she called. 'Cabal? Are you all right?'

He turned his head to look at her. 'Never been better,' he said, too exhausted to put even a whit of the sarcasm he would usually have employed into it. 'Give me a moment to catch my breath, and I'll join you.'

'Yes, about that . . . I was thinking, actually, maybe if I came back.' Something bent and snapped in the line guide's swivel mount, making it swing and tilt by a few more degrees

319

from the horizontal. Miss Barrow suppressed a cry, and tightened her grip until the metal edges dug painfully into her fingers. 'It's just . . . I don't think I feel very safe over here.'

'You shouldn't feel safe anywhere aboard,' replied Cabal, truthfully if undiplomatically. 'Stay where you are.'

'I think . . . it's going to fall off,' she said in a very careful and moderated tone, as if the line guide might hear her and fall off in spite.

'That is the idea,' said Cabal. He got painfully to his feet, grunting at his sprains and bruises. 'It will come off easily on impact, not before. It is our best chance to survive this. Stay where you are and . . .' He paused as he glanced forwards. '*Ach, Scheiße*,' he snapped. With seconds to spare he glanced at the shattered pylon with the line guide wagging slowly at its tip and decided he would never make it in time. Instead, he ran forward on to the landing strip and threw himself full length at the nearest arrestor cable slot. He hooked his fingers around the cable, pressed his face against the deck, and hoped for the best.

The rocky outcrop Cabal had seen jutting proudly out of the hillside, like a glacier awaiting the next unsinkable ship, smashed into the forward dining-room windows and tore through the structure, rupturing the next deck up. The sound of the smash of rock, metal, and glass meeting in a cacophonic orgy was visceral in its force. Cabal gripped the arrestor cable with the fierce determination of a man who knows that there is no second chance. His head was jerked down as his body snapped straight behind him, and for long, long seconds, the roar of destruction and the black rubberised decking were his entire world.

Gushing coolant, hydraulic fluid, and root vegetables from her dreadful wound like a gut-shot haemophiliac, the *Princess Hortense* crashed downwards, spearing her belly on the great trees in that rarely travelled deep forest. But her momentum was massive, and she tore trees up by the roots in her headlong charge down the hillside, and those that wouldn't be uprooted were ripped atwain.

Miss Barrow had followed Cabal's glance and was already securing her grip on the line guide housing as he'd run for the landing strip. She saw Cabal hang on for his life and, just momentarily, thought he glanced up at her, but then she had to put her own face down against the metal of the line guide and braced herself. She closed her eyes, cherishing and fearing every second to come.

The incredible roar of destruction battered her, the dreadful tones of disintegration buffeting through her like a fierce, endless beat upon a bass drum, the resonations pouring through her, making her stomach and her heart feel as if they would explode in sympathetic vibration, and that she would welcome such a rapid release. Beside her, the aeroship lost its first and last battle, fought against an implacable and invincible foe. The *Princess Hortense* died screaming her last as the Earth itself tore out her guts and smeared them across the hillside.

When it suddenly became quieter, Leonie Barrow assumed she had been fatally injured, life and senses ebbing from her. She couldn't bring herself to lift her head for the longest time, afraid of what she might see. But even fear can be defeated by curiosity or, failing that, boredom, and she looked.

Almost a mile ahead of her, the *Princess Hortense* was still sliding, but slowly, so slowly. She would smash into a tree and start to roll up it until her immense weight cracked the trunk, and the ship lurched on again with small shreds of rediscovered momentum until she struck the next. She was alight, angry orange flames boiling out from rolling circular clouds of evil black smoke, that moiled and hovered in the air like the Devil's fingerprints. Amid the smoke, Miss Barrow thought she once saw the figure of a man standing at the forward end of the flight deck, black jacket fluttering about him, but then the black clouds closed around him and she wasn't even sure if she had seen anybody there at all.

Then the aeroship hit several trees simultaneously, and this time they bent, but they did not break. The ship lay still, and burned.

Leonie Barrow stood atop the shattered remains of the line guide, lying where a tree had interceded between hull and the guide itself and neatly bisected the supporting pylon. She stood and she watched the ship burn. She chose to ignore the bodies she could see scattered along the path of crushed trees, bark and branches stripped upwards by the passage of the aeroship over them.

She was still standing there an hour later when a flight of Senzan combat entomopters flew overhead and started circling. One sighted her and flew low, dropping the pilot's pack of survival supplies by her with a hastily scribbled note that the terrain was too difficult for the fighters to land, but that help was on its way. Miss Barrow did not react, even when the rescue mission arrived. They could get little sense from her, but this was only to be expected; a wreck is a traumatic event, an air wreck doubly so. She was drugged and removed from the site of such carnage, flown back to Parila in the company of doctors while the search for other survivors continued.

But they found only corpses.

Miss Leonie Barrow, a British national, was the only known survivor of the catastrophe. In the two days of bed rest she had before her doctors declared that she could be questioned for short periods, the investigators at the crash site had already begun to have grave suspicions that the *Princess Hortense* was not what she appeared to be. Senzan mechanics and engineers would not be fooled as custom officers might: they studied the line guides and levitators, and found them to be of military grade; they examined the aeroship's skeleton exposed by collision and fire, and noted the concealed frames and hard points where armour could be welded and weapons mounted. So when Miss Barrow told them of Marechal's subterfuge, it came as no great surprise to them. When she told them of his death, it came as no great sorrow.

They had found Marechal's remains – 'body' was altogether too composed a description – and tentatively made an identification based on clothing and artefacts. It was good to have his unexpected presence and death confirmed. Now all they required was an explanation. Some useful data had come from the man Roborovski, but when it was realised how deeply he was involved in the Mirkarvian armament programme, he was spirited away by Senzan intelligence, and the crash investigation saw no more of him. The Ambersleigh woman had been even less helpful, saying that she wasn't interested in local politics, crossing her arms, and demanding to be taken to the British consulate in increasingly strident terms until the investigators acquiesced for no better reason than to be rid of her.

This left Miss Barrow, and even she was evasive, pleading that shock had affected her memory. She asked to see a list of casualties, which they were reluctant to give her at first until she suggested that it might help her recall. It turned out to be a very short list; the *Princess Hortense* had burned fiercely and consumed flesh and bone. Marechal, despite being reduced to a smear, was one of the few they had been more or less sure of.

Miss Barrow read the few names and the short physical descriptions and effects of those still unidentified, and she bit her lip. 'He may still be alive,' she said quietly to herself.

Not quite quietly enough to escape the attention of the

police officer assigned to her; a chit of a girl barely out of the academy, but who burned with an intelligence and perceptivity that would either see her to the top of the force, or resigning in disgust. 'Alive, Signorina?' she prompted. 'Who may be alive?'

Miss Barrow started, and then relaxed. It would be a relief to tell somebody, she realised. The only consideration was how much to tell. 'It's time . . .' she began slowly. 'It's time to tell you what happened. Time for you to know. I think I've put it all together properly in my mind now.' The officer had already produced her notebook and flipped it open. She sat, pencil hovering and eyes intent upon her charge. Miss Barrow hesitated a moment longer, unsure if she was being wise. Then trusting to fate and judgement, she began.

'There's a man central to all this. He may still be alive. You have to find him. Dead or alive, you have to find him.' And, with Officer Frasca's shorthand flowing, Leonie Barrow told her story.

Through the forest, he walked alone. His jacket still stank of smoke and it reminded him of another time, not so long ago, when he had been walking home smelling much the same albeit with a more sulphurous note to it. He hoped this wasn't going to become a recurring feature of his life.

His escape from the stricken *Princess Hortense* had been so pathetically simple that he felt faintly ashamed to have placed Miss Barrow on the line guide. She was probably dead now, he thought, which was his fault. His conscience prickled him and, for once, he did not chide it into silence. To be fair to himself, he had thought the aeroship would explode on impact, but instead it had burned and that had given him time. Time, as the ship ground along the hillside at little more than a fast walking pace, to take up station at the end of the pylon at the shattered tip where once Miss Barrow's line guide had been, time to wait for a likely tree bough to approach, and time to grab it as it passed. That part of the operation had been no more difficult than boarding an escalator or a paternoster; descending the tree after all of its branches beneath him had been torn away by the passage of the aeroship proved more exercising. He had finally managed it by going back to the trunk and clambering gracelessly around to the undamaged side of the tree.

Once on the ground, he had contemplated going in search of the missing line guide to check whether Miss Barrow had survived or not, but the arrival of a flight of Senzan entomopters had dissuaded him. By the time he worked his way back up the hillside, he decided, rescuers would be arriving in force and he had no desire to answer their questions. Besides, if she was dead, she was dead. That didn't put her beyond his particular brand of help, but he doubted whether she would appreciate anything he could do for her. Well, then. Her fate was her fate, and his was his.

His looked like it would involve a lot of walking.

Through the towering trees, dismaying the wildlife by his very presence and never pausing to apologise, went a pale man. Johannes Cabal was walking home.

An Afterword of Sorts

On the subject of Cabal's journey home, some commentators have enquired as to whether anything noteworthy occurred en route, to which the author has replied that there was very little to concern oneself with on that subject. The journey was uneventful in all respects, unless one counts the business with the spy and the bandits and the Elemental Evil and the end of civilisation as we know it. So, no. Nothing one might call noteworthy.

Ah, *said the commentators, who plainly don't know when to leave well enough alone,* some people might like to hear about spies and bandits and all that. *This, the author finally admitted, is a fair point. If, therefore, you are a person of such low appetites, here follows an account of a further adventure of Johannes Cabal. Read it or ignore as you are minded.*

JLH

The Tomb of Umtak Ktharl

Just round the corner from the Haymarket, the knowledgeable Londoner will note a discreet and understated portico, under which stands a discreet and understated doorman in a discreet and understated hat. By the door is a small brass plaque, which – for the sake of completeness – shall be described as discreet and understated. The plaque declares, quietly, that the establishment it marks is called *Blakes*. It says no more, because the knowledgeable Londoner needs no more.

Within its portals (which are not 'hallowed', because enhallowment suggests some fame, and this is anathema to the establishment) lie facilities of comfort and convenience for the rare variety of clubbable men who do not care for clubs. In all conceivable senses, it is a club for gentlemen, but in a single ineffable sense, it is not, and this is what attracts a particular caste. Nor is it sheer coyness to say that this exotic factor is ineffable – it is a *je ne sais quoi* of which one literally does not know what. The nature of this curious factor is neither germane to the following narrative, nor even to the jealousies of rival clubs, which are simply aware of the existence of 'Blakes men' and are content to leave them in Blakes.

Certainly, there was little beyond its doors, hallowed or

otherwise, to mark it out as anything but one of the smaller clubs of the great metropolis. There is a dining room, studies, some rooms for members to stay overnight should the need arise, and a library which, despite its books going untouched from one year to the next, is the most popular room in the place. Here the members slouch in overstuffed chairs, hold desultory conversations, and read (newspapers, that is, although the otherwise unloved books get the occasional perusal providing they are either a volume of *Wisden's* or, intriguingly enough, Quiller-Couch's *Oxford Book of English Verse*).

On a wintery evening, the members had concluded a pleasant dinner – the majority enjoying an excellent Beef Wellington followed by spotted dick and custard, finishing with a good port served with a varied cheeseboard – and had retired to the library to finish the evening with brandy and cigars. There, they occupied their habitual seats and settled into a warm and happy glow as they chatted about politics and sport. Chiltern, who seemed to spend every morning memorising the newspaper so that he should never be without a topic for conversation, was setting forth his views on the marbles that the Greeks seemed to regard as theirs. These views seemed uncannily similar to those of that morning's editorial but that was Chiltern; he regarded the newspaper as a useful alternative to having to evolve any opinions of his own.

'They're ours,' he said, waving his pipe stem at Protheroe, who seemed to be asleep. 'How dare those Grecians start laying down the law to us. To *us*. If we hadn't removed the blessed things, the Turks would probably have blown them up or something.' He glowered. 'You know what the Turks are like.' Chiltern had read history and had yet to forgive the fall of Constantinople.

'How much does a Greek earn?' asked Tompkinson

abruptly of anybody. 'I mean, what does a Greek earn?'

'Drachmas, I should think,' said Munroe, sketching Chiltern in profile. None too flatteringly, at that. 'That's what they use instead of money over there.'

'No, no, no,' said Tompkinson, shaking his head emphatically. 'I mean, what's a Greek earn?' He looked around until he caught somebody's eye. On this occasion, the poor unfortunate was Kay, the professor of chemistry. 'About five bob!' said Tompkinson. Kay looked at him blankly. 'It's a joke,' Tompkinson explained. 'What's a Greek earn?'

'About five bob?' Kay ventured.

'No! You're supposed to say, "It's a bit of pottery" or similar. It's a pun! A . . . a . . . thingy. *Earn* E A R N and *urn* U R N. Sounds the same but it's different.'

'Homophone,' supplied Munroe.

'Well, good Lord, if you can't take a joke,' said Tompkinson and subsided into an aggrieved silence, for which they were all very grateful.

'One should be very careful with archaeology,' said Enright from where he stood by the fireplace. Everybody stopped and looked at him.

Enright was something of a mystery. Blakes was, as has already been intimated, a club of slightly unusual attributes, this slightness being of such a degree that nobody was sure exactly which attributes were specifically the unusual ones. There had been the incident of the whiskers in the water closet, and some of the members became very tight-lipped should the words 'clockwork' and 'Lord Palmerston' ever accidentally find themselves in the same sentence, but these were no more than the common eccentricities of any establishment. Enright, by comparison, was a riddle, wrapped in a mystery, inside a very tasteful Holland & Sherry suit. None knew very much about him. He came highly recommended from a former member, and sailed gracefully and somewhat laconically through the selection committee. It seemed that the club was perhaps his only social indulgence, as he was never seen at any of the many parties that one attends in and about town. Attempts at gentle investigation into his past by having a word with his primary sponsor came to naught when that gentleman took a nosedive off Beachy Head after some share options turned out to be less than on the square. Even the committee had been reticent in discussing Enright's background. They made noncommittal noises about salt of the earth and confidentiality but seemed discomforted and eager to change the subject. Thus, it may be understood that all were intrigued as to anything to do with Enright, and all listened attentively as he spoke on this occasion.

'Careful with archaeology?' echoed Chiltern. 'What's that supposed to mean? One might as well say, "One should be circumspect with ornithology," or perhaps, "There are dangers incipient in accountancy."'

'Here, here,' said Wilson, whose wife had run off with a chartered accountant.

'Sorry, Wilson. Still, what do you mean, Enright, "careful with archaeology"?'

'Just what I say. No more, no less.'

'Good heavens,' said Clifton, folding his newspaper and putting away his reading glasses into his top pocket, 'I do believe there's a story here.'

'A story?' Enright took a spill from the pot on the mantelpiece, lit it from the fire and used it to rekindle his cigar. 'Perhaps there is. There is certainly a salutary warning to the curious.'

'Don't be so dashed mysterious, Enright,' chimed in Kay. 'Is there a tale to be told or isn't there?' Perhaps it was the impatience in his tone, but Enright shot Kay a warning glance that the chemist didn't like at all. It was too late for discretion, however; the others had the scent of a yarn and would worry Enright like terriers with a rat until they had it out of him. To his credit, he knew an impossible position when he saw one. He warmed the brandy in his glass and took a sip as he considered his words. Then he began.

'I appreciate that I seem something of a dark horse amongst you,' said Enright. 'Only the committee know anything of my background, and them I swore to silence upon their words. I fear I shall have to ask the same of you.'

This demand raised no eyebrows; if a shilling had been entered into a fund every time a member of the club had agreed to tell a story only under the most sober promise of secrecy, it would by now contain two pounds, seventeen shillings, and sixpence (to cover Battersby's tale of his cuckolding. *Everybody* knew all about that well before Battersby did, so it was only worth half a bob). The assembly made its usual collection of incoherent mumbles to signify agreement, and he continued.

'I have seen a great deal of the world in my forty years, sometimes rather more than any Christian would want to see. I was at Panisha in the year 'eight-five, I was in the Guasoir Valley shortly after the Desolée Suppression and, on the occasion I am thinking of, I was in Mirkarvia during the rioting after the assassination of Emperor Antrobus the Second. I should point out that, at all these times – and others too numerous to mention – I was acting as a private citizen. My loyalties, however, lie with the crown in all affairs. I am, I like to think, a patriot and I believe it is my duty to see what is to be seen, and report it to the proper authorities.'

'Good Lord!' interjected Chiltern at this point, 'You're an amateur spy!' He looked around aghast. 'Another one!' He was always put out to discover yet another fellow member was a spy, as he was about the only member who had never been one. He did, however, maintain hopes that one day a coded letter might accidentally make its way into his hands, or a desperate government agent might hoarsely whisper some vital secret into his ear before succumbing to a knife between the shoulder blades. Then, he was sure, he would show his mettle and save the day. Towards this happy adventure, he read a good many yellow books, and bought a bowler hat containing a concealed camera. The others shushed him and Enright continued.

'The rioting was very ugly and threatened to turn into civil war at any moment. I stayed as long as I could, but foreigners quickly came to be regarded as agents provocateurs by elements of both sides and I found it necessary to leave. My departure was neither as ordered nor as leisurely as I might have hoped and I found myself on horseback with a few belongings heading for the neighbouring state of Senza in the wee small hours of the morning.

'There was a . . . *misunderstanding* at the frontier, the border guards made fractious and suspicious by the events of the moment, and I was forced to ride on with bullets threading the night air behind me. I made it through unscarred, but my horse was less lucky. She was a skittish mare, all I could lay hands on at short notice, and she was creased upon her left flank by one of the guards' wild shots. The combination of her fragile nature and the mild but stinging wound conspired to drive her into a frenzy of fear and she bore me deep into the dense forest that is common in that part of the world.

'I'd venture to say I am not a novice in the saddle, but that nightmare's ride filled me with apprehension as she bore me through the closely packed trunks of ancient and twisting trees as if the Devil himself was at our heels. There was no hope of controlling her; her neck was iron and she cared little for the bit that I pulled fiercely back into her mouth. She was beyond fear of a mere man. I was no longer her rider but simply a passenger. I clung on to her as long as I could and, as she tore blindly through the forest, I could not help but think of the tales my old Scottish nanny used to tell me of the water horses of her country that tempted the unwary on to their backs and then ran insanely along the banks of the loch, terrifying their hapless victim before plunging into the waters and drowning them, the easier to feast upon their flesh. This recollection started me worrying about the streams that criss-cross the valleys there, running off the mountain ranges that delineate the many pocket states.

'And then, suddenly, it was morning.

'I've been knocked unconscious before and am familiar with the small loss of memory that comes with it, so I was not unduly concerned that I could not recall precisely how I had lost my horse. Indeed, a wound on my brow suggested I had been swept off her back by a low bough. I was, however, *very* concerned to discover that my clothes were filthy and I found that I had a beard of several days' growth.

'As I lay there, I heard voices and, looking to one side, realised I had been laid out in a clearing in the woods. My horse, that wretched beast, was tied up by a tree with two others and, by a small fire, two men were going through my saddlebags. I have a small gift for languages, but their parochial dialect of Mirkarvian German was difficult to follow – salted as it was with Katamenian words – and I could only make out with difficulty what they were talking about. What I heard filled me with anger but made me apprehensive for my own safety. They appeared to be bandits and had happened across me – they consistently referred to me as the *baromarcu' Ausländerfotz*, a singularly insulting term for 'foreigner' – in a state of confusion. Seeing that pickings rarely got easier than an amnesiac upon an injured horse, they had ridden after me and knocked me from the saddle. They kept speaking of me in the past tense and I realised that they believed this second fall had killed me. In fact, it had restored me to my senses.

'I remembered reading Mallory in my youth and thought of the mad Lancelot lost in the forest. I couldn't remember what happened to him, but I doubted he had recovered his wits to discover a pair of thieves bickering over his field-glasses. I lay doggo and considered my next move. If they discovered me to be alive I had little doubt they would cut my throat and consider it small inconvenience. I felt weak and my wound – I had been fortunate that the bandits had not seen me stir and touch it – burned abominably, suggesting some infection. Fighting them was out of the question. Thus, I was left with little option but to continue to lie quite still and play dead.

'After some further argument, the two villains finished splitting my belongings between them, took their horses – and mine – and made to leave. One briefly wondered whether they should bury me, but the other said to leave me for the wolves and bears. The first was unhappy about this and I had the sense that he was superstitious about mistreatment of the dead, a courtesy he notably didn't extend to the living. Thankfully, his companion was made of sterner stuff and belittled him for his fears until they both left, the former in a nervous dudgeon.

'For safety's sake I lay still there for several minutes after the sound of their movement had faded away. I was in a dilemma: injured, weakened and lost without food or water. What was I to do? I've been in a good few scrapes in my time but, to be frank, none had seemed this hopeless and it took a few moments to fight a sense of despair that arose in me as the gravity of my situation made itself perfectly apparent. Of course, I was able to rein such sensations back – despair is an enemy just as any other but at least it can be fought with action. At which point I heard an animal moving close by.

'I stayed perfectly still. Most bears, no matter what the bandits had said, are not especially interested in dead meat until it has become a little gamy. They are, however, easily antagonised and, judging by the sounds the animal was making, it was more likely to be a bear than a wolf. I lay absolutely still, eyes shut, and listened as the animal came closer and closer by degrees, obviously suspicious of the clearing. There would be silence for seconds, sometimes minutes on end, and I would think it had moved on. Then I would hear it again, still cautious, still closer. The blood was pounding in my head as my heart raced, goading me to leap to my feet and either fight or run. I knew either course would almost certainly result in my death. There was nothing to do but wait.

'Can you imagine what it felt like? Even now, I remember with perfect clarity what it was to lie there and hope against hope that whatever was interested in my prone form was not hungry at that moment. Then I felt its shadow fall across me and I knew that everything would be settled one way or the other in a few moments.

' "You are quite the least convincing corpse I think I've ever clapped eyes upon," said the creature, causing my own eyes to snap open with surprise.

'The "creature" was a man, standing over me and giving me a look of such sour criticism that I felt faintly ashamed, as if caught in the commission of a puerile practical joke. I sat up and immediately regretted such rapid movement as my head whirled and I felt dangerously nauseous. "Somebody's been using your head as a punchbag," said the man, studying me coldly as if I were but a microbe upon a microscope stage. He knelt by me, pulled back my eyelid, and studied the white. "Mild concussion," he said, "you'll live."

' "You're a doctor?"

335

'He smiled and it was like a bloodless cut. "No," he replied, amused by something.

' "No, not a doctor. I haven't the bedside manner for it."

' "But you've had medical training?"

'He seemed to be finding this line of questioning boring. "Self-taught, largely," he replied in a dismissive tone before adding, "Look, we're both a long way from civilisation and those brigands have horses. I suggest we appropriate them."

' "Yes, you're right, of course." After I'd floundered around on the ground for a moment he deigned to help me up. "My name's Enright." He nodded and set off across the clearing in the direction the thieves had taken. He showed no indication of answering my implicit enquiry. "And your name is . . . ?" I called finally as I stumbled after him.

' "A closely guarded secret. *Do* keep up, Enright." '

Protheroe, apparently snoozing by the fire muttered, 'A curious cove,' before lapsing back into gentle snores.

'As I walked with the stranger, I took the opportunity to study him. He stood around the six foot mark, perhaps a little taller, perhaps a little shorter but not by much in either direction. His hair was blond, a very Nordic blond that matched the faint German accent I'd detected in his speech. He didn't seem to have shaved for a few days. His clothes were an odd choice for travelling through dense forest, too; he was wearing a city suit, and a conservatively cut one at that – it was as if a civil servant had been plucked from the streets of the government district and dropped in the wilds. I remember noting he had a sorely battered and ageing red carnation in his buttonhole; when I pointed it out, he looked at it with surprise and said something about forgetting that it was there. He then plucked it from his lapel and tossed it away into the undergrowth with a sour remark about life having seemed to be a good deal more agreeable on the morning he bought it. All this said, I must have looked as ill prepared for the rigours of the forest as he, and I made the natural assumption that he, as I, was a refugee from the troubles.

'"You don't talk much," he said suddenly.

'"I thought we were trying to catch them unawares?"

'"Just so. Based on the evidence, however," he indicated a clear trail running through some bushes leading across a slope, "we're not dealing with the world's most cunning criminals. I'm hardly frontier material myself but this . . . this really is pathetic."

'"They probably think that they're safe this far from the beaten track."

'"Well," said the stranger, "we'll simply have to disabuse them of that notion."

'We followed the trail until it met with a small stream running out of the hillside and turned up the slope. I was about to continue the hunt when I noticed my mysterious companion had paused by the stream. I guessed he wanted to get some water, which seemed to be an excellent idea. I crouched by the bank, scooped up a cupped handful of water and supped.

'The liquid was barely in my mouth before I spat it out again. I cannot communicate how foul that water was.'

'Well, at least have a go,' prompted Munroe. 'Can't be as bad as one of Kay's gin slings.'

'I say!' Kay said.

Enright shook his head, and continued, 'It didn't simply taste bad; it *was* bad. As it touched my tongue it was as if all the world's corruption had gathered there, a horrible rancorous sensation that made my heart quail and touched my soul. I staggered back from the stream, retching violently.

'"As I was about to say," commented the stranger evenly, "I wouldn't drink from this stream if I were you." He gestured to take in the banks and I saw what he had already seen, what had attracted his attention. They were barren, completely devoid of plant life up to their upper edges where a few stunted and somehow unwholesome specimens clung disconsolately. "There's something very wrong with the water here."

'"You might have said something earlier," I coughed.

'"I didn't realise what you were doing until you'd done it," he said and smiled that cold smile again. I was about to remonstrate that he'd had every opportunity to stop me when I abruptly realised something that left a taste in my mouth almost as filthy as that accursed water.

'He hadn't stopped me for a reason. He *wanted* to see what effect the water would have.'

There was a pause while the usual mutters of 'Cad!' and 'Bounder!' were aired.

'Then, to add insult to injury, he produced a notebook, presumably noted the results of his little experiment, and said "Let's see where this comes from." We followed the stream up the hill in silence until it vanished into the earth in a hollow, overshadowed by an embankment. My companion knelt at the edge of the stream and tried to see exactly where the water bubbled out from, but there seemed to be a cave, for want of a better description, barely large enough to kennel a dog, overgrown with weed that hung down from the slope above, safely away from the herbicidal qualities of the spring. Displeased with his vantage point, he lay flat out and peered into the gloom.

'"It's just a spring," I said, exasperated with his behaviour.

'"Just a spring," he repeated. He took some sort of small black leather folder from his pocket and opened it to reveal the heads of several test tubes. Selecting one that contained a clear liquid and an eye-drop pipette, he took a small quantity of water from the stream. He held the tube and the pipette up for me to see and then, without fanfare, let a drop of the stream water fall into the tube. The result was immediate and dramatic. The two liquids reacted violently, fizzing furiously and flashing with a strange cobalt blue phosphorescence that lasted for a few moments after the initial hissing had calmed.

'"Good Lord," I said. I may have said something stronger, I was so moved by the idea I'd had that filthy liquid in my mouth however briefly. "What is in that tube?"

'"This?" He stoppered the tube and put it in his breast pocket. "It's holy water. And *that*," he pointed at the stream, "is very *un*holy water." He craned to look into the tiny cave again. "There's writing in there." He produced his notebook and started laboriously transcribing what he could see.

'I stood over him, uncertain what to think. "Unholy water," I ventured at last. "I've never heard of it."

'"It's not the sort of thing Mother Church tends to advertise. And with good reason – you can combust a bishop with this stuff. Just as well for the serried ecclesiasticals of the world that it's so uncommon. All of which makes such water bubbling out of the ground by the gallon all the more interesting, wouldn't you say?"

'"Who are you?"

'He didn't look up but I noticed that he stopped writing. "Does the name *Johannes Cabal* mean anything to you?"

'It didn't even seem familiar and I said as much.

'He started writing again. "Then that is who I am."

'When no further elucidation was forthcoming, I said, "You behave as if I might know you."

'"I make enemies easily. I have a good memory, but it gets difficult to keep track of all the people who might have an interest in me. It's a substantial list. To return to the matter in hand, however," he sat up and studied the writing that he had transcribed. I looked at them over his shoulder, but they simply looked like chicken scratchings to me, no alphabet that I'd ever seen. "The head of the spring isn't natural. It's worked stone and looks more like a drain to me. These markings are carved into the stone of the head. Look a lot like Ugol letters, wouldn't you say? Rather pithy too. Look at the figure that starts and finishes the inscription: that's a triple imperative, the so-called 'black exclamation'. Failure to obey carried the death penalty back in the time of the Hass. As to what it's enforcing . . ." He paused, frowned and looked up at me. "*Do not block.*"

'"They took their plumbing very seriously," I joked, but Cabal was not in the mood.

'"Seven hundred years ago, you couldn't move in these valleys for Ugol raiders with fur hats and ridiculous little horses. They swept westward, carving swathes through several empires en route, and nobody seemed to be able to stop them. The incursion started to slow down not long after they came through here before petering out entirely. Their leader, the Great Hass Majien, was an old man by that point. His ill health was probably what stopped the hordes in their tracks. He's supposed to have died somewhere around here and they buried him and all his wealth beneath a hill. Unimaginable riches just sitting there, waiting to be found."

'I couldn't help but look at the hill upon whose slopes we were standing with widening eyes. "Good heavens, Cabal! You don't suppose . . . ?"

'"Perhaps." He shrugged and seemed maddeningly unconcerned at the possibility. "One cannot but help wonder, however, why any treasure trove would require running unholy water, only to let the stuff pour down a hillside. The answer lies closer to the summit, I fancy, along with those thieves and their horses." So saying he continued up along the trail. Biting back all too many questions, I had little choice but to follow.

*

'Within a few minutes, however, Cabal resigned the lead as the bandits' den hove into view. A cave mouth ahead of us showed signs of frequent congress; footprints and hoofprints led in and out and, as we listened, we heard a horse neigh from within. Cabal started to say something but I tersely gestured him to silence as a pair of the brigands walked out, chattering with foolish disregard for their own security. I recognised them immediately as the two who had robbed me of whatever belongings had remained with me through my period of amnesia. My grim anger at seeing them again must have been apparent, as I looked sideways at Cabal to discover him smiling quite openly at me. *Friends of yours?* he mouthed with faux innocence. I glared at him and turned my attention back to the men. One was hanging close by the cave mouth, the one who had been so concerned that I might return from the dead to punish them. The other was already heading for the treeline down the slope. He said something dismissively and plunged into the gloom. After a moment, and with clear misgivings, the other followed him. As soon as they were out of sight, Cabal was up and running for the cave. I followed him closely.

'"Careful!" I warned him. "There may be more."

'"No," said Cabal, pausing to check that the woods seemed clear. "They were arguing about leaving the cave again when they're supposed to be guarding it. Apparently, the rest of the merry men are off taking advantage of the refugees driven from Mirkarvia in the recent unpleasantness. Theirs is an ugly, mongrel tongue but the meaning was quite apparent. Come on, Enright, we may not have long."

'We ducked around the corner and ran inside.

'I wasn't expecting the cave of Ali Baba and I wasn't disappointed. The first thing that struck us was a near-palpable wall of stench, human as well as horse ordure.

What little light there was in that foul place was provided by a few torches and many crudely formed clay lamps burning animal fat through coarse wicks. The atmosphere was oppressive with smoke and I wondered aloud what sort of men would willingly choose this kind of life over one in the open air.

'"The usual sort," said Cabal, taking a torch from the crack into which it was wedged, "desperate men. Just like you and me."

'Ignoring him and his pretensions toward profundity, I went straight to the horses and quickly chose the two most promising. The mare that had caused me all this trouble in the first place could stay there for all I cared. I turned to pass the reins of his mount to Cabal only to find him gone. A flickering light down a rocky side passage showed where he'd vanished. I called after him in an urgent hiss but he failed to respond. Cursing him and his misjudged and ill-timed curiosity, I tied off the horses again and followed him at a trot. I found him at the end of the passage examining the cul-de-sac he'd ended up in.

'"Are you mad, Cabal? If they come back, we'll be trapped. The treasure of the Great Hass can wait for some future date, can't it? If those fools are still resorting to horse theft, then it hardly seems likely they've found it, or will any moment soon. Come on! We don't have time to dally!"

'I might as well have been talking about the weather.

'"Convincing, isn't it?" he said, blithely unconcerned with our danger.

'"What is?" I asked impatiently.

'"This," he said and moved the torch close to the rock face.

'"What *are* you blathering about, man?' I started to say. And then, the words froze in my throat. The natural rock face, lined with the cracks of ten hundred thousand nights of cold and as many days of warmth, was no such thing. Under the oblique light cast by the flickering torch, the cracks resolved themselves into regular markings . . . *letters* . . . just like the ones I'd seen Cabal transcribe by that curious stream. In fact, some were *exactly* alike. "The black exclamation," I breathed, caught up in the mystery of the moment despite myself.

'"Just so," said Cabal, distracted. "The black exclamation. But the warning is different this time. Still terse, though. *Do not enter*. Not very equivocal, is it?' He experimented for a few seconds with the torch, altering how its light fell as he tried to tease the secrets out of the other hidden letters. " *'Know this, thou foolish . . . thief . . . no . . . interloper, know that to go beyond here is to suffer not only death in this life but . . . the one that is to follow."'*

'"A curse?"'

'"No, the Ugol liked their curses to go on for several stanzas. This is a warning. They believed in reincarnation, you see. *Not only death in this life but the one that is to follow*. It's saying that you will be killed so very thoroughly that your reincarnation will die by it too. That's not the kind of thing they'd say lightly."'

'It is not for me to say I am a brave man, but I believe I can at least claim not to be a coward, physically or morally. Yet, as we stood in that close passageway and read those dire words of warning, inscribed seven hundred years before and likely never read until then, I felt a sense of nervous tension that I had never experienced before. The walls, lit by the fitful dancing flame, were covered in strange shadows that seemed to crowd about us, the air was thick enough to touch. There, gentlemen, within the living stone of that hill, I think I felt the slender, strong fingers of mortal, nameless fear close around my heart.'

Enright paused in his narrative to light another cigar. We

waited in utter silence for the minute that the commonplace ritual lasted. When he spoke again, it was a shock.

'Thus when the bandits returned in force, it was actually something of a relief.

'A relief to be confronting a foe I understood on terms I was familiar with. A relief to face a known quantity. Admittedly, they would probably murder us in cold blood but that, at least, was something I could understand and fight against.

'First we heard the clatter of hooves on the stone floor of the cave entrance and the laughter of men back from a successful day's butchery. Leaving Cabal searching for the entrance implied in the warning for a moment, I walked quickly and quietly up to the opening of the passage into the main body of the cave, and looked cautiously around the corner. There were a dozen of them if there was one – dangerous men, of evil-aspect. The pair they'd left behind to guard the hideout were obviously the least of them, lowered still further by their evident dereliction of duty. Their leader looked around and his snarling countenance showed his displeasure at their absence. A moment later, they ran in. The cockier of the two affected to slow to a saunter as he came to his leader's notice. There were some barked derogatory remarks that left the less self-assured guard cowering and begging. The rest of the surly gang gathered around as the other guard stood up to his leader and spoke dismissively. The cave was safe, he seemed to be saying, why the complaints? Who was the leader to second-guess the man on the spot? The coxcomb actually swaggered back and forth as he spoke, taking the dark smiles of the other bandits as approbation. I did not. I knew their look, had seen it on the faces of righteous executioners and priests watching the innocent burn, seen it too many times to mistake it or the horrid sense of foreboding that always came with it. It wasn't approval I saw in their eyes. It was anticipation.

'And then the leader, an ugly bear of a man, swept a curved dagger from its sheath, held it up just long enough for the guard to see it, to understand its import, then smashed it down into the hapless man's chest.

'The blow was brutal, but it was not efficient. I think it took the guard almost a minute to die, sobbing and pleading for help as his blood ran free and hot over his fingers. A minute of laughter and derision as his "comrades" watched his life flow across the floor to mix with the filth. Sickened, I quietly returned to Cabal.

'I found him behaving oddly, using his fingers like a cartographer's dividers to measure out distances on the rock face. He listened as I told him about the number of bandits and pursed his lips. The fate of the guard he greeted with a nod and, "Good. One less to worry about."

'"No man deserves to die like that," I said, angered by his insouciance.

'"Or kicking on the end of a length of state-owned rope. Or blown to pieces on a battlefield. Or quietly in bed surrounded by *loved ones*." He spat out these last words venomously. "One cannot pick and choose. You shouldn't be railing against the manner of death, Enright."

'"And you find nothing to fear in death, I suppose?"

'"Only one thing." He drew a line with his left fingertip along a crack and then continued down to where his right waited, having finished its curious measurings. He mouthed *Perfect* and pushed hard. There was a hollow grating sound of stone on stone, and the end of the passage swung in and back. Cabal looked at me, said, "Its *inevitability*," and plunged into the darkness beyond. I admit I stood gawping at the secret entrance, so perfectly concealed, for a long moment until Cabal's irritated voice demanding the torch broke me from my daze.

'The passageway continued down for only perhaps another ten feet or so before opening out abruptly. I stepped into this new cave and held the torch high. I admit, I was harbouring some childish expectations of what the tomb of the Great Hass Majien would look like. I'd envisaged a cavern, its soaring vaulted ceiling supported by cyclopean columns, heaped piles of treasure of unimaginable worth and, at the centre of it all, a great golden sarcophagus, perhaps standing by the famous war chariot of legend.

'Instead I found we were in a roughly hemispherical cave perhaps forty feet across with a pond in the middle of it. High on one wall, a V-shaped hole vented water that ran down the rock in a steady flow into a gutter. The gutter, in turn, fed a square pool that lay exactly in the middle of the floor, perhaps six feet along the edge the gutter ran over and ten in the other dimension. At the other end of the pool, another, deeper gutter took the overflow and ran it off into a sinkhole. Much time and effort had clearly been spent in the excavation, construction, and concealment of that place yet its purpose was, to me at least, unfathomable.

'Cabal went to where the water flowed into the room, took some in his cupped hand and tasted it. "If you still have a thirst, Enright, you can slake it here. The water's good." He walked round the pool to the other gutter and, taking the tube of holy water from his pocket, allowed a drop to fall from it into the run-off. There was a brief flash of blue fire as the two liquids mingled. He nodded, clearly pleased the little experiment had performed as expected. "And this is the source of that remarkable stream. Now I wonder what it is," he said, going to one knee by the pool, "that lies in here and has been preternaturally corrupting spring water by the tun for seven centuries." I didn't like the calculating way he said it, and was glad to find something to distract him.

'"Cabal! Look!" In the torchlight, I had made out more of

the carvings, this time plainly written. He was with me in a moment.

'"This one looks quite simple. No triple imperatives, no flowery discursions, just *Thou who hast entered here, know thy folly. For the sake of thine soul and the sanctity of life upon life, leave now. This is the tomb of . . .*" It was hard to tell beneath the unsteady light of the torch, the unshaved chin, the dirt of the woods and his own sallow complexion, yet I had the distinct impression that Cabal paled. ". . . *Umtak Ktharl*," he said finally, in a ghastly thin voice.

'"What did you say?" I demanded.

'My voice seemed to shake him out of the state of mental paralysis he'd retreated into and he turned to me with a new, urgent vitality. "I said," he said, snatching the torch from my hand and heading for the entrance, "we're leaving. *Now!*"

'Remonstrations were pointless as he gained the exit and moved out of sight. Cursing my impetuous companion, I went after him.

'I caught up with him at the corner of the passage and the main cave where he was glaring at the bandits from concealment, apparently trying to will them into non-existence. "Who's Umtak Ktharl?" I whispered urgently.

'"That doesn't matter," he whispered back. "We should be concerning ourselves with how to escape."

'"No, it *does* matter. Why are you so scared?"

'He glared at me. "I am *not* scared," he barked, rather too loudly.

'The bandits all turned to look at us.

'Cabal looked at them, then looked back at me. "Now look what you made me do," he said, exasperatedly. Then, he got up as if we had every right to be there and walked up to the nearest bandit. "*Guten Abend*," he said. The bandit looked at him with sheer disbelief. "We're so very sorry, but we've

347

rather been forced into precipitate action. A thousand pardons." So saying, he pulled the bandit's revolver from his belt and shot him through the head. He backed towards me firing twice more, snatched up a rifle that was lying to hand and threw it to me. "We'll just be holing up down here. Feel free to try and winkle us out." He turned and ran back down the passage with me close at his heels. I swear there was a count of three before the bandits fully appreciated what had happened. Our unexpected appearance and Cabal's easy resort to great violence had quite discomforted them. Then the bullets started flying.

' "Now what?" I asked him as we sought cover in the tomb cave.

' "I'm no military man, thankfully," replied Cabal as he laid himself flat behind a partially emergent boulder, "but, in their place, there are two obvious plans. The better of the two is simply to ascertain that there is no exit from here and then seal us in. In a couple of weeks, they can wander in with complete impunity."

' "And the second?" although I was sure I already knew.

' "The second is purest folly. A frontal assault. Here they come!"

'The villains, unappreciative that everything comes to he who waits, had massed on the other side of the entrance and were running in, zigzagging across the floor in an attempt to reach cover. Cabal fired and missed the first through. I took a little more time in the poor light of a few torches that had been thrown in and put a bullet in the wretch's chest. Cabal fired once more at the entrance and then I heard his revolver clack uselessly. He snapped the cylinder out and studied the chambers. "A cautious man. He didn't carry a live round under the hammer. Five shots. I'm out." He closed up the pistol resignedly and dropped it to the floor. "Make your shots count better than I did mine, Enright."

'A couple of the bandits had reached cover and were firing over our heads, probably trying for a lucky ricochet. They stood an excellent chance of getting one too, given the confines within which we found ourselves. Happily, ammunition became a concern and they slowed to some desultory sniping. I lay there behind that boulder knowing what it was to really be between a rock and a hard place. My rifle's magazine only held another four rounds and there had to be at least eight bandits left. Our death was a certainty and the only choice left to us was how easy we made it for them. I'd made up my mind to make it as difficult as possible and I suspected that Cabal was of the same liver. After a few minutes, the ringing in my ears from the close gunfire had reduced to the point that I could hear the surviving bandits arguing amongst themselves. "What now?" I asked Cabal again, with less urgency this time. There hardly seemed much point.

'He sighed, picked up the useless revolver and fidgeted with as he replied. "We wait while the better option occurs to them and they wall us in, I suppose."

'"That's not very optimistic."

'He laughed humourlessly. "I don't see many grounds for optimism." He looked past the edge of his boulder at the pool. "You wanted to know who Umtak Ktharl was."

'"If we're to die in his tomb, I might as well know who I'm going to be sharing eternity with."

'Cabal nodded. "That's fair. Very well. Every schoolboy knows of the Great Hass Majien and his Ugol hordes. The stories talk of vast hordes of horsemen sweeping down from the Irthat Steppes with Majien at their head in his ubiquitous war chariot. Nothing could stand before their unparalleled ferocity, expert horsemanship, uncanny archery, little ponies, comedic moustaches, and so on and so forth, ad nauseam. Utter rot. I researched this period in some detail and I'm confident that the horde barely exceeded a thousand undisciplined men. Any defending army worth the name would have wiped the floor with them."

' "You're saying the history books are wrong?"

' "I'm saying the history books have rationalised how a bunch of foul-smelling thugs managed to defeat every force thrown against them. The truth is too ugly for the historians in their ivory towers, so they've come up with the myth of an unbeatable army. The Ugol *were* unbeatable but that's the only true part of it."

' "They had a secret weapon?" I ventured.

' "No. Yes, actually. Yes, in a sense, they did. A secret weapon. Umtak Ktharl. He was the Great Hass's vizier, adviser, major domo. Actually, I think he ran everything and the Hass was just there as a more acceptable figurehead. The Hass could roister and doister and do all that nonsense. Umtak Ktharl, on the other hand, was evil incarnate." I looked questioningly at him, but he was disassembling the revolver for his amusement and wasn't aware of me. "I first became aware of him when I read of something called the Red Snow," Cabal continued. "Red snow that fell from a clear sky and where it touched human flesh it dissolved it. And every flake sighed as it ate away the meat from a man's bones, the sigh of a tiny ribbon of vital essence leaking away into thin air. Entire armies were reduced by it, kings lived in fear of it, and it was only one of the novelties in Umtak Ktharl's bag of tricks. Some were much, much worse. Who would stand against an army backed by a warlock like that?'

' "A necromancer," I corrected.

'For a moment, he seemed to be about to lose his temper and took a moment to swallow his irritation. I affected not to notice.

' "No," he said finally and his voice betrayed no emotion. "Not a necromancer. They are men of a very different stripe. This *warlock* was the reason for the horde's success. The only reason. Kingdoms would be abandoned at the very whisper that the Great Hass and his *éminence grise* were coming. If Umtak Ktharl was entombed here, it explains why the horde withdrew soon after they passed through this land. They very wisely appreciated that the jig was up and it was time to cut and run."

' "Not a pretty story."

' "No."

' "There's still something about this place that I don't understand. Why the pool, the spring?"

'Cabal looked at me again and smiled that ugly, cold smile of his once more. "Isn't it obvious?" He looked over at the pool and made as if to speak. Then his expression suddenly became horrified. "Enright! What's that by the gutter? Over there, man!"

'I followed his glance. Near the gutter that fed spring water into the pool, there was something dark and ophidian. As I watched, it moved slowly and cautiously towards the running water. I blinked and then appreciated the illusion. The tail of the black snake ran back towards the body of the bandit I had shot, the flattened perspective, of course, it was obvious. "It's blood, Cabal. Only blood."

'The effect on Cabal was astounding. He sat up, presenting himself as a beautiful target and started yabbering at the bandits in furious German, pointing frantically at the dead man. Fortunately for him, my reactions were better than our persecutors'. I dived across between cover and tackled Cabal, flattening him behind his boulder even as a shot whizzed through the space he'd been in a moment before. I hadn't been expecting gratitude, but I was unprepared for the vitriol Cabal blazed at me. Not much of it was in English, or even German, but what little I could make out doesn't bear repeating.

' "I just saved your life, Cabal!" I bellowed in his face. "They would have had you otherwise!"

'"Them?" he barked back. "I'm not afraid of *them*. The worst they can do is kill us!"

'Suddenly, I became aware of a bubbling sound, like a great cauldron coming to the boil. Risking a peek by the boulder, I was astounded to see that the water in the pool was boiling. Beside me, Cabal said with sharp anger and desperation. "Blood! It's too late, there's blood in the water!" And so there was; the slow trickle of blood from the bandit's body had finally reached the gutter and thence the pool.

"I was never very bright at school in my divinity classes. Our teacher, Dr Chatt, was a patient man, but even he must have been sorely tried by my complete inability to absorb anything at all. Or at least I'd always believed none of it had stuck until, looking at that extraordinary pool, its surface boiling fiercely and seeming to glow with subdued red like the sea over a submarine volcano, I heard dear old Chatt's voice speak to me over the distance of years. It was a lesson about John the Baptist and somebody had asked what baptism meant. "It is the washing away of our sins," Chatt had replied in that dark, wooden voice of his. The washing away of our sins. And then I understood.

'Umtak Ktharl had been having his sins washed away for seven centuries. Seven hundred years of pure water driving over him as he lay at the bottom of that strange pool, seven hundred years of corruption being sapped from him. And he, a seemingly bottomless well of sin, hadn't been purified one whit. In an instant I saw it all. The Great Hass finally realising that his vizier's goals surpassed those of any mortal man; the secret construction of this place; the luring of Umtak Ktharl here under some pretext and then plunging him into the pool before he recognised the trap. As generations had been born, flourished, and died away, Umtak Ktharl had lain here, rendered powerless by the never-ending purity of a mountain stream, powerless but still rotten to the core of his foul soul.

'At least, the purity had *been* never-ending. Until the blood of a wicked man had spilled into it and it had been polluted.

'As I watched the boiling increase in intensity, Cabal slumped down behind the boulder and commented, rather flippantly I thought, "Oh, well. *There's* the end of the world as we know it."

'"Is there nothing we can do?" I started to ask him, but he hushed me with a raised finger.

'"I'm thinking," he said. And, as he thought, Umtak Ktharl rose from the waters.

'"He seemed to half climb, half float from the pool, an Oriental who should – judging merely from the elements of his face – have been in his forties. But there was something wrong in the way they worked together, perhaps caused by the uncertain light or my own state of mind, something that made him seem ancient beyond belief. The water streamed from his high brow as mercury across glass, and fell hissing like drops of lave to the rocky floor. He was dressed in a long heavy robe of the type favoured by the Ugol in centuries past, but it was dark and featureless, hanging about him like a bed of weed, dank and horrid. It had no right to have survived its long immersion, of course, but mere physics were of little consequence in that cave at that moment.

'All of which were mere details beside those eyes. I cannot even begin to describe them for as soon as I saw him I looked away. But I know one thing of a certainty and that is that they were not human. I knew nothing of this . . . *man's* history and have never gone to pains to find out since, for I have no desire to learn what precisely takes a man's eyes and replaces them with the voids that I glimpsed. Perhaps his eyes were black orbs in his skull. I hope so, for the alternative was that he had no eyes at all but saw through sockets filled by something so wrong for this world that they were not simply beyond description, but beyond apprehension.

'My sanity was saved by the bandits who, seeing only the warlock's back, opened fire. Umtak Ktharl staggered very slightly under the rain of bullets, like a man snagging his toe in a loose carpet but catching himself in plenty of time. He seemed, if anything, faintly exasperated. Then he turned and set foot on dry ground for the first time in thirty-five generations. The instant they saw his face, the firing stopped. There was a moment of utter astonishment and then one man made a horrible high whining scream of terror and bolted.

'It was the signal for a general rout. The surviving bandits threw themselves back into the passage, kicking and trampling those who were too slow. I saw Umtak Ktharl lazily wave his hand and the hindmost bandit burst into fire, an unnatural fire of grey flames that consumed him within seconds. Yet he continued to scream even as he fell into ashes and for some moments afterwards. His fate inspired his companions to yet greater exertions and, in a moment, they had gone. Their nemesis followed with insolent leisure. Cabal and I were left alone listening to their dying screams echoing in the entrance cave.

'"Bullets don't hurt him," I said somewhat hopelessly.

'"No, they don't. It would be a salutary lesson to those vermin that violence doesn't always get them what they want. Of course, it helps to be alive after a lesson to appreciate the nuances."

'His flippancy was starting to irritate me and he saw it. "Look at the bright side," he added. "I think I have a plan."

'"Yes? What is it?"

'"Can't tell you. In the first place there will be a lot of improvisation. In the second, I don't have time for explanations it we're to keep up with Ktharl. We mustn't lose him. Come on!" He threw the disassembled revolver aside and, having seen that devil's imperviousness to bullets, I made to do the same with my rifle but Cabal stopped me. "It

354

might not kill him but it can certainly attract his attention. Hold on to it."

'We moved quickly but cautiously back up the passage to the entrance cave and happened upon the remains of some of the hapless bandits.

'No two of them had died in the same fashion: one's body lay unwounded but gelatinous beside a pile of steaming bones that I took to be his skeleton; another sat upright leaning against a stalagmite, his head brilliantly alight, the flame consuming his flesh as a candlewick does the wax; yet another lay sprawled on his back having apparently vomited up his heart. These were men who only minutes before I would willingly have killed myself, yet at least I would have offered them a quick and humane death. This, however, was far, far beyond the pale.

'"Why?" I asked Cabal. "Why has he done this? Surely he has it within his power to kill quickly and painlessly? Why these . . . these *monstrous* acts?"

'"Fear. With his power, he can vanquish an army. With his reputation, he can conquer the Earth. And he's probably rather out of practice anyway, I should think. These are the equivalent of piano exercises to him." Cabal looked at a human arm protruding from the cave's wall, a victim it would take pickaxes to extract. "These are simple party tricks for somebody like Umtak Ktharl. He's still working the cricks out. We must catch up with him before he gets back into his stride."

'Another scream from outside showed he hadn't got far. From the shadows of the entrance, we watched as the last of the bandits was dangled by his ankles from a tree at the edge of the clearing. For a moment I thought Ktharl had somehow bound him there when, with a sick sense of horror, I realised the even the trees were doing his bidding. The bandit wasn't tied to the branch – the branch was actually wrapped round his ankles like a black snake. The tree leaned slightly making a ponderous creaking and then, with unbelievably rapidity, swung the terrified man at the trunk of a neighbour. His screaming stopped the instant his brains were dashed out.

'"Your plan, Cabal," I whispered, still shaken by what I'd seen, "quickly, what is my rôle?"'

'"Are you good at thinking on your feet?"'

'"As good as any, better than most."'

'"Good. Get to those bushes over there. Act when you see my signal."'

'"What signal?"'

'"You'll know when you see it." With this, he walked once more straight towards an enemy.

'Umtak Ktharl saw him coming and turned to watch, mildly interested. He raised a hand to make one of the lazy gestures I now associated with an ugly death at which Cabal did the most remarkable thing. He threw himself prostrate before the warlock and started babbling at him in some odd tongue. Ugol, I suppose. An obviously educated man – and a European to boot – grovelling in such a way before an Oriental was a demeaning sight and it even seemed to take Umtak Ktharl aback slightly. He lowered his hand and listened to what Cabal had to say. Then he spoke back – a question by the sound of it – in a strange high voice, thin and complex like birdsong. It was fascinating and I could have watched for some time, but I remembered Cabal's plan, such as it was, and crawled on my belly to the cover of the bushes, my rifle held firmly in my hands for instant action. Reaching them, I climbed to my knees and furtively parted the leaves to see how Cabal was getting on.

'He appeared to be making some headway as he was now on his knees with his head bowed. There seemed to be some sort of question and answer session going on. I guessed that this was the first part of Cabal's plan, to gain the monstrous lich's confidence. Then what, I had no idea, nor could I guess my part in it.

'As it happened, I didn't have to wait long. Cabal had somehow so ingratiated himself in the space of fifteen or twenty minutes that he was allowed to rise to his feet, although he had to maintain a respectful distance and his head stayed bowed. He was speaking quite loudly and fervently and reminded me of adherents of those religions less civilised than our own.

'Then suddenly, unbelievably, he pointed straight at my hiding place. I was stunned for a moment and then the true import of Cabal's "plan" struck me. There had never been any intention to stop Ktharl, only to save his own neck in the apocalypse that he knew was coming. And I was to be the first sacrifice to his survival.

'Swearing bitterly, I brought my rifle up, aimed straight at Cabal and fired. I'm a good shot and my aim was true, but the bullet never arrived. That accursed Ktharl, that disgusting abomination that should have been dead seven hundred years ago, simply reached out and plucked the ball from the air. He studied it, lying in his palm, for a second or two – eminently unimpressed by the best modern science had to throw at him – and then he raised his hand to his mouth and blew gently. Some instinct made me dive to one side, but not fast enough to avoid being winged by that selfsame bullet as it shot back at me as fast as from any rifle barrel.

'It was plain that I couldn't fight him. My only chance was to escape from him and his new cur, Cabal, in the forest, get back to civilisation and try and convince the authorities of this incredible story. I slung the rifle over my shoulder and started running. I risked a look back and saw Umtak Ktharl sweeping after me across the leaf litter as if he were gliding across ice, Cabal running doggedly in his wake.

'My only advantage was speed but even that would be lost

if I became exhausted. Ktharl was inexorable, his steady progress indefatigable. I considered my options and decided to forget about losing them amid the trees, and instead try to find a dwelling with, I hoped, a horse. I finally understood why it had been so important in Cabal's plan for me to leave the cave because in doing so, I had also left behind any chance of reaching the horses stabled there. Furious with myself for trusting him, I ran and ran and ran. My path was along and down the side of the hill in the direction I guessed the Senzan border lay. On reaching the base, I struck out across the forest floor and hoped for the best.

'Every time I looked back, Umtak Ktharl was there. I didn't know why he didn't just kill me there and then; it must certainly have been within his power. Perhaps he had another use for me and that was something I didn't wish to think about, and which spurred me onwards with still more desperation. It was a nightmarish situation, one that I hope never to repeat and, God willing, never will except within nightmares. My wounded arm bled steadily, my headlong flight preventing any hope of it closing. As the seconds of running turned into minutes, I had the unappealing thought that Umtak Ktharl was somehow tracking me by the drops of blood I left in my wake, that he could smell them, perfumed with my fear.

'It was by the merest good luck that when I found the gorge, I didn't fall headlong into it, so harried was I. It was deep enough to kill a man, perhaps eighty feet into a fast-moving torrent with sharp rocks on either side. Scaling the side was impossible without equipment and the time needed for the descent. I had no choice but to run alongside it. The ground started to angle upwards and I started to fear for my endurance again as every step became a torment in itself. The incline wasn't great, but in my exhausted state it was the last thing I needed. Then, thank God, I saw the bridge.

'The bridge was a rope affair, obviously not meant for carts nor horses or other beasts. Even to a man, the crossing of sixty feet or so across the ferocious drop would have been a little daunting. Anything, however, *anything* was better than staying on the same side of the river as Umtak Ktharl, and I quickly crossed, the bridge swinging and twisting beneath my feet as I firmly gripped the rails and ran like a tightrope walker with the Devil on his coat-tails.

'Perhaps Umtak Ktharl would not be able to cross the bridge, what, with his weakness for running water? Perhaps, like a vampire, he wouldn't be able to pass over it? Second, even if he could, it would be my delight and my privilege to cut the guy ropes loose when he and, I hoped, Cabal, were halfway across. I enjoyed the prospect of the pair of them tumbling all that way into the angry white waters below. I fear I may even have been laughing a little hysterically by the time I reached the far side.

'Barely had I attained a hiding place by the mooring posts when Umtak Ktharl swept majestically into view and, without even a pause, moved on to the bridge. It would seem that my first hope was to be confounded. The sight of Cabal staggering exhaustedly up to the mooring posts on the other side and leaning on them while he wheezed unhappily reminded me of the second. I reached into my pocket for my clasp knife with murder in my heart. My hand found nothing but an old receipt and the stub of a pencil. The knife wasn't there.

'I almost cried out loud with frustration. Of course it wasn't. Those damnable and damned bandits had stolen it from my "corpse" back when they'd also relieved me of all my other belongings and my horse.

'I looked behind me; the path rose in a sharp zigzag up a very steep forested slope. I couldn't hope to get far. My reserves were gone and the jig was up, but I was damned if I was going to go down without a fight. Anger making my thinking clear, I unlimbered my rifle from my shoulder and took careful aim at the approaching sorcerer. I breathed gently and, just as my breath was on its cusp, squeezed the trigger.

'My first shot caught him square in the chest, but made him pause only momentarily, as if he'd forgotten something and then decided it was not important.

'The second bullet struck him in the face; I think I had some vague thought of puncturing one of those eyes in the hope they were where his power lay. That is how desperate I had become. I heard the bullet ricochet off him as if it had struck rock. He shook his head as if bothered by an insect and advanced.

'I was down to my last bullet and all hope had run out. Umtak Ktharl was clearly utterly invulnerable to mundane weapons. On the other hand, I doubted the same could be said for that turncoat Cabal; I decided to let him have the last shot.

'I was grateful that the bandit whose rifle it had been had shown more concern with the maintenance of his weapon than his personal hygiene. Every shot I had so far fired had gone exactly where I had placed it. Despite the bandit's peripatetic lifestyle, the barrel was well maintained, the action was reliable, and the sights were perfect. I trusted them implicitly as I placed foresight 'twixt back leaf and centred the whole upon Cabal. I aimed at his head with the expectation of the bullet's trajectory taking it into either his throat or upper chest. Either would be satisfactory. He was still wheezing pathetically, his whole frame heaving with the effort of drawing breath as he stood half slumped against the mooring post. Then I paused. There was something peculiar here, something odd in the way he was moving. I lowered my sights and was delighted and ashamed by what I saw. His body wasn't heaving with exhaustion at all, but exertion . . .

exertion as he sawed fiercely through the guy supporting one side of the bridge with a small pocket knife. The whole thing had truly been a ruse; Cabal had been looking for such an opportunity, and had now taken it with both hands.

'Without a further second's hesitation, I brought my rifle back up to the target and fired.

'It wasn't a clean shot, I'm embarrassed to admit; I can only plead unfamiliarity with the weapon at that range. But still, it clipped the second guy rope nicely, severing a good half of its strands. Cabal almost dropped his knife with surprise, but saw what I had tried to do and waved at me. He redoubled his efforts and the rope he was working on parted with a woody snap. The bridge leaned crazily to that side and Umtak Ktharl showed more emotion than I'd seen up to now; he actually seemed quite angry. The weight of the bridge was too much for the rope I'd damaged and, with a musical twang, that gave way too. Now anchored only on my side of the gorge, it fell and swung to smash against the cliff wall. Bits of wood and debris rained into the stream to be instantly carried away.

'Umtak Ktharl, however, was not amongst them. With a countenance of utter fury, he hung in the air in the middle of the gorge defying both gravity and our fondest hopes.

'I was at my wits' end and had been for some time. Cabal was not and that is something we should all be grateful for. He reached into his breast pocket and threw something at that remorseless monster. "Umtak Ktharl!" he shouted as whatever it was glittered and shone in its arc. "Catch!"

'I like to think it was Ktharl's utter arrogance, his total belief in his invulnerability, that proved his downfall. He should have done almost anything except catch what had been thrown to him. I think in his brief acquaintanceship with Umtak Ktharl, Cabal had seen it in his character and played upon it. What is they say comes before a fall?

'At any rate, Umtak Ktharl caught it. The object had barely been in his hand a moment when it flashed an angry cobalt blue that illuminated that warlock so strongly I had the absurd impression that I could see his bones within him. With rising hope, I realised what it was. A tiny thing . . . nothing at all in the usual way of things.

'A small phial, two-thirds full of holy water.

'The water must have boiled in its tube because it broke with the distinctive "plink" of fracturing glass I remembered so well from my dawdlings in chemistry as a boy. It must have been like a tube of acid shattering in his hand. Not enough to kill him or even really hurt him, but more than enough to engage his full attention, to break his concentration and really, at that point, that was all that was necessary. The holy water flared and steamed like St Elmo's fire where it splashed upon him, he made some small, pathetic effort to beat the supernatural flames from his hand and arm, and then he was falling. It took only a moment to plummet the distance before he was gone, lost in the frothing waters.

'Cabal and I ran downstream, eager to make sure that he didn't make the bank. This time I'm sure I was laughing, laughing with sheer relief. There would be a tomorrow. It wasn't the end of everything.

'I saw Umtak Ktharl first. Just the hint of an arm waving in the turbulent water of an eddy pool. Pinned against a rock underwater, once again having his sins washed away constantly.

'"He's finished!" I shouted with delight across the roar of the river.

'"He's no such thing," Cabal shouted back. "He could get washed free, the water level could drop in high summer, somebody might find him, anything could happen. He's contained for the moment but he isn't finished by a long chalk." He started walking back upstream. "I need to think."

'I could barely get a word out of him for the next couple of hours as we trudged along each on our respective side of the gorge. Then the river started to rise and the gorge to become shallow and, finally, we found another bridge, a properly metalled road bridge this time, and joined our paths. It was clear that we were leaving the wild lands and towards nightfall we reached – quite unexpectedly but very welcome all the same – a customs post. We were on the border between Senza and Mirkarvia, actually on the Senzan side; I had crossed the border days earlier while delirious. We must have looked very disreputable as we approached the building and a couple of officers came out to greet us. We went inside and were glad of their offer of a pot of coffee while they processed us. About the only thing the bandits had left me with were my papers and these the commanding officer took and studied closely.

'Satisfied, he turned to Cabal and asked to see his passport. Cabal sighed and shrugged. "I'm afraid my papers were lost in my escape." Then he looked the officer in the eye and said, "My name, however, is Gerhard Meissner. I was formerly a docket clerk first class in the Mirkarvian Department of Administrative Coordination. I am claiming political asylum." I looked at him aghast until he sent me a warning glance that made me compose and comport myself more neutrally.

'The customs officer looked at him oddly and started flicking through the sheets on his clipboard. He found what he was looking for and nodded. "Of course, Herr Meissner, you have been expected."

'Cabal's face was a picture. He looked utterly blank for a moment. Then he pulled himself together. "I am? That is to say, excellent. I must admit, I was worried about the loss of my documents . . ."

'"Inconsequential, mein Herr. The Minister of the

Interior will need to speak to you, of course. You must be interviewed."

' "Of course," replied Cabal, but I could see his confusion.

'They organised a horse and trap for us and we rode in silence for the few miles to the nearest town, Sadile. The only time Cabal – I assume his real name *was* Cabal – spoke was to point out the watercourse running parallel to the road. "If that ever dries up," he said, "we're all in a lot of trouble." '

'And that's your story, Enright?' asked Chiltern in the silence.

'That's my story,' replied Enright. 'At least, it's most of my story. There is a small coda. Two unusual things happened that first night in Sadile. At about two in the morning the whole town was woken up by an explosion. A distant thing it was, several miles away, but the rumble travelled through the earth and tumbled people out of their beds and tiles from the rooftops. Those who had been awake at that hour said that there was a strange flash in the sky to the south, that turned to an angry cobalt glow hanging over the forest that took minutes to fade.'

'Oh!' said Tompkinson excitedly, 'I know what that was.' He pondered for a moment and then shook his head. 'No. No, I don't. Carry on.'

'And the second thing?' asked Munroe.

'Well, I only found out about that the next morning. Cabal – I'm sure Meissner was a pseudonym – was gone, vanished into the shadows. He obviously had a few secrets he didn't want the authorities to learn. Nobody was much concerned about his absconding nearly as much as the outrage that had been committed the night before.

'The Archbishop of Parila was visiting the parish. Shortly after midnight, a mysterious stranger had dragged him out of bed at gunpoint. The poor archbishop been forced into his robes, and driven down to a small river that runs by the town.

There his assailant had put a gun to his head and told him to bless the river and to keep blessing it until he was told to stop. The archbishop, quite reasonably under the circumstances, blessed the river waters for all he was worth. At about two o'clock, there was the blue flash in the sky, reflecting upwards from some sort of explosion in the forest. The archbishop's assailant seemed very pleased, said something about being able to sleep now, and left him there. The archbishop's description sounded awfully like Cabal.'

There was a respectful silence, broken by Tompkinson saying, 'No, I don't understand.'

'I'll explain it to you next week,' said Munroe. 'I'm tired now, though, so I'll take my leave of you, gentlemen. Good night, Enright. Thank you for that fascinating story.'

They broke up, and started to make their varied ways home. In the cloakroom, Kay bumped into Enright putting on his overcoat. As they made their way across the foyer to the exit and the city night, Kay asked him, 'Johannes Cabal. Did you ever find out who he was?'

'I made enquiries when I got home,' he replied. 'Turned out he's a little infamous in some circles.'

'A spy?

Enright smiled and leaned towards him confidentially. 'A *necromancer*,' he whispered. He seemed to find Kay's expression of shocked outrage still more amusing. 'Look on the bright side, Kay. I'm very glad he turned out to be a necromancer rather than, say, a docket clerk, even a first-class one. So should you. A lot of use he would have been then. Good night!'

Acknowledgements

The Cabal Cabal, for their enthusiasm, and for making me feel like the cool kid – a rare experience for me.

My agent, Sam Copeland, without whom none of this would have happened, so blame him.

Everybody at Headline, in particular my editors, Jane Morpeth and Claire Baldwin, for their professionalism, humour, and taking me out to lunch.

John Betancourt, Marvin Kaye, and George H. Scithers for first unleashing Cabal upon an innocent and unsuspecting world in *H.P. Lovecraft's Magazine of Horror*. Warrants have been issued.

Linda 'Snugbat' Smith, for producing the chapter heading art, and patiently weathering the blizzard of reference pictures and tweaking requests I threw at her as I fretted about Spanish police hats and barrel tops.

Graham Bleathman, for going away with my prose descriptions and clumsy scrawls, and coming back with wonderful pictures.

Andrew 'G' Goddard, a very clever man, for the best nineteenth century that never was.

My best friends, Michael and Marsha Davies, and Katharine Long, for their support and advice.

And Louise and Maddy, for being Louise and Maddy, which they do very well.